WHEN
TWILIGHT
BREAKS

Books by Sarah Sundin

SUNRISE AT NORMANDY SERIES

The Sea Before Us
The Sky Above Us
The Land Beneath Us

WINGS OF GLORY SERIES

A Distant Melody
A Memory Between Us
Blue Skies Tomorrow

WINGS OF THE NIGHTINGALE SERIES

With Every Letter
On Distant Shores
In Perfect Time

WAVES OF FREEDOM SERIES

Through Waters Deep
Anchor in the Storm
When Tides Turn

WHEN TWILIGHT BREAKS

SARAH SUNDIN

Revell

a division of Baker Publishing Group
Grand Rapids, Michigan

Published by Revell
a division of Baker Publishing Group
PO Box 6287, Grand Rapids, MI 49516-6287
www.revellbooks.com

Printed in the United States of America

Library of Congress Cataloging-in-Publication Data
Names: Sundin, Sarah, author.
Title: When twilight breaks / Sarah Sundin.
Description: Grand Rapids, Michigan : Revell, a division of Baker Publishing
   Group, [2021]
Identifiers: LCCN 2020024621 | ISBN 9780800736361 (paperback) | ISBN
   9780800739713
Subjects: GSAFD: Historical fiction.
Classification: LCC PS3619.U5626 W48 2021 | DDC 813/.6--dc23
LC record available at https://lccn.loc.gov/2020024621

Published in association with Books & Such Literary Management, 52 Mission Circle, Suite 122, PMB 170, Santa Rosa, CA 95409–5370, www.booksandsuch.com.

This is a work of historical reconstruction; the appearances of certain historical figures are therefore inevitable. All other characters, however, are products of the author's imagination, and any resemblance to actual persons, living or dead, is coincidental.

21   22   23   24   25   26   27   7 6 5 4 3 2 1

In loving memory of my grandfather

John F. Ebelke.

I wish I'd known you.

ONE

Evelyn Brand had done a crack bit of journalism, and she hadn't even had to dress like a man to do so.

She perched her hip on the desk in the American News Service office in Berlin, while Hamilton Chase III, the European bureau chief visiting from London, reviewed her article.

George Norwood, the Berlin bureau chief, paced the office, glaring at Evelyn with each turn. If he'd arrived in Vienna on time, the story of the year would have been his, not hers. But he hadn't, so it wasn't.

After Adolf Hitler bullied the Austrian government into allowing Nazi Germany to annex the country, German troops had marched across the border without firing a shot.

And Evelyn would get the ANS byline.

She'd stood under the blood-red swastika flags as the Führer's cavalcade rolled into Vienna to thunderous cries of *"Heil, Hitler!"* In her story, she'd described the little girl in native costume tossing flowers and the black-uniformed SS officer handing the bouquet to the Führer.

But she'd also described the scene on another street, where a

7

mob forced two dozen Jews to scrub anti-Nazi graffiti from the sidewalk. She could still see the silver-haired man down on his knees, still see the jeering boy knock the gentleman's hat into the gutter. The man had reached for his hat, then thought better of it and returned to work.

When Hamilton Chase set down the article, Evelyn gave him a triumphant smile. "It's good, isn't it?"

He ground his cigarette in the ashtray. "Yes, it's good."

"Good?" George Norwood flung a hand in her direction. "She shouldn't have been there. She's assigned to Munich. She lives there."

"I'm in the room, Mr. Norwood." Evelyn sent her boss a thin smile. "I did call the Berlin office beforehand. Mr. O'Hara said no one from ANS was in Vienna. But I was already there."

"I was on my way." Norwood wasn't even thirty, but he glowered at Evelyn as if she were a naughty five-year-old.

Silver fanned back in Chase's sandy hair. "Why were you in Vienna, Miss Brand?"

Evelyn rearranged her houndstooth check skirt over her knees. "My roommate is a flautist, and she wanted to attend a certain concert in Vienna. I didn't think she should travel alone, given the tensions." More like she'd used the concert to lure Libby into accompanying her to Vienna. Bait and switch, Libby had said. She wasn't incorrect.

"She tried to sneak into the press conference." Norwood ran his hand through chestnut hair almost the same shade as Evelyn's.

"I didn't sneak. I presented my press pass and asked politely. With no one from ANS in town, it was worth a try." Instead of asking why Evelyn was in Vienna, Chase should have asked why Norwood wasn't. The only major news service or paper without a correspondent in town. Almost criminal.

Norwood blew out a roiling cloud of cigarette smoke. "She knew she wouldn't be admitted. She wasn't on the list."

Evelyn crossed her arms. "Bert Sorensen from the New York

Press-Herald wasn't on the list. He got in. But he's a man. I should have—"

"Don't even think about it." Chase speared her with his gaze. "I will not have a repeat of the Paris fiasco. You made the ANS a laughingstock."

Evelyn lowered her chin. "Yes, sir." If only she'd used more pomade and bobby pins that day. With her fence-post figure and a man's suit, she'd been admitted to the press conference given by that woman-hating French official. No one would have been the wiser if tendrils of hair hadn't sprung from under her fedora.

Chase handed Evelyn's article to Norwood. "Clean it up and send it to New York."

Evelyn clutched her hands in her lap. "Please keep the part about the man and the hat."

Norwood's nostrils flared. "That's the part that needs cleaning."

She'd never forget the desolation in the gentleman's eyes. He'd reminded her of Grandpa Schmidt, who had been born Jewish. He'd converted to Christianity, but the Nazis wouldn't care. To them, Judaism was about race, not religion. If Grandpa hadn't come to America, he would have been forced to scrub sidewalks too.

"Please, Mr. Norwood," Evelyn said. "The story needs to be told. America needs to know. I owe it to him."

"To him?"

"The man on his knees." If Libby hadn't held her back, Evelyn would have rushed to his aid. And she would have failed, one woman against a mob.

"Fight with words," Libby had told her. "Your words have power."

Not if edited to death by George Norwood.

"Keep as much as you can, Mr. Norwood," Chase said. "And remember, Miss Brand, we American correspondents are guests of the German government. They don't censor us, but they do have limits."

"They certainly do." In other countries, correspondents wired their stories to the US. But the Nazis screened telegrams, and they only transmitted stories they liked. So American reporters usually phoned their stories to their London or Paris bureaus to be wired home.

Chase fished a cigarette case from inside his vest. "Never forget. You're not in the US."

Evelyn's shoulders slumped, but she rolled them straight again. "I know. No freedom of speech. No freedom of the press. No freedom of anything."

"Yes. So, what are you working on next?"

"I have an assignment for her." Norwood rummaged through a folder on his desk. "A feature on the American students at the University of Munich and their experiences here."

Evelyn tried to find a smile but failed. Another softball assignment.

Norwood handed her a slip of paper. "Peter Lang is one of my oldest and closest friends. We were roommates at Harvard, and his father served with mine in the House of Representatives. Peter's earning his doctorate in German."

Another East Coast prep school Hah-vahd man, like Norwood and Chase and every bigwig at ANS. Evelyn tucked the piece of paper into her purse.

"Lang can introduce you to the other American students. He's a fine fellow."

"Of course, he is." Somehow she kept the sarcasm from her voice.

Hamilton Chase stood. "I'm looking forward to that article."

"Thank you, sir." After she shook his hand, she went out into the newsroom full of clacking typewriters, lively banter, and the actual news.

This was where she belonged.

Even with all the huge stories happening around the world—the Great Depression, civil war in Spain, Japan's invasion of China, and Stalin's purge of tens of thousands of his own people—Berlin was every reporter's top choice. But Evelyn was exiled almost four hundred miles away in Munich writing softball stories.

"In trouble again, Brandy?" Frank Keller stopped typing and pointed his cigar at her. "You know what you need? A husband to keep you in line."

Exactly why she'd never marry. She hated lines.

Evelyn leaned against Keller's desk and batted her eyelashes at the pudgy, middle-aged reporter. "Volunteering for the assignment?"

"Not on your life." His carriage return hit Evelyn in the hip.

She pressed the back of her hand to her forehead. "My poor little heart is wounded."

Keller laughed. "Beat it, sister."

Gladly. Across the room, Mitch O'Hara beckoned to her.

She grinned and joined him at his desk.

O'Hara pulled over a chair for her, always a gentleman. Pushing sixty, he'd reported the news in every major city around the world. Too bad he'd turned down Norwood's job. For O'Hara, Evelyn would be willing to stay within the lines—on occasion.

"What'd you do, Ev?"

He was the only person she let call her that. "Nothing. I got to Vienna before Norwood did. And I called here first, you know that. I tried to get into the press conference but was turned away. If any of you fellows had done the same, you wouldn't have been summoned to Berlin."

O'Hara scratched at his gray mustache. "You've only been in Germany six months."

"Seven, and two years in Paris before that. And I did my stint at the copy desk in New York."

He dipped his chin, his silvery-blue eyes fixed on her. "You're still paying your dues."

Her lips wanted to pout, but she restrained them. "My dues are twice as high as a man's."

11

"Yes, and the penalties are twice as high as a man's. It isn't right, but that's how it is."

Evelyn's jaw worked back and forth, and she glanced to the closed office door. "Norwood's going to edit the heart out of my story. I should be free to write how I want."

"You are." O'Hara tapped his pen on Evelyn's wrist. "And ANS is *free* to fire you. And the Nazis are *free* to kick you out of the country if you make them look bad."

"It isn't hard to do."

He chuckled. "True."

Evelyn drummed her fingers on the red leather purse in her lap. "Getting expelled from Germany might not be so bad. Dorothy Thompson was expelled, and she's more famous than ever."

"She was famous to begin with, established in her career. You're in your early twenties."

"*Late* twenties."

He laughed and leaned back in his chair. "I've been married long enough to know that only a very young woman will argue that she's older than people think."

Evelyn had to laugh too.

"You can do it, Ev." O'Hara rested his elbow on his desk. "You're a good writer, you've got the nose for news, and you've got drive and gumption in spades. Just keep your head down and try—please try—to follow the rules. The Nazis can do far worse things than expel you."

"I know," she said with a sigh. Her rights as an American citizen wouldn't do any good if she met with a fatal "accident" staged by the Gestapo.

She stood and slung her purse strap over her shoulder. "Thanks for the pep talk. I have a train to catch. Norwood wants me to interview exchange students, pat the hands of the Ivy League mommies and daddies, let them know their little dah-lings are safe and happy in their junior years abroad. Softball assignment."

O'Hara picked up a half-eaten apple from his desk and grinned at it, then at Evelyn. "You look like the kind of gal who knows how to play ball."

"Yes . . . ?"

He mimed winding up for a pitch. "What do you do with a softball, Ev?"

She returned his grin threefold. "Hit it out of the park."

TWO

Peter Lang removed the wax cylinder from his Dictaphone, slid it into its cardboard tube, and wrote a number on the tube. "*Sehr gut*, Fräulein Wechsler. You made good use of the winter semester in your junior year abroad. Your German has improved much since I saw you in September."

"*Danke schön.*" The Mount Holyoke student fiddled with a light brown curl. "I look forward to your class next semester."

"Starting a week from today." Peter shook her hand. "Thank you for helping with my research."

"I'll help in any way I can. *Auf Wiedersehen.*" She left Peter's office, sending a smile over her shoulder.

At his desk, Peter checked his research log. With the thirty-four American students about to enter their second semester at the University of Munich and the following year's class which would arrive in the fall, he'd obtain plenty of data for his dissertation.

"*Guten Tag*, Peter." Professor Johannes Schreiber entered the office. "*Wie geht's?*"

"*Sehr gut*, Herr Professor." Peter shook the hand of his favorite

14

professor from his own junior year in Munich. The man had lost some hair since then, but he'd kept the same warm smile. "Only three more recordings to make. The students have been generous with their time on their semester break."

Professor Schreiber fingered the flexible steel tubing on the Dictaphone's mouthpiece. "I'm glad, but I wish your research were more conventional. I fail to see how this will improve language learning."

Stifling a groan, Peter straightened books on his desk. "I've found it helps if a student listens to himself and then to proper pronunciation. Also, I can compare recordings before and after the semester to show the effect of my teaching methods."

"Your methods." Professor Schreiber rubbed his chin and frowned at the machine. "Students learn best from immersion."

"Naturally. That's why my research compares my students at Harvard who did not have the benefit of immersion with the students here who do. That's why I met this class in New York and recorded them before they sailed to Hamburg. I also recorded Harvard students with a different instructor—"

"It isn't too late to find a new approach. You are here for a year."

Peter drew a deep breath. Without Professor Schreiber's blessing, he'd never receive his PhD. "What if I help Hans-Jürgen?"

"My son?"

"Ja. His English is good, but his accent is . . . not."

The professor got a faraway look in his pale blue eyes. "I would like him to study in England or America."

Peter spread his hand on the cool black Dictaphone case. "If I can improve his accent, may I continue my work?"

A smile dug into one cheek. "He is fond of you."

"And I am fond of him. Do we have a deal?"

"Very well. Now you have a reporter visiting, ja?"

"Ja. A favor for a friend."

After the professor departed, Peter checked his watch. Three minutes if she were the punctual sort. He closed his log and filed it away.

Poor George. He'd called to say he'd given Peter's number to a firebrand female reporter who didn't know her place. George was heaping on assignments to keep her out of trouble.

"Good luck." Peter closed his file drawer. By definition, trouble-makers made trouble.

"Entschuldigung?" A slender brunette knocked on his open door. Not a pretty woman, but . . . arresting. "Professor Peter Lang?"

"Just Mr. Lang until I receive my doctorate," Peter said in English, and he strode over. She had a firm handshake born of working in a man's profession, no doubt. "You must be Miss Firebrand."

Medium-brown eyes looked up at him, lit by intelligence and humor. "My reputation precedes me."

What had he said? "Pardon?"

"My name is Evelyn Brand, not Firebrand, despite what Mr. Norwood says."

For heaven's sake. "My apologies, Miss Brand. I assure you, the mistake was mine, not George's."

"No need to apologize." The pleasure in her expression told him she'd probably repeat this story to all her friends.

"Please come in." Fumbling for the remnants of his manners, he motioned her inside. "Would you rather go outside? The weather is chilly, but I enjoy it that way."

"I do too, but I'd like to start in here. You can learn a lot about a person from his surroundings." She shrugged off her overcoat.

Peter helped her and hung her coat on a hook. "All right, Miss Brand. What can you learn from my miniature graduate student office?"

At his bookcase she pulled out a few volumes. She cut a stylish figure in a gray suit and a red blouse with a red belt around her waist. Her hat had a man's cut but with a feminine tilt, gray with a red bow. Even her shoes were gray and red.

Miss Brand slid a book back onto the shelf. "Your books tell me nothing that Nor—Mr. Norwood didn't tell me. You're studying the German language. But despite your recent arrival, everything is unpacked."

This could be interesting. "I don't procrastinate."

"A Dictaphone?" She stroked the machine with the reverence it deserved. "What for?"

"My research. I'm—"

"Ah, your research. You'll tell me about it in exceptional detail, I'm sure. But may I ask my questions first?"

He grinned. After the giggling junior year girls, Miss Brand was refreshing. "In my defense, I was answering your question."

She chuckled. "You were."

Peter leaned back against the wall and crossed his ankles. "Let the interrogation begin."

"Your chair is beside your desk, not behind it."

"I was meeting with a student."

"And you prefer a non-adversarial role. May I?" Miss Brand gestured behind the desk.

"Be my guest. Watch out for the exploding cigars in the top drawer."

She shot him a sly smile as she passed, dropped a red purse into his chair, and picked up a framed photograph from his desk. "Your family?"

"Yes."

"Well, aren't you all Aryan looking?" she said in a teasing voice, as she compared Peter to the photo. "All blond and—yes—blue-eyed."

"One hundred percent German."

"I'm 75 percent German, and I don't look like that. Let's see. You're the third youngest of four boys. You look about ten in this photo. Have you always worn glasses?"

"I was nine, and I've worn glasses since first grade when I couldn't see a thing on Miss Hathaway's blackboard."

Miss Brand squinted one eye at him. "Sometime between then and now, you broke your nose."

Peter sucked in a breath, hearing again how that fist had crunched into his face, feeling rough hands shove him to the floor, seeing more rough hands beat his father to death, while Peter had lain there, too much of a weakling to save him.

"Fraternity brothers?"

Peter blinked and forced his focus onto the young lady, who held up a photograph of Peter with his three closest friends in their fraternity sweaters. "Yes. Now all of us are in Europe."

"Nor—Mr. Norwood hasn't changed."

Peter stepped closer. "That's Henning—Baron Henrik from Denmark. And Paul Aubrey runs an automobile factory near Paris."

"That's you." She glanced him up and down quickly. "You've changed."

Meaning he wasn't a skinny weakling anymore. He'd made sure of that.

"You don't have a Boston accent like my bureau chief."

"I come from New York, the Albany area."

"No picture of a wife or sweetheart. Either you're unattached or you keep your wife's photo at home, the better to lure pretty coeds."

Peter heaved a mock sigh. "If only I were that scandalous. It would make a better story."

"It would." She scanned the office. "You're very organized. *Alles in Ordnung.*"

Everything in order, as it should be. "Any more analysis, or shall we go for a walk?"

"A walk would be nice."

Peter helped her on with her coat, slipped on his own coat and hat, and led her down the hallway. "Now it's my turn."

"Your turn?"

He squinted at her pointedly. "You're from the Midwest, probably Chicago, judging by how you pronounce your *R*s."

Brown eyebrows rose. "Chicago born and bred."

"You come from money, judging by your outfit."

Miss Brand wrinkled her nose. "Well . . ."

"But you're uncomfortable with being wealthy, which speaks well of your character, as does the fact that you chose a career rather than marrying your escort from your debutante ball."

"I didn't *have* a debutante ball." She looked quite pleased about that.

Peter pressed a hand to his chest. "And your mother was sorely disappointed."

Her mouth flopped open. "How did you . . . ?"

"Nor did you pledge a sorority."

The hallway emptied into the atrium with its dark marble pillars and high white dome. Miss Brand's heels clicked on the tiled floor, and she gave him a look both suspicious and admiring. "You could be a reporter, Mr. Lang."

He bent in a small bow. "I'll presume you mean that as a compliment and accept it as such."

She laughed, low and melodic and not silly at all. "That's enough. I'm here to interview you and to ask for contacts with other American students."

"Happy to oblige. I'm teaching the German language course next semester for the junior year program. We have thirty-four exchange students."

"Wonderful." She climbed broad marble steps to the landing, pulling a notepad from her purse.

"Shall we find a bench?" He headed down the steps on the other side of the landing.

"I can walk and write."

"Good. I'm a firm believer in fresh air and exercise." He opened the door of the main building.

Unlike American universities with their sprawling, park-like campuses, the University of Munich had two long buildings facing each other across Ludwigstrasse, with a circular plaza in the middle. In the center of the plaza, a dozen students perched on the side of a large fountain, laughing and flirting.

Peter turned left on the path around the plaza. "I love how Germans are walkers and hikers."

Miss Brand drew in a deep breath. "I like that too. My roommate and I go hiking in the Alps whenever I can tear her away from her music."

"She's a musician?"

"A flautist. A bit of a darling in the Munich music scene."

"Not Elizabeth White?"

Miss Brand raised a smug smile. "I've known Libby since second grade."

"Goodness." He'd heard much about her but hadn't heard her play.

"Once again, I'm here to interview you. Name—Peter Lang. Age . . . ?"

"Twenty-seven." He led her beside the elegant, cream-colored building. "Harvard class of '33, bachelor's in German, working on my PhD in German at Harvard. Arrived in Munich on March 8 for a year of teaching and research, studying under the esteemed Dr. Johannes Schreiber, who was my professor during my own junior year here from 1931 to '32. Does that take care of your preliminary questions?"

Miss Brand scribbled frantically, either in shorthand or in atrociously bad handwriting. "I'm adding 'thorough' to my description of you. And 'slightly impudent.'"

Why on earth did George dislike this woman? "Only slightly impudent? I'll have to try harder. Next question, Fräulein?"

"Just . . . a . . . minute." She continued to scribble. "Johannes Schneider?"

"Schreiber." Peter inhaled the crisp air under the cloudy sky.

"All right, Mr. Lang. What has been your greatest challenge here?"

George had warned that Miss Brand was determined to paint Germany in a bad light and to not let her lead him down that path. He shrugged. "Finding a car to purchase."

"A car?"

"I love to drive."

"I thought you loved to walk."

"Yes, and I like to drive places where I can go walking." He pictured Miss Evelyn Brand beside him in his Opel Admiral convertible, a kerchief tying back her hair, as he sped down the Olympic Road to hike through the wonders of the Partnach Gorge.

"Mr. Lang?"

"Hmm?" Had she asked another question?

One corner of her mouth twitched. "I asked if you'd had any other difficulties. Other than listening, that is."

They'd reached Ludwigstrasse. Peter turned left and led her down the street toward the Siegestor. He was certainly making a fine impression. "Difficulties? Can't say I have. I'm fluent in German, and I'm familiar with the culture. Although everything's vastly different from when I was here in '32."

"I can imagine. I'd ask more about that, but your return is rather recent."

"Long enough to see." Peter strolled down the clean street, past shiny cars and smiling students. Back in '32, Germany had been mired in poverty and unemployment, the people demoralized, while communist mobs spread terror.

The Siegestor rose before him, the triumphal arch as solid and sure as Germany's recovery, crowned by a statue of Bavaria, her chariot drawn by four lions.

Now in 1938, the rest of the world struggled with the Great Depression, with strikes and riots and despair. But Germany prospered, with no unemployment, the people happy and secure. For all of Hitler's reputation in America as a clownish gangster, he'd turned the country around.

Miss Brand flipped a page in her notebook. "How is the university experience different from in the US?"

Peter tipped his hat to two female students. "It's coed, for one. I like that."

21

"Of course."

"But the academic calendar confuses most Americans, with a winter semester running October through February and a summer semester April through July."

"That is confusing." She glanced around and lowered her voice. "Any problems with the German Students' League?"

Fishing for criticism. Peter stifled a smile and led her onto the roundabout circling the Siegestor. "No problems at all."

"I suppose teaching language wouldn't violate Nazi policy. How about your experience living in Munich?"

"*Wunderbar.* Sausage, Bavarian sweet mustard, hiking, the opera." An idea formed. "Although I haven't heard Miss White perform."

"You must. She's incredible."

"Aren't you tired of hearing her play?"

"Never." Miss Brand pushed a brown curl from her cheek, burnished red in the muted daylight. "I was practically raised at the symphony, so—"

"Wait. Brand? Chicago? You wouldn't be related to Ernest Brand, the conductor?"

Her grin shone with pride. "My father."

"Your . . ." Why, this woman only grew more interesting. "I took the train out to Chicago for one of his concerts."

"He'll be pleased to hear that."

His idea solidified. "Do you know when Miss White is performing next?"

"This Saturday."

"Would you do me the honor of accompanying me?"

Miss Brand stopped and studied him, framed by the Siegestor's central arch. "On one condition."

"Anything," he said, his hand to his heart.

"You need to be a good boy, stop getting distracted, and answer my questions."

"I promise." Although how on earth could he avoid getting distracted around such a fascinating creature?

THREE

Munich
Thursday, March 31, 1938

"For someone who says she despises fashion, you have exquisite taste." Libby White followed Evelyn out of the boutique on Maximilianstrasse.

"The higher the quality, the less often I have to go shopping." Evelyn hitched her purse strap up on her shoulder. Thank goodness the shop would deliver the evening gown to her apartment so she wouldn't have to lug it home.

Libby patted the coil of dark brown braids at the nape of her neck. "The gown is gorgeous. Your date will love it."

Evelyn searched for their streetcar. Her date would probably like it very much. Peter Lang had looked at her with interest, which wouldn't last once he got to know her. All for the best, and she smiled.

"Is he handsome?" Libby's deep brown eyes fairly twinkled.

"No, but he isn't unattractive. And his nose is crooked. I like that."

Libby hooked her arm through Evelyn's. "Have I mentioned how odd you are?"

"Not often enough. But Mr. Lang is clever and has a good sense of humor. He'll be interesting company."

"You do collect interesting people."

"Like you." Evelyn squeezed her friend's arm.

Libby rolled her eyes, then brightened. "There's our streetcar."

They boarded, and Evelyn chose seats facing the center so she could watch and listen. She'd found good story ideas and sources while riding the streetcar.

Even better, a man one row back was probably Gestapo. Bland-looking man in a bland-looking suit, peering over a folded newspaper.

Evelyn choked back a laugh. The newspaper was upside down. Definitely Gestapo. Who was he watching? Or was he just scouting for leads as she was?

Closer to the front, two young men held on to overhead straps, and the taller boy grumbled in a low voice about his upcoming six months of compulsory labor service after he turned eighteen.

Not a low-enough voice. Such talk could land him in prison, and Evelyn had to help.

"I just love my new dress," Evelyn said loudly and in English. Europeans thought Americans were boorish anyway.

Libby gave her a strange look. "Yes, it's beautiful."

"The instant I saw that silver brocade, I fell in love. I adore how the bodice is gathered on the sides. What did you call it? Ruching?"

"Yes, ruching." Libby's forehead rippled, imitating the ruching.

But it worked. Mr. Gestapo's gaze swung from the boys to Evelyn.

"That silver." Evelyn raised wiggling fingers in glee as she'd seen other women do. "Oh my! It'll look stunning with my rubies. I have the perfect shoes. Maybe that little red satin bag. Or would that be too much?"

"I . . . I think . . ."

"And red lipstick—oh no, that's right. Lipstick is forbidden in Germany, isn't it?"

The streetcar stopped, the two young men exited, and Mr. Gestapo sprang to his feet.

Evelyn bolted up, grabbed Libby's hand, and aimed her backside to block the secret policeman's path. "I saw another shop I simply *must* visit."

Libby had been tricked into enough adventures to recognize Evelyn was up to no good. Despite that, she followed. "Then visit it we must."

Evelyn strolled down the aisle and stopped at the foot of the steps. A quick scan for the boys, of the shops, of the sidewalk. "That jewelry store is divine."

Mr. Gestapo cleared his throat behind her.

"I'm sorry," Evelyn said in loud English, like a typical American tourist who thought volume could crush language barriers. Then she meandered down the sidewalk under the chestnut trees, dividing the space between Libby and the storefronts. She spread her arms wide. "I love how the skirt twirls, don't you?"

"Entschuldigung." Mr. Gestapo tried to get around her.

Evelyn spun and stood in front of him. "Ent-shoo—I know that word. It means 'excuse me,' right?"

"Yes," Libby said. "Yes, it does."

Evelyn clapped her hand to her cheek. "Oh! Am I in your way, sir? I am. I'm sorry. Ess tut mer lide." She deliberately mangled the phrase *"Es tut mir leid."*

"Ess toot meer light," Libby said as if correcting a child.

"Ess toot meer light. Oh! I'm still in your way." Evelyn stepped aside. "I'm sorry, Herr—sir—how do you say it?"

Mr. Gestapo strode a few paces, but the boys were gone. His shoulders sagged.

Evelyn pulled Libby into the jewelry store.

"What was that about?"

Evelyn glanced out the window. "He's Gestapo."

"What? Evelyn!"

"He's harmless to us, but not to those boys grumbling about labor service."

"Oh." Libby peered out the window too. "Did they get away?"

"Yes, thank goodness. What a horrid country if you can be arrested for grumbling."

Libby blew out a long breath and frowned at Evelyn. "You take too many chances."

"Only to help someone or to get a story. And God will keep me safe."

Libby's eyebrows rose higher than notes from her flute.

"Jesus is the way, the truth, and the life." Evelyn gave her friend a saucy smile. "He'll help me find a way to get the truth, and he'll keep me alive."

A laugh sputtered out. "That isn't what the verse means, and you know it."

Yes, but Evelyn liked her version.

"Darf ich Ihnen helfen?" A portly dark-haired man called from across the counter.

"Nein, danke." Evelyn smiled at the jeweler, but then she fingered the gold cross around her neck. "Actually, would you be able to tell me about my cross? My grandmother is German, and she went to America in the 1880s. The cross has been in the family for generations."

His eyes lit up. "May I see?"

"Ja, bitte." Evelyn undid the clasp and laid the cross before the jeweler.

He inspected it with his jeweler's loupe, murmuring as he worked. "Beautiful, but it is not German."

"It isn't?" Perhaps Grandma Brand's family had come from another country before settling in Germany. She never talked about her life in Europe.

"Nein." He pointed to a mark on the back of the cross. "It is American."

"It is?"

"Ja, and it is not old. This baroque style was fashionable in the 1880s."

"Grandma lied to me?"

Libby laughed. "Why are you smiling about that?"

"Because that means I've found a story."

Friday, April 1, 1938

Peter pointed to the sentence on the blackboard—"The water is wide."

"Da oo-ater is oo-ide." In the front row of the classroom, seventeen-year-old Hans-Jürgen Schreiber concentrated on his pronunciation.

"Much better." English had many difficult sounds for the native German speaker, but the *w* and *th* sounds topped the list. After only one hour, Peter had cured Hans-Jürgen of saying "vide," and soon he'd coach the "oo-ide" to "wide."

Peter wrote more phrases on the board. "Write these down and practice. Don't worry about any sound except the *w* for now."

Hans-Jürgen groaned and stretched gangly limbs clad in the black shorts and long-sleeved tan shirt of the Hitler Youth. *"Ich habe kein—"*

"In English," Peter said with a smile.

"I have no time to practice. We must stay after school every day for physical conditioning, and every Wednesday night and every Sunday are for the *Hitlerjugend*."

In the seat next to his son, Professor Schreiber frowned. "Hans-Jürgen."

"I know, Vati, but it is difficult to study for school, and I have no time to read."

Since membership in the Hitler Youth was practically mandatory, the boy needed encouragement. Peter sat on his other side. "You get to camp and hike and play sports, right? That's good."

The boy lowered his blond head, and his eyes darkened. "I do not want to be a soldier. I want to be a professor of mathematics."

Peter crossed his arms. "When I was your age, I stayed inside and read. I didn't play sports, and I was skinny and weak."

Professor Schreiber peered around his son and chuckled. "You were still skinny when I met you."

Hans-Jürgen stared at Peter's arms. "You are not skinny now."

The cords in Peter's neck tightened. Not since that day in 1933. "One day I learned why it isn't good to be weak, and I decided to be strong of both mind and body. A strong body helps the brain work better. *Verstehst du?*"

"*Ja, ich verstehe.*" Something in the boy's light eyes said he did indeed understand.

Professor Schreiber glanced at his watch. "It is time for your meeting."

Hans-Jürgen stood and grabbed a rucksack from under his seat. "Ja, hiking and the rifle range. I shall exercise my love of mathematics by calculating my rate of fire—while exercising my body." He grinned at Peter.

After Hans-Jürgen left, Peter wiped down the blackboard. "He is improving."

"Yes, but you give him private lessons," Professor Schreiber said. "I do not see how your techniques will work for larger groups."

Peter's shoulders stiffened. Such a small influence to have. His father had wielded great influence in the House of Representatives and in his business, an influence adopted by Peter's brothers—and expanded. They could reach the nation through their work. Peter couldn't.

"Perhaps your dissertation could focus on the phonetic differences between the regions of Germany." Professor Schreiber stood and tugged down his suit vest.

Peter rubbed his hands together to remove the chalk dust. He'd dedicated his life to this work since the age of twelve, including almost five years of graduate research. To start in a new direction?

A topic he had no passion for? A subject that would have no effect on the world?

Absolutely not.

He straightened his shoulders. "Thank you, but the German department at Harvard approved my topic, and I've already started my dissertation." If Dr. Schreiber withheld his approval . . .

The professor went to the window. "Do not be inflexible, Peter. When the storm comes, the reed bends but the stick breaks."

Peter picked up his attaché case. "A thin, weak stick perhaps, but not a thick, strong rod."

Dr. Schreiber gazed into the tree-filled courtyard flooded with morning sunshine. "Many thick, strong rods have fallen."

"What do you mean?"

The professor raised a sudden smile. "*Auf Wiedersehen*. Until Monday."

"Until Monday." Peter followed him out of the classroom, then turned toward his office to review his lesson plans for the first week of classes.

"Peter!" Fellow graduate student Otto von Albrecht jogged down the hall in the brown uniform of the National Socialist German Students' League.

"*Guten Morgen*, Otto." Peter preferred to offer the first greeting to remind his friends that as an American he wasn't required to give the "Heil, Hitler" greeting and salute.

Otto gave the greeting anyway. "Do you want to go skiing this weekend?"

"You know I would, but I have tickets to the symphony." And a date with an intriguing woman.

"Too bad. We'll miss you." Otto raked back the lock of light brown hair determined to reside between his eyebrows. "Are you free Monday evening? I'd like you to meet the fellows in the Students' League. They want to learn about life in America."

Peter had been warned about fanatics in the League, but Otto was a good egg. Besides, one of the purposes of studying abroad was to teach Germans about America and foster goodwill between the nations. "I'd like that."

"*Wunderbar.*" Otto raised the stiff-armed salute and jogged away.

Peter smiled as he returned to his office. This was shaping up to be an interesting year.

FOUR

After a pat to the ruby-studded comb in her hair, Evelyn opened her apartment door. "Good evening, Mr. Lang."

"Good evening, Miss Brand." He wore white tie attire with a top hat in his white-gloved hands, and a slow sweep of his gaze led to a slow smile. "You look . . . radiant."

"Thank you. Please come in while I fetch my things." She stepped inside, the silver brocade brushing her ankles.

Peter Lang didn't look half-bad himself. The black cutaway coat accentuated his tall, athletic build, and his wavy blond hair shone.

"That dress is stunning," he said. "And please call me Peter."

"Thank you. Please call me Evelyn." She transferred items from her daytime black leather handbag to a red satin clutch, cramming her smallest notebook inside.

She'd enjoy his appreciative looks and words while they lasted. The first date eliminated men who didn't like intelligent women. The second date weeded out those who assumed a modern career woman had loose morals. On the third date, if the man hadn't realized Evelyn was too much to handle, she helped him figure it out.

"Is this where you work?" Peter frowned at her Smith-Corona typewriter and the papers strewn about.

31

Perhaps she should have picked up, but she refused to hide who she was even to get a full three dates from a man.

"Yes." She pulled on long white gloves. "But when Libby's not home, it's too quiet, and I work at a darling café on Gärtnerplatz."

Evelyn reached for the cape draped over her desk chair.

Peter laid it around her shoulders, then he held open the door.

"Thank you." She descended the stairs and stepped out into the chilly evening, the smell of spent rain in the air. A black cab awaited. "I'd hoped you'd bring that car you're so fond of."

"I would have if I knew I could find parking on Türkenstrasse." He opened the cab door for her.

Evelyn slid in and gathered her skirts inside.

Peter circled to the other door, climbed in, and leaned forward to speak to the driver. *"Das Tonhalle, bitte."*

He settled back in the seat with his top hat in his lap. "With a conductor for a father, you must have had musical training."

Her cape pulled across her throat, and she adjusted it. "I play the viola, but not well. I have no patience for scales."

The cab passed a streetlamp, which illuminated Peter's amused expression. "I played the cello and not well at all. But I did enjoy it."

"That's what matters."

"Did your father want you to follow in his footsteps?"

"At first." Evelyn shrugged. "Then I told him words are my music. He understood, and now he's my greatest champion."

"Good. My father supported my goals too."

He spoke in the past tense, and his wistful tone hinted at a story. But Evelyn buttoned her lips. This was a date, not an interview.

"Speaking of your musical words, how is your article on the students coming along?"

"Good. I've interviewed a dozen students, and I hope to interview a few more." Surely she could find one student who'd seen past the shiny façade of Nazi prosperity to the darkness underneath. Although the juniors had been in Munich since September, all were bewitched.

"Is that why you agreed to come tonight? Follow-up questions?"
A teasing note lifted his voice.

"Oh no. I'm afraid I extracted every interesting morsel from
you."

He heaved a sigh. "I tried to manufacture a scandal but failed."

"Perhaps you could have an affair with the wife of a Nazi bigwig."

"Sorry. I'm afraid I'm the chivalrous, churchgoing sort."

Like Evelyn's father, brother, and grandfathers—a good sort.
Evelyn played along and heaved her own sigh. "Too bad. How
about theft? Murder?"

"What's the story, dollface?" He affected a gangster voice. "Who
do you want me to knock off? Say the word and—" He snapped
his fingers.

Evelyn couldn't resist. "George Norwood?"

Peter broke out laughing. "He's my oldest friend."

"Very well, but it sure would help my career."

"He warned me about you. I should have listened."

Somehow the warmth in his voice melted her more than a hundred compliments would have. For one moment she pictured a
fourth date. A good-night kiss.

Who was she kidding? Next thing she knew, he'd be ordering
her to wear florals and to stop speaking her mind on unfeminine
topics like current events.

The cab arrived at the Tonhalle, and Peter helped her out and
offered an arm sturdier than expected from a professor-in-training.
With her free hand, Evelyn lifted her skirts so she wouldn't fall
flat on her face climbing the steps.

Inside the concert hall, Peter checked in his hat and Evelyn's
cape. The lobby chandeliers cast light on women in colorful gowns
and men in uniform or white tie. So many hands knifed up in the
Nazi salute it was a wonder no one was hurt.

A tall man in a field gray Army officer's uniform smiled at her.
"Ah, Fräulein Brand. Heil, Hitler!"

Evelyn dropped a curtsy. "*Guten Abend*, Herr General. May I introduce Herr Peter Lang, an American doctoral student at the university. Herr Lang, this is General Ulrich Gerlach."

The men shook hands, then the general introduced the very young woman at his side as Fräulein Magda Müller. Fräulein Müller's platinum hair didn't match her dark brown eyebrows, and she certainly wasn't Frau Gerlach, mother of the general's four grown children.

Evelyn greeted her warmly. Disgruntled mistresses often became her best informants.

Peter smiled over Fräulein Müller's head. "I didn't know they'd be here. Excuse me, Herr General, Fräulein, but I would like to introduce Fräulein Brand to a dear friend."

After they said good-bye, Peter led Evelyn across the lobby to a middle-aged couple. "Professor Schreiber, Frau Schreiber, what a pleasure to see you."

"*Guten Abend*, Peter." The professor beamed and turned to Evelyn. "Who is this lovely lady?"

"May I introduce Fräulein Evelyn Brand. She's a correspondent with the American News Service."

Despite her shock, Evelyn managed to say her how-do-you-dos. In a social setting, men never introduced women with their job titles. They only did so for fellow men.

A friendly smile creased Frau Schreiber's round face. "How long have you known our Peter?"

"Only a few days. I interviewed him for a story on Monday."

"Have no fear, Fräulein." Crinkles radiated around the professor's light eyes. "Peter will take care of those *R*s and *L*s for you. U-umlaut too, Peter?"

His expression sobered. "I'm afraid so, Herr Professor."

Evelyn turned a quizzical look to her date.

He grinned. "I'll explain. Shall we find our seats?"

Peter tucked Evelyn's hand in the crook of his arm and led her through the lobby. "I grew up speaking both English and

German. My mother's family emigrated from Germany when she was eighteen. After the Great War, she was treated poorly because of her thick accent. I wanted to help her, so I analyzed how we Americans pronounce certain phonemes and how she pronounced them. Then I trained her, and we eliminated her accent almost entirely."

What a sweet picture that painted. "How kind of you."

He led her into the hall and down the aisle lit by chandeliers and resounding with the orchestra's warm-up. "When I took German in high school, I analyzed the other side, why my American friends had troubles with sounds in German. My teacher didn't like my meddling, so I started a German club and taught my classmates."

"Extraordinary." How many young people would do such a thing?

He dipped his head modestly. "That's the focus of my dissertation. I hope to revolutionize the teaching of foreign languages."

"That's fascinating." She found her seat and arranged her skirts. "By the way, I despise u-umlauts."

"Most Americans do, but the sound isn't that difficult. I could teach you." The invitation curled his lips in an enticing way.

However, the night was young, so Evelyn gave a noncommittal nod and studied the chamber orchestra. "I love this sound."

"You do?" Peter smiled at her. "It's a mess."

"Yes, but the mess means beauty is coming."

His smile deepened, and he leaned back in his seat and closed his eyes.

Evelyn had told Libby he wasn't unattractive. She'd have to amend that—he was definitely attractive, even if many women would disagree. The wire-rimmed glasses gave him the look of a kindly professor, but the crooked nose and a scar on his chin lent his face character. And his eyes were the deep gray-blue of her mother's Wedgwood vases.

She tapped her white-gloved fingers on her gray silk lap—one finger, two fingers, three. One date, two dates, three. Her pinky settled down to her lap, and her thumb lowered.

No. She tucked it into her palm. No fourth date. Absolutely no fifth date.

The orchestra silenced, and so did the audience. The first violinist came out to applause, and then the conductor. Then came Libby, resplendent in a floor-length black gown with her long brown hair done up in curls and loops like a Grecian goddess.

Evelyn resisted the urge to applaud uproariously, but she exchanged a grin with Peter.

The chamber orchestra began to play Carl Philipp Emanuel Bach's Flute Concerto in D minor, and Libby swayed with the music, her flute bobbing and circling. The notes flitted like a flock of butterflies, darting and weaving and sweeping, always in motion. Evelyn heard her practice every day, but with an orchestra behind her, the effect was glorious.

For her second piece, Libby played Handel's Sonata in F, one of her favorites, and it showed. All too soon, the conductor lowered his baton for the intermission.

Evelyn and Peter rose. She took his arm, and they headed up the aisle.

"I can see why Miss White receives so many accolades," Peter said.

"I remember when she started flute lessons and cried because she couldn't make a sound."

"She certainly overcame that. I wish my friend Paul Aubrey could hear her. He traveled to Chicago with me for your father's concert."

Paul Aubrey . . . she'd heard that name before. "One of your Harvard pals?"

"Yes." Peter sent her an appreciative look. "He runs a factory in Paris, a subsidiary of the family business."

Evelyn smiled at memories of the Seine and baguettes and

stimulating café conversations. "I lived in Paris for two years. It was wonderful."

"Not anymore. Aubrey's having a terrible time."

"Really? How strange."

Peter led her to an open spot in the lobby and faced her, his expression stern. "The communists have ruined everything."

"Communists?" She spoke in a low voice—not a word one wanted to use in Germany.

"Have you heard? They're striking in Paris, rioting, occupying factories, including Aubrey's."

"I—I've heard."

"That's the problem with them." The hardening of Peter's face and voice was swift and startling. "They have no respect for property, for negotiation, for *life*."

Evelyn eased back and gazed around the lobby filled with Nazis. The same could be said of other factions.

"That's what's so refreshing about Germany," Peter said.

Evelyn's gaze jumped back to him. "Refreshing?"

"Yes. When I was here in '32, communist mobs roamed the streets. No one was safe."

She fought to keep the shock off her face. Had he forgotten the Nazi mobs of the time?

"But not anymore," Peter said.

Only the presence of so many Nazi uniforms kept Evelyn from speaking her mind. The communists didn't roam the streets anymore because they were in concentration camps. So were the socialists and the Social Democrats and anyone who dared speak against the regime, even pastors and priests.

Peter adjusted his glasses, and the glare concealed the blue. "Now the streets are safe, the people are happy, and there's order in the land."

American and British correspondents constantly complained about the tourists and students who saw the low unemployment and the new buildings and declared the Nazis weren't as bad as the mean old newspapers said.

For some reason, she'd expected better from Peter Lang.

Evelyn's hand rested flat by her side against her brocade skirt, and she rolled her fingers around her thumb. One, two, three, four. She would be charming and polite for the remainder of the evening, but there would be no second date.

FIVE

Peter strolled around the circular park in the middle of the round-about. Colorful flowerbeds spread out in loops around a fountain, even and proportioned. No wonder Evelyn Brand liked the Gärtnerplatz.

Buildings with curved façades rimmed the park, painted in shades of pink and cream, and an elegant neoclassical theater sat in the seat of importance.

Only one café overlooked the plaza, its outside tables abandoned in the unseasonal cold weather. Peter checked his tie and opened the door.

A gentleman approached, small and trim, with gray seasoning his black hair. "*Guten Morgen.* Welcome to my café."

"Good morning. I am looking for my friend." There she was, her brunette head bent over a clacking portable typewriter.

"Ach," the gentleman said. "Fräulein Brand? Come with me."

Evelyn sat at a small square table, her back to the wall and papers in disorder around her.

"Fräulein Brand, I bring you a friend." The café owner swept his arm toward Peter.

She raised her head, and her eyes swam into focus. "Herr Lang."

Peter removed his hat and smiled. Unlike many Americans, Evelyn remembered the formality Germans used in public. "Good morning, Fräulein."

Evelyn turned to the café owner and pressed her hand to her heart. "Why would I need another friend when I have you, Herr Gold?"

"Ach, but look at your Herr Lang." Herr Gold clapped him on the shoulder. "See how tall he is, how his hair curls. Is he not a fine friend?"

Peter gave her what he hoped was a fine smile.

She patted her papers. "I would invite him to join me, but as you see . . ."

Herr Gold snapped a brown-eyed gaze to Peter. "Then I will be your friend. Please sit."

"Thank you, *mein Herr*. You do me an honor." Peter sat at the table beside Evelyn's, his back also to the wall, and he set down his attaché case.

Herr Gold sat across from him and flapped his white apron over his lap. "So, my friend, please tell me why a good Münchner like you has never visited my café."

"Because I am not from Munich. I am an American."

"American?" Herr Gold pressed back in his chair. "You do not sound American."

"My dear mother came from Munich."

"Outstanding. She taught you well." Then he gasped. "Ach! I sit here being your friend, and you have nothing to eat or drink. What would you like?"

"Coffee, please."

"I am making fresh *Krapfen*. I will bring one, no charge, for my new friend." Herr Gold hurried into the kitchen.

Peter slid his gaze to Evelyn, and she raised a half smile. Was she amused? Annoyed? A little of both?

He pointed with his thumb toward the kitchen. *"Das ist Gemütlichkeit."*

Evelyn zipped her paper out of the typewriter and perused it. "Yes, *Gemütlichkeit*, the famous Bavarian hospitality."

"It's more than hospitality." Peter switched into English. "It's opening the home and the heart, inviting the stranger into the coziness."

"Speaking of my *gemütlich* café, what brings you here?" Her tone was anything but cozy.

"You said this was a fine place to work, so I thought I'd give it a try. I have papers to grade." He lifted his attaché case to the table. He'd also come to figure out why the electric connection with Evelyn had fizzled after the concert.

She rolled a new sheet of paper into the typewriter.

"What are you writing about?" he asked. "The concert?"

"I already turned that in. Even Norwood will like it. Now I'm working on the article about your fellow students." She straightened the paper in the roller. "Yesterday I interviewed two more students and found what I needed."

"Good." He set his elbow on his attaché case. "Please tell me what George Norwood has done to wound you."

"To wound me?" She riffled through the mess of papers. "To start, he sent me to Munich. All the other ANS correspondents are based in Berlin. That's where the news is."

"Hmm. Is that because you're young?"

"Young?" She set aside a stack and picked up another. "Norwood must be close to your age, and you're twenty-seven."

"He's a year older." His fingers itched to straighten her mess, but he restrained himself.

"I'm twenty-six, and we have a new fellow, all of twenty-three. He's in Berlin. And I'm here."

"Because you're a woman."

Her gaze met his, and thin brown eyebrows lifted. "Yes."

"I'm sorry. That isn't right."

Evelyn selected a paper. "If a man hunts down a lead, he's called bold. I'm called pushy. If a man finds an unconventional way to get a story, he's called clever. I'm scolded for breaking the rules."

"That's a shame."

She frowned at the paper. "Don't you dare breathe a word of this to your pal."

Peter studied her in her brown tweed suit, her brown curls brushing her jaw, leaving her slender neck bare and somehow vulnerable. "May I tell George how polite and professional you were? How your questions were intelligent and reasonable?"

Her eyes widened, and sunlight through the window allowed him to admire the shade of brown—coffee with a splash of milk.

"For you, my friend." Herr Gold set down a coffee cup and a plate with a *Krapfen*, a fragrant ball of fried dough sprinkled with powdered sugar.

"Thank you. Everything smells delicious." After the café owner returned to the kitchen, Peter added a splash of milk to his coffee and held up the cup to Evelyn. "Cheers."

She raised her cup and a genuine smile. "Cheers."

No, two splashes of milk, and Peter added another splash to match her eyes.

Good. He'd restored the connection. He took a sip of coffee, rich and warm. "You said you enjoy hiking and that you'd like to see my car. Would you like to drive to Garmisch-Partenkirchen on Saturday? We could hike through the Partnach Gorge and have dinner at the Olympia Haus. The cheese spaetzle is excellent."

"No, thank you." Evelyn set down her cup and resumed typing.

"If you're busy, we could go another day."

"No, thank you." She hit the carriage return lever and slid it across.

Hmm. He took a bite of the *Krapfen*, light and sweet. The problem wasn't the activity. It wasn't the day. It certainly wasn't the spaetzle. Ah, it was the company.

He wiped his sugar-powdered fingers on his napkin. What had

he said or done? He'd never been smooth, but he'd had his fair share of romances.

Peter stroked the walnut-brown leather of his attaché case, opened it, and pulled out the quizzes from the first day of class. The quizzes wouldn't count toward grades, but they'd show him what the students already knew.

A pause in the typing, then a frenzied outburst.

When had things changed with Evelyn? Peter took another bite of the Bavarian donut. He'd noticed a distinct chill after the concert. They hadn't talked during the performance, of course.

Intermission? They hadn't talked much. Evelyn had excused herself to the ladies' room, and Peter had chatted with the Schreibers until she returned right at the end of intermission.

Something he'd said? Something about Aubrey or Paris or the communists?

He ventured a glance in her direction. A red purse hung from her chair. Every time he'd seen her, she'd worn something red.

Peter grinned, feeling like a schoolboy about to tug a girl's braids. Instead, he tugged the purse strap. "Is the red a fashion statement or a political one?"

She glanced down at her purse, and she chuckled, low and resonant. "You think because I'm a reporter, I'm a communist." She mouthed the word silently.

"Are you?"

"I assure you, Mr. Lang, I am not. My views are traditionally American, based on freedom. Freedom of speech. Freedom of the press. Freedom of assembly. Freedom of religion."

"Very patriotic." He sipped more coffee.

"You said you were a churchgoing man, so you must have some respect for Christian values like liberty and mercy, values I cherish."

"I do. I also have respect for the Christian values of law and justice and order."

A spark lit Evelyn's eyes and smile. "The purpose of the law is to preserve freedom."

Peter shook his head. She hadn't been there. She didn't know. "It's to limit freedom. Without order, freedom leads to chaos and destruction. It leads to mobs, rioting, murder."

"Your father."

Peter sucked in a sharp breath.

She lowered her head. "I'm sorry, but he was a public figure. I called the bureau, and they wired me an article about his death."

His vision darkened, and he forced himself to breathe. "Did— did the article mention his son was present?"

Now she sucked in a loud breath. "You?"

Peter sorted the quizzes into alphabetical order by student last name. "I was home for the summer after I received my bachelor's. My father asked me to accompany him to the factory. The communists had taken over the union, the workers were striking, and Father wanted me to learn about negotiation. Except you can't negotiate with unreasonable and violent men."

Townsend's quiz went after Schultz, before Wechsler. "They wouldn't even listen to my father's offers. They shouted him down. He saw it was useless and tried to leave. That's when they started hitting him."

"Oh dear," Evelyn said.

"I tried to help, but they—" He touched his nose, the sharp angle to it, then back to sorting. "They punched me, knocked me down, held me back. I—I had to watch as . . ."

"I am so sorry." Evelyn's voice quivered. "How awful for you."

Peter tapped the stack of papers on the table to straighten it, then lifted his red pencil and bent over the first quiz. "You have work to do, and so do I."

A long pause, and typewriter keys tapped, but slowly.

Peter crossed out a *der* and changed it to *die*, corrected the declension of the adjective, but then he set down his pencil. It wasn't fair to the students to analyze their work when he was agitated.

Mutti's letter. He still hadn't read it, and he pulled it from a pocket in the lid of his attaché case. It started *"Mein lieber Peter."* Of her four sons, Peter loved the language most, so Mutti always wrote him in German.

My dear Peter,

Tomorrow I will write with news from home and pleasant things, and I will ask about your studies and your life in my beloved city of München.

But today I write what is on my heart, what I've prayed about for weeks.

My dear Peter, of all my sons, you were the one with the sweetest heart. You were the boy who couldn't stand to see his mother mocked for being German and who taught me how to speak like the other mothers. You were the first to help when anyone was hurt, the first to speak up when anyone was wronged, the first to step in when anyone needed assistance.

I write this with tears in my eyes because I write in the past tense.

You have changed since your father's death. Naturally, the loss of such a great man has affected us all. Your older brothers have had to assume his roles in Congress and the company, and I have had to learn to live without the man I love. But you, my Peter, have changed the most.

I have seen a hardening in you due to unforgiveness.

My darling Peter, I have forgiven those men for what they did to your father and to you. I have done this out of love for my Lord. Was my sin not also responsible for the blows that rained down on my Savior's precious head?

As the Lord has forgiven me, I have forgiven those men. I pray you will too and will rediscover compassion and mercy.

Peter pulled off his glasses and rubbed the inside corners of his eyes. Compassion and mercy? Compassion drove Father to make generous offers to his workers. Mercy urged him to negotiate even after the men turned violent.

Forgiveness? He'd consider it when those murderers were locked behind bars.

"Mr. Lang?" Evelyn stood before his table, typewriter case in hand. When had she packed?

Peter put on his glasses, worked up a smile, and stood. "Leaving?"

She smiled back, soft and tentative. "I have an appointment. I hope you liked my café."

"I do. It's . . . *gemütlich*."

"It is." She extended her hand. "Good-bye."

He shook her hand, then returned to his seat and stared at the letter and quizzes. A brisk walk to strengthen body, mind, and soul—that's what he needed.

Herr Gold came out with a tray and collected Evelyn's cup and saucer. "She will not be easily won."

Peter's mouth drifted open. Was he that transparent? Of course, he was.

Herr Gold pointed a finger and a smile at Peter. "Those are the women most worth winning."

"Ja." Peter put away his papers and laid out his payment and a tip that more than covered the cost of the *Krapfen* as well.

Between his memories and Mutti's letter, the last thing he needed in his addled brain was romance.

SIX

SUNDAY, APRIL 10, 1938

Snow in April and on a day when Evelyn had a chance to get a story. She stamped her feet on the sidewalk outside the church the government had commandeered as a polling place—on a Sunday, no less.

Three women walked out, and Evelyn approached with her notepad. "*Guten Morgen.* I'm Evelyn Brand with the American News Service. May I interview you about the plebiscite?"

"For America?" A white-haired woman smiled up at her from under a fur-trimmed hat. "Ach, how exciting."

"Imagine our names in a newspaper in America," the youngest lady said, clad in a fashionable green coat.

Evelyn led them away from the entrance. The correspondents in Berlin would get the main bylines for the articles on the national election, but only Evelyn would write about the women's angle. ANS might actually pick it up.

"Are you related?" Evelyn asked. "You have the same lovely shade of blue eyes."

"My daughter and my granddaughter," the oldest woman said. "We voted 'Ja.'"

Evelyn took notes. "You voted in favor of the *Anschluss*, the unification of Germany and Austria."

"It is all Germany now." The daughter's heavyset face glowed. *"Ein Volk, ein Reich, ein Führer."*

One people, one empire, one leader. Evelyn wrote the slogan she'd heard innumerable times.

"Hitler has made Germany strong again. He is undoing the disgrace of Versailles." The grandmother puckered her mouth.

Evelyn murmured. The Versailles Treaty at the end of the Great War had gutted the German military and imposed severe reparations. The Germans blamed the treaty for the poverty Peter Lang had observed six years earlier. The chaos.

She frowned and took notes. "And now . . . ?"

"Now we hold our heads high." The granddaughter lifted her chin. "The world can see how great our Führer is and how good he is to us."

The grandmother patted Evelyn's arm. "You Americans should follow our example. All the gangsters! And the soup lines." She clucked her tongue.

Evelyn's jaw tightened. Yes, times were hard in America, but a dictatorship wasn't the solution.

After she took the ladies' names at their request, they went on their way.

Evelyn adjusted her leather gloves. Snow frosted the street in white, with shiny black tracks where cars had driven. She'd heard reports from farmers about the cold snap causing a loss of blossoms from fruit trees, and the government predicted a fruit shortage. So much for apple strudel and plum cake.

A woman left the polling place, her gaze darting about, and she gave the storm trooper guards at the door a wide berth.

A woman with a story. Evelyn met her about twenty feet from the door. *"Guten Morgen.* I'm Evelyn Brand with the American News Service. May I interview you?"

The woman startled. Thin lines cupped around her mouth, and

gray streaked the brown braid coiled around her head like a halo. "An—an American reporter?"

"Yes." Evelyn gave her a soothing smile. "May I interview you about the plebiscite?"

"Nein." She stepped around Evelyn and hustled down the sidewalk.

Bother. It would have been nice to have had one dissenting voice, even a cautious voice. Evelyn wouldn't have taken her name.

Over the next hour, she interviewed several dozen ladies. The vast majority spoke with enthusiasm about the Anschluss and their Führer. A smaller number spoke the same words but with stiff voices and furtive glances to the brown-uniformed SA storm troopers, even though Evelyn conducted her interviews well out of earshot.

The correspondents predicted a 99 percent "Ja" vote as in every other Nazi plebiscite. Every day the Germans lost a little more freedom, but they had jobs, and that was all that seemed to matter to them. But freedom mattered to Evelyn.

With plenty of interviews, Evelyn closed her notepad. She'd write her article and phone it to Berlin this afternoon. Norwood insisted on editing her work first. Only hers. Completely insulting. After all, the staff in New York edited all articles before publication.

Evelyn slipped her notepad into her purse.

"Excuse me, Fräulein. You dropped your handkerchief." A lady held out a white hankie.

Evelyn hadn't used hers. "No, I—"

The woman grabbed her hand and stuffed the fabric into her grip—the skittish woman with the halo braid. The handkerchief crinkled.

And Evelyn understood. "Oh, it *is* mine. *Danke schön.*"

"*Bitte.*" She slipped away.

Without looking, Evelyn stuffed the handkerchief and the enclosed note in her purse. She'd read it in the privacy of her apartment.

She turned the corner. The street was strangely empty, and she peered ahead.

Two blocks up, red and black standards bobbed. A parade.

Evelyn glanced around for a place to hide. A butcher shop, and she ducked inside. It didn't matter who was parading—military or SA or Hitler Youth—everyone watching was required to raise the Nazi salute.

Sure, the German government had issued numerous decrees stating that foreigners weren't required to salute, but Evelyn didn't exactly wear the flag of the United States as a shawl. In the past five years, dozens of Americans had been beaten up for not saluting at parades. An official apology didn't mend broken bones.

She browsed the butcher case. Might as well buy meat for dinner, but the pickings were slim. The government's insistence on making the German economy self-sufficient had led to food shortages.

The sound of drums and trumpets and cheering built, and Evelyn feigned indecision, although she knew what she wanted. It was her night to cook, and she craved meatloaf.

When the din peaked, Evelyn asked for half a pound of *Hackfleisch*, the German equivalent of ground beef.

The butcher weighed out the meat and wrapped it in paper, and Evelyn slowly picked out coins for payment.

By the time she finished, the little parade had passed. After checking both directions, Evelyn hurried home.

Flute music wafted from inside the apartment—Johann Sebastian Bach's Suite no. 2 in B minor. Evelyn flung open the door, tossed the meat on the table, plopped into a kitchen chair, and snatched the note from her purse.

The music stopped. "Well, hello to you too."

"Hi, Libby." Evelyn unfolded the paper—*"Brot, Käse, Kraut."* A shopping list. She flipped it over. "A woman sneaked me a note at the polling place."

"How exciting." Libby came over, flute in hand, her hair bound in a braid down her back. "What does it say?"

Evelyn peered at it. Not only was German handwriting script difficult to decipher, but the woman had written small and had filled every space. Evelyn read aloud for Libby's benefit.

I will not tell you my name, but I want you to tell our story, the true story no one dares voice.

You asked my opinion on the plebiscite. It is a sham. No Jews are allowed to vote, but everyone else is required to. If you don't go to your polling place, they bring you by force.

The ballot asks, "Do you agree with the reunification of Austria with the German Reich, and do you vote for the policies of Adolf Hitler?" One vote on both questions. A large circle in the center of the ballot is marked "Ja." To the side is a small circle marked "Nein." To vote no is not only disagreeing with the Anschluss but opposing Hitler and his policies. To vote no is treason.

The voting is not secret. A long table stands in the open, and brownshirts watch over our shoulders as we mark our ballots. Those who vote no will be arrested. In case anyone sneaks past, the ballots are marked. When I checked in, they wrote a number beside my name on the elector list. I felt bumps on my ballot and inspected them surreptitiously. It was the same number, as if someone had typed it without a ribbon. If you vote no, they will track you down.

To vote no is to offer yourself to the Gestapo for arrest, torture, and a trip to Dachau.

I voted yes, but I hate Hitler and his regime. I work as a secretary at a government ministry, and I hear many things. If you are interested in hearing them too, meet me tonight at 10 p.m. in the Maximiliansanlage by the Angel of Peace monument.

"You have a new informant." Libby squeezed Evelyn's shoulder.
"I think so. You have to be careful with informants, especially

the eager ones. They're often sent by the Gestapo. But I think this woman is genuine." After Evelyn wrote her article, she'd feed the note to the fire.

"Are you going to meet her tonight? It'll be cold."

"Of course, but first I have an article to write." At her desk, Evelyn shoved aside papers and hefted up her typewriter case. She'd last used it on Thursday at Herr Gold's café.

Peter Lang had visited the café again, which was bothersome. Yet she was glad to see him in good spirits after how she'd treated him on Tuesday.

She could still see the shock and pain on Peter's face when she'd mentioned his father. Just because she had access to information didn't give her the right to invade his privacy. His grief.

How horrendous for him to have watched his own father's murder. Now she understood why he felt the way he did—although she'd never agree with him.

Evelyn opened her typewriter case. A piece of paper remained in the roller—she never did that. She twisted the knob to roll it up a few lines.

"Dinner tonight?" was typed, and Evelyn laughed.

The flute music stopped again. "What's so funny?"

"This." Evelyn took the paper to Libby at her music stand. "Peter must have typed it when I went to the kitchen to say good-bye to Herr Gold. You know me—I pack so quickly, I didn't even see it."

"That's sweet. You should give him another chance."

"Absolutely not." Evelyn returned to her typewriter and rolled the paper back in. "He has a certain charm about him, but we don't agree on the important things. Besides, I don't need a man to lean on."

"I know. You can handle anything."

"I can." She typed "No, thank you." If Peter returned to the café, she'd give it to him. It was rather rude of her not to have replied.

"You and the Lord together can handle anything." Libby's tone implied that her statement was a wish for Evelyn, not the truth.

Her fingers settled onto the keys, each finger pad nestled in round black lacquer.

"'The Lord is my strength and song,'" Libby quoted, "'and is become my salvation.'"

"Yes." Evelyn loved God. He was indeed her song and her salvation. She rejoiced in how he'd freed her from sin.

But she didn't need him for strength as Libby did. Still, she was glad the Lord was there to help in a pinch.

Libby's metronome ticked away, and notes from Bach's suite tumbled out.

Evelyn added her own music in time to the metronome, the music of her typewriter keys, the music of her words, of truth.

SEVEN

The pageantry thrilled Peter's heart, and the eloquence of the human form in motion pleased his eyes. The most spectacular movie he'd ever seen. He'd bought tickets to the premiere of Leni Riefenstahl's *Olympia* for Evelyn's sake, but he was glad he'd come.

"Let's go," Evelyn whispered in the darkness beside him.

"Now?" The movie was coming to a sweeping finale.

"Before the national anthem. Come on."

She had a point. Staying bent over, Peter ducked into the aisle and followed Evelyn. As Americans, they weren't required to sing "Deutschland über Alles" or the "Horst Wessel Song," but he didn't want to offend anyone by refraining.

In the lobby Evelyn started putting on her coat, and Peter helped her.

"That was the longest movie I've ever seen," she said.

"It was." Peter slipped on his own overcoat. Even with an intermission, three and a half hours gave the film a marathon-like feel appropriate for a movie about the 1936 Berlin Olympics. "I'm starved. Shall we get dinner? The Hofbräuhaus isn't far."

Evelyn's chin jutted out. "I only accepted your invitation to the movie, not dinner."

"And you only accepted so you could write an article about the movie. However"—he tapped his wristwatch—"it's late. Do you want to cook dinner? I don't. I'd rather have sausage and potato salad."

She hesitated, then pressed a hand to her stomach. "I do like potato salad."

"Great." The triumphant strains of "Deutschland über Alles" poured from the theater. "If we hurry, we'll beat the crowd."

Outside, snowflakes dusted the night air. Talk of the unseasonal cold hovered on his tongue, but he wanted something deeper.

"You were very kind to get me the ticket." Evelyn plunged her hands into her coat pockets. "ANS assigned me to cover the premiere, but when I couldn't get tickets—well, you already heard me gripe about this."

He chuckled. "Thank goodness you griped, or I wouldn't have known. And thank goodness I went to the Students' League meeting when they sold tickets."

"The German Students' League? You went to a meeting?" Evelyn's eyes grew enormous.

"I'm not a member, if that's what you were thinking. And you were."

She gave him a mischievous smile. "Do you blame me?"

He smiled back and led her across the street, his shoes crunching in the snow. "My friend Otto invited me. They want to learn about America. That's part of the purpose of studying abroad."

Snowflakes glittered on her dark gray hat. "What I wouldn't give to attend. What a story. But I don't suppose women are allowed."

Peter grimaced. "Come to think of it, only men attend. But they mostly talk about classes."

They reached the Hofbräuhaus, a Munich landmark. Traditional Bavarian music greeted them, the tuba and accordion leading the other instruments in frolicking tunes. Peter and Evelyn were led through the maze of rooms, under elaborate signs for the *Stammtische*, the tables reserved for regulars. Waiters in lederhosen and waitresses in dirndls carried platters of beer and savory food.

Their table stood by a tall arched window. After Peter hung their coats on hooks, they both ordered bratwurst, sauerkraut, potato salad, and coffee. It gave him hope that they could find other things to agree on. Although bantering with her was fun too.

Peter scooted his chair in. "The movie was incredible."

"It was." Evelyn adjusted the sleeves of her burgundy dress. "I've never seen anything like it."

"I looked for my friend Henning. He rowed for the Danish team, but he must not have been photogenic enough."

"Henning?" She narrowed one eye. "One of your Hah-vahd friends?"

"Right." He grinned at her Midwestern disdain for the Ivy League. "Did you get enough material for your article?"

"Yes, and I figured out my angle."

"Angle?"

Evelyn rested her forearms on the table and leaned closer, lowering her voice. "As a guest, I have to be careful not to insult my hosts, or I'll be escorted out of the house. *Gemütlichkeit* has limits."

One day at the café, she'd mentioned the risk of getting expelled. "How would . . . our hosts know what you've written?"

"The embassy in DC reads our newspapers." Evelyn shot a furtive glance at a long table, where a group of older men raised beer steins and sang "Du, du, liegst mir im Herzen."

With the boisterous music and conversation in the room, Evelyn had no need to worry about anyone listening, but Peter leaned in, more than willing to play her game of low voices and code words. Anything to study her face at close range. "All right, but when your hostess serves a tasty dessert of a movie, how can any guest find fault?"

"No faults to report." Thick dark lashes swept over her brown eyes. "I can honestly praise the beauty of the production, the innovative camera angles, the splendor, all that."

"It was gorgeous." So was Evelyn, in her own unique way.

"But it was also about subverting the individual to the will of the community. About conformity and uniformity."

Peter tilted his head. Perhaps some saw it that way. He hadn't.

"That's my angle." She patted the table. "Phrases like uniformity and the loss of individuality will please our hosts. They cherish those values. But the phrases will have the opposite effect at home. What do Americans fear most? Loss of freedom. Loss of individuality. After all, what's our founding document? The Declaration of Independence."

Peter tipped his glasses higher and smiled. "'We the people of the United States, in order to form a more perfect union.' We're more than individuals. We're a group."

"A union of *individuals*."

"Yes, but a *union* of individuals, bound in community. Besides, community is a Christian concept. The body of believers."

"True." Evelyn rested her chin on her palm with a spark in her eyes. "Yet our hosts destroy church communities—Catholic and Protestant alike. They've arrested hundreds of priests and pastors—especially in the Confessing Church. Men who preach the Bible instead of Party doctrine—like Martin Niemöller." She whispered the name.

Peter frowned at the red-and-white print tablecloth. He'd heard about Niemöller. And Otto had told him the official German church rejected the Old Testament and the Apostle Paul's writings as too Jewish. They even preached an Aryan Jesus. That all bothered Peter . . . deeply.

"Our hosts put the Party above the Lord, a political leader above the Lord." Evelyn's voice barely crossed the divide between them. "And look how they treat God's chosen people."

He raised a heavy head and met her gaze. "I don't agree with that. Not at all. No one should be treated unfairly due to his race."

Evelyn's face sobered. "We've found something we agree on."

"Yes." He drew in a deep breath. "But I wouldn't worry. It's a passing phase."

She blinked rapidly. "A passing phase?"

"Germany has had difficult times, and in difficult times people seek scapegoats. It's wrong, but it happens. It happens in America too."

Her brows bunched together. "That's true."

"Now that prosperity has returned to this land, they'll stop seeking scapegoats and the pressure will ease."

"I hope you're right. But our hosts have given up so much freedom in exchange for that prosperity. Where do you draw the line?"

Peter clenched his hands together on the table. Where *did* he draw the line?

Evelyn grabbed her purse and dug around inside. "How did Roosevelt word it?"

"Roosevelt?"

"He gave a Fireside Chat last week to reassure people about the latest economic setback. You wouldn't have read it—the German papers are censored—but the bureau gets reports straight from New York." She pulled out a notebook.

Peter smiled. "I read an article about that speech in the *Münchner Neueste Nachrichten*."

"Only the parts approved by Joseph Goebbels's Ministry of Propaganda." She flipped a page. "Here we go. The president said, 'Democracy has disappeared in several other great nations—disappeared not because the people of those nations disliked democracy, but because they had grown tired of unemployment and insecurity, of seeing their children hungry while they sat helpless in the face of government confusion, government weakness—weakness through lack of leadership in government. Finally, in desperation, they chose to sacrifice liberty in the hope of getting something to eat.'"

The waitress came over with plates heaping with food, and the steam wafted tantalizing scents into Peter's nose.

After the waitress left, Evelyn pulled the pot of Bavarian sweet mustard close and slathered some on her bratwurst. "What do you think of that quote, Mr. Lang?"

"I think you should be careful, Miss Brand." He aimed a mock stern look at her. "Careful not to put a political leader above the Lord."

She stared at him, then burst out laughing, right in time with the accordion.

Peter grinned and scooped a forkful of potato salad into his mouth, pungent with vinegar. Herr Gold was right. She was worth the winning.

EIGHT

Tobacco-scented words drifted to Evelyn through the moonless night in a wooded area in the English Garden. "Almost a hundred men from Munich hauled to Dachau for being beggars or 'work shy.' The Nazis have gone too far."

This was the third time Evelyn had met this informant, a member of the "Kripo," the criminal police, as opposed to the Gestapo, the state police. Or so he said.

His previous tips had proven correct, although not enough for a story, Norwood said.

"You must write this. We were ordered to arrest fifteen hundred men throughout the Reich."

"I'll do what I can, *mein Herr*." But she didn't completely trust this man she'd dubbed *"Ein Knopf"*—"one button"—for his habit of buttoning only the top button of his overcoat. He was either too cheap or too vain to buy the larger size needed to accommodate his belly.

"You can verify with your other sources, right? Surely you speak to others in the Kripo."

Her guard went up. "I speak to all sorts of people."

"Anyone in the Kripo? I would be glad to meet like-minded men."

That guard sounded the alarm, but she schooled her voice to a sympathetic tone. "I can't reveal my sources."

"I understand." Cigar smoke wafted her way. "The Nazis are cruel to those who oppose them. So cruel."

Evelyn knew better than to agree or disagree. She just took notes. "Do you have any other information?"

"Not today, but let's walk. It is good to speak freely."

More alarms rang. Her other sources spent as little time with her as possible. "I understand, but it's late and my roommate is holding dinner for me."

"All right." His sigh seemed to come from the tips of his toes. "If only I had a comrade to talk to, who shared my opinions. Then I would not feel alone. Surely you know others. I know you can't give names, but if I knew where they worked, what they looked—"

"I'm sorry, but I must go home. My roommate will worry and call the police. Good night."

"*Gute Nacht*, Fräulein."

Evelyn followed the path out of the woods and through the gardens, dimly lit by streetlamps. If Ein Knopf was not Gestapo, he was certainly reporting to them. No dissident who wanted to keep his head attached to his body would ask for information on others. But it was typical for the Gestapo. She would not meet him again.

Although the temperature was above freezing for the first time in ages, Evelyn shivered. She scanned every shadow, every tree, every bush, acutely aware of how alone she was, how empty the paths.

What was wrong with her? She'd walked the streets of Chicago, New York, and Paris alone at night without a tremble. Journalism was no place for a woman who needed a big, strong man to feel safe.

And why did Peter Lang's big, strong form flash through her mind? Evelyn walked faster and broke through to Mandlstrasse.

Even if she did want a man in her life, it wouldn't be Peter. Sure, it was flattering how he asked her out every time he visited the café, how he keyed his date ideas to her interests. Sure, he received her polite refusals with amusement, almost as if he preferred a refusal to an acceptance. And sure, she was entranced when he talked, not just because of the pleasing shape of his lips, but how they moved with almost exaggerated precision, probably due to his research.

"For heaven's sake." Then she clamped her mouth shut. Talking to oneself in public wasn't wise in a nation that prized physical and mental perfection. A nation that forcibly sterilized people with psychological disorders or hereditary diseases.

How could Peter approve of a single policy from such a regime? In that moment, all she wanted was to find him and have that spirited argument. And watch him speak.

If only Peter Lang's opinions were as finely formed as his lips.

She groaned and turned onto Herzogstrasse. Even if his opinions were better formed, she knew better. She knew.

Peter might praise her independence at first. But so had Howard and Clark and Warren. Howard had called her lively, Clark amusing, Warren refreshing.

Then Howard asked if it would hurt her to wear something pretty and feminine for once. Then Clark said it embarrassed him when she challenged professors, although the male students did so all the time. Then Warren demanded dates when he knew she had deadlines, told her to put aside fantasies and stop pretending to be a man.

A stinging across her mouth, and she rubbed away the sensation, the memories. Never again would she let a man silence her.

Evelyn tromped up the steps in her apartment building. She was all sharp points, and when men failed to file down those points, they tried to break them off by force.

The scent of past-prime roses from Libby's last performance greeted her.

Her roommate sat curled up with a book while the radio played Beethoven's *Pastoral Symphony*. "You're home late."

"Met with a source." Evelyn hung up her coat and hat.

"There's potato soup on the stove."

"Thanks, Lib. I'll cook tomorrow." She untied her black lace-up pumps and worked her toes into slippers.

"You received a letter from home."

"Great." Evelyn ladled a bowl of fragrant soup, sliced some rye bread, and sat at the table. A letter awaited—from Mother.

She opened it and set aside clippings of her articles. Mother took two subscriptions so she could keep one copy and send one to Evelyn.

News from home made her smile—Papa's latest concert, Mother's club happenings, her younger brother Roger's college classes, her older sister Francie's house decorating, and the antics of Francie's darling children. For once, not a word asking when Evelyn would have a house to decorate or children to have antics.

She flipped the page.

I'm not surprised your cross was made in America. I'm only surprised Grandma Brand continues to tell that story.

As you know, my father was Jewish and became a Christian as a boy. My father was never ashamed of his heritage, unlike your father's parents, who were also born Jewish.

Your Grandma Brand actually came from Russia. When her family was wiped out in a pogrom, she fled to Germany, where she met your grandfather and begged him to emigrate to America. Here they converted and were married in the church. She was terrified they might also be persecuted in the US, so they vowed to pretend they had always been Christian. Your grandmother bought that cross and told everyone it had been in the family for generations.

I've always thought the charade unnecessary, but I've

followed your father's wishes. However, I refuse to allow you to believe a lie at your age.

Evelyn laid down the letter. "I'm three-quarters Jewish."

"Hmm?" Libby raised her head from her book. "I thought you were one-quarter."

"So did I." She read that part of the letter to Libby.

Her roommate's face grew pensive. "Your poor grandmother. Imagine losing your whole family. Imagine being so afraid that you'd give up everything you knew and believed."

"I can imagine." Evelyn rolled her fingers around the cross at her neck. All through Germany and Austria, Jews were converting. Since many nations only granted visas to Jews with baptismal certificates, they saw conversion as a chance to escape.

The fullness of the meaning of it all wormed into her stomach and slithered there. "If I—if I weren't an American citizen, the antisemitic laws would apply to me."

Libby's eyes widened. "Oh my."

To distract herself, Evelyn folded the letter and picked up the newspaper clippings—her article from the Anschluss in Vienna and her article about the students. Both had run!

She dashed to her desk. She liked to compare her original articles to the printed versions to see how they were edited. Sometimes cuts were made for the sake of space, but many changes were stylistic. Evelyn wanted to improve her writing and adapt to ANS style.

She scanned the Anschluss article. As she'd feared, Norwood had cut the story of the Jews forced to scrub sidewalks. Even worse, the article read as if Evelyn were reporting on a Christmas parade. He'd even changed "blood-red swastika flags dripped from every pole and balcony" to "crimson banners waved."

"For heaven's sake." She picked up the article on the exchange students. All reports of misgivings or disapproval were absent— although Evelyn had written subtly. Only the glowing reports remained.

And what? Evelyn gasped. She'd written, "When asked if they'd observed any persecution of the Jews, two students said they had and the others said they hadn't." Norwood had changed it to "When asked if he'd observed any persecution of the Jews, graduate student Mr. Peter Lang said he hadn't and had heard no complaints."

"What!" Evelyn shoved back her chair. "How could he? I didn't even ask Peter that question. For a reason. He'd only been in Germany two weeks. Norwood's making things up."

"Pardon?" Libby said, curled up with her book again.

Evelyn took the articles to her. "These! He—I know he has to remove anything that would anger the Germans. Fine. But he did more than that. I tried to be neutral, to show both sides. But he—these read like travel brochures. 'Come to scenic Germany and hike the Alps in lederhosen with a stein of beer and a blonde.' I can't believe it."

"Let me see."

Evelyn handed her the Anschluss article. "You were in Vienna. Is this what you saw?"

Libby read the article, then looked up to Evelyn, her mouth dangling open. "It reads as if Joseph Goebbels had written it."

"With my byline." She jabbed at it. "I sound like a fascist."

"What are you going to do? Are you going to talk to him?"

"I have to." Her jaw tightened. "I won't let him silence me."

65

NINE

"Ich gehe in die Oper," Peter wrote on the blackboard. "I am going to the opera. Past imperfect—Fräulein Blackstone?"

"Ich ging in die Oper."

"Very good." Peter wrote the past tense underneath. "Past perfect—Herr Schultz?"

"Ich bin in die Oper gegangen."

"Yes, indeed. Past pluperfect—Fräulein Wechsler?"

"Ich war in die Oper gegangen."

"Very good." After Peter finished, he wrote the homework assignment on the board.

Now in their second semester at the University of Munich, these junior year students were close to fluent. In the past month Peter had been teaching them, he'd noticed improvement in grammar and vocabulary, but mostly in diction.

Energy coursed in his veins. The students were engaged and responding. He had an influence on their lives. Was this how his brother Richard felt when crafting legislation? How his brother Karl felt when running the business?

But Rich influenced tens of thousands in the House of Representatives. Karl influenced thousands. Soon their youngest brother, Albert, would influence many as a lawyer, a judge.

Peter influenced thirty-four students. A wall slammed down and stopped that energy in its course.

He set down the chalk. "Class is over. I'll see you Wednesday."

The students made their way out of the classroom, speaking a mishmash of English and German.

Fräulein Wechsler approached the desk, holding her textbook on her hip. *"Am Samstag werde ich in die Oper gehen."*

"Very good." Peter set his papers inside his attaché case and grinned. "But I gave you past pluperfect."

A flush raced across her cheeks. "I really am going to the opera on Saturday, with Tom and Irene." She gestured to the couple behind her.

"The Magic Flute?"

"Yes." She inclined her head, and a light brown curl slid over to meet her smile. "Would you like to come with us?"

Peter pressed shut the latches on his attaché case. As he'd suspected, Fräulein Wechsler had a crush on him. The instructors often took groups of students to cultural events as part of their education, but Peter had a policy not to date students.

He smiled at the girl. "Thank you for the invitation, but I'm afraid I must decline. However, I look forward to attending the music festival in Düsseldorf with your class."

A quick hike to her eyebrows, and she gave him a thin smile and turned to her friends. A girl that pretty probably wasn't used to men not falling at her feet.

After the students left, Peter wiped down the blackboard. He'd wanted to attend *The Magic Flute* with Evelyn. He'd purchased two tickets hoping she wouldn't turn him down with tickets in hand. But she had.

He chuckled. She seemed to enjoy the game, and so did he. Twice a week he joined her at the café. Twice a week he asked her out. Twice a week she turned him down. She never seemed bothered that he asked—and if she did, he'd stop asking.

Peter inspected the board for stray marks. He and Evelyn

worked well together at their adjacent tables, occasionally pausing to share stories, to banter, or to chat with Herr Gold.

Evelyn seemed to enjoy his company, and—this intrigued him—she still came to the café on his now-regular days.

Maybe someday.

After the room was ready for the next class, Peter put on his coat and hat, picked up his attaché case, and headed into the hallway.

A man marched toward him wearing a Hitler Youth leader's uniform—a brown jacket, black trousers, and tall black boots. He saluted. "Heil, Hitler! Are you Herr Peter Lang?"

"I am. As an American, I offer you a simple '*Guten Tag*' and a handshake."

The man, about Peter's age, accepted the handshake. "I am Bannführer Wolfgang Diefenbach. I came to ask about Hans-Jürgen Schreiber's English."

Peter gestured down the hall. "I have an appointment, but will you walk with me?"

A nod of his square jaw, and he fell in beside Peter. "This Sunday I heard the boy speak English to his friends—with an American accent. I visited New York, so I recognize it. He said you were teaching him."

"I am. Diction is my field of expertise. I help American students improve their German."

"And you help Germans improve their English. That is good. I would like you to teach my other boys. It is a useful skill."

Useful? Although Peter loved teaching, something about the request didn't sit right. "I am honored. But with the demands of my research and teaching, I can't take on additional responsibilities."

"We can pay you handsomely."

"Ah, but I'm short on time, not money." Peter stopped at Professor Schreiber's open office door and extended his hand. "Thank you again, Herr Bannführer. *Auf Wiedersehen*."

Diefenbach slipped a card into Peter's hand. "My phone number. Please think about it. This would be a great service to the *Vaterland*."

Peter's fatherland was the United States, not Germany, and his stomach squirmed. Diefenbach was only asking him to help boys with English—something he would enjoy. Why did it feel as if he'd been asked to do something wrong?

Diefenbach faced into the office. "Heil, Hitler!"

Professor Schreiber sprang to his feet, papers fluttering to the floor, and he returned the salute and heil. "What brings you here, Herr Bannführer?"

Peter came inside with a smile. "He is impressed with Hans-Jürgen's English and wants me to teach the other boys. But I am too busy." At least Diefenbach's offer validated his work.

Diefenbach remained in the doorway, stiff as a tin soldier. "Hans-Jürgen was not at the meeting last Wednesday."

The professor picked up the papers from the floor and set them on his desk. "It was his grandmother's birthday."

"You have many birthdays and anniversaries."

"We are a large and close family."

Diefenbach frowned. "His family is the Hitler Youth. You selfishly held him back and did not allow him to join until last year. He is behind the other boys and must catch up. It is your duty to the Reich."

Professor Schreiber stood still, his hand on the desk. "He will come when able."

"See that he is able every Sunday and every Wednesday night, Herr Schreiber." Another heil and salute, and he left.

Peter frowned at the empty doorway. Surely the Bannführer knew to address him as Professor Schreiber or Herr Professor.

The professor sat in his desk chair, his face pale.

Peter opened his mouth to ask more, but Dr. Schreiber's gaze shifted to Peter and brightened. "How was your class?"

"Very good." He took his seat across from his mentor. "They learn quickly."

"Good." He opened a desk drawer and handed an envelope to Peter.

The return address was from Harvard University. "What's this?"

"You went to Harvard, as did your father and brothers, ja? Your family has influence there."

"Yes." They were all generous with donations and active in the alumni group.

"This is an application for Hans-Jürgen. Would you write a letter of recommendation?"

"Yes, but . . . I know you want him to study abroad, but I thought you meant for graduate school. It's so far away."

"Yes. Very far." He gazed to a baby picture on the desk, and his forehead furrowed.

This from a man who kept his son home from youth meetings, a man with a close family. And Hans-Jürgen was his only child.

"If you can help him get accepted, it would mean the world to my wife and me." His tone was light, but then he raised his gaze—tinged with urgency and a flicker of fear.

Peter swallowed hard. "I'll do my best, Herr Professor."

TEN

Like a gourmet feast spread before her, and Evelyn savored it. Five ANS correspondents sat around a table in the Berlin bureau, pitching story ideas and discussing meetings with diplomats, officials, generals, business leaders, and dissidents.

For almost two months, Evelyn had been careful to follow the rules. How long until she was allowed to report from Berlin, where everything exciting happened?

"Last we come to Miss Brand." George Norwood crossed his hands on top of the table. "What are you working on?"

"I have a new informant, the mistress of a general. He tells her everything, and he is not pleased with Hitler." Magda Müller, the bottle blonde Evelyn had met at the symphony with Peter, had mailed Evelyn an invitation to have coffee, which Evelyn leaped upon.

"Well . . ." Evelyn paused for effect. "We all know Hitler wants to annex the Sudetenland, the German-speaking region of Czechoslovakia, and the Sudeten Nazis are causing trouble. Well, my general friend says Hitler has drawn up plans to invade Czechoslovakia."

71

Mitch O'Hara gave Evelyn a pleased look. "I've heard similar rumors."

It felt good to have her tip confirmed. According to Magda, Gerlach and many other generals strongly opposed invasion. Maybe they'd stand up to Hitler and overthrow the regime.

"I will not publish rumors, especially warmongering rumors." Norwood ground his cigarette into an ashtray. "Military matters are over your head, Miss Brand. We'll follow up here in Berlin. What else are you working on?"

Over her head? Evelyn could barely see—and she certainly couldn't talk.

Norwood shuffled notes. "Mother's Day is on the fifteenth here in Germany, and the first mother's crosses will be awarded. That article needs feminine sensibilities."

Frank Keller broke up laughing. "Feminine sensibilities? From Brandy?"

Evelyn found her voice, rested her chin in her hand, and batted her eyelashes. "Mr. Norwood, I'm afraid I don't have any feminine sensibilities."

Norwood growled. "Find some and write the article."

"Find feminine sensibilities," Evelyn murmured and wrote down her stupid assignment.

"Also, there's a music festival in Düsseldorf late in May. I want you to cover that."

Evelyn turned to O'Hara and mouthed "Softball."

O'Hara made a tiny batting motion with his pen.

After a good eyeroll, she wrote down the other assignment. "I'm working on an article on the new law requiring Jews to—"

"No." Norwood shook his head. "Old news."

"It's a new law."

"But an old story. The American public is tired of reading about such things."

"You don't understand the way things are, Miss Brand." Edgar

C. Reeves, who was far too proud of his C, gave her a condescending smile.

Evelyn had to put every ounce of strength into keeping the shock off her face at being lectured by a man three years her junior, with a paltry four months experience as a reporter.

"You see," Reeves said in a voice as oily as his pomaded strawberry-blond hair, "when the American public hears stories of persecution, it reminds them of the atrocity stories the British used to trick us into fighting in the Great War. Americans are cynical, and rightly so. They don't believe a word. Even those who do believe it want to let the Germans handle their own problems."

"Reeves is right," Norwood said. "Besides, writing about such things is the quickest way for a reporter to get expelled from Germany. Maybe to get the entire ANS expelled."

"My angle will work." Evelyn kept her voice level. "I'm interviewing both Aryans and Jews, and I'll quote the German press release. That's fair game."

"That might work," O'Hara said. "How about I help her with the article, show her how to tweak it to pass muster?"

Evelyn's back stiffened. "I don't need—"

O'Hara held up one hand to silence her. "Would that be all right, Mr. Norwood?"

Norwood's jaw worked back and forth. "Fine, but watch her like a hawk."

Evelyn was used to Norwood talking as if she weren't in the room, but O'Hara too? She shot him a dirty look, but he didn't glance her way.

Norwood dismissed the meeting.

Evelyn gathered her things and followed O'Hara to his desk.

"Don't blow up at me, Ev." He pulled over a chair for her and sat behind his desk. "Do you want to write that article or not?"

Evelyn remained standing and glaring. "Not by being babysat, I don't."

"Listen." O'Hara leaned his forearms on his desk. "Write it. Phone it to me. I'll wave my magic stamp over it. After Norwood approves it, I'll tell him I didn't alter a single comma. That'll put an end to it."

"Will it? Does any other correspondent here have to run their articles by Norwood?"

O'Hara's mouth pursed. "You know the answer to that question."

Evelyn plopped into the chair and leaned close so she could talk low. "Not even Reeves. He got a degree in English literature, not journalism, then spent the past year gallivanting around Europe on a grand tour. Then he thought, 'Wouldn't it be a lark to be a foreign correspondent?' His daddy calls Norwood's daddy, and here he is. He didn't even have to work the copy desk first like the rest of us."

"He isn't a bad reporter."

Evelyn sharpened her glare.

O'Hara sighed. "Yes, you're better."

"But he's a man, and his family knows the right people."

O'Hara jabbed his finger at the desk. "Look. Do you want that article or not?"

Something inside her deflated, and she leaned back in her chair. "I do. It—it's personal. I just found out I'm three-quarters Jewish."

"You are?" Reeves's voice—behind her.

Evelyn sucked in a breath and whipped around. How much had he overheard?

Edgar C. Reeves stood with a stack of notebooks in hand and a slight curl to his thin lips. "You're Jewish?"

"I'm Christian, but three of my grandparents were born Jewish." She turned back to O'Hara. "If I were a German citizen, all those antisemitic laws would apply to me."

O'Hara's face went grim. "Don't repeat that outside this room, Ev. You hear? Your passport might protect you from those laws, but not from getting beaten up—or worse. Don't mess with these fellows. They're dangerous."

"I—I know."

"Hmm." Reeves walked away. "That explains a lot."

Evelyn gasped. "Why, that little—"

O'Hara grabbed her forearm. "Save your outrage for your writing. For the Nazis."

Speaking of outrage, she had a confrontation to make. She turned a smile to O'Hara. "Thanks. What would I do without you?"

"You probably would've throttled that antisemitic twit. As much as I would have enjoyed that, he and Norwood are thick as thieves."

"Don't worry. I'll behave."

"Good. Meet me and the wife at the Adlon for dinner? At seven?"

"I'd love that. Your wife is a gem. You . . . ?" She squinted at him.

He laughed.

"Oh, you're a gem too. I'll see you at seven."

Now to confront Norwood. Evelyn paused halfway to his office. Perhaps she should cool down first. But the day was almost over, and she needed to take the first train back to Munich in the morning.

She resumed walking. Originally she'd planned to catch a train this evening, until she realized she was doing it so she could be in Herr Gold's café on Tuesday morning. When Peter always came.

That's when she'd decided to stay in Berlin overnight. She couldn't let herself be drawn in by Peter Lang and his finely formed lips.

Evelyn knocked on Norwood's open door. "Excuse me? May I speak with you?"

"Of course." He waved her in.

Evelyn shut the door behind her. Libby would tell her to pray, and Libby was right. She shot up a prayer for guidance and to keep her temper.

She sat in front of the desk, opened her portfolio, and pulled out Mother's clippings. "I always look at the published versions of my articles to see how they were edited. I want to improve my writing and align to ANS style."

"Good for you." A smile increased the roundness of his face.

Evelyn pulled in a deep breath to remain calm. "In my article on the Anschluss, you removed my story about the Jewish people being forced to scrub sidewalks. I was disappointed, but I do understand we can't anger the Germans."

"I'm glad you understand."

She smoothed the newsprint. "However, the tone of the article changed as well, from neutral to very positive."

He made a scoffing noise in his throat. "The Austrians were rejoicing."

"Not all of them." Evelyn switched to the other clipping. "In my article on the students, you removed anything negative, even minor things like the girl who was tired of sauerkraut and the boy who missed jazz clubs. And you put words in Peter Lang's mouth."

Norwood's green eyes went hard. "I beg your pardon."

"You inserted a sizable paragraph where Mr. Lang praised the changes in Germany and stated he'd never seen any persecution of the Jews. He never said those things."

"He said them to me." Norwood gripped his pen in both hands as if to snap it in half. "That was your fault for not asking those questions. Very negligent of you."

Evelyn fought the tightening of her jaw. "I didn't ask Mr. Lang those questions on purpose. At that point, he'd only been in Germany two weeks. The whole article—I strove to be balanced and impartial, but now it reads like a press release from Goebbels."

Abandoning his pen, Norwood set his elbows on the armrests of his leather chair and slapped one hand over the fist of his other hand. "As Mr. Reeves so pointedly said, you don't understand the way things are."

Evelyn made her own fist, in her lap under her portfolio.

Norwood massaged his knuckles as if he'd just punched someone. "Times are hard in America. Unemployment is high, the communists are stirring up strikes and riots, and businesses are struggling. One of the few bright spots in our economy is trade with Germany. This country is booming, and many US companies have invested and are seeing excellent returns."

Did the man honestly think she wasn't aware of all that?

He gave her a flat smile. "What happens when the papers print atrocity stories? The people get riled up, especially the Jews. The Jews have political power, economic power, and a lot of pull in the media, and they're good at making noise. Then what happens? Boycotts and protests and mock trials of Hitler and other nonsense."

Nonsense? With great effort, Evelyn kept her eyebrows from rising and her jaw from falling.

Norwood spread his hands wide. "That jeopardizes our investments in Germany, investments that benefit both nations, mind you. However, when we highlight the many positive aspects of Germany, we encourage investment and tourism and study abroad. Those foster good relations and peace between our nations. I would think peace would interest you." He raised a patronizing smile.

After all, weren't her feminine sensibilities inclined toward peace above all?

Not at the cost of freedom, but she sent a patronizing smile of her own to tell him to get on with it.

Norwood settled his hands in his lap. "I hope you understand things better now."

Evelyn stood and gathered her clippings. "I understand perfectly. Good day, Mr. Norwood."

She understood that truth had taken a backseat to profits for Norwood Industries Inc.

ELEVEN

Several high-ranking German officials were on their way to Munich. Wouldn't Evelyn love to know?

Peter leaned back in his chair at the German Students' League meeting and grinned at the imagined look on her face. Surely he could inform her so she could "happen" to be at the right place at the right time.

But Otto von Albrecht, the leader of the league and highly involved in the local Nazi Party, said the information was secret. The students were only told so they could make preparations. Peter didn't want to violate the trust Otto had placed in him by welcoming him into their midst.

Peter would have to find another way into Evelyn's good graces.

Otto adjourned the meeting, and the young men in brown uniforms stood and chatted.

Several undergrads gathered around Peter.

"Thank you for telling us about American universities." A tall young man with a thatch of brown hair stood too close. "I am glad so many are for men only."

Peter smiled and eased back. "Many are coed."

"You should do what we Germans did." Another young man lifted his pointed chin. "Only 10 percent of admissions go to women, and they must do a year of domestic service before starting their studies."

The first student nodded briskly. "That would cut your unemployment and remind your women they belong in the kitchen."

Peter smothered a laugh. His own mother hired kitchen help because she was a lousy cook. And what if someone had kept Evelyn Brand from college? That would have been a crying shame. "Our women are free to make their own choices about such things."

A third student frowned, making his deep-set eyes almost disappear. "That is the problem with your country—you place individual freedom above the good of the community."

In a way, he was right, and Peter sighed. Too much freedom had flung the nation into decadence, then into violence that struck down innocent men protecting private property.

Otto approached and clapped Peter on the shoulder. "Excellent talk. You are a great speaker, a natural leader."

The other boys murmured their agreement.

Otto crossed sturdy arms. "With your abilities and connections, you could have great influence."

That energizing thrill resumed its course. "Thank you."

"You are in the right place." Otto raised a winning smile. "Here you see how we have established order, how we build roads and businesses and museums—how we flourish. You can teach your people to do likewise."

That was Peter's firmest hope.

TUESDAY, MAY 10, 1938

The bells of the glockenspiel tinkled their tune from the balcony of the town hall as wooden figures jousted and rolled out beer barrels. Peter would never tire of the show at the Neues Rathaus or the wonder on the faces of those who filled the Marienplatz.

Like the little towheaded boy tugging on his hurried mother's hand and tripping over his feet trying to watch.

The wooden rooster crowed three times, and the crowd went on its way.

So did Peter. He always timed his walk to the Gärtnerplatz so he passed through the Marienplatz when the glockenspiel played.

He craned his neck to take in the three-hundred-foot tower of St. Peterskirche, or *Alter Peter*, as the locals dubbed it—"Old Peter." His mother had Munich's oldest church in mind when naming her third-born son.

Before arriving at the café, he had a decision to make. On what sort of date would he invite Evelyn and how would he ask her? And how would she turn him down?

Wind curled around the ancient stone of the church, and Peter worked his hat lower on his brow. Although he enjoyed their game, he still hoped to entice her on an outing.

He bypassed the bustling Viktualienmarkt. He'd buy fresh produce on the way home, but not now.

The date would have to be in the evening, because he had to run errands on Saturday. The heels of his brown oxfords needed to be replaced, and a few suits needed dry cleaning. He could use a haircut too.

Then he laughed. Why not ask her to accompany him on his errands? He'd never asked her to join him in the mundane. It wouldn't work, but it'd make her laugh, and she had a beautiful laugh, low and rich.

Peter turned onto a side street. A blur of motion and noise ahead, and he halted.

Half a dozen policemen yanked and shoved someone toward a black car, pounding him with fists. An arrest.

Something stiffened in Peter's chest. Good. That's how they kept Munich's streets peaceful, by putting away rabble-rousers.

A few of the officers backed away as they reached the car, clearing Peter's view.

His breath froze. The prisoner had to be in his eighties, with tousled white hair and stooped shoulders. A rivulet of blood ran down his temple.

"What did he do?" Peter's words tumbled out.

"Hmph." A heavyset woman in an apron leaned against the doorjamb of a grocery store. "He called Hitler a swine, right here in my store. He has been my customer for years, but I won't stand for such talk about our Führer." She marched into the store, head high.

The black car pulled from the curb.

Peter's vision fogged over. His feet couldn't move.

An elderly man. His crime wasn't rioting or murder but speaking his mind.

Blinking over and over failed to clear his eyesight. Peter had justified an arrest, a beating, without knowing the facts. What was wrong with him? When had he become so callous?

He pried his feet from the sidewalk and forced himself onward. How could the police treat an elderly man like that? How could they treat *any* human being like that?

His breath came hard. How many times had Peter criticized President Franklin Roosevelt—or Herbert Hoover before him? What if that were a crime?

His black oxfords pounded the pavement. He wanted order on the streets, but did order require arresting people for criticizing the government?

Yes, free speech had its problems. Free speech could work people into a frenzy, leading to violence. Lives and property needed to be protected.

But where did you draw the line?

Everything in his head was a gray putrid mess. All he knew was the German government had drawn the line in the wrong place.

He stopped on a corner. Where was he? He turned in a circle. The brilliant greens and reds and pinks of the Gärtnerplatz seemed garish today, like a vaudeville suit at a funeral.

The café lay behind him. Maybe he should go home. He was in no mood for repartee.

However, he backtracked and entered the café, empty except for Evelyn.

She sat at her usual table with a teasing smile. "You decided to come in after all. You marched past as if you were late to an important meeting."

Peter sat at his table and set down his hat and attaché case. "Just preoccupied."

"Deep scholarly thoughts, I'm sure." She sipped her coffee, eyeing him over the rim of the cup. "I'm glad you didn't storm past because you're angry with me."

"Angry?" He snapped open the clasps of his case and pulled out a folder of essays to grade. "Why would I be angry with you?"

"You have every right." She swept a finger along the space bar on her typewriter, and the corner of her mouth puckered. "After I turned down your invitation to *The Magic Flute*, Libby brought home tickets for the same performance. I attended with her. That was rude of me."

"Hardly. I'm glad you went." He pulled out his red pencil.

"I didn't see you there."

"I gave my tickets to the Schreibers." He couldn't be witty, couldn't even grade the essays. "What are you working on?"

"An article about small businesses and some new laws. Would you . . . would you like to see? I only have one more paragraph to write."

"I'd like that." She'd never offered before.

Evelyn pulled out the paper and gathered two more sheets. But then she held back the bundle and gave Peter a penetrating look. "Are you all right?"

"Sure." He held out his hand for the article.

"Preoccupied?"

"Yes." He set down the papers, wiped dust from his glasses with his handkerchief, and began reading.

The café has stood in the neighborhood for decades, bright and cheery and fragrant. "I expect an increase in business thanks to the new laws," the proprietor told this reporter. "The government is clamping down on unfair competition."

His wife agreed as she rolled out a batch of spaetzle noodles. "No more will Germany allow swindlers and dirty business practices."

A few blocks over, another café has also stood in the neighborhood for decades, bright and cheery and fragrant. "My father built this café," the proprietor told this reporter. "But soon I shall lose my livelihood and his legacy."

What is the difference between the two cafés? The rst is owned by a man with "pure Aryan blood," and the second by a man of Jewish blood.

In 1933, over 100,000 companies in Germany were owned by Jews. Due to governmental and economic pressure, almost 70 percent of these have been closed or sold to Aryans.

On April 22, Germany passed the Decree Against the Camou age of Jewish Firms, which made it a crime to conceal the ownership of a Jewish-owned business or to change the name. The intent was to label Jewish-owned companies so Aryans would take their money elsewhere.

On April 26, Germany required Jewish business owners to receive authorization to sell a company, giving the government control over the "Aryanization" process.

Also on April 26, the Order for the Disclosure of Jewish Assets was issued. Under this law, Jewish people must register assets over 5000 Reichsmarks, approximately $2000, less than the price of an average business.

For the Jewish business owners who remain, revenue will decrease and the pressure to sell will increase, but the new regulations mean they will receive below market price.

More stories and examples filled the remaining pages. At the end, Peter took off his glasses and rubbed the bridge of his nose. The German economy was strong, and the people were secure. Why a new law against the Jews? Several new laws?

"What do you think?" Evelyn asked. "Is it too long?"

"No. It's good. The article—it's excellent."

"Is it biased? Incendiary? I asked you to read it because you approve of German policy."

Peter winced. "Not this. I don't approve of this. Of that." He waved in the direction of the street where an elderly man had been beaten and arrested for voicing an opinion.

Evelyn was quiet for a long time. "You know Norwood. What do you think he'll say?"

Peter handed it back to her. "He'd be a fool to alter it. It's balanced and factual, but deeply personal. You're a gifted writer."

"*Guten Morgen*, Herr Lang." Herr Gold approached the table, wiping his hands on his apron. "I didn't hear you arrive. Please forgive me. What would you like?"

"Only coffee. I'm not hungry."

"One minute." Herr Gold's smile was more subdued than usual, his step less sprightly as he returned to the kitchen.

Oh no. Realization slammed into him. "He's the second café owner, isn't he?"

Evelyn nodded, her brown eyes solemn.

Herr Gold was Jewish. He entered the dining room and set a cup and saucer on the table. "Coffee for you, my friend."

Peter stood and clasped the man's hand. "I am sorry. Fräulein Brand just told me about the troubles you're facing with your café."

"You are very kind." He patted the table. "Please. Please sit and drink."

"Herr Gold?" Evelyn said softly. "Please tell Herr Lang how things are for you."

"Ach." He waved her off. "He does not want to hear."

"I do." Peter motioned to the opposite chair. "Please sit with me. Please tell me."

Herr Gold paused, then lowered himself to the chair. "It is strange not to belong in your own home."

Peter rested his forearms on the table, thirstier for the man's words than for coffee.

"My family has lived in Munich for three hundred years." Herr Gold gazed out his window. "But I am no longer a citizen of Germany. Of—of any nation."

"The Nuremberg Laws of 1935," Evelyn said.

Peter knew about them. They were meant to bring peace between the Aryans and the Jews by building a wall between them, separating the races. But the wall kept shifting.

"I fought in the Great War, and at a higher rank than the Führer, but we Jews are no longer allowed to serve in the military. We aren't allowed to work in civil service, as teachers or judges."

Peter chewed his lips and lowered his head. Professor Schreiber said two of Peter's favorite professors from his junior year had been fired because of their race. He'd been shocked, but now the magnitude of the situation sank in.

"My café has been boycotted, vile slogans painted on my walls. Every table used to be full, every *Krapfen* sold by nine." Herr Gold frowned at the empty tables. "My brother-in-law is Aryan. He will buy the café, but the state controls the price. My brother-in-law will change the name of the café, and customers will return. I will work here as an employee, but . . ."

"But it isn't the same," Peter said, his voice rough. "It isn't right."

"There is no right or wrong." Herr Gold spoke softly and with a faint smile. "There is only the will of the Führer."

Peter's head ached. This was all supposed to blow over. But it hadn't. It was blowing harder than ever. When would it stop? Or would it? "I'm sorry, my friend. This shouldn't be happening to you. To anyone. It's wrong."

Herr Gold swept his arm to Peter and his smile to Evelyn. "Our Herr Lang is a good man. Next time he asks you to dinner, you accept, ja?"

On an ordinary day, Peter would have jumped on that, but not today.

Evelyn raised that sly smile of hers. "You forget. If Herr Lang and I were both German, a romantic relationship would be forbidden under the Nuremberg Laws."

Peter frowned. A cross glimmered around her slender neck, and she always talked as if . . . "I thought you were a Christian."

"I am. But three of my grandparents are converted Jews. German law is about race, not religion, so I would be considered Jewish. You wouldn't dare ask me out." Her mouth smiled, but something in her eyes challenged him.

"But my dear Fräulein." Herr Gold pressed both hands over his heart. "You are both Americans. These laws do not apply to you, so be thankful."

"I—I am."

"All the more reason to have dinner with good Herr Lang— because you *can*."

Evelyn's face darkened, and she inserted paper into the typewriter. "It isn't that simple."

Peter's stomach fell. No, it wasn't. Why would she want to date a man who'd praised a regime that would strip away her rights, the rights of her friends?

Herr Gold stood, set his hands on either side of Evelyn's typewriter, and leaned close, right in her startled face. "Do not tell anyone. You are too free with your words. Who else knows?"

Evelyn's eyelids fluttered. "My—my roommate. A couple of fellows at the bureau."

"No one else. Do you understand?"

"Yes, *mein Herr*."

Herr Gold skewered Peter with his gaze. "And you—tell no one."

Peter found his breath. "I won't. Not a soul."

The café owner returned to the kitchen, and Evelyn watched Peter warily. The poor woman probably realized she'd shared a dangerous secret with a man she didn't even care to share a meal with.

Peter filled his gaze with the truth that he'd protect her and never let any harm come to her, as much as it depended on him. "No one will ever know."

Evelyn's shoulders relaxed. "Thank you." She returned to her work.

If only Peter could return to his.

Everything felt inside out. He'd thought of the new Germany as a fine cheese—once you cut away the ugly rind, you could savor the richness inside.

But it wasn't. It wasn't at all.

He felt as if he'd been given a beautiful pastry, only to bite in and find the filling rotten.

TWELVE

GARMISCH-PARTENKIRCHEN, GERMANY
SATURDAY, MAY 28, 1938

Evelyn waved to the hikers as they wended their way down the Alpine path. "Thank you for talking to me. Enjoy your vacation."

"You're welcome. We will," they called back.

She breathed deep the cool air fresh with the scent of pine. Below her, hikers greeted each other on the path that ran past the Olympic Ski Stadium. Built for the 1936 Winter Games, a giant ski jump ramp slashed down a green slope, ending in a meadow framed by grandstands and the charming Olympia Haus restaurant.

Behind her, Libby White thumped her hiking stick on the ground. "This was supposed to be a day off."

Evelyn tucked her notepad into the pocket of her serviceable gray dirndl skirt. "When a story leaps into my lap, I can't very well toss it back out, can I?"

Libby tried to look stern, but she was too cute in her dirndl and sweater, with her big brown eyes and her braid hanging over her shoulder. The corners of her mouth twitched. "Your chief will like this one. Light and happy."

"I won't even have to stretch to make it positive. It pains me to admit, but Germany did something good with the *Kraft durch Freude* program." Wouldn't Peter Lang love to hear her talk like that?

"Strength through Joy," Libby said. "It does have a nice ring."

"Those hikers—they're factory workers from Essen. Before the KdF program, none of them had ever been on a vacation. Now they can stay at an Alpine resort for dirt cheap—hikes, boating, tours of Neuschwanstein Castle, the works."

Libby headed toward the entrance to the Partnach Gorge. "Well, today's a nice respite after the tension of this past week. I thought there would be war."

"Everyone did." A week earlier, the Czechoslovakian army had mobilized in response to rumors that German troops were massed at the border. Hitler appeared ready to achieve union with the Sudetenland by force, possibly to conquer the rest of Czechoslovakia as well.

A few days later, Hitler said the rumors were false, and tensions were defused. For now.

Magda Müller had fed Evelyn more tidbits about German military plans, but oh no, her feminine sensibilities couldn't possibly understand complicated military matters.

She strode harder, slowing only to duck pine branches. George Norwood would find some way to make her KdF article even more positive. After all, he'd skewed her article about the *Olympia* movie, changing her talk of the will of the individual coming under the will of the state to "the joy of camaraderie."

How would he ruin her article about Herr Gold's café? O'Hara proclaimed it her best work yet and gave Norwood his approval, but she didn't trust the bureau chief. "Not one bit."

"Hmm?" Libby faced her, then peered past her. "Don't even think of interviewing this group—oh, wait. They're American tourists. We're safe."

About two dozen young people approached, laughing and speaking English, probably college students on their grand tours of Europe.

One of the men waved. Was that . . . "Peter? What's he doing here?"

"Ooh!" Libby said. "The famous and elusive Peter Lang. Now I can finally meet him."

Nothing for Evelyn to do but wave back.

Peter strode up, wearing a green felt Bavarian hat, brown corduroy trousers, and a V-neck sweater that was probably the same blue as his eyes. She'd never seen him wear anything but a three-piece suit or white tie, and the sporty look was good on him. Unfortunately.

"Good morning, Miss Brand. Class, you remember Evelyn Brand."

Yes, the exact same blue. Also unfortunate.

"Good morning." Evelyn smiled at the students she'd interviewed for her article and had seen the past week at the Düsseldorf Music Festival.

"I'm so glad to see you again." A petite blonde clutched her hands together before her chest. "I forgot to tell you in Düsseldorf, but my parents loved your article. They were nervous about sending me to Germany—the reports in the newspapers are awful. I keep telling them we're happy and safe, but they didn't believe it until they read it in the paper."

"You're welcome." Evelyn found a smile for the girl. That was the purpose of the article. At least Mr. Norwood's purpose.

Time to be polite. "Libby, may I introduce Mr. Peter Lang? Peter, this is my dear friend, Miss Libby White."

"It's a pleasure to meet you, Miss White. I had the honor of hearing you perform." He turned to the students. "Everyone, I'd like to introduce Miss Elizabeth White."

Gasps swept the class. "The flautist?"

They surrounded Libby, peppering her with questions and praise.

Peter backed out of the crowd. "Walk and talk, everyone. We came to exercise more than our vocal cords. And please give Miss White space to breathe."

The exchange students swept Libby up the path. Evelyn frowned, but Libby was laughing and fielding questions. No need to rescue her yet.

That left Evelyn alone . . . with Peter.

He tilted his head toward the group. "Shall we?"

She fell in beside him. His compassionate response to Herr Gold had softened her opinion of him. However, even though he wasn't a fascist, she still didn't want to date him.

The path climbed beside the Partnach River, narrow and roiling, and the mountains folded in closer with each step. "Second field trip with the kiddies this week?" she asked.

Peter chuckled. "Did you get good material for your article on the music festival?"

"Two articles. I interviewed the wife of a Nazi bigwig. The husband won't talk to me, but the wife was flattered that someone thought she was important too. She told me all sorts of interesting things."

"See, that's an advantage you have as a woman. And you found a creative solution."

Oh, why did he have to wear a sweater that made his eyes even bluer? She gazed down to the river instead, almost a mint green. "Creativity born of necessity. Did your little flock enjoy the festival?"

"They did."

"You didn't take them to the"—she affected a stage whisper— "*Entartete Musik* concert, did you?"

"The Degenerate Music concert?" Peter crossed a little bridge over the river. "I did. And I enjoyed most of it. Surprised?"

Yes, she was. The Nazis had staged the concert to mock music they said violated the German spirit—works by Jewish and Negro composers and many modern works.

A new music met them as they entered the gorge, the music of swishing, tumbling water. The river churned down from the Alps through a narrow channel, edged by steep rock walls, dark and mossy, soaring almost eighty feet. At the top, pine trees framed the ribbon of sky. A footpath had been carved into the rock, with a wooden railing to keep tourists from taking icy and deadly tumbles.

Peter led at a nice slow pace that allowed Evelyn to admire the scenery.

If only the scenery didn't include Peter's back, encased in snug wool that accentuated his build. It was time to start an argument. A good-natured argument, but an argument, nonetheless. "You said you liked *most* of the music?" She raised her voice to compete with the river.

Peter smiled over his shoulder. "I like jazz, but some of the modern works are too atonal and chaotic for my taste. Classical music will always be my favorite."

"Of course. As neat and orderly as your desk."

"That's what makes it beautiful. It follows the rules." He stepped close to the wall to let a young couple pass.

Evelyn pressed against the damp, cold rock. After the couple passed, she resumed her walk and her argument. "Yet true beauty comes from that one minor chord, the note that's sharp or flat. My father says those are the elements he has his orchestra stress—a little drawn out, a little more volume. Those are the elements that sink in your heart and pull on your emotions."

Behind his glasses, Peter's eyes narrowed. "I see. I see what you're saying."

Winning was even more fun than arguing. "True beauty comes when rules are broken."

The path passed through a tunnel, thick with the smell of damp stone. On the other side, the path cut under an overhang.

Peter ducked his head. "When rules are broken too often, it creates dissonance. The only emotions it produces are discomfort, anxiety. That might be the composer's aim, but it doesn't produce the same sense of awe."

A thin stream of water plunged down the overhang beside the

trail, and Evelyn wiped mist from her face. He was right. Bother, but he was right.

Peter faced her under the little waterfall, his expression intense. "I see it now. The best music has both order and disorder, rules and the perfectly placed breaking of the rules."

His eyes reflected what she felt in her heart—the pain of shattered assumptions and the light of new understanding.

"I see it too," she said. They were talking about more than music, weren't they? They were talking about life, about meeting in the middle, about seeing the other side of things and joining, there under the waterfall, not as far apart as she'd thought.

His lips bent, those fine lips, in a smile soft and intimate, from a man of rules and order, but also a man of kindness, of deep feeling.

In the cool, feathery mist, she swayed toward him, her heart leading, her body following, and her mind screaming to stop, stop, stop!

"Herr Lang! Herr Lang!"

Peter's head jerked up and bonked the rock ceiling.

A pretty young woman dashed up the path, laughing and waving, light brown curls bouncing against her chin.

Evelyn caught her breath and stepped back, her heart ramming her rib cage. Saved by the belle.

Peter removed his hat and rubbed his head. "Yes, Fräulein Wechsler?"

"Come join the fun." Laughing, she tugged on Peter's arm. "Chip composed a song for Miss White, and it's a scream. We've decided to serenade her. It'll echo in the most gorgeous way. You simply must join us."

Peter slid the girl's hand off his arm and smiled. "I'm afraid I'll ruin the effect. I sing horribly. But we'll catch up in a minute."

Miss Wechsler peeked around Peter to Evelyn with a quick look, a malicious look.

Evelyn choked back a laugh. So Little Miss Socialite had a crush on the teacher.

That socialite straightened her shoulders, lifting a bustline many times larger than Evelyn's, and she sauntered away with a pronounced sway to her rounded hips.

Despite all that swaying femininity, Peter turned to Evelyn with that same intimate smile.

This time she resisted. "Walk and talk. We're here to exercise more than our vocal cords."

Peter laughed at her imitation of him, and he continued down the path. Up ahead, it widened, and he dropped back to walk beside her. "When are you and Miss White returning to Munich?"

"Later this afternoon."

"I am too. May I take you out to dinner tonight?"

In the past two months, he'd asked her out at least a dozen times. But his tone this time was so earnest. As dangerous as the moment under the waterfall, and she had to shatter the intimacy.

Evelyn stopped, set both hands on her hips, and gave him a saucy look. "Why do you keep asking me out, Lang?"

A flash of a smile, and he mimicked her posture. "Because I like you, Brand."

"Why don't you ask Miss Wechsler? She has a crush on you."

He grimaced and returned to walking. "No, thank you."

Evelyn trotted back to his side. "She's far prettier than I am. She comes from the right family and goes to the right school and vacations in the right places, and she'd hang adoringly on your every word."

Peter sent her a half smile that was more than half attractive. "I don't like her. I like you."

What an utterly maddening man. "All you have to do is open your arms, and she'll jump right in."

With his gaze fixed on Evelyn, Peter opened his arms toward Miss Wechsler, then crossed his arms with a slap and lowered them to his chest.

Goodness, he was funny. And cute. And he wouldn't take his eyes off her.

She laughed and lifted a finger. "I figured it out. She's too easy to catch, isn't she? Men are hunters. You like the chase, and you don't like prey that's easily caught."

Peter's face screwed up. "I wouldn't put it that way."

"It's true." Winning another argument made her smile. "Every man who's ever pursued me liked that about me. I'm not easily caught. I'm a challenge."

He shrugged. "I can't disagree with that statement."

"See? But as soon as men catch me, they want to change me, tame me, put me in a cage. I won't have it."

His eyes widened, and his lips parted. "Did—did someone try to do that to you?"

She squirmed a bit. "Don't look so shocked, Lang. You'd do the same."

"No." He shook his head slightly, his expression dazed. "I wouldn't. I wouldn't want to."

Evelyn fought for control, and she set her hands in front of her as if holding a box. "You say that now, but you like your rules, your neat little boxes and folders and everything in order. I'd never fit. You'd try to make me fit, and I'd fight you, and we'd both be very unhappy. Trust me, I'm doing you a favor by turning you down."

"Herr La-ang!" Miss Wechsler called, this time with a whine. "Tom wants to go right and Chip wants to go left, and I say we need to stay together."

"I'll be right there." Peter turned back to Evelyn with a look of stunning gravity. "I'm so sorry, Evelyn."

Then he strode up the path to his students.

Evelyn stood there alone. She folded her arms across her belly, which churned like the water beside her.

Was he sorry for being a man and for what he'd do to her? Or was he sorry . . . for her?

THIRTEEN

WEDNESDAY, JUNE 8, 1938

Ten o'clock sharp. Peter slid the essays into a folder, alphabetized and graded, with the scores entered in his grade book.

He leaned back in his desk chair. Golden lamplight shone around his apartment, on his neat little boxes and folders. Made him want to mess things up to prove Evelyn wrong. Except it wouldn't convince her.

And it would drive him crazy.

Rain pattered on the window. Peter put the essay folder in his attaché case for Friday's class, and he added a folder of homework to grade at the café in the morning.

He paused with his thumbs on the brass clasps. Perhaps he shouldn't go to the café anymore. His pursuit had labeled him a hunter, determined to trap her.

"Cage her," he said. That was the phrase she'd used.

Who would do such a thing? And why? Independence and drive were what made her Evelyn. What made her beautiful. So beautiful he'd almost kissed her at the Partnach Gorge. For one heady moment, he'd thought she'd welcome a kiss. Now he knew she would have kneed him in the groin.

"Cage her." He scratched at his scruffy jawline.

He hadn't asked her out since that day, almost two weeks earlier. For her to see he wasn't a hunter, he had to call off the hunt.

Of course, for her to see that, she actually had to see him. Tomorrow he'd go to the café. He snapped his briefcase shut and turned off his desk lamp.

The phone jangled, and he frowned at it. Who would call so late?

He picked up the receiver. *"Hallo?"*

"Otto here. Great news. I'm calling everyone in the league."

Peter eyed his bed and his nightstand. He liked to read for half an hour before bed. This had better be great news indeed. "What's happening?"

"You remember how Hitler was in Munich a few days ago? Well, the Führer saw that monstrosity, the so-called Great Synagogue at the corner of Maxburgstrasse and Herzog-Max-strasse, impeding traffic to his beautiful new House of German Art."

Peter's fingers curled around the armrest.

"Tomorrow it will be demolished." Excitement lifted Otto's voice. "By order of the Führer. Today they told those filthy Jews, to give them time to clear out. More time than I would have given them. Tomorrow morning, down it comes. Soon we will have a new parking lot in its place. A great day for Germany."

A hard lump filled Peter's throat. He'd never heard Otto speak like that. How could such vile thoughts live in the head of a man he liked?

Otto groaned. "I want to be there tomorrow, but I teach two classes."

Peter shoved down that lump. "You must be in class. To teach."

"Ah well. There will be other days. I must call Klaus now. Goodbye."

Peter sat like stone, the receiver clamped to his ear. More injustices. It was supposed to stop by now.

How could he have been so blind? Evelyn saw. She saw through them from the start.

Evelyn! She'd want to be there, to write the story, to report the injustice.

He slammed down the receiver, picked it back up, and dialed her number.

"Hallo?" The woman didn't sound like Evelyn—or Libby.

"I would like to speak to Fräulein Brand."

"I am the cleaning lady. Fräulein Brand is not here. May I take a message?"

Strange time for a cleaning lady to work. "Yes, please. Tell her—no, never mind."

He hung up. He stood. He paced.

How could he stand by and do nothing? But what could he do, one man against a government order and heavy machinery and dozens of workmen?

Peter shoved aside his curtain and peered into the night, into the rain.

Those poor people. They had so little time to empty the synagogue. What sort of items would they have? Sacred scrolls and candlesticks and records of congregational life for generations. Their heritage.

He could help save that heritage. He marched to the door and threw on his hat and raincoat without bothering to put on his suit vest and jacket.

Peter climbed into his Opel and pulled away from the curb. As he drove the half mile to the synagogue, the windshield wipers beat in time with his heart.

How could they tear down a house of worship? Would they demolish St. Peterskirche? The Frauenkirche? He didn't know anymore.

He turned onto Maxburgstrasse. Up ahead, a crowd had gathered. Rain slashed through the faint light of the streetlamps.

Peter parked his car and jogged down the street. About two dozen men stood outside the massive old stone building, shouting and jeering.

A mob.

Peter's pace slowed. Weak. Gangly. Like the night Father died. A sharp pain in his nose.

No. He wasn't that weakling anymore.

He ran harder. This was why he lifted dumbbells and did calisthenics every morning.

Raindrops on his glasses distorted his vision, but he kept running.

On the sidewalk by a side door to the synagogue, two men hunched, one shielding the other, while men kicked and hit them.

"Lord, help me." Peter ran up to them. *"Halten Sie! Halt!"*

The thugs looked over. Hitler Youth. Schoolboys.

Peter grabbed the biggest boy by the collar and jerked him away. "How dare you defy Party orders?"

"I—I'm not." The kid's voice squeaked.

Peter shoved him aside and yanked another boy away. "The order was to tear down the synagogue—in the morning. And to let them clear out tonight. Not to beat people up."

Someone pushed Peter from behind. "Ah, let them have their fun."

Peter wheeled around and glared at the man, shorter than Peter but powerfully built. "Will you tell the Führer his order was defied? Will you?"

Fear skittered across the man's face. "Nein."

Inside the open doorway, a line of men and women held boxes and candelabra and scrolls.

Peter turned to the mob and motioned them back. "Back away. Let them leave. Party orders. You'll have your fun tomorrow. Don't make trouble for yourselves."

Thank goodness, it worked. Mumbling, the crowd dispersed and slunk into the night.

"Herr Lang?" One of the men on the ground looked up.

"Herr Gold!" Peter fell to his knees beside them. "Are you all right?"

Herr Gold shoved up from his position shielding an elderly man. "I'll be fine, but the rabbi . . ."

The rabbi lay moaning, blood glistening in the lamplight.

Peter laid a hand on the man's shoulder. "*Mein Herr?* Can you walk?"

"I—I think so."

"Let's get you to safety. My car's one block down." He nodded to Herr Gold, and the two men helped the rabbi to his feet.

As the synagogue community hurried their treasures out into the night, Peter made his way down the sidewalk. The rabbi slumped against his side, and Peter tightened his grip. "Only a little farther. Where's the nearest hospital?"

"Nein," Herr Gold said. "I do not trust them. Take him home. We'll call a Jewish doctor."

Peter's stomach tightened. Surely doctors would be above cruelty, but everything was upside down in the world.

The rabbi lifted his bearded chin to Peter. "You are Jewish?"

"Nein. I'm a Christian."

The rabbi stiffened and pulled away.

"Nein," Herr Gold said. "Herr Lang is a good man. We can trust him."

"This! This is what Christians do."

Everything in Peter wanted to protest. No, this was not what Christians did. Not what Christians were supposed to do. And the Nazis didn't even claim to follow Christ. But Peter had no right to argue with what the rabbi had experienced at the hand of Aryans.

Two storm troopers approached, fists rising, an evil light in their eyes.

"Nein!" Peter thrust out his arm like a linebacker on the charge. "Party orders! They are free to leave. Do not interfere."

They stepped aside and glowered. "Jew-lover!"

A spitting sound. It hit Peter's shoulder. He didn't care.

"Here's my car." He shifted the rabbi's weight to the café owner and opened the back door.

Peter and Herr Gold helped the rabbi lie down on the backseat, then they slid into the front seat. Peter hit the gas before the storm troopers could change their minds.

"You Christians . . ." The rabbi's voice drifted over the seat, strangely forceful in its weakness. "You say you read the same holy Scriptures we do, but you do not follow them. '*Higgid leka adam mah-tov; umah-Yahweh doresh mimmeka, ki im-asowt mishpat, veahavat hesed, vehatzneah leket im-elohikah.*'"

Peter shot a questioning glance to Herr Gold. "What does that mean?"

"It comes from the Prophet Micah." Herr Gold pressed his handkerchief to a gash on his cheek. "In German it says, 'It is known to you, O man, what is good, and what does Jehovah require of you but to do justice, to love kindness, and to walk in humility with Elohim?'"

Peter had heard that verse, although he didn't know the reference.

To do justice. He believed in that, worked for it.

But kindness? Mercy? Forgiveness?

"Oh, Lord," he whispered. "Where have I gone wrong?"

FOURTEEN

Evelyn hurried home with a newspaper tucked inside her raincoat. Frau Engel was the smartest and best informant imaginable.

Evelyn's feet were damp despite her umbrella, and the wet sidewalk shimmered in the cold light of the streetlamps.

Engel meant *angel* in German, an appropriate nickname for the woman with the halo braid who had fed Evelyn information since the plebiscite. Every week, Evelyn went to a train station or streetcar stop, and Frau Engel would be there reading a newspaper. When the train or streetcar arrived, Frau Engel would say she was done with her paper and did Evelyn want it?

Yes, she did, thank you. Frau Engel tucked messages inside the papers, including the time and location of their next meeting. Every tip had been as golden as those heavenly streets.

Evelyn opened the door to her building, climbed the stairs, and set her umbrella in the hall to dry. Light came from under the door, meaning Libby was home early from her concert. She opened the door.

"Ach!" Helga, the cleaning lady, stood at Evelyn's desk. She startled and dropped some papers. "You are already home?"

Something was very wrong. "Why are you here?"

"Ach! You and Fräulein White!" Helga clucked her tongue and

shuffled papers. "She is here the whole day, and you come and go. I waited for you both to leave so I could finally clean."

Evelyn clutched the newspaper to her chest under her damp coat, her blood as chilly as her feet. "You're reading my papers."

"Ach, nein." She fussed with those papers, hiding what she'd been reading, no doubt. "You are messy, Fräulein. And I am a simple cleaning woman. I do not read English."

"Those are my private papers. Put them down."

"Why?" Helga frowned over her shoulder at Evelyn. "Do you have something to hide?"

Evelyn pointed to the door. "That is all for today, Helga. Thank you."

"But I—I'm not done." She patted the scarf tied around her graying blonde hair. "I haven't—"

"That is all for today. Thank you."

Helga grumbled, grabbed her bucket of cleaning supplies, and departed.

Evelyn locked the door behind her. She'd tell her landlord to hire a new cleaning lady. Many of the foreign correspondents complained about cleaning ladies placed by the Gestapo to spy on them. Some reporters had been questioned by the Gestapo and expelled from Germany.

Evelyn shrugged off her raincoat, set her purse and newspaper on the desk chair, and inspected the papers. A dozen letters from home were interspersed with story notes and drafts.

A sick feeling filled her stomach. She might not be organized, but she knew what was on her desk and what wasn't, and those letters had been in a drawer.

Helga had been snooping—and she'd lied about not speaking English. Maybe Evelyn should buy a lockbox to store anything sensitive.

"Lord, I could use some help." A morsel of guilt plunged into that sickness. Libby teased her about only praying in emergencies. But praying for help when she could do very well on her own felt silly.

Regardless, a spy reading her papers was an emergency.

A pounding on the door.

Evelyn jumped. The Gestapo?

"Oh, Lord. Oh, Lord. Oh, Lord." Her heart raced, and she opened the door.

Peter? What was he doing here? And so late?

And so wild-eyed.

"Peter?"

He charged past her, no hat, his unbuttoned raincoat flapping open. "Where's your notebook? Your purse? Your coat? Come on, let's go. A story."

Crimson stains covered one side of his chest. "Peter! You're bleeding!"

"What? No." He lifted his elbow and inspected his raincoat.

"Where are you hurt? How badly?" Evelyn grabbed his lapels and tugged off his coat.

"Not me. The rabbi."

He wasn't making sense, and he wasn't wearing his usual jacket and vest. She patted down his chest, looking for the injury, but no blood marred his white shirt. "You're not hurt?"

"We need to go. Before it's over." He moved to step around her.

Evelyn planted both hands on his chest. "I'm not going anywhere until you tell me what's going on."

Peter's gaze darted around above her head, and his chest heaved, warm and very firm beneath her hands. "The synagogue. The Nazis are going to tear it down."

"What? No!"

"I—I went to help."

Her hands recoiled as if burning. "You did what!"

"No. No." He raked his fingers through his rain-darkened hair. "I went to help the congregation get their things out. The government gave them until tomorrow morning."

Evelyn clapped her hands over her mouth. Oh no! How could she have judged him so wrongly? So quickly?

"Come on. Your purse, your coat." He edged past her and grabbed her purse from her desk chair. "Notebook inside?"

"Yes, but Peter—the blood."

He shook the purse by the strap. "You're the only correspondent for the ANS in town, right? I'll drive you to the synagogue to see, to interview the mob."

She waved her arm toward his coat in a heap on the floor. "The blood. Peter—where did it come from?"

He grabbed her heavy winter coat from the rack. "It's raining."

Evelyn took the coat and exchanged it for her raincoat. "If I come with you, will you tell me?"

Without helping her, without his own coat, he opened the door and left. "Come on. No time to waste."

Evelyn pulled on her coat and followed. She had to. He had her purse.

At the curb, he opened the passenger door to a black four-door convertible. After they were both seated, he raced down the street.

Evelyn buttoned her coat and tried to decipher the man beside her. "What happened?"

"The synagogue. There was a mob. They were beating up a rabbi. Herr Gold was protecting him."

She gasped. "Herr Gold? He was there? Is he all right?"

"Some cuts, bruises. He'll be fine. But the rabbi—they beat him badly. And he's elderly."

"Oh no. It was his blood. You—you helped him."

Peter cranked the car around a corner. "I got the mob to back off. Just had to talk tough. Then I took the rabbi and Herr Gold to the rabbi's house. We called a doctor. Then I came here."

"And you? You're all right?"

Peter didn't look at her, hadn't really looked at her since he'd barged into her apartment. He just shook his head a bit, his face agitated.

Evelyn took a deep breath to calm her racing emotions. Peter

Lang had stood up to a mob. To the Nazis. To help the Jews. And why was she so relieved that not one drop of that blood was Peter's?

He wheeled around another corner.

She braced herself on the dashboard. "You're taking me to the synagogue?"

"The mob will come back. You can interview them. Then I'll take you to the rabbi. You need both sides, right?"

"Yes." Evelyn stared at him in his white shirtsleeves and tousled hair. Men usually tried to hold her back from danger—not drive her into the middle of it.

"Both sides. Both sides." Peter rapped the steering wheel with his palm. "Justice, kindness. Order, liberty. Both sides."

"Peter?" She fought an urge to smooth his hair, to straighten his tie, to make him neat again, Peter again.

He pushed his glasses higher on his crooked nose. "Freedom without order, without justice—it leads to chaos and violence. I know that."

Evelyn bit her lip. She'd heard him talk like this, but never in such turmoil.

"Why couldn't I see?" He thumped the steering wheel again, making the car swerve a bit. "But order without freedom, without kindness—it makes you hard. Cruel. It leads to chaos . . ."

"Violence," Evelyn murmured.

Peter raised one finger in the air. "Once you asked me where I draw the line. Well, I draw it here. Now." He stabbed that finger into the seat between them.

"All right . . ."

"I want to do something. I need to help."

"You—you did. You helped the rabbi and—"

"More. I need to do more. I'm going to help you."

"Me?" She didn't need help.

Peter slowed, peering into the night. "Otto and his friends in the German Students' League—they trust me, think I'm one of them. Of course! Of course, they do!"

How could Evelyn disagree, when she'd thought the same thing?

"Otto keeps inviting me to local Nazi Party meetings. He wants to draw me in deeper. I'll go. I'll be your ears and get you leads, tips, whatever you call them."

Evelyn's mouth watered with the possibilities. Foreign correspondents couldn't attend those meetings, but boy, did they want to.

Peter made a right turn. "You always say how hard it is for you as a woman. Well, this will help even things out."

It would, but it didn't sit right. This would be different from using an informant. "I don't need help."

He glanced at her, the first he'd really looked her way all evening. "Sure, you don't need help, but don't you want it?"

Yes. No. She groaned and looked out the window, at the shivering trails of raindrops across the glass. Depending on others made her feel weak. It felt confining. And she'd be bound more closely to Peter, which didn't seem wise.

"I'll find out who's coming to town," he said. "I'll find out about events like this. Then you can just happen to be there. Maybe I can get you some interviews. Please. I need to do something."

He parked the car. A streetlamp illuminated his face. Turmoil still rippled across his forehead, but his eyes shone with a strong and steady light.

Evelyn wet her lips. "It'd be dangerous. If they find out you're feeding me—"

"I know. I don't care. I want to do this. I want to help you speak out."

All she wanted was the chance to speak, to stop having her voice stifled in insipid articles. "All right."

"Great. Thank you." Peter got out of the car and held open her door. "It's one block down. I'm coming with you."

For heaven's sake. She leveled her gaze at him. "I don't need a chaperone."

"For crying out loud." He flung his arm to the side. "I'm not— I'm not trying to stop you. I brought you here, didn't I?"

The rain had stopped, and Evelyn's posture softened. "You did. Thank you."

"But there's a mob. A violent mob." His expression managed to be gentle and firm at the same time. "Yes, you can handle it yourself. But you don't have to handle it alone."

Now her heart softened, her gaze, everything inside her. He wasn't standing in her way—he was standing beside her.

Peter's arm drifted back down to his side. The top button of his shirt was unbuttoned, his tie hung loose, and his hair was a riot of damp waves.

She fastened that button. "If you insist on coming along, let's make you as presentable as possible in just your shirtsleeves. Do you have a comb, Lang? You're a mess."

He reached into his shirt pocket, his hand brushing hers, and he pulled out a comb and went to work with it.

Evelyn wiggled the knot of his tie into place and made the mistake of meeting his gaze.

All turmoil erased. Only that strong and steady light. "Let's go, Brand."

FIFTEEN

Munich
Tuesday, June 28, 1938

In Hugendubel's bookstore on Salvatorplatz, Peter browsed the selection. Since he'd arrived in Germany, he'd been building his collection of German-language books. At first, he'd been pleased to find so many. Today all he could see were the missing authors. The banned authors.

Thomas Mann. Lion Feuchtwanger. Alfred Döblin. Erich Maria Remarque. Hermann Broch.

Some were Jewish. Some spoke out against the Nazis. Some were deemed unpatriotic. All had been banned in their home country.

Peter's stomach tightened, and he left the store without making a purchase.

He strode down the street. Ahead of him, the Frauenkirche lifted twin domed towers in the muggy air.

How could a nation that produced wonders like cathedrals and glockenspiels and bratwurst also ban her best authors and put dissenters in concentration camps?

Peter heaved a sigh and marched ahead. In a few minutes, he rounded the Frauenkirche's red-brick façade, made his way down a narrow lane, and crossed the Marienplatz. He was too early for the glockenspiel, but he didn't care.

"Peter Lang!"

Otto von Albrecht approached with an older man wearing the tailored black uniform of the *Schutzstaffel*, the SS. "Vater, this is Peter Lang, the American graduate student I told you about. Herr Lang, this is my father, Standartenführer Ludwig Graf von Albrecht."

A colonel and a count. Peter shook his hand. "I'm pleased to meet you, Herr Standartenführer."

Otto adjusted his brown kepi cap on his square head. "Where are you going?"

He couldn't very well say he was going to a café owned by a Jewish man to report on the Students' League meeting to an American correspondent. "Gärtnerplatz. I'm preparing next week's final examinations for my students, and there's a little park where I like to work."

"We will walk with you." Count von Albrecht had the same stocky build and quick gait as his son. "You should go to the Englischer Garten. It is bigger and more beautiful."

"It is, but I like this one too." Peter turned left beside St. Peterskirche, the high stone walls cooling him on the street below.

Otto nodded to his father. "Herr Lang comes to all the Students' League meetings, and he has come to several Party meetings this month."

"Good." Gray eyes assessed Peter. "Otto tells me you are impressed with the Reich."

"Very much. You have achieved great order. I can only hope my nation follows suit." He hated lying, but the more he talked like Otto and his friends, the more they welcomed him and the more information he obtained for Evelyn's articles.

Otto grinned at Peter. "Your students will return to America with good reports."

"Naturally." Peter strode down the cobbled pavement in step

with the black boots of Otto and his father. But in the two weeks since the destruction of the synagogue, he'd engaged the students in discussions of the issues he was mulling over. He hoped to raise questions, to encourage speaking up, and to remind them not to brush away concerns, but to address them.

The three men crossed the street into the busy Viktualienmarkt with its stalls of fresh produce. However, the spring cold snap had depleted the stock of fruit.

Otto frowned at the meager offerings in one stall. "It is important that Americans hear the truth about Germany, to overcome the lies of your Jews."

Bile rose in Peter's throat, but he swallowed it and prayed for forgiveness for the words he had to speak. "Yes, it is."

The count stopped at a produce stall under a blue-and-white striped awning. He hefted a potato. "Most Germans dismiss America as of no importance to us. Your nation is young, weak, far away. But they have misjudged you."

"Thank you." Peter shifted his attaché case from one hand to the other. By skipping the glockenspiel, he was ahead of schedule, but not if his companions insisted on grocery shopping.

Count von Albrecht set the potato in a scale, then added two smaller potatoes on the other side. The balance wobbled. "France and England oppose everything we do, but they are weak willed."

"Yes, Herr Standartenführer." Peter couldn't deny that. Both nations had been bloodied in the trenches in the last war and had no taste for another war.

"But America . . ." He held up a potato to Peter. "You like to stay on your side of the ocean, *nicht wahr?*"

"That is true."

"Good." The count swung the potato back and forth above the two pans of the scale. "If you stay on your side of the ocean, you let things settle the way they should. But if you choose, you can tip the balance one way or the other. That is why we need friends in America."

"Herr Lang is a friend," Otto said. "He will be an excellent voice for us."

That old longing for influence tugged at him, but now he tugged back and in new directions. Like exercising a weak muscle, he did so carefully but diligently, knowing the discomfort would make him stronger.

"That is my goal," Peter said. "I want people to know the truth about Germany. Now, if you'll excuse me, I have an appointment with my favorite park bench." Actually, it was his favorite reporter, but they didn't need to know that.

After pleasantries were exchanged, Peter continued south.

For the past few weeks, everything had felt off-kilter. He'd always been a straightforward man, but now he talked in different ways depending on the company. It was for a good cause though, to obtain information for Evelyn.

He left the marketplace and headed down Reichenbachstrasse, lined by stately five-story buildings. Such a clean street, free of mobs and chaos.

Guilt squirmed in his stomach. Some days, he felt as if he was betraying his father's memory.

For years, he'd believed any enemy of his enemy was his friend. But just because the Nazis opposed communism didn't make them right. They were simply wrong in a different way. Peter didn't have to choose one side or the other—he had to choose what was good.

And what was good?

"'To do justly, and to love mercy, and to walk humbly with thy God.'" He repeated Micah 6:8, which he'd memorized since the rabbi quoted it.

Peter was trying to walk that new way, that humble way, that both-sides way. Lately, he'd spent a lot of time in the Old Testament, which the Nazis rejected.

Exodus and Numbers and Leviticus and Deuteronomy were full of laws from the Lord. Many were laws of order, to restrain and punish evildoers. But many were laws of mercy, to protect the vulnerable, the poor, the widows, the orphans, and the aliens in the land.

Peter pushed his glasses higher on his nose. Both order and mercy were required for a harmonious society. When one was chosen over the other, only suffering resulted.

Peter had seen that suffering firsthand. His father's death. The synagogue's destruction.

Herr Gold had told him the rabbi was recovering. Most of the synagogue's treasures had been saved, thanks to the congregation's hard work. That night after taking Evelyn home, Peter had returned to help. He only had two arms and a car, but every bit made a difference.

He turned onto the roundabout, and the garden of the Gärtnerplatz filled his nose with freshness. Soon the smell of coffee and pastries added to the pleasure. The only good thing missing was Evelyn.

"Ach! Herr Lang." Herr Gold rushed to greet him, with another man by his side. "I would like you to meet my dear brother, my sister's husband, Gottfried Werner."

"I am pleased to meet you, Herr Werner." Peter shook the man's hand. Herr Werner was as tall and plump and blond as Herr Gold was small and trim and dark.

"I am pleased to meet you too." Herr Werner gave a polite little bow. "Please—which table would you like?"

"It is such a warm day. I will sit outside."

Herr Gold opened the door for him. "Coffee and a *Krapfen*?"

"You know me well." Out on the sidewalk, Peter found a table shaded by the awning. He took off his hat to let the breeze cool him, and he pulled his folder from his attaché case.

After the summer semester ended in early July, Peter would make the final set of recordings from this class.

This summer, before the winter semester started in October, he would write his lesson plans for the incoming students and work on his dissertation. The background material could be written before he had his final data.

"Your coffee and *Krapfen*." Herr Gold set out Peter's refreshments, then he gazed over the plaza.

Peter added two splashes of milk to his coffee. "Your brother-in-law seems kind. How goes the sale of the café?"

Herr Gold sighed and sat at the adjacent table, where Evelyn would have sat. "The government wants me to sell but makes it difficult and expensive to do so."

"I am sorry. But then you will still work here, ja?"

"As long as I am able."

"Able? Are you sick?" He looked hale and hearty.

"I am not sick. I am Jewish." Herr Gold sent him a wry smile. "First they banned us from civil and military service. Now they've banned us from working in industry. Soon there will be no work for us."

This in a country that locked people up for being "work shy." Peter turned the plate around and around. "Why do they want you all unemployed?"

"They want us out. They want us to leave Germany."

How horrible to be unwelcome in your home country. "Have you considered leaving?"

"We are trying. But where to go?" Herr Gold shrugged. "My people do not have a homeland. England rules Palestine, and they have strict quotas so as not to anger the Arabs."

Peter murmured his sympathy.

"Shall I go east?" Herr Gold gestured in that direction. "Poland and Hungary and Romania have antisemitic laws too. Shall I go south? Italy only allows baptized Jews, and Spain is in the middle of a civil war. Shall I go west? To France? England? America? Everyone has quotas. My wife and I are on many waiting lists, but they are long. No one wants us."

Peter did. He would gladly welcome the Golds, the entire synagogue congregation, into his community. "If I can help in any way

. . . my family has connections." But those connections felt flimsy in the face of such obstacles.

Herr Gold slapped his hands on his thighs and smiled at Peter. "It is too beautiful a day to talk of ugly things. Now, where is your Fräulein Brand?"

"I don't know, but she is not *my* Fräulein Brand."

"I thought—after that night you helped us—"

"She is a friend." Peter took a sip of coffee. "It is good to have friends."

Herr Gold grinned and whacked Peter on the arm. "It is better to have a wife. Keep pursuing her. You will wear her down."

That would be the worst possible thing to do to her, the least compassionate.

Peter bit into his donut. He would help her with his reports on the Students' League and Party meetings. He would enjoy the friendship, even savor the attraction. Maybe someday she'd fall for him.

Probably not.

Regardless, he refused to be another hunter on her trail.

Perhaps he should leave the café before she arrived. A strange and sad idea, but right and good.

Peter finished the pastry and pulled an envelope from his attaché case—his report from the meeting. He handed it to Herr Gold. "This is for Fräulein Brand. Please give it to her."

"You will not wait?"

Peter returned his papers to his attaché case. "I shall return to my dark little office where warm breezes and colorful flowers do not distract me from my work."

Herr Gold waved the envelope with a teasing look. "A love letter?"

Let him think what he wanted. Peter set down his payment, stood, and shook the café owner's hand. "For her eyes only."

Attaché case in hand, he strolled down the sidewalk around the park.

"Peter?" Evelyn stood by the fountain in the center of the park, wearing a summer dress.

"Good day, Evelyn." He smiled and waved. "Don't worry. I saved a *Krapfen* for you."

"Are you leaving already?" She almost sounded disappointed.

"I am. Herr Gold has something for you." Another wave, and he continued on his way.

Everything in him wanted to turn around and resume the chase, but he urged his feet homeward.

"Compassion," he muttered. "Kindness. Mercy."

SIXTEEN

On the street before Evelyn, six horses draped in colorful blankets towed a float bearing a statue of a giant eagle perched on a swastika.

Seated in the grandstand beside Libby, Evelyn took notes for her article on the Day of German Art.

What a relief to sit among snide-talking foreign correspondents, with no expectations to cheer or salute.

A band marched past playing martial music, followed by men of the Nazi Motor Corps on their motorcycles.

Libby flipped through the parade program. On the cover, a bare-chested man held up a torch and a swastika flag. "The parade's almost over."

"Good." The rain had cleared and the weather was cool, but Evelyn had had enough.

Today wrapped up the three-day Festival of German Art, with concerts, lectures, and a spectacle of fireworks to Beethoven's "Ode to Joy." Part of it was impressive, even beautiful, but the militarism and propaganda nauseated her.

Hundreds of shirtless young men marched past in dark green

trousers, shovels propped on their shoulders like rifles, the members of the Labor Service, who dug ditches and built roads and worked the farms in their mandatory six months of service.

This was probably all up Peter's alley.

Or was it?

Evelyn made notes. The old Peter might have liked this, but not the new Peter. He brought her good information from the Nazi meetings, most of it too good to use. An article about the Party recruiting men to go to Czechoslovakia and incite the German speakers to riot would be sensational, but Evelyn would get pitched out of Germany and Peter would land in jail.

The cynic in her wondered if Peter's spying was only a ploy to win her heart. Except he hadn't asked her out for ages. Since the hike at the Partnach Gorge a month and a half earlier.

Evelyn tapped her pen on her notepad as SS troops marched by in sharp black uniforms.

She shouldn't miss his invitations, but she did. His attention had been flattering, the mutual attraction stirring. But she'd directed her sharp points at him too many times, and he'd given up. Strangely enough, that hadn't ended their friendship. He still came to the café, and they still had spirited conversations.

Dozens of women glided down the street in long white robes and flowing capes—the *Edelfrauen*, the noble or ideal women. Curvaceous, gentle, domestic. Evelyn's opposite in every way.

Libby leaned her shoulder against Evelyn's. "What's going on with the other correspondents?"

Evelyn glanced around at the men and a handful of women. None met her eye, even those she knew from Paris or Berlin. But then she'd been exiled to Munich for almost a year.

"They keep pointing at you. Some are snickering." Under the brim of her spring hat, Libby's brown eyes narrowed.

Evelyn grumbled. "I'll never live down dressing like a man at that Paris press conference."

Libby chuckled.

But stories of the Paris incident usually led to ribbing, not snubbing, and Evelyn frowned.

One last horse-drawn float passed, a giant statue of a naked man with the ubiquitous torch and flag, and the correspondents exited the press area.

Evelyn and Libby strolled down the street toward the *Haus der Kunst*—the House of Art, which had opened a year ago. Built in the massive, chunky style the Nazis favored, the museum stretched in a long limestone box with marble columns that led the locals to dub it the *Weisswurstpalast*—the White Sausage Palace.

In the morning, Hitler had made a grandiose speech opening the 1938 Greater German Art Exhibit, which would run through October 16.

At the museum entrance, Evelyn showed her press pass and Libby handed in her ticket.

The ladies wandered through the spacious rooms past an enormous portrait of Hitler, busts of Hitler, a painting of Hitler at the infamous 1923 Beer Hall Putsch.

A painting of corpulent Hermann Göring in hunting garb, with dead birds piled beside him.

Evelyn exchanged a glance with Libby and turned away quickly so she wouldn't laugh.

They passed pastoral scenes of farmers in the field, militant scenes of marching brownshirts, and nudes.

So many nudes. Well-muscled men in heroic poses and well-rounded women lounging in gardens and homes.

Libby giggled. "Apparently clothing violates Nazi ideology."

Evelyn smothered her own laugh and entered the next room.

The works were competent without genius, without creativity, without innovation. And certainly without modernism. Only Nazi-approved artists and Nazi-approved subjects and Nazi-approved techniques.

Libby sighed and frowned at yet another nude female statue. "I want to go home."

Evelyn sighed back. "I have to see the whole exhibit for my article, but you don't have to stay."

"No, I want to go home to the States." Libby faced her in the middle of the sterile white limestone room.

"But you're a sensation here."

Libby gestured with a graceful hand around the room. "My wings are clipped as much as these artists' are. I love Mozart and Bach and Beethoven. But I also love the Russian composers and the Jewish ones, even the moderns—not my favorite, but I like the challenge."

Evelyn twisted her red purse strap and stifled her protests, all of which were selfish. Libby had welcomed her into her apartment when Evelyn had been sent to Munich, and rooming with her had been wonderful, just like college. "How much longer will you stay?"

"A few more months. I have offers in New York. I feel awful leaving you in the lurch with our apart—"

"Never mind that. I should be in Berlin soon. If not, I can afford it. But I'll miss you, of course."

They resumed their tour, and Evelyn paused in front of a portrait of Dr. Joseph Goebbels. The artist had captured the intelligence on the man's gaunt face, but he'd imbued him with a thoughtful spirit. Evelyn had only attended a few of Goebbels's press conferences. The Minister of Propaganda had surprising wit and a grin that transformed his face from sharp to genial, but occasionally something sinister flashed in his eyes, chilling Evelyn to the bone.

"Admiring your boyfriend, Brand?" a male voice said behind her.

Evelyn turned to Bert Sorensen of the New York *Press-Herald*. "Pardon?"

Sorensen flicked his pointy chin to Goebbels's portrait. "Gonna plant a kiss on those lips, Gigi?"

Evelyn hiked up an eyebrow. "Gigi?" No one had ever called her that. She didn't even have a G in her name.

The reporter's gray eyes sparked with a mean sort of teasing. "That's what we call you—Goebbels's Girl."

"Goeb—what! That's disgusting. They don't think I'm—" She waved a hand toward the portrait.

"Making little Nazis with him? No. Just living in his back pocket."

Evelyn's chest filled with churning, burning heat. "Why on earth would anyone think that?"

He barked out a laugh. "We see your articles. We read them to ourselves when we want a laugh—'each athlete reveling in the joy of camaraderie' and all that."

Norwood. Evelyn's lips pressed tightly together. How could she be both honest and diplomatic? "That is not how I wrote those articles. They were edited. Heavily."

"Sure, they were." He winked. "You fit in at the ANS—Adolf's News Service."

Evelyn's mouth hung open, and she slowly turned to Libby, whose mouth also hung open. "Now *I* want to go home. I have a phone call to make."

———

"Mr. Norwood's in France," the receptionist at the Berlin bureau said. "Mr. O'Hara's in charge in his absence. Would you like to speak to him?"

"Yes, please." Evelyn stood by the phone, drumming her fingers on the table, reminding herself to speak cautiously in case the phone line was tapped.

A few clicks. "Hey, Ev. What's up?"

All caution went up in flames. "Goebbels's Girl? Adolf's News Service? Have you heard this?"

Mitch O'Hara groaned. "I have."

"Because of Norwood."

"He's afraid we'll get kicked out and—"

"It's more than that. Have you seen my articles, how he's edited

121

them? He doesn't just make sure the Nazis don't look bad—he makes them look good."

"I've only seen a few."

"Listen." Evelyn spread out a clipping and an original article. "This is what I wrote about the movie *Olympia*—'The athletes march in precise formation. The camera skims past faces and shows muscled arms and legs swinging in uniformity, the individuals blending into a mass.' That would have passed, wouldn't it?"

"Yes," O'Hara said. "That works."

"This is how Norwood edited it—'They march in precise formation. Riefenstahl's camera shows the beauty of muscled arms and legs swinging in unity, each athlete reveling in the joy of camaraderie.'"

"You've got to be kidding me."

"There's so much more." Evelyn put her hand on her hip. "Everything negative deleted. Everything neutral made positive. Everything positive expanded."

"What'd he do to your café article?"

"Rejected it."

O'Hara fell silent. No, not silent. Low curses flowed through the telephone line.

Evelyn strode to her desk, as far as the cord allowed. "Now I have two articles to write, on the art festival and the art exhibit. He'll edit those to death too."

"He's at the Evian Conference this week."

"Of course, he is. Plum assignment like that."

"Not so plum. Nothing's coming out of that conference."

Evelyn picked through papers on her desk. As pressures increased on the Jews to leave Germany—and as life became increasingly difficult for them—they were seeking new homes. But quotas and restrictions in other nations hindered their escape.

President Roosevelt had called an international conference to resolve the problem, but since the US State Department refused to increase America's immigration quota from Germany, the US had lost moral leverage.

"Say, Ev. I'm in charge while he's gone."

She smiled. "You'll edit my stories?"

"I don't have time for that nonsense. Send them to New York, same as the rest of us do."

Evelyn restrained a childish cheer—on the outside anyway. "I would love that."

"Tell you what. How many articles are you working on? Finish them fast. I don't expect Norwood back until the eighteenth. Get as many articles to New York as you can. You know how to follow the rules now."

"I do." She'd make sure no Nazi would squirm—but Americans would.

"Say . . . that café article. You didn't throw it away, did you?"

"No. It's too close to my heart."

"Update it. You know what I mean."

"I do." On July 6, Germany had passed a law requiring all Jewish-owned businesses to be closed or sold by the end of the year. "I'll update it and send it tomorrow."

"Good. I have an idea."

Evelyn grinned at her piles of articles, soon to see the light. She didn't know what O'Hara's idea was, but she knew she liked it.

SEVENTEEN

MUNICH
SATURDAY, JULY 23, 1938

Although dozens of people roamed the Forstner mansion, Peter picked out Evelyn across the room by the grand piano. Even if she hadn't worn red, he would have noticed her, but she had worn red, deep and rich as a fine wine.

"Many thanks for coming to my soiree," Katarina von Forstner said to him. "Fräulein Brand insisted we invite you. She said you'd be a lively addition to our guest list."

Peter pried his gaze from Evelyn and bowed his head to his hostess, an elegant widow in her sixties. "I can only hope to live up to such expectations. I am honored to be welcomed into your home."

"Ach, here is our Fräulein Brand."

Evelyn glided over, her slim hips swaying. Her dress hugged her figure down to her ankles, and a filmy collar traced the V-shaped neckline and fluttered on her bare shoulders. Her lips rose in a brilliant smile.

Lord, help me. Peter straightened his tuxedo jacket. He took her hand, outstretched for a handshake, and he bowed to kiss it in the Bavarian fashion, letting himself linger. "Good evening, Fräulein Brand. You look stunning."

"Good evening, Herr Lang. Doesn't he have lovely manners, Frau von Forstner?"

Their hostess smiled, fine lines radiating around her blue eyes. "He's perfectly charming."

"I shall introduce him around so others may enjoy his charm." Evelyn plucked her hand from Peter's, tucked it into the crook of his arm, and led him away.

"Be careful," Peter said, "or my head will swell with pride."

"Not to worry. I'll throw an insult or two your way."

"Better make it three. You slathered it on thicker than jam."

Evelyn laughed. On one side, her hair fell in waves to her chin, and on the other it was held up by a ruby-studded comb. "You'll like it here. Frau von Forstner throws soirees with the most interesting people. This is one place in Germany where people are free to speak their minds."

She led him through a salon decorated in the ornate baroque fashion popular with Germany's upper class. Chairs and settees and low tables formed intimate areas for conversation, and a gentleman played Beethoven's *Moonlight Sonata* on the piano.

Peter patted the breast pocket of his tuxedo jacket. "I brought that poem for you."

"Thank you. I'll get it before I leave." Evelyn had insisted they find different ways to pass reports on the Nazi meetings.

If it allowed Peter to see her in social settings, so be it.

Evelyn drew up to three people standing in conversation. "Fräulein White, you remember Herr Lang. Everyone, this is Herr Peter Lang. He's studying for his doctorate in German at Harvard and is teaching at the University of Munich."

Peter smiled at the group and greeted Libby, who looked lovely in a long pale pink gown.

Evelyn nodded toward a gorgeous, full-figured blonde. "Fräulein Anneliese Vogelsang sings in operettas, and Herr Wilhelm Heinecke is a gifted novelist."

"It's a pleasure to meet you, Fräulein." Peter kissed her hand. He had a hunch Vogelsang was a stage name, since it meant *birdsong*. Then he shook Heinecke's hand.

"Please excuse me." Evelyn departed.

Peter's arm felt naked and lonely, but he knew how to mingle. "Fräulein Vogelsang, are you currently in a production?"

"I am." She raised a smile that had probably claimed hundreds of men's souls. "I play Rosalinde in *Die Fledermaus* at the Bavarian State Theater."

On Gärtnerplatz. Peter's favorite Platz.

"There you are, *Liebchen*." Bannführer Wolfgang Diefenbach pressed a kiss to Fräulein Vogelsang's cheek, then extended a hand to Peter. "We haven't had the pleasure of meeting."

Yes, they had, not only in regards to Hans-Jürgen Schreiber but at numerous Party meetings. However, Peter shook Diefenbach's hand as if they'd just met. "Peter Lang."

"Wolfgang Diefenbach." He wore a tuxedo rather than a uniform, unusual for a Nazi.

Frau von Forstner came over, whispered to Libby, and the two ladies excused themselves.

Heinecke turned sleepy-lidded eyes to the operetta singer. "You must find music stifling lately."

Peter tensed. Heinecke didn't know a fervent Nazi stood beside him. Complaining about restrictions on the arts could land him in prison.

She leaned against Diefenbach's shoulder. "What do you mean?"

Heinecke's mouth screwed up, about to spew words that would probably condemn him.

"If you'll excuse me, Fräulein, I'm not familiar with Herr Heinecke's work." Peter turned to the author. "Please tell me about your latest novel."

His expression relaxed, then grew to satisfaction, and he described the plot of his book, which sounded dreary and ponderous. However, since it had been accepted for publication under Nazi rule, the topic was safe.

A woman in ice blue approached and tugged on Heinecke's arm. "Are you boring everyone with your stories, Willi? Come with me. I want you to meet Herr Janvier from Paris."

Diefenbach patted Fräulein Vogelsang's waist. "*Liebchen*, please fetch me some wine."

"Naturally." She gave him a flirtatious look and sashayed away.

Diefenbach stepped closer, his eyes level with Peter's. "It is good to see you here, good to see someone of like mind."

"It is." Peter felt off balance and adjusted his stance. It was vital that Diefenbach believe he was a Nazi sympathizer, and just as vital to protect the guests from the danger.

Diefenbach surveyed the room. "Anneliese told me about the inappropriate conversations that occur here. I came to see for myself."

With his civilian attire, no one would suspect he would report to the Gestapo. But if Peter kept him occupied, Diefenbach couldn't spy on the others. "Did Hans-Jürgen Schreiber tell you he was admitted to Harvard University?"

"Yes." Lettuce-colored eyes hardened. "I will not grant him permission to go."

Peter's chest constricted. "Why not?"

He snorted. "He is not a good Nazi. The students we send abroad must be dedicated to spreading our ideology."

Professor Schreiber hadn't said so, but clearly the boy was being sent abroad to escape that ideology. Peter scrambled for a solution. "The Schreibers are quiet. The boy's beliefs run deeper than you realize."

Diefenbach shrugged massive shoulders. "The Labor Service will be good for him."

"He has a brilliant mind, and he is growing stronger of body, ja? If he convinces you his ideology is correct, you would be wise to let him go. Harvard could use a young man like him."

"Very well." But his tone said he wouldn't be easily convinced. Tomorrow, Peter would visit the Schreibers and urge Hans-Jürgen to spout every bit of Nazi ideology, no matter how vile. Or else he'd never leave.

A twinge of guilt. It wasn't fair that Aryan Hans-Jürgen Schreiber might be able to travel to America while Herr Gold couldn't, but student visas fell outside the quota of immigration visas. The boy wouldn't take one of those valuable slots.

"May I have your attention?" Frau von Forstner stood by the piano with Libby. "It is my pleasure to announce that acclaimed flautist Fräulein Elizabeth White will play for us."

Libby inclined her head modestly as applause filled the salon. "Thank you for the kind welcome. I'd like to play selections from an American composition. It was composed for piano and orchestra, but I will play it on my little flute. *Rhapsody in Blue* by George Gershwin."

"How dare she?" Diefenbach said through gritted teeth. "It's banned."

"Because it's jazz?" Peter whispered.

"Worse. Gershwin was Jewish."

Peter grunted as if disgusted with Libby rather than with Diefenbach. "She's American. She might not know."

"Your land is so infested with Jews and Negroes you don't even see the infestation."

"That is why I am here. To learn your ways and bring them to America." Peter's stomach squirmed, but he had to play his role. He had to help Evelyn spread the word so the Nazi infestation would *not* come to America.

Fräulein Vogelsang returned with two glasses of wine.

"Come, *Liebchen*. The air is bad here." Diefenbach sniffed in Libby's direction and drew his girlfriend to the far end of the room.

Peter had to sound the alarm without letting Diefenbach know he'd sounded it.

Where was Evelyn? Peter weaved among the chairs and guests.

Libby's music wafted through the salon, so masterfully played it sounded as if composed for flute. And Gershwin's syncopation broke the rules—in the right way.

Evelyn sat on a settee in the back of the room, and all he wanted was to draw her close.

Yes. That would work. She'd hate it, but it would work.

Peter sat beside her and draped his arm on the back of the settee. "You look beautiful."

She raised one corner of her mouth. "You already said that."

"I said you looked stunning." He settled his arm around her shoulders and leaned close to her ear. "Don't move. I have something urgent to say."

"Pardon?" Her muscles stiffened beneath his touch.

"Urgent and private. Your friends' lives may be at stake. Understand?"

A pause, then she nodded slowly, her hair brushing Peter's nose.

"I'll pretend to flirt, and you'll pretend to welcome my advances," he murmured into her ear, bared by the ruby comb. "When I'm done, you can tell me off."

"I'm looking forward to that." But her relaxing shoulders and a lilt in her voice said she was playing along.

"Miss Vogelsang has bad taste in dates. Bannführer Wolfgang Diefenbach is—"

"Bannführer?"

"Shh." He shook his head, his forehead in her soft hair, his lungs filling with the smell of her, clean and fresh. But he had to concentrate on his mission. "Don't talk. Listen. He's a regional leader in the Hitler Youth. I met him through Professor Schreiber's son, and I've seen him at Party meetings. Miss Vogelsang told him about these parties. He's here to spy."

"I see." She stroked his fingers on her shoulder and nestled closer, a perfect fit in his embrace.

She'd let him have it later, but for now he surrendered. Savored. Even as his heart hammered at the dangers all around.

Peter nuzzled her ear, let his lips touch her warm skin, forced his brain back to his speech. "Your friends need to be warned. They are not free to speak. Probably never were. That is all. You may now slap me."

Evelyn rolled her shoulder to disengage his hand, and she stood and gave him a sassy look, her color higher than usual. "You're cute, Herr Lang, but I'm not looking for a college boy. I'm looking for a man." She chucked him under the chin as if he were five years old.

Peter clapped a hand to his heart as if wounded. "I did ask you to insult me."

"Two more insults to go." She sauntered away in time to Gershwin, lean and leggy.

He blew out a long breath. Touching her like that hadn't been wise, but it had been wonderful.

Peter tried to watch Libby play, but his gaze kept slipping to his rhapsody in red, now chatting by the kitchen door with Frau von Forstner.

The hostess stepped into the kitchen, and Evelyn leaned back against the wall by the door and smiled at her friend's performance.

When Libby finished, Peter joined in the applause.

Frau von Forstner came to the front of the room. "Isn't she a delight? Now, where is Fräulein Vogelsang? There you are. Would you be willing to bestow a song upon us?"

The singer beamed and made her way forward. "Why, yes. Thank you."

"Have a seat here, dear. Before she sings, I've been told by our Fräulein Brand that our new friend, Herr Lang, does an interesting party trick."

Peter laughed. "Party trick?"

Evelyn smiled smugly. What on earth did she mean?

"Come, Herr Lang." His hostess beckoned.

Peter obeyed. The ladies had their reasons. As he made his way to the piano, he passed Diefenbach and his date, who took seats up front.

Frau von Forstner welcomed him by the piano. "Herr Lang teaches Germans to speak with an American accent and Americans to speak with a German accent."

Peter checked his wristwatch. "I'm afraid your party will not be long enough."

Laughter circled the room.

Frau von Forstner patted his arm. "Perhaps a demonstration?"

"Very well. How can I refuse so charming an invitation?" Peter smiled at the guests in their evening wear. "In America, I'm called Peter Lang." He pronounced his last name the American way, rhyming with *rang*. "In Germany, I'm called Peter Lang." He pronounced it the German way, like *long*.

Peter rested his hand on the piano. "The difference in pronunciation goes beyond the vowel. Fräulein Brand, since you put me on the spot, I shall put you on the spot. Please say the word *Onkel*."

Still leaning by the kitchen door, Evelyn gaped at him but then recovered. *"Onkel."*

"Very good. She pronounced every sound properly, and yet every German in this room knew immediately she was American or British, *nicht wahr*?"

Murmurs of agreement floated through the room, and Evelyn frowned in confusion.

A maid passed Peter with a tray of wineglasses.

He stepped out of her way and swung a smile to the hostess. "Frau von Forstner, you speak excellent English. Would you please say *uncle*?"

She did so, and the Americans and British in the room murmured.

"You hear it, don't you?" Peter tapped his ear. "It's the letter *L*. The sound labels you instantly, and yet it's one of the easiest sounds to teach. All you need is an understanding of how we use the tongue and teeth and lips as we speak."

The maid picked her way between two chairs, tripped, and cried out. Wine streamed in red arcs, glasses shattered, and everyone gasped.

"My gown!" Fräulein Vogelsang cried.

Diefenbach threw up his hands. His shirt front bloomed red as if he'd been shot in the chest. "Foolish girl!"

"Oh no!" Frau von Forstner rushed over. "Greta! What have you done? Fetch towels at once."

The maid backed away, babbling apologies, and she scampered to the kitchen.

Frau von Forstner dabbed at Fräulein Vogelsang's white dress with her handkerchief. "I am sorry. She is young. I will pay to have your clothes cleaned or replaced. Come with me, please. Rudi?" she called to a man by the door. "Bring the car around so we can send them home."

Peter glanced to Evelyn, who gave him the slightest nod. That was no accident, and young Greta was in no danger of losing her job.

Frau von Forstner ushered her soiled guests to the foyer, waving over her shoulder. "Please continue, Herr Lang."

Peter spread his hands wide. "As we say in America, 'The show must go on.'"

He described the difference in the position of the mouth when Americans and Germans pronounced the letter *L*. Around the room, guests said *Onkel* and *uncle*, foreheads furrowed in concentration.

"Let's break into groups of three to four people. Make sure you have a mix of nationalities in your group. Take turns working on this. I'll circulate and help out."

Over the next fifteen minutes, the groups worked together with much laughter and crying uncle. Peter visited the groups and gave pointers. Everyone seemed to enjoy themselves, and he even heard improvement.

Soon the groups were simply conversing, mingling resumed, and Peter enjoyed meeting various people. Evelyn flitted in and out of his vision, listening, laughing, connecting people, telling stories, completely in her element.

He resisted the urge to go to her, but his eyes were less obedient than his feet. Never once did her gaze turn his way, which told him all he needed to know. Relenting from the pursuit hadn't swayed her heart any more than the pursuit itself had.

A lady sat at the piano and played a Chopin polonaise with feeling and talent, and Peter sat in an armchair to listen. Was Chopin banned or not? How could musicians keep it straight?

"I might be offended." Evelyn perched on the left arm of his chair.

She'd sought him out, and pleasure surged through his chest. "Offended? How so?"

Evelyn lifted one shoulder under that filmy ruffle. "You visited all the groups to give pointers—except mine."

That pleasure built in strength. She did notice him, after all. He rested his elbow on the right arm of the chair, deliberately leaning away from her. "I didn't dare risk another insult."

Her eyes flashed with fun. "You asked for insults. I still owe you two."

Peter held up his hands in surrender. "Fire away."

Her gaze roamed his face, and she brushed a curl away from her ear—the same ear Peter had nuzzled. "I—these things take time. Inspiration."

"Shouldn't take long." He glanced around the room. "Get any story leads?"

"I did, and now I can write what—oh." Her forehead and lips puckered. "I might have caused problems for your pal Norwood."

Peter heaved a mock sigh. "What did you do to poor George?"

"Poor George, my foot." She gave her head a shake, and curls sprang back over that sweet little ear. "I told you how he edited my work to death. Well, last week he was in France, and Mitch O'Hara was in charge. O'Hara let me send my stories straight to New York. Even a story Norwood had rejected—the one about the cafés."

Peter's eyebrows rose. "George rejected that? It was excellent."

"Thank you." Evelyn adjusted her perch. "The editors in New York were shocked at the change in my articles. And . . . pleased."

"Pleased?"

She gave him a hesitant look. "ANS thought my articles had a pro-German slant."

"Because of George's editing." Peter's heart sank. What was his friend thinking?

"Yes. They called Hamilton Chase—he's the European bureau chief in London. He called O'Hara in Berlin, and O'Hara told him everything. Yesterday, Chase told me to mail him the carbon copies of my original articles so he can compare to Norwood's versions."

"And George is in trouble?"

"I don't know. Maybe. His family has a lot of pull though. But there's a big difference between not insulting your host and praising your host."

Peter drummed his fingers on the armrest. "George and I have always seen eye to eye. He likes the same things here that I do—I did."

Evelyn's eyes widened.

"I admit I like certain things here, but not at this cost. Not when you can't perform Gershwin or when elderly men get arrested for calling Hitler a swine or when synagogues get razed."

Evelyn studied him, her brown eyes intense.

Peter leaned back. "You still don't trust me."

"I trust you." She cocked her head to the side. "Your tips have checked out."

"You check up on me?" He had to smile.

"It's my job. I check up on all my sources, especially the . . . the annoying ones."

Peter laughed. "Now you only have one insult left."

Evelyn stood and smiled down at him. "I'll have to make it a doozy."

EIGHTEEN

The aromas in Herr Gold's café usually stimulated Evelyn's appetite and creativity, but today both were squelched.

Across the road, on a bench in the Gärtnerplatz park, sat a man in a tan coat and a tan hat, reading a tan book. This wasn't the first time Evelyn had seen him there.

Peter would arrive in five minutes. From her seat, she could see the path he always took.

Herr Gold came out with a coffeepot and refilled cups for the half-dozen customers.

Evelyn held up her cup, even though it was almost full. "Would you please open the curtains all the way? It's a dreary day, and I'd love more light."

"Yes, Fräulein." He pushed aside the blue-and-white striped café curtains, then sat across from Evelyn and leaned his elbows on the table, on her papers. "May I make an observation?"

"Please." Evelyn blew on her coffee.

"This is the third time you have asked me to open the curtains. The two previous times, Herr Lang did not make his regular visit."

"What a strange coincidence." Evelyn met the café owner's gaze over the rim of her cup.

Herr Gold flicked a glance to the window without moving his head. "That must be a very good book."

"It must, to read outside on such an unpleasant day."

"This café is your home. If you ever want sunshine, please don't hesitate to open the curtains." He stood and returned to filling cups.

Evelyn riffled through her notes, though she could barely remember her topic.

Right on time, Peter came into view in a light gray suit and hat, his stride strong and sure.

"Go away," she whispered as if he could hear her.

He turned and crossed the street toward the *Apotheke* in the next block as if the pharmacy had been his destination all along.

Evelyn released a pent-up breath. Thank goodness, Peter was smart and vigilant.

The Gestapo had been watching her more closely, and she didn't want them to see her with Peter, lest the Nazis suspect he was informing on them. Peter had planted red herrings with his friends, saying he was using Evelyn to spread pro-Nazi propaganda. As proof, he'd shown them the Norwood-mangled article on the exchange students, full of glowing quotes from Peter.

But why take chances? Better not to be seen together in the first place.

Frau Engel understood. Last week, she'd passed Evelyn a message folded in a newspaper, which stated it would be the final message. She'd observed the extra eyes on Evelyn. Although Evelyn hated to lose an informant, she refused to risk Frau Engel's life.

The café door flew open. Magda Müller dashed to Evelyn's table. "Fräulein—"

"You shouldn't be here." For Gestapo benefit, Evelyn had to pretend Magda was a complete stranger. She gestured to her overflowing table. "I'm sorry, Fräulein. I have no room."

Magda plopped into the chair and scooted close, her brown eyes huge. "This is urgent."

With her smile fixed, Evelyn worked hard to keep her voice firm and low. "Nothing could be urgent enough to justify the chance you took. What if we're being watched?" She didn't dare draw Magda's attention to Herr Gestapo, but out of the corner of her eye, Evelyn saw the agent sit up straighter and peer through the café window.

Magda shook her head, her hair dull from too much bleach, and she opened her purse. "Ulrich gave me—"

"Close your purse," Evelyn said in the sharpest tone she could muster at low volume. "This is what we'll do. In a moment, I will spill coffee on my papers. You will open your purse and pull out a handkerchief to help clean up. You will add your papers to mine. Do you understand?"

"Yes, Fräulein." Magda folded squat-fingered hands atop her purse.

Evelyn sipped coffee, keeping an unrelenting gaze on the young woman. "After I pack, we will talk for a few minutes. Then I will leave. You will order food and stay here at least another hour. That is very important. Do you understand?"

She nodded, but annoyance flickered over her pretty features. "No one followed me."

"How do you know I'm not being watched? Never do this again. You know how to contact me. You put both our lives at risk, and your man's as well."

Magda's tiny chin poked out, then she drew it back in and sighed. "I understand."

"Good." If only Magda were as careful as Frau Engel. Evelyn closed her typewriter case to protect the machine. Then she drank some coffee and set the cup down off center so it sloshed. "Oh dear!"

"Ach!" Magda gasped and opened her purse.

Evelyn whisked her napkin off her lap.

Their hands met on the table—a handkerchief, a napkin, Evelyn's soiled article, a new set of folded papers. In the dabbing process, Evelyn slid her papers on top of Magda's.

Herr Gold peeked out of the kitchen.

"It's all right. A small spill, all taken care of." Evelyn sent him a smile. "But in a few minutes, the Fräulein would like to order. She doesn't know what she wants yet."

"Very good. I will return shortly."

After Evelyn blotted up the coffee, she gathered the papers into her portfolio. For the next ten minutes, she made boring small talk about movies, Magda's hat, and the weather.

Herr Gestapo still sat there. If only it would pour down rain.

Evelyn had to leave first so he'd follow her and not Magda. She picked up her typewriter, purse, and portfolio. "It was lovely meeting you, Fräulein. Enjoy your lunch."

Outside, cool mugginess pressed down, low and gray. She strolled north, sweeping her gaze over the Gestapo man as if he were as invisible as he thought he was. On her way home, she'd meander through the Viktualienmarkt and buy potatoes or something, as if in no hurry at all, as if she didn't carry incendiary papers.

Two weeks earlier, Magda had given her information about a military plot to arrest Hitler the moment he activated the plan to invade Czechoslovakia. The report had included the names of General Gerlach and other officers involved in the coup plan. Evelyn had burned the papers. Didn't Magda know those men would be executed if the report fell into Gestapo hands? And Evelyn would be executed for espionage.

Evelyn had rebuked the young woman. She'd better have learned her lesson.

Everything in her wanted to run home, read the papers, and destroy them before the Gestapo caught up with her. But a casual attitude was her best defense, so she strolled at a leisurely pace and didn't once look behind her.

In the farmer's market, bright stalls beckoned but held almost no fruit and few vegetables.

Cabbages—perhaps she could make coleslaw. She picked up a head and hefted it.

"That one looks good, Fräulein." Peter's voice.

So much for him being smart and vigilant. Without looking up, she examined more cabbages. "You shouldn't talk to me."

"Don't worry. Your shadow is gone."

"Hmm?" She glanced up.

A smile bent those fine lips. "Right after you left, another woman departed. He followed her—I made sure. I had no trouble catching up with you."

Evelyn squeezed the cabbage so hard, she'd have to buy it. "Oh no. The other woman—was she young, blonde, curvy?"

Peter frowned. "I believe so."

Bother. Why hadn't Magda listened to instructions? Evelyn would have to be careful meeting her in the future or stop meeting her entirely. She couldn't afford reckless informants.

"Someone you know?" Peter asked.

"Go look at the radishes across the way." Evelyn sloped the broad brim of her hat to shield her face. She pulled a string bag and cash from her purse, paid for the cabbage, and put it in her bag.

Peter hadn't left. "I don't need radishes. But don't worry. Even if Mr. Shadow were here, he'd find our conversation boring."

Evelyn went to the next stall with its bins of potatoes. "Boring? Why? Are you going to lecture me on the correct pronunciation of the u-umlaut?"

Deep, rich laughter welled up. "I've been waiting for the third insult for almost three weeks. That was worth the wait."

Evelyn smiled with satisfaction, but her chest warmed at her memories of Peter's anything-but-boring lecture at the soiree. He'd been so engaging, speaking with authority and warmth and humor. He had . . . presence.

That evening, when he'd asked for another insult, she'd been stumped. The only adjectives that had come to mind had been complimentary. Manly. Captivating. Tempting.

Those would not have done. Not at all.

Evelyn wheeled to the potatoes, and the heat spread up her neck. "What is this boring conversation you have for me?"

"I said it would bore Mr. Shadow, not you. George Norwood called last night."

"He did?" She scrunched up her face. "He must be furious."

Peter angled to reach around her, and he picked up a potato with long, supple fingers. "Most men are when they lose their jobs."

"He didn't lose his job. He was demoted, but the ANS is letting him stay in Berlin as a correspondent. That was generous of them."

"It was. I told him so." He picked up another potato. "I know he was being cautious and thought he was representing American interests, but he went too far."

Norwood's bias surpassed caution and protecting business, but she let Peter off the hook since Norwood was his oldest friend. "He must be angry with me."

Peter set down the potato and brushed dirt off his hands. "Yes, but he's mostly angry at your friend O'Hara. George says O'Hara sabotaged him to get his job."

Evelyn let out a laugh. "Hardly. O'Hara turned down the job before they offered it to Norwood. He's only filling in as chief until ANS sends a replacement."

Peter glanced at her sidelong, his hat shadowing his eyes. "I imagine you'll be in Berlin soon."

"No, I'm staying here." Not long ago, she would have fumed about that. "O'Hara says I've made good connections and I'm getting good stories. He likes having a correspondent in southern Germany. It makes ANS more flexible."

"I'm sorry. I know how much you wanted Berlin." His voice sank in compassion.

"Thank you, but I don't mind. I like Munich. I have friends here." She tucked her hair behind her ear. The same ear.

How many times since the soiree had she exposed that ear to Peter, as if inviting him to caress her again with his warm breath, his rumbling voice, his soft lips?

Far too many times, and she whirled to the potatoes and flagged down the woman behind the stall. *"Zwei Kartoffeln, bitte."*

Evelyn paid the lady and added the two potatoes to her string bag.

"Well, I'm glad you're staying." Peter inclined his head, and the shadow rose from his eyes, revealing disarming warmth in that blue.

That warmth flooded into her smile. "Thank you. I . . . I should go home now."

"May I help? You have your arms full."

"No, thank you. I can handle it myself."

"Of course, you can." Peter tipped his hat and a smile. "Auf Wiedersehen."

Evelyn frowned at his back, that strong back. She threaded her arm through the loop of the string bag, clutched her portfolio, and picked up her typewriter case from between her feet. Her purse strap slipped off her shoulder, and she rearranged everything.

She did have a lot to carry, and it was heavy. Peter had offered to help, not because she wasn't capable, but because he was capable.

Evelyn headed toward her apartment, the string cutting into her forearm. What was wrong with her? Would it have hurt to have allowed Peter to help?

No. No, it wouldn't.

Or would it? True, Peter hadn't asked her out in ages, but . . . the soiree. Libby said he hadn't taken his eyes off her. And when he'd embraced her . . .

Oh my! Evelyn blew a breath upward to cool her heating face. Not just the way he'd nuzzled her ear, but the feel of his arm around her, the way he'd stroked her shoulder, the warmth of his solid torso against her side. It had felt very good.

Evelyn stopped and shifted her gear between arms. Yes, embraces felt good. Kisses felt even better. But everything had felt good with Howard and Clark and Warren.

She couldn't let herself be fooled by strong arms and fine lips and engaging banter. What if Peter was like Howard and Clark and Warren?

Evelyn didn't want to find out the hard way.

NINETEEN

Peter listened intently at the Nazi Party meeting. At home he'd write down his notes for Evelyn.

She'd be interested in tonight's proceedings. Even if she couldn't write an article about it, she'd want to know.

Three men were visiting from Czechoslovakia's Sudetenland region, which curved around the western flank of the nation.

The visitors stood at the swastika-festooned podium, describing how they incited riots and prompted clashes with the Czechoslovakian police. It didn't matter if people were hurt—in fact, they wanted injuries. Then they could point fingers and say the Sudeten minority was oppressed. The German newspapers trumpeted stories of brutality in the Sudetenland, most of them false, the speakers stated.

Peter pushed his glasses higher. Clearly, Hitler meant to take the Sudetenland by force, perhaps the rest of Czechoslovakia. All the talk about diplomacy was a ruse. The Nazis were provoking a crisis to create an excuse to invade.

Sitting next to him, Otto von Albrecht sent him a grin, and Peter returned it despite the uneasiness in his soul.

Would it be wise for Evelyn to have this information in written form? Recently he'd asked whether she wanted him to censor out things that would be dangerous if found in her hands—or to let her decide for herself. She'd seemed surprised by his inquiry, even touched. Then she'd thanked him for trusting her, and her softened gaze had invigorated his hopes.

Peter stifled a sigh and shifted position in his chair. With the rising talk of war and with the Gestapo tailing Evelyn, romance needed to be shoved far from his mind.

The Sudeten Germans took their seats, and the leader of the Munich block of the Party came to the podium and ran through routine business of no interest to Evelyn. Or Peter.

He couldn't wait to see how Evelyn would use tonight's information. She had an incredible talent to tell the truth, often raising doubt as to whether it was truth or rumor, and artfully concealing her sources.

For all she'd complained of George's editing, he'd taught her discretion. Now O'Hara let her write freely.

Poor George had to learn the opposite lesson, to be less discreet.

After business concluded, everyone stood to sing the "Horst Wessel Song," honoring an early martyr for the Nazi cause.

Everyone but Peter saluted. He sang some, pretending to forget the words when they pained him. His reputation as a friendly American allowed him liberties.

The meeting adjourned, and the men broke into groups to chat.

Otto adjusted the leather strap that crossed diagonally over his brown uniform shirt. "Exciting times, ja?"

"Ja." War would indeed be exciting—but terrifying and tragic.

Otto nudged him with his elbow. "Have we convinced you to join the Party?"

"If only I could." Peter twiddled his hat in his hands. "I will have more influence in America if my allegiance remains secret. Then I can share all I've learned here."

"That makes sense." Otto raked back a lock of light brown hair from his forehead. "I miss seeing you on campus. How goes your summer?"

"*Wunderbar.* My dissertation is coming along. And the new class of American students will arrive soon, and I'll make my recordings before the winter semester."

"Good. Are you free this weekend? My father asked me to invite you to our lake house."

"A weekend of swimming and boating in the Alps? Yes, please."

Wolfgang Diefenbach approached. "*Guten Abend*, Herr Lang."

"I'll see you later." Otto nodded to Peter and headed for another group.

A smile crossed Diefenbach's chiseled face. "I understand our young friend Hans-Jürgen has sailed for America."

"Yes. I attended his going-away party." The joy and grief on Professor and Frau Schreiber's faces had torn at his heart. "The Schreibers are grateful that you helped him obtain his exit visa."

"My pleasure." Diefenbach's green eyes lit up. "After you talked to him, he spoke up at meetings. We saw he's a good German after all."

"Good. He will help Americans see the truth about Germany." Although not the truth Diefenbach wanted.

"He was sad to miss the Nuremberg Rally though," Diefenbach said.

"Naturally, but American universities start in September rather than October, so it couldn't be helped."

"A shame." He beckoned to an army officer. "I told my friend about your work with Hans-Jürgen and your demonstration at the Forstner party—what I heard before I left."

Peter clucked his tongue. "That was too bad about the wine."

Diefenbach sniffed. "Frau von Forstner assured me the maid would be fired. Clumsy idiot. A Jew, I'm sure."

Peter murmured. On the contrary, Frau von Forstner had given the maid a week off with pay, and she'd crossed Fräulein Vogelsang and Bannführer Diefenbach off future guest lists.

The army officer joined them in a field gray uniform. He stood several inches taller than Peter, his brown hair peppered with gray.

Diefenbach introduced Oberst Heinz-Eugen Eberhardt.

The colonel raised a friendly smile. "The language expert."

Peter lowered his chin. "The Bannführer may have overstated my abilities."

"Herr Lang is too modest," Diefenbach said. "I have heard the results of his teaching. Not only does he have a knack for teaching pronunciation, but when he speaks to a group, he commands the room. Very impressive."

Oberst Eberhardt clasped his hands behind his back. "You teach Germans to speak with an American accent."

"I have, but the focus of my research is teaching Americans a German accent."

"Those are useful skills."

"Yes, they are." Peter's blood ran cold. Like many useful things, his skills had military applications, didn't they? Either nation could use his techniques to train spies.

Eberhardt narrowed one eye a fraction of an inch. "How long are you in Germany?"

"A year, through February when the winter semester ends. I have been soaking up as much German culture as I can and eating more than my share of *Wurst*."

Diefenbach chuckled. "Herr Lang is attending the Nuremberg Rally next week."

"Good." The colonel's broad grin broke free. "You will find it stimulating."

Peter shook the men's hands and left the Führerbau, the new Nazi Party building.

A cool rain descended in the night, and Peter scrunched his hat lower. His breath grew ragged, and he rubbed his fingers together as he walked the slippery granite slabs paving the Königsplatz—no, the Nazis had renamed it the Königlicher Platz.

All his life Peter had striven for order, and now he lived in chaos—chaos he'd deliberately created.

His personal views had swung far from the Nazis, but in the presence of Nazis he spoke more like them than ever. Even though he hedged his words and avoided lying, he was being deceptive. He was misleading them as to his true beliefs.

The wind shifted, and the rain came straight at him. He tilted his head and turned up his jacket collar.

Even more disturbing than his own deception was Eberhardt's interest in his work.

What if an American military or consular officer had overheard that conversation? How could they have known he was working undercover for an American reporter? They might have thought Peter was a spy for Germany. They might have seen him as a traitor.

Peter's upper lip tingled, and he swiped away rain. No, sweat.

Black and white he knew. But this gray in-between land felt foreign and messy.

And dangerous.

TWENTY

Flames raced up, darkening ink and paper until both turned black, and Evelyn dropped Peter's notes into the kitchen sink. With a fork, she poked every bit of his neat handwriting into the flame. When only black flakes remained, she rinsed them down the drain.

She'd typed up his notes as soon as she'd come home from the café, editing so it sounded less Peter-like and deleting revealing details. Since her landlord had refused to fire Helga, the snooping maid, Evelyn stored anything suspect in her new lockbox. Peter would be in great danger if the Nazis found out what he was doing.

At her desk, Evelyn opened the curtains to admit the late-afternoon sun. Then she penned a u-umlaut in the corner of the typewritten page, secretly marking Peter as the source.

Never once had she pressed him to tutor her in the frustrating sound. It would mean watching Peter's lips as they rounded around words like *fünf*. And he'd hold that position, only making her want to kiss those rounded lips.

"That would be stupid." Evelyn folded the paper in half.

Now that Peter's fondness for fascism had dissolved, nothing repulsive remained in him.

Therein lay the danger. He might have changed, but she hadn't. She still wouldn't fit in his neat little boxes. Especially the marriage box. Not with her career, her ambition, and all her sharp points.

Evelyn headed for the bedroom to lock up his notes.

The phone rang. She laid the notes on the phone table and answered. *"Hallo?"*

"Hi, Ev. O'Hara here."

Evelyn smiled and rested her hip against the table. The past weeks with O'Hara in charge had been idyllic. "Hi there, chief."

He grunted. "Not anymore. I'm transferring to Rome."

"Rome?" Mussolini had once been the talk of the world, but now Italy was a sideshow. "Why would you leave Berlin?"

Silence fell, and Evelyn fiddled with the cord. The line might be monitored, so they both had to be careful.

He cleared his throat. "Do you remember that gift our friend Sigrid received?"

"Yes . . ." Sigrid Schultz was the Berlin bureau chief for the *Chicago Tribune* and a pioneer for women in journalism. In 1935, she'd received an envelope in the mail containing secret designs for a German aircraft engine. Immediately, she'd burned them. Soon after, she'd intercepted Gestapo agents and informed them she'd burned the papers, she knew what they were trying to do, and she was on her way to the US Embassy to tell them about it. If she'd been caught with those plans, she could have been executed as a spy.

"I received a similar gift." O'Hara's voice was taut.

Evelyn clenched the receiver in her fist. "You did? What a lovely surprise." They didn't just want O'Hara out of Germany—they wanted him dead.

"I've told you about my ailments. New York thought a warmer climate might help."

"I'm sure your wife will love Rome. But we—we'll miss you here."

"Chase will send a replacement. In the meantime, call Keller if you need anything."

"Not Norwood?" She couldn't keep the sarcasm out of her voice.

"He's on his way to Nuremberg for the rally. A test."

"I see." Apparently Chase wanted to find out if Norwood could write a balanced article about the Nazi Party's big yearly spectacle. Peter would be there too. Maybe he could set his Harvard chum straight.

"Ev? You might want to consider a warmer climate too."

From any other person, she would have bristled at the suggestion, but not from a man who'd narrowly avoided arrest for espionage. "I'll keep an eye on the weather."

"Good. You know how quickly it can change."

When she hung up, a sensation swept over her, unmoored and floating, like when she'd gotten lost at the fair when she was five. A sensation of being small and alone and vulnerable.

"Nonsense." Evelyn pushed away from the table and brushed ash from the sleeve of her red-and-white print blouse. She might have lost her champion, her mentor, one of her best friends in Germany, but she could handle herself. Even after Libby returned to the States.

A knock on the door, and she smiled. "See? I'm not alone."

After she exchanged her house slippers for gray pumps, she opened the door.

Two men stood in the hall in unbuttoned trench coats—Herr Shadow from the Gärtnerplatz and a smaller man. Evelyn's breath turned solid and plugged her throat.

"Fräulein Evelyn Brand?" the shorter man asked. "We are with the *Geheime Staatspolizei*. May we come in?"

The Gestapo agents stepped right in, not waiting for a reply.

Evelyn backed up out of necessity, and her heart rate skittered out of control.

Herr Shadow closed the door and leaned back against it.

Caged.

Lord, help me! Evelyn struggled to breathe, but she schooled herself to look unconcerned.

The other officer, short and nondescript, with a thin layer of beige hair, removed his hat and strolled around her apartment.

To keep up her spirits, Evelyn would privately call him Herr Zero.

"Please have a seat, Fräulein." Herr Zero gestured to Libby's favorite chair.

Offering her a chair in her own home? "How kind of you." Her knees wobbled, and she lowered herself into a chair—a different one, just to be contrary.

The Gestapo hadn't arrested her, hadn't taken her in for questioning, so she forced herself to relax, to pray, to remember all she'd been taught about dealing with the Gestapo. Show no fear. Reveal nothing. If they talked tough, talk tougher.

Evelyn dramatically crossed her legs. "To what do I owe the pleasure of this visit?"

Zero stood at her desk and inspected the paper in her typewriter. "You are a reporter with the American News Service."

"Ja." Oh no. Her transcription of Peter's report. Had she locked it up? No, it was still on the phone table. With every ounce of strength, she kept her gaze on Zero, not letting it fly to the phone. Even with her care to conceal Peter as the source, the material was raw, too dangerous to put in an article—or to be seen by the Gestapo. *Lord, keep them away from Peter's notes.*

Herr Zero looked up and sniffed. "Do I smell burning?"

Evelyn pointed with her toe to the ashtray on the coffee table. "My roommate and I have friends who smoke."

His lip curled. "That is the smell of burning paper, not tobacco."

"Oh, that." She lifted one shoulder. "I have a suitor who writes annoying love letters. I burn them."

He huffed and sifted through papers on her desk. For the first time in her life, she was glad she was messy. With so many papers lying around, he was less likely to find Peter's notes.

Zero picked up a paper and scanned it. "I once liked your writing, Fräulein."

"What a pleasure to meet a fan."

His gaze darted to her over the paper. "I no longer care for it."

"Oh dear." She frowned as if that were the saddest thing she'd heard all year.

"Dr. Goebbels is not pleased. You were one of the few reporters who were fair to Germany. Now you are like the others, spreading lies and hatred."

What hypocrisy, coming from a regime that thrived on lies and hatred. "I report only what I hear."

"Then you listen to liars." He tossed the paper on the desk, came closer, and put one foot on the coffee table. "Who are your sources?"

My, my, my. Not even subtle. She gave a casual little shrug. "I hear things around town."

Zero whipped a notepad from his coat pocket and flipped it open. "In your article of August 12, you stated that German troops were preparing to invade Czechoslovakia."

Magda's information. Evelyn raised her sweetest smile. "Aren't they?"

"You mentioned plans. Who told you such lies?" His pale little eyes glared.

Yet she felt no intimidation. She rolled her eyes heavenward and sighed. "With so many men in my life, it's difficult to remember who says what."

Zero's upper lip curled. "I find that hard to believe. You are not an attractive woman."

Strange how unattractive men felt perfectly comfortable condemning women for being unattractive. She gave him a stiff smile. "It's interesting how beautiful a woman becomes to a man when she flatters him." Better for him to think the information came directly from a military officer. If he thought her a tramp, so be it.

Herr Zero kicked away from the coffee table and sauntered behind her chair. "In your article of August 4, you mentioned a delegation being sent from Munich to the Sudetenland. That information was known only by Party members."

And by Peter Lang. She gazed at Zero over the back of her chair. "Is that so?"

"I need his name." He marched around to stand directly in front of her chair.

With her elbow on the armrest, she rested her chin on her fingertips. "You assume it's a man. Never underestimate the vengefulness of a scorned wife or a jealous mistress or an underpaid servant. You should remind your men to treat their women more kindly."

"What's her name?" His face reddened.

Evelyn flapped her hand to the side. "Oh dear. These long, complicated German names—*von den Hohenuntenkleinengrossenburg*—oh! They're so confusing."

Zero raised his hand as if to slap her.

Everything in her wanted to cower, but she refused. Heart pounding, mouth tightening, she stared him down.

His fingers curled, claw-like, into a fist. He lowered his arm, and his facial expression flattened. "You are a woman, Fräulein. You should be more careful."

Evelyn sharpened her gaze to a razor and stood, her pumps lifting her above him. "On the contrary, *mein Herr*. You should be more careful. I am an American citizen and—as you noted—a woman. If anything were to happen to me, it would be bad for German-American relations. Right now, no American wants to get involved in this insanity in Europe. Not again. We learned our lesson twenty years ago. Your Führer likes it that way. He likes it when America minds her own business. You do not want to be the man responsible for changing that."

Not a hint of understanding or fear or doubt flickered in the man's bluish eyes, and he strode to the door. "Be careful what you write, Fräulein, or we'll have to meet again. Since I visited your place this time, next time I'd have to reciprocate and invite you to my place. I doubt you'd find my place as . . . pleasant."

Evelyn dropped a curtsy. "I'll bring a bottle of wine for your wife." Then she directed a big smile to Herr Shadow at the door. "I hope I see you again soon at the Gärtnerplatz."

He blinked, and his chin jutted out.

Zero motioned to the door, Shadow opened it, and Evelyn followed to lock it.

Libby was coming up the stairs. She passed the Gestapo men with wide eyes and a polite *"Guten Abend,"* and she darted inside the apartment.

Evelyn pushed the door shut and threw the lock.

"Who are they?" Libby whispered.

Evelyn snatched up Peter's notes, gestured for Libby to follow her, and dashed to the bedroom. "Gestapo. They're Gestapo."

"Evelyn! No!"

"I'm all right. I'm all right." She yanked open the middle drawer of her dresser and pulled the lockbox from under stockings and slips. "They wanted my sources, but I told them nothing."

"Oh my goodness. Did they hurt you?"

Evelyn shook her head, sank to her knees by the bed, and spun the dial on the combination lock. But her fingers jerked and didn't cooperate.

Libby knelt beside her. "You poor thing. You must have been terrified."

"I wasn't. I—I wasn't." But the jerking spread up her arms, shaking as if she were out in a Chicago blizzard without an overcoat. "I—I *was*. I was."

Libby hugged her from the side. "It's all right to be scared, sweetie."

Evelyn clutched her hands together on top of her knees, but her arms trembled out of control. "They didn't know I was scared. I didn't let them know."

"Of course not." Libby leaned her head on Evelyn's shoulder. "You're a strong woman, and the Lord was with you."

"He—he was." She pounded her clenched fists on her knees. "I hate it. I hate depending on others. It makes me weak."

Libby chuckled.

What was funny about that? Evelyn sat up straight.

Libby's brown eyes warmed with compassion and amusement. "Don't you know God makes us strong? He didn't create us to be completely independent, but interdependent. That's why he gave us families. That's why he gave us friends. That's why he gave us himself."

Evelyn frowned. Although she enjoyed her friends and family, she didn't need them for strength. But for Libby's sake, she nodded.

One more squeeze and Libby got to her feet and straightened the skirt of her green-and-white floral dress. "Go wash your face, and I'll make tea. Then we'll pray together. We'll read some Psalms."

Psalms? Libby had a Scripture for everything.

Libby rested her palm on the doorjamb, and a smile glowed. "David wrote many of the Psalms, you know. He was a warrior, and he leaned hard on the Lord. That didn't make him weak. It made him—"

"Strong." Evelyn's mouth hung open. She knew the stories. All her life she'd heard them. Why had she never seen?

TWENTY-ONE

In the night sky, beams from dozens of searchlights shot straight up to the clouds, outlining the rectangular Zeppelinfeld, four times larger than a football field.

Beside Peter in the grandstand, George Norwood tipped his head to the spectacle, holding on to his homburg. "It looks like a great Grecian temple."

Peter nodded, but he saw a prison. Bars of light and dark. No way out.

On the field, over one hundred thousand brown-uniformed Party members stood in rank with standards held high. Martial music played as Party leaders marched down the center of the field.

"Isn't this incredible?" George said. "Even better than a Harvard football game."

Peter managed to crack a smile. "Considering Harvard's record when we were there, that's not much of a statement."

George laughed. Despite their differing views, it was good to see George happy. And maybe one of the stories he wrote during the Nuremberg Rally would open his eyes.

Peter had told George he was attending the week-long rally to have the full German experience. It was better if George didn't know about his activities on Evelyn's behalf. Not only was he helping George's nemesis, but his infiltration into the Nazi Party could be misinterpreted.

Peter's foot tapped in time with the trumpets and drums, but he forced it to stop. The pomp stirred something within him, the majesty of the uniforms, the music, and the people united under a common purpose. But the purpose was skewed, polluting the entire spectacle.

At least tonight, sitting in the press section with the foreign correspondents, he didn't need to spout beliefs he hated.

Hermann Göring marched by, encased in a uniform bedecked with ribbons and medals.

A reporter behind Peter laughed. "Look at that fat pig in his Halloween costume."

"Some people have no manners," George said, and not quietly.

"Say, Cal," the reporter to Peter's left called to the heckler. "Have you read Evelyn Brand's latest articles? Can hardly believe ANS's best reporter in Germany is a girl."

"She's a rising star," Cal called back. "Ever since Norwood got the boot, that is."

As thrilled as Peter was to hear about Evelyn's success, he cringed for George's sake.

George's hands fisted between his knees, and he scooted his feet in, ready to stand.

Oh no. A fistfight would destroy George's career.

"Say, George." Peter gestured to the main grandstand. "Tell me who's who. I can identify some of them, but not many."

George's gaze slid to him, rough with anger.

Peter gave him a calm smile. "Tell me who's important. We know who *isn't* important."

One corner of George's mouth flicked up, he straightened his posture, and he pointed out the Party luminaries.

The music shifted, and Adolf Hitler marched by with his entourage. Peter and George and the correspondents stood, as they would for any world leader. The rest of the stadium cheered and applauded.

Peter had heard Hitler speak earlier in the week, but never this close.

All around, reporters whipped out notepads. Evelyn would have done the same, those brown eyes sharp in concentration, those chestnut curls falling over her cheek as she wrote, one slim hand whisking those curls behind her ear.

Boy, did he miss her.

"I see your smile," George said. "Hitler's impressive, isn't he?"

Peter studied the man who seemed to hold the world's fate in his hands. Not a big man or a strong man or a handsome man, yet one who had drawn an entire nation under his will.

"Yes," Peter said. "He certainly makes an impression." But not a good one.

Hitler strode up to the concrete platform that jutted out from the main grandstand.

His influence didn't come from his physical presence, but from his voice. His voice rose and fell and shook with emotion. His gestures accentuated his message, jabbing a finger, knifing his hand, pounding his fist.

"Say, Tony." Cal tapped the shoulder of the reporter to Peter's left. "Bet you five Reichsmarks he'll rant against the Czechs."

"You're on." Tony grinned back at him. "He's saving it for the closing ceremony on Monday. Get ready to cough up some dough."

Tony would win that bet, but Peter clamped his lips together. Going deeper into Nazi Party circles gained him information these reporters would love to have.

Based on that information, he could predict Hitler's upcoming speech on Monday night. The Führer would list injustices committed by the Czechs against the Sudeten Germans—although the land had been peaceful until the Nazis incited violence. He would lambast the leaders of Czechoslovakia, making Germany sound like a pitiful victim and Czechoslovakia a bully. He'd say the

Sudeten Germans deserved self-determination, and Hitler would see they had it.

In the giant stadium, before the adoring crowd, Hitler rose in pitch, bouncing on his toes, stabbing the night sky. He thrived on power, craved it.

Peter's face tingled. If Hitler's army invaded Czechoslovakia to "help" the Sudeten Germans, France was bound by treaty to aid Czechoslovakia and the Soviet Union was bound by treaty to aid France. Although Britain talked about appeasing Germany, surely honor would drive them to fight as well.

Another European war.

Peter swallowed hard. Everything in him recoiled, but maybe it would be best.

Germany was strong, but not strong enough to fight four of the best armies in the world. If Germany lost, the Nazis would fall. Hitler would fall.

Peter stared down the red-faced, gesticulating man at the podium. *Go ahead and invade, Adolf. I dare you.*

NUREMBERG
SATURDAY, SEPTEMBER 10, 1938

Outside Peter's hotel, it smelled like rain. But the clouds held back, their cheeks puffed full, waiting. The deluge would come and soon.

Peter strode across the Hauptmarkt plaza. His navy blue civilian suit was out of place among the numerous uniforms, just as those modern Nazi uniforms contrasted with the ornate medieval fountain and the Gothic brick church.

"Peter! Peter Lang!"

He turned around. George Norwood and his older brother, Charles, approached from the same hotel, and Peter waited for them to catch up.

"Where are you going?" George asked.

Peter tilted his head south. "To meet my friend Otto and his father at the Deutscher Hof."

"Where Hitler is staying. Must be a nice hotel." George adjusted his hat. "I'm interviewing Hugh Wilson, the new American ambassador to Germany. Charles arranged it for me." Charles's job at the US Embassy in Berlin provided excellent connections.

"Sounds great." Peter resumed walking, and the Norwood brothers fell in beside him.

"You'll like the ambassador, Georgie." Charles never let his brother forget he was seven years older.

"Far better than the previous ambassador." George wrinkled his nose. "William Dodd."

Charles shook his head and puffed out cigarette smoke. "Didn't know the first thing about diplomacy. But Wilson does. He's here for the rally. Dodd could never be bothered."

A crowd of boys in tan-and-black Hitler Youth uniforms ran by, laughing and shouting, and Peter stepped aside to let them pass. Evelyn had called Ambassador Wilson's attendance controversial. Since the rally was a Party function, not a government function, a diplomatic visit implied official US approval of the Nazi Party.

Charles led the way across a little bridge over the Pegnitz River. "A good diplomat knows the less we antagonize Germany, the better it is for business."

"True." Peter frowned upstream at the Heilig Geist Spital, a picturesque medieval building that spanned the still waters. Building bridges between nations might be good for business, but perhaps Hitler needed less business and more censure.

"True indeed." George gestured toward the street ahead, where red-and-black swastika banners hung from each building. "Let Germany be. They're doing well. Far better than America."

A suspicion wormed inside, and Peter tested it. "If only we could follow Germany's example."

George laughed and tapped his brother's arm. "I told you Peter was smart. He'll let people back home know how good the Germans have it."

Peter's stomach shriveled, but he worked up a smile for his old friend. His fraternity brother. "You're in a better position to do that than I am."

George's face darkened. "Not if ANS has its way. I can't believe they haven't reinstated me, even with O'Hara out of the way."

What had happened? "Out of the way?"

George's shoes slapped the cobblestones. "He and that Brand girl conspired against me so O'Hara could get my position. Then the old fool got in trouble with the Gestapo, and he transferred to Rome."

"Oh no." Evelyn hadn't mentioned O'Hara's troubles—and he knew for certain there had been no conspiracy.

"Don't feel sorry for O'Hara." Charles gave Peter a look as if tutoring a child. "He had it coming."

"And Brand." George's eyes flashed. "Typical pushy Jewish broad. The way she's writing lately, she'll get herself expelled. Or worse."

Peter glanced away to conceal his expression. His worry for Evelyn. His disgust at the Norwood brothers. Peter's father had often joked that it was great to have the Norwoods as friends—because you didn't want them as enemies. Now he understood.

"Here we are." Charles stopped in front of a hotel. "We'll see you later, Peter."

"See you later." Peter couldn't manage to say, "Hope your interview goes well." Not after George had shown no concern for Evelyn or her mentor.

He continued on his way, over the cobblestones, under the crimson banners. Perhaps he should call Evelyn and warn her.

Warn her of what? That her writing could put her in danger? She already knew that. Peter would sound like an overbearing, caging sort of man.

A banner hung low in his path, and he whapped it aside.

He was sick of banners. Sick of swastikas. Sick of parades and spectacles. Sick of rants against the Czechs and the Jews.

Sick of Nuremberg. Sick . . . of Germany.

His groan settled deeper. If he didn't have meetings scheduled at the rally, he'd return to Munich. And if he didn't have a fellowship and a commitment to teach and research to complete, he'd return to the States.

But his meetings might yield information for Evelyn. Even if she couldn't write the stories while she was in Germany, perhaps she could after she left. If George was correct, that could be soon.

Peter breathed out a prayer for her safety and her ability to continue as a foreign correspondent—even if it took her farther from him.

In a few minutes, he arrived at the Deutscher Hof, a grand red brick building. He took the stairs, found the Albrechts' suite, and knocked.

A servant led Peter to a parlor, where two men were seated.

In his black SS uniform, Standartenführer Ludwig Graf von Albrecht rose and greeted Peter. "Otto won't be joining us. He's participating in the athletic games." He turned to the other gentleman, who was wearing a field gray army officer's uniform. "Herr Oberst, may I introduce Herr Peter Lang. Herr Lang, this is Oberst Franz Ziegler with the Abwehr."

Military intelligence? Why did they want to meet Peter?

After Peter declined offers for cigarettes and drinks, he settled onto an overstuffed sofa and Albrecht returned to his armchair.

Ziegler stood by the fireplace, an unusual-looking man in his forties, with close-set eyes and the most triangular face Peter had ever seen. "You probably wonder why we invited you here."

"I do." Peter shifted in his seat, seeking a comfortable position.

Ziegler cradled the bowl of a pipe in his hand. "Word has come to us of your high regard for our country and of your personal attributes."

The count swirled amber liquid in his tumbler. "At my lake

house I had the pleasure of spending several days with this young man, and I've observed him at numerous Party meetings. However, I've never seen him give the Hitler greeting."

Peter crossed his ankle over his knee. "I apologize, Herr Standartenführer, but as an American citizen, it wouldn't be proper for me to swear allegiance to a foreign leader."

Both men grinned. "That is good," Ziegler said. "And useful."

"Useful?"

"Tell us of your interest in Germany and our regime." Ziegler set his pipe in his mouth.

Why did Peter feel as if he were interviewing for a job—a job he hadn't applied for? Yet an air of anticipation in the room drove him onward. "My mother came from Germany, as did my father's parents. I grew up speaking both German and English and knew from a young age I wanted to be a professor of German. When I spent my junior year in Munich, I fell in love with the land and the people, but I hated the poverty and chaos. Now I have returned. I have seen the order, the prosperity, and the happiness of the people."

When Ziegler narrowed his eyes, they almost disappeared. "Do you have a more . . . personal reason?"

Something told Peter this was a doorway, and he wanted to know what lay on the other side. He lowered his gaze to his lap, and his fingers clenched. "My father was killed by a mob of communists. I—I saw him die." He raised a hard gaze. "Germany does not have a problem with communists."

The men smiled. The doorway opened.

"Didn't I tell you, Herr Oberst?" Albrecht sipped his liquor. "He's articulate and amiable. Studious but strapping. Assured but not arrogant. And Otto says he is a gifted speaker."

"Thank you, Herr Standartenführer." Peter draped his elbow over the back of the sofa. "But I haven't been told why I'm being questioned and flattered."

Ziegler plucked his pipe from his mouth. "When do you return to America?"

"In February, after the winter semester."

"Would you like a project? One that will benefit both our nations?"

Peter's heart thumped as if he were tiptoeing through that doorway, apprehensive, curious. "I would need more information."

Ziegler laughed and strolled behind Albrecht's chair. "Have no fear. We would never ask you to commit treason. Your allegiance to your country is a benefit to us."

What an odd thing to say. "Continue."

"Many Americans have a dim view of Germany. We need men to speak on our behalf."

"You have the German-American Bund in the States."

Ziegler huffed, sending fragrant gray smoke into the room. "Most Americans see them as clowns. As thugs. The swastikas and uniforms and goose-stepping appeal to Germans, but not to your people. The Bund will never have a broad influence."

Peter murmured. Thank goodness for that.

"We need more subtle influence, and we need to organize those who believe as we do." Ziegler gestured to Peter with his pipe. "We believe you are our man. Not only your personal qualities, but your connections in politics and business and soon in the legal field."

Even as his heart stalled, Peter raised half a smile. Ziegler had researched his family and already knew about his father's death.

Ziegler strolled back to the fireplace. "You would press our case with your contacts, students, and colleagues. You would give lectures about your experiences in Germany."

Peter's fingers rubbed together. "Please define this case you'd like me to press."

"Simple." Ziegler shrugged. "First, counteract the bad reports about Germany with the good. Second, remind Americans of the dangers of interfering in Europe again."

"Promote isolationism."

"Yes. It is popular in America. Make it more so." Ziegler rested his forearm on the mantel. "Third, remind them of the dangers of communism and of the importance of a strong Germany as a hedge against the Soviet threat."

Peter licked his drying lips. "And ideally to bring National Socialism to America, ja?"

Ziegler smiled. "That would be good for your nation. What do you think, Herr Lang?"

While his thoughts spun, Peter rose and headed for the bar, where he poured himself a cup of coffee. Six months ago, he would have accepted eagerly. But not now.

What good would it do to accept? Evelyn couldn't write about this meeting—Peter would be revealed as her informant and they'd both be in great danger. But declining might alert the Nazis to his true allegiance. The smartest choice would be to accept with no intention of following through.

What new dangers might that introduce?

"Tell him the most important part," Albrecht said.

Peter turned around and sipped his coffee, trying to look casual.

Ziegler pulled an envelope from his pocket. "I have a list of men in America, reasonable and respected men in positions of power. All have contacted us and stated sympathy with our cause. You would be our liaison. You'd give them points to proclaim in the media, in their organizations, through legislation, in talks with their congressmen. You would connect them—not an official organization, but a loose network. Subtlety is vital."

Peter stared at the envelope. His thoughts slowed in their clockwise spin, stopped, and began spinning counterclockwise.

Ziegler tapped the envelope on the mantel. "We would communicate with you by letters, friendly letters written by fictional university students to their former instructor. They would mention things about Germany or pleas for peace or complaints about communism."

Breathing deeply to keep his mind clear, Peter returned to the sofa. "Those would be the points to stress."

"Yes, and if we had a new contact for you, we'd scatter the

hometown and first and last names throughout the letter and underline them. For example, '*Herman* and I went hiking the other day,' and 'How was your trip to *Detroit*?'"

"Clever." Peter set his cup and saucer on an end table. His jangled nerves didn't need extra stimulation.

Ziegler held the envelope to his chest. "This also lists two German agents in America in case you need to communicate with us. You must contact them only if necessary and with the greatest delicacy. Your nation just passed a law requiring all foreign agents to register with your State Department, but these two agents will not comply. They must remain secret."

Peter nodded slowly. "I understand."

Albrecht swirled his tumbler, and his gaze speared Peter. "That list must not fall into the wrong hands."

"The FBI." More than anything, Peter wanted that list so he could place it in FBI hands.

"You would have to memorize everything in this envelope and burn it. You must not bring it into the US."

"Indeed not." Yet that was exactly what Peter planned to do.

"I like you, Peter." Albrecht gave him a thin smile that argued with his words. "But if you were to cross us, it would be very bad for you."

"Think carefully." Ziegler gave the same thin smile, even more sinister on that sharp-cornered face. "You are not bound yet, but once you agree, once you receive the list . . ."

Peter shot up a prayer for guidance, and the urge within him strengthened. The danger was great, but the benefits were greater.

He stood, straight and tall, his chin firm. "I agree."

The greatest service he could now perform would be to break his word.

TWENTY-TWO

Evelyn and Libby strolled into the grounds of the Oktoberfest along with the new Junior Year in Munich students, with Peter in the lead.

Under a clear, warm sky, crowds swarmed the main road. Children laughed from an airplane ride to her left and from a Ferris wheel to her right. Gigantic brewery tents flanked the road, their wooden façades topped by giant beer steins or kegs. In the distance, the Alps raised snowy, craggy heads above the roller coaster and pavilions.

"I'm glad you thought to come with Peter's class." Libby wore a pale green dirndl, and a braid circled her head. "I really wanted to attend, but it didn't seem safe just the two of us."

"I understand." Evelyn adjusted the embroidered red bodice over her white puffed-sleeve blouse. If only she had the bosom for a dirndl.

Libby nudged her. "Interview the students. I know your pen is itching for paper."

Evelyn laughed and passed a stall selling big soft pretzels stacked high on poles. "The interviews can wait. Today is for you and me. I—I'll miss you."

"I'll miss you too." On Monday morning Libby was taking the train to Hamburg, and then she'd sail for New York. "Are you disappointed that I'm not as brave as you?"

"Brave? Or stark raving crazy?"

"Both." Libby winked at her. "The closer we get to war, the more excited you get. When the bombs start falling, you'll probably run around like a child in a snowfall."

The image almost made Evelyn laugh. "I won't. But you have to admit, it's exciting to be in the middle of something big and watch it unfold before your eyes."

Libby gazed to the tent tops, each with a Nazi flag waving high. "I'd prefer to watch from a safe distance."

Unless something happened soon, Germany would be at war in a week.

After Hitler's incendiary final speech at the Nuremberg Rally, the Sudeten Germans had rioted, leading the Czechoslovakian government to declare martial law.

Britain and France had begged Czechoslovakia to cede the Sudetenland to Germany, and British Prime Minister Neville Chamberlain had met with Hitler twice. Czechoslovakia's President Edvard Beneš had accepted Hitler's demands—but then Hitler had raised them. If his latest demands weren't met, he would invade Czechoslovakia on October 1.

About fifteen feet ahead, one of the students, a lanky young man in a gray suit, caught up to Peter. "Why do they call it Oktoberfest when it's September?"

Peter chuckled. "It ends in October."

A petite brunette leaned in. "This year it isn't called Oktoberfest but the *Grossdeutsches Volkfest*." She gave Peter an expectant "did I earn an A?" look.

Evelyn frowned. The Greater German Folk Festival, celebrating the union with Austria and the soon-to-be union with the Sudetenland.

168

"So . . ." Libby gave Evelyn a mischievous smile. "When will you give Peter a chance?"

Evelyn pressed her finger to her lips and lowered her voice. "Never."

"Come on. He even looks good in lederhosen."

Libby was wrong. Peter didn't look good. He looked great. The leather pants hit above his knees, showing off well-muscled calves. He wore a white shirt with the sleeves rolled up, forest-green suspenders with colorful embroidery, and the green Bavarian hat he'd worn when hiking in the Partnach Gorge.

"I know you like him," Libby whispered.

Evelyn leveled her gaze at her friend. "You were there when I dated Howard and Clark. I told you what Warren did to me."

"He isn't like them. There are good men in this world."

Evelyn shrugged. There were for soft and sweet women like Libby, but not for her.

Up ahead, Peter stopped and turned to the side. "Have you ever seen so much sauerkraut in your life?" he said loudly.

Sauerkraut? Evelyn caught her breath, grabbed Libby's elbow, and tugged her to the nearest booth, where a lady sold beribboned floral wreaths. "Aren't these pretty?"

"Yes, they are." A question stretched Libby's voice.

True, Evelyn never fussed over ribbons and flowers. Out of the corner of her eye, she saw Peter talking to a sturdily built young man in a brown Nazi uniform, possibly from the Students' League. They'd chosen *sauerkraut* as a code word in case they ran into certain people.

They had a good cover story. The ANS would welcome an article about the American students' first impressions of Germany, but it was better if Peter's Nazi friends and Evelyn's Gestapo buddies didn't see them together.

Especially now that Peter had the list. Evelyn fingered the colorful paper flowers on a wreath, and she shuddered.

What would the Nazis do if they learned Peter's plans for that list?

Her chest warmed at his courage, at his principles. He could have declined the list without any repercussions, but he'd taken it.

Peter was a fine man. But that didn't mean he was fine for her. The only way to determine if monsters lurked in dark waters was to dive in. Then it would be too late.

"The red one." Peter's deep voice rumbled over her shoulder, down into her heart. That was no monster's roar.

She pulled herself together and inspected a yellow wreath without turning around. "Who was that?"

"Otto von Albrecht. Don't worry. He's going home."

Oh. The son of the SS officer who had arranged for Peter to get the list of American Nazi sympathizers—and German spies.

"Which one would you like, Libby?" Peter asked. "My treat. A going-away present."

"How sweet of you." Libby sent him a beaming smile, then selected a wreath with green ribbons and yellow flowers.

"And you, Evelyn?" he asked.

Part of her wanted to pick any color but red, but . . . she picked one with red ribbons and red and white flowers.

Peter paid the lady, and Libby pinned her wreath over her braid.

"May I?" Peter settled Evelyn's onto her head like a crown. "Very pretty."

"Thank you." She rearranged bobby pins to hold the wreath in place.

Peter smiled in a way that made her want to dive into those dark waters—a big tumbling, somersaulting Olympic dive. "Very pretty."

He'd already said that. It wasn't true. As Herr Zero had so kindly reminded her, she wasn't an attractive woman.

But at that moment, with Peter smiling at her, she felt beautiful. Feminine.

The lanky student leaned in. "There's dancing in the next tent. May we?"

Peter grinned at the boy. "You're adults. You don't need teacher's permission."

Libby laughed and pushed Peter along the path. "They're not asking for your permission but your company. Let's go."

"Great idea." He hooked arms with both Libby and Evelyn, and he strode ahead.

Evelyn leaned back to shoot Libby a poisonous dart of a glance, but Libby deflected the dart with a smug smile.

The class stepped into a giant tent, striped in sky blue and white, the Bavarian colors. At the front, a traditional band played a rollicking tune. Couples whirled past, feet stomping, skirts swinging.

Libby circled behind Peter and Evelyn, and she leaned close to Evelyn's ear. "My going-away present to you." Then she found a tall, good-looking junior.

The student erupted in a smile and spun Libby away.

Peter bowed to Evelyn and kissed her hand. "May I have this dance, Fräulein?"

Warmth flowed from the back of her hand up her arm. "I don't know the steps."

"Looks like you just gallop in a circle."

Evelyn's feet did itch to dance. "I can gallop."

"Great." Peter gathered her in his arms and whirled her away in a flurry of feet and laughter.

He led with confidence but not force, his body solid and strong, his arm about her, his shoulder warm beneath her hand, his long legs bumping hers as they galloped and twirled.

A riot of color all around her, and Evelyn gave in to the joy of it, the abandon of it. Peter's face shone with the same joy, and she laughed with him.

If only, if only, if only. What would it be like to let go, to surrender herself to the depths? What if he stayed as he was, kind and accepting? What if he could live with her sharp points?

A strange look crossed Peter's face. Alarm. Disgust.

He stopped abruptly and brushed at a ribbon that had fluttered across her throat. "Maybe red ribbons were a bad choice."

"What?"

Peter pulled her toward the wall away from the throng, his eyebrows drawn together under the brim of his hat. "Here. Turn your back to me."

She did so. "I don't understand."

He gathered the ribbons behind her. "Let me tie these. It—it reminded me. In the—in the French Revolution, women wore red ribbons around their necks to mock . . ."

To mock those headed to the guillotine.

Evelyn's hand flew to her throat. Here in a land where the guillotine was used to silence political foes.

Used by these galloping, twirling, laughing people.

———

Peter tied the ribbons in a knot at the nape of Evelyn's slender neck, and he grimaced. Why had he mentioned the guillotine after she'd been visited by the Gestapo, after her mentor had been targeted? "I'm sorry. I don't usually . . ."

"I know." Her voice trembled.

He raised his hands to her shoulders, hesitated, then settled them in place. Her shoulders felt both strong and delicate. "I really am sorry."

Evelyn spun into the dancing position, her head lowered. "Let's dance before we get trampled."

His lips longed to kiss her forehead, but he swung her back into the maelstrom.

The levity was gone. The innocence.

The song ended, and everyone applauded. Then the band started a slower number, and Peter held out his arms. "Shall we?"

Evelyn scanned the crowd and stepped back into position. "We're less conspicuous dancing than we would be watching."

Conspicuous. Peter waltzed her deeper into the crowd and

searched for familiar faces, like the agent who prowled the Gärtnerplatz. His arm tightened around the gentle curve of Evelyn's waist.

If she transferred, the ANS would send her to London or Paris or Moscow, and he'd never see her again. However, she needed to leave and soon. "How long do you plan to stay in Germany?"

She frowned at him. "I'm not planning on leaving."

Peter twirled her past the band. "Maybe you should consider transferring."

Sparks flew in that coffee-with-two-splashes-of-milk brown. "That's my decision to make. No one else's."

Peter huffed. He'd never known anyone so resistant to suggestion. "For heaven's sake. I want to leave myself."

The sparks fizzled out. "You do?"

"That—delivery. The longer I keep the cargo, the more dangerous it becomes, the more likely I'll slip and reveal which side I'm on. The sooner I deliver it, the better."

"That's true." Ripples flowed over her forehead.

Peter edged around an elderly couple. "But the winter semester hasn't even started. I can't leave until it's over. I made a commitment to teach. And for my dissertation, I need both sets of recordings of this class—before and after."

"Libby's going home. Could she make the deli—"

"Absolutely not. What if they search her before she boards? They do that. I'll take that risk, but I won't let anyone else take it for me."

Evelyn studied him as they swayed to the music.

Peter held her gaze, watched her emotions shift, and knew deep inside he mustn't release her.

She blinked rapidly. "I—I apologize. I shouldn't have snapped. You were being a—a good friend."

Warmth flooded through him. At last, he'd earned her trust. And he sensed a shifting, her affection bending toward him, her resistance lowering.

He lifted a little smile. "I understand. You don't like it when you think someone's trying to put you in a cage."

Her eyebrows jolted upward. "No. No, I don't."

That was now Peter's greatest fear—her work could land her in a cage. But saying so would be foolhardy.

A strange sensation developed between his shoulder blades, as if someone were pushing him—pushing him to push Evelyn.

Talk about foolhardy. But the pressure increased. Should he? Peter waltzed Evelyn past the door, and he drew a deep breath. "What did he do to you?"

She cocked her head to the side. "Norwood?"

He kept his voice gentle. "Whoever tried to tame you and cage you. What did he do?"

Evelyn's step hitched, and her gaze darted away. "I never said anyone did that."

"You spoke with the voice of experience."

The muscles of her back squirmed beneath his hand. "None of your business."

Another push between his shoulder blades. Was that the Lord? He'd never had anything like that happen before.

He frowned at Evelyn's beflowered, stony profile. She was already annoyed at him. What did he have to lose by obeying?

Peter gave her stiff hand a squeeze. "It's very much my business. You've placed all men in the same category as this other man, just because we're males."

Evelyn's jaw thrust forward.

Ideas rolled through his head in beautiful, logical order. "In your job, you're often dismissed because you're a woman. It isn't right. I used to hate all communists because of what happened to my father. It wasn't right. And our hosts hate those who hold different religious or political beliefs. It isn't right."

Evelyn gasped. "It isn't the same."

Peter rocked her in a turn. "Isn't it? Treating an individual a certain way because he belongs to a certain group—sounds the same to me."

Her eyes flitted back and forth, doubting, questioning, defying. "But—"

"But if you prize individuality, as I know you do, consider treating men as individuals. Not all men fit in your neat little box." A smile played on his lips as his words played with hers.

Evelyn sucked in a breath, and confusion and comprehension battled for control of her face.

More words welled up. Words he'd longed to say for months and other words he only now knew to be true.

Pressure built on his throat. Not choking, but restraining.

Mercy. The word drifted like the fragrance of Evelyn's hair.

He swallowed his words, gathered her close, and danced.

Mercy. Mercy to give her time to contemplate what he'd said. Mercy not to speak those words. Not yet. Maybe not ever.

So he said them in his head. *I'm not just another man. I'm a man who loves you.*

Certainty blended with mercy and with deep sadness. For one moment, he allowed his cheek to brush her hair. *I love you so much.*

TWENTY-THREE

Evelyn paused with her fork halfway to her mouth.

The radio in her apartment played the news while she ate dinner.

It couldn't be.

Not in Munich. It had to be Berlin.

But the broadcaster repeated it. With the British Navy and the armies of Germany and Czechoslovakia and France mobilized and ready to strike, Prime Minister Chamberlain had called for an international conference on the fate of Czechoslovakia, and Hitler had agreed.

In Munich.

Tomorrow.

She dropped her fork and dashed for the phone to call Frank Keller at the Berlin bureau.

Before she could reach the phone, it rang. She grabbed it. The operator had a call from London. Would she like it?

Would she ever! "Hello?"

"Miss Brand? Hamilton Chase here."

"I just heard about the conference tomorrow."

"It's yours."

Her feet did a little dance, but she restrained her glee. "You aren't sending Mr. Keller?"

"You're already there. Besides, Keller and Reeves can hardly keep up in Berlin. I'm transferring Bukowski from Paris as soon as he can pack, but we're undermanned."

Evelyn frowned at the dial face. "Where's Mr. Norwood?"

"Oh. I thought you would have heard by now. We let him go yesterday. His reports from Nuremberg were unprintable."

"My goodness." Evelyn didn't want him to be fired, only to keep his red pen off her articles.

"Call your stories straight to New York—never mind the expense. I can't tell you how important it is for the ANS to get good material out of this conference. Our stories out of Germany aren't being picked up by the papers as they should."

Because of Norwood, and Evelyn scrunched up her face.

Mr. Chase blew out a loud breath. "New York has been impressed with your work lately, but honestly, they're not sure you have the chops for a story like this."

Evelyn's jaw set. "I can do it."

"Don't blow it." He all but growled.

"No, sir. I won't."

She hung up. His threat was clear. She needed a top-notch article, the best of her life. If she wrote a mediocre report, she could be fired. If she were restricted from important meetings because of her sex, she'd be fired. But if she broke the rules, she'd also be fired.

If only she had someone to talk to. Her life felt empty with Libby gone.

She could almost hear Libby laugh. Yes, she always had someone to talk to.

Evelyn set her hands on her hips and gazed at the ceiling. "Lord, the bases are loaded. If I strike out, I'm out of the game forever. Help me. Tomorrow I need a home run."

Thursday, September 29, 1938

If only she could get closer.

With dozens of correspondents, Evelyn stood outside the Führerbau, the imposing Party building on Königlicher Platz. On the red-carpeted steps coming down from the portico, Hitler talked with Benito Mussolini of Italy. On the paved plaza, Neville Chamberlain talked with his men, and French Prime Minister Édouard Daladier talked with his.

The correspondents couldn't get within shouting distance. Helmeted, rifle-toting, black-uniformed SS men stood shoulder to shoulder, cordoning off the area.

The officials filed back into the Führerbau for the second round of negotiations.

Not a single press conference had been held since the meeting started at twelve thirty. Until then, no one would get any material. And then everyone would get the same material.

Evelyn groaned. Sure, she could add her own flair, but it would be a base hit, almost identical to every other news report today.

She tucked her notepad into her purse. Worrying about her career seemed selfish today. In the Führerbau, leaders of four nations were deciding the fate of a fifth nation—and that fifth nation hadn't even been invited to the conference. Appalling.

Chamberlain had promised to represent Czechoslovakia's interests, but the proposals he'd given Hitler earlier in the month at Berchtesgaden and at Bad Godesberg had appeased Germany and ceded them the Sudetenland.

Meanwhile, the British were evacuating children from London in fear of German air raids. Two days earlier Chamberlain had made a radio broadcast, stating, "How horrible, fantastic, incredible it is that we should be digging trenches and trying on gas masks here because of a quarrel in a faraway country between people of whom we know nothing."

Evelyn frowned. Not the words of a man who had those people's interests at heart.

For the next two hours, she mingled with the correspondents, all waiting and bored.

By six thirty, the sun neared the horizon. Since the conference lunch break hadn't started until three fifteen, the dinner break would be late as well. Evelyn's stomach rumbled. Might as well get her own dinner, then return.

She weaved her way through the thick crowd.

"Hey, Brandy." Cal Monroe of the Boston *Ledger* grinned at her. "The ANS is letting little girls play with the men, huh?"

"No." She tipped her hat to him as she passed. "They're letting grown women play with little boys."

Evelyn headed toward a restaurant on Maximiliansplatz, a few blocks away.

If she were a man, a bland article would suffice. But she wasn't. She was held to loftier standards, paid higher dues, and took stiffer punishments.

Her pace quickened under the cloudy sky. It wasn't right to be treated differently just because she was a woman.

Evelyn stumbled on a flagstone. She could still hear the accordion and tuba, still feel Peter's arm around her, and still see his gentle expression. Even as his words pierced like daggers. *"Not all men fit in your neat little box."*

She'd wrestled with that. She hadn't put all men in the same box as Howard and Clark and Warren—only the men who pursued her. Something about her attracted the hunter and his cage.

But . . . Peter. Yes, he'd pursued her, but he'd stopped. He'd become a good friend. He took great risks to bring her story leads.

His attentiveness at the Oktoberfest told her his interest hadn't waned. Interest without pursuit? Completely baffling.

Evelyn crossed the Karolinenplatz with its black obelisk monument. Who was she kidding? She couldn't date him anyway. Not when they had to cry "sauerkraut" to attend the Oktoberfest together.

Yes. A smile rose as she strolled past tall buildings hung with German, Italian, French, and British flags. All correspondents knew better than to date informants. Problem solved.

A crowd formed up ahead, another line of black uniforms. They'd cordoned off the Regina Palace Hotel.

"That's right," she murmured. The British delegation was staying there. She'd have to find a different restaurant.

Five women in maid's uniforms approached the hotel. They talked to an SS man and were let in the back door.

Evelyn crossed her arms and tilted her head. What must those maids be hearing and seeing? And if one shift was about to start, another shift would soon leave.

A hunch. Only a hunch. But what else did she have?

Evelyn loitered behind the crowd, keeping that back door in view. Soon five young ladies stepped out, and the guards let them through. No one paid them any attention.

Except Evelyn. In the twilight, she followed at a short distance down the side street. The girls turned right and crossed the street to the park in Maximiliansplatz.

Evelyn caught up to them under the trees. "*Entschuldigung. Guten Abend*, ladies. My name is Evelyn Brand. I'm a reporter with the American News Service. Do you work at the Regina Palace Hotel?"

The girls looked at each other, confused.

A tall brunette addressed Evelyn. "We do. Why would you want to speak to us?"

Evelyn grinned at them. "You are eyewitnesses to the biggest news story of the year, and none of the other reporters thought to talk to you. But who knows better what's happening than women?"

A plump blonde smiled. "True. I—I'm cleaning Prime Minister Chamberlain's room."

Evelyn asked the blonde about herself and her experience, and soon the other maids chimed in with stories of the British envoys and the talk they'd heard. Nothing terribly useful, but the girls were fun to talk to.

The tall brunette nodded to the one girl who hadn't spoken yet. "Lida has the best stories. She speaks Czech, so she was the only one allowed in the room with the Czechs."

"The Czechs?" Evelyn's head jerked up from her notes. "What do you mean? They weren't invited to the conference."

Lida tucked a lock of frizzy brown hair under her cap. "They arrived late this afternoon. The Gestapo brought them in a police car. They're under guard in their rooms. They aren't allowed to leave."

Evelyn could hardly breathe, hardly talk. "Who? Do you know who they are?"

Lida's gaze darted to the other maids. "One is Dr. Vojtech Mastny—he's the ambassador to Germany. The other is Dr. Hubert Masarik of the Foreign Office."

Evelyn scribbled the names, hoping she'd spelled them correctly. "They're not allowed to leave their rooms? They can't participate in a conference that decides the fate of their nation?"

"Of course not." The blonde sniffed. "Our Führer gave them a generous offer, and they refused."

The maids nodded, but Lida's expression disagreed with the blonde's statement.

No one else knew Czechoslovakian officials were in town— much less confined to their rooms—and Evelyn's fingers tingled as she wrote.

Lida stepped forward with a glint in her eye. "Would you like to meet them?"

The brunette squealed. "We could dress her in one of our uniforms. Wouldn't that be fun?"

An interview? Evelyn clutched her notepad, and her mouth hung open. An exclusive interview? This was more than a home run. This was a World Series winning grand slam that everyone would talk about for years. "Yes! Yes, please."

"Come." Lida motioned her through the park. "My apartment isn't far."

Evelyn fell in beside her. This scoop would make her career forever. And it only required a little bending of the rules.

"I don't know," the blonde said from behind. "What if our boss finds out?"

"Don't worry," Evelyn said. "I won't name any . . ."

Oh no. She stopped in her tracks. "No. No, I can't."

"Why not?" The brunette nudged the blonde. "Don't listen to Brigitte. She's a coward."

Evelyn shook her head. This would be worse than getting caught dressed like a man at the Paris press conference. That time only Evelyn had caught grief. "No. Lida will get in trouble."

Lida grabbed Evelyn's arm and tugged her away from the other girls, her dark eyes intense. "I don't care. I want to do this," she whispered. "They're destroying my homeland, and no one cares. No one listens. But you do. You'll tell the world what happened today."

"I will," Evelyn whispered back. "But not like this. If I write about meeting those men, everyone will know who let me in. You would be in grave danger."

Lida's chin quivered. "I don't care."

"But I do." She raised her voice for the group's benefit and gave Lida a pointed look. "No. You're right. Why would I want to meet such men?"

Lida's expression cleared, and she raised her chin. "I don't blame you. It makes me sick talking to those ungrateful swine. Turning down the Führer's offer."

"They must have said outrageous things. Would you like to tell me more?" Then Evelyn smiled at the other ladies. "No need to keep you from your dinner. Thank you for talking to me."

The maids smiled and waved good-bye.

In the falling light, Evelyn led Lida to a bench and interviewed the Czech immigrant who grieved for her nation.

Half an hour later, Evelyn raced for her apartment to place a call to New York. While she waited for the call to be returned, she'd write up her article.

Evelyn might not have an exclusive interview, but she had a scoop.

FRIDAY, SEPTEMBER 30, 1938

Sitting in the press conference room long after midnight, Evelyn rubbed her eyes, exhausted but energized. New York had been thrilled with her story.

Everything in her wanted to trumpet her scoop to the dozing correspondents, but if she did, it would no longer be a scoop. Besides, they'd find out when her article came over the wire.

She'd worded it so the maids would be above reproach, stating they thought it was common knowledge that the envoys were confined and that they believed the envoys had been treated exactly as they deserved.

Evelyn stifled a yawn. The correspondents had been told an agreement had been made, so she waited.

What would happen to the army officers' plot to arrest Hitler when he ordered the invasion of Czechoslovakia? No invasion, no arrest.

Evelyn couldn't ask Magda Müller. After yet another reckless report from General Gerlach's mistress, Evelyn had stopped meeting her.

Footsteps at the doorway, and the reporters poked each other awake. The German foreign press chief entered the room.

Evelyn readied her notepad.

At the podium, the press chief read off the details of the Munich Agreement. They'd done it. They'd sacrificed the nation of Czechoslovakia on the altar of peace.

Evelyn scribbled down every detail. The lost territory contained the nation's natural mountainous defenses, its military fortifications, its munitions factories, and most of its industry. The Germans would begin occupying the Sudetenland the next day, October 1, with the occupation to be complete by October 10. Those who chose to leave the occupied territory were not allowed to take property or livestock—only what they could carry.

Shocking. Absolutely shocking.

Czechoslovakia would be weakened defensively and economically and inundated with impoverished refugees, especially Jews.

Evelyn's eyesight blurred, but she kept writing. Hitler had bullied the world into giving him his demands, and it had worked. It had worked again.

Austria. The Sudetenland. What would be next?

Because something would be next.

If you gave a bully your lunch on Monday, he wanted your lunch on Tuesday and Wednesday and every day forever.

Hitler needed someone to stand up to him. He had complete freedom to do whatever he wanted. He needed a fence, containment, the restraint of law and order imposed from the outside.

Evelyn groaned. Peter was right. Freedom without limits was as dangerous as order without limits.

When the press conference concluded, the reporters rushed to the phones.

But Evelyn headed home to place her call to New York. What was brewing inside her needed to percolate before she could pour it out.

TWENTY-FOUR

"I hear it now." Jim Purcell's eyes widened as he sat in front of Peter's Dictaphone.

"Good." Peter opened the sleek black case and removed the wax cylinder.

"That's fantastic." Jim grinned at Professor Johannes Schreiber seated beside him. "I mean, '*Das ist fantastisch*.' When I speak, in my head I sound like you. But when I listen to the recording, I hear how bad my accent is."

"It isn't bad." Peter smiled at the junior year student and slid the cylinder into its numbered cardboard tube. "And you will improve."

"With you teaching me, I will." Jim stood and pumped Peter's hand. "Thanks a million, Teach."

Peter chuckled and said good-bye.

Professor Schreiber fingered the corrugated steel tube that connected the mouthpiece to the Dictaphone. "I am finally convinced."

Peter placed the tube in its slot in the crate and suppressed a smile. "Convinced about this contraption or about my techniques?"

"Both. They go together. Now I see that not everything new is bad."

Peter perched on the edge of the desk and gave the professor a teasing smile. "Flexibility, ja? Didn't you tell me that when storms come, the reed bends but the stick breaks?"

Professor Schreiber blinked a few times, his brow furrowed, but then he smiled. "I did."

"I'm glad my techniques have won you over." Peter crossed his arms. "The problem remains that they work best in small groups. I can partly overcome this by training teachers in my methods and by placing diagrams of the mouth in textbooks."

The professor scratched his chin. "You will include this in your dissertation, ja? How is it going?"

"It's going well." Peter opened the file drawer in his desk, pulled out the draft, and handed it to the professor. "I have fifty pages already."

"Good." Schreiber flipped through. "Your background section . . ."

Peter resumed his perch. "I describe the strengths and weaknesses of current teaching methods and the difficulties native English speakers have with the German language."

"Excellent, then a section describing your teaching techniques."

"Yes. I've also made a good start on my study methodology, and I'm typing up the data from my earlier recordings."

"You will send this case to America soon?" He nodded to the crate full of recordings from the beginning of the winter semester.

"Tomorrow." Peter had rated each recording from one to ten, beginner to fluent. Since he knew the students, he wasn't impartial, so professors at Harvard also rated the recordings.

"If only Frau Schreiber and I could stow away." He smiled wistfully at the case.

"Any word from Hans-Jürgen?"

"Ja." His face brightened. "He loves Harvard. He has met some of your former students and has made friends. But he is . . . surprised."

"Surprised?"

The professor stroked the edge of the desk, his mouth shifted from side to side, and he stared hard at the telephone. "He has met many Americans who hold to Nazi ideology."

Peter followed Schreiber's stare. Did he think there was a listening device in the telephone? "It is popular at American universities. However, students are allowed to hold other ideologies as well." He flicked his head to the phone to let the professor know he'd received his message. "In this you see America's great strength and great weakness."

Professor Schreiber lifted a partial smile. Peter's statement could be interpreted in two opposing ways.

The phone rang. Both men startled, then laughed.

The professor stood. "I will let you take your call. Auf Wiedersehen."

"Wiedersehen. Give Hans-Jürgen my best." Peter answered the phone. "Hallo?"

"Peter, old man, old friend."

"Hi, George." Peter settled into his desk chair. He could practically smell the whiskey through the telephone line. Why was George drunk at one o'clock in the afternoon? Celebration or dejection? "Have you found a job?"

George cussed.

Peter raised one eyebrow. George had never been one for cussing. "I'm sorry."

"I don't understand. You and I—we have family in Congress, friends in power. Why can't we get control of the papers? All owned by communists. That's why they won't hire me."

Even when Peter was most virulently anti-communist, he wouldn't have agreed. "Are you still in Berlin?"

"Uh-huh. Writing freelance articles. Sold a few."

Clamping the phone receiver between his shoulder and ear, Peter stacked the pages of his dissertation and filed it. "That's good. You'll get a job."

"No. No. They only want drivel from hacks like that Brand girl."

Peter's hand clenched around the drawer handle. Evelyn was no hack. "There's no need—"

"D'you know how much I had to edit her work? Full of lies and warmongering and sensationalism. Now she's the darling of the news world."

"Is that so?" Peter smiled to himself.

"ANS let her cover the Munich Conference. Can you believe it? And what'd she do? Wrote a bunch of lies about Czech envoys being confined. Garbage."

Peter took off his glasses and rubbed the inner corners of his eyes. "George—"

"All the world was rejoicing. Dancing in the streets in Berlin and Paris and London. You saw. Chamberlain said they'd achieved 'peace for our time.' He's right. Peace. And that Brand girl's articles sounded like funeral dirges."

Peter sighed. Evelyn's articles had been masterpieces. Instead of stating opinions that could have gotten her expelled, she'd raised questions to provoke thought. What was more important—one nation's desire for peace or another nation's desire for sovereignty and freedom?

The tone was indeed somber, as it needed to be. German troops had occupied the Sudetenland without firing a shot, and Hitler had been emboldened. He would keep nibbling away at surrounding nations until someone slapped his wrist. Meanwhile, the German military grew stronger, which would make future wrist-slapping far deadlier.

"That Brand girl." A sound of liquid sloshing. "She messed with the wrong people."

Peter's jaw tightened, and he pushed back his chair and got to his feet. He'd been afraid Evelyn would be expelled for her scoop about the Czech envoys, but she hadn't been. Meanwhile, George needed to be talked down. Maybe a change in subject.

He circled the desk, raising the phone cord so it wouldn't knock books off his desk. "Say, have you talked to Charles lately? Has the embassy made any progress getting a visa for my friend Jakob Gold?"

"You're wasting your time, old boy." More sloshing. "You know how many Jews are clogging up the waiting list? We have a quota for a reason. Charles might be able to bring in a scientist or an industrialist, but a baker? With ten million unemployed in America, we can't let in people like that."

People like that? Peter couldn't stand another minute. "I need to go."

"Sure. Good old Peter. What would I do without you?"

"Good-bye, George." He hung up.

His head throbbed, and he rubbed his temples. How could George talk that way about Evelyn? About Herr Gold? Was it due to unemployment and whiskey? Or had the unemployment and whiskey merely unmasked meanness that lay beneath the surface?

Peter put his glasses back on and returned books to his bookshelf. The sooner Herr Gold left Germany, the better.

Things grew worse for the Jews every day. Germany had revoked the licenses of almost all Jewish physicians and lawyers, with the remainder only allowed to aid fellow Jews. The Reich had also revoked all passports for Jews and required them to obtain new ones, stamped with *J* for *Jude*—Jew. Jewish people were even required to have "Jewish names" by the first of the year or to add new names—Israel for men and Sara for women.

At least Herr and Frau Gold had obtained visas for Bolivia and were collecting the documents required for exit visas.

Herr Gold might not have been a scientist, but he was a bright and funny man who gave generously to friends. And his definition of friend was wide and long. Due to shortsighted politicians and their quotas, the US wouldn't benefit from those fine traits. Bolivia would.

At his desk, Peter pulled out his research log and made sure the data was complete for the recordings he'd ship to the States the next day.

After he finished, he'd go to the café and tell Herr Gold the bad news. Maybe he'd see Evelyn. However, she'd started visiting the café at a later time. Too dangerous to see him, she insisted in the notes she left with Herr Gold.

With a groan, Peter closed the logbook. Too dangerous because of the Gestapo or because of him?

He'd pushed too hard at the Oktoberfest, but he'd do it again. He loved her too much not to push.

"*Entschuldigung?* Herr Lang?" Two army officers entered his office.

Peter greeted the men in gray. He'd met Oberst Heinz-Eugen Eberhardt at Nazi Party meetings, but not the older officer. Eberhardt introduced him as General Rolf Richter.

Peter showed them to the chairs in front of his desk, and the general sat, removed his peaked cap, and smoothed pewter strands of hair over the top of his head.

Eberhardt closed the office door. "I will get to the point, Herr Lang. I investigated your credentials and brought you to the general's attention."

Peter strolled behind the desk, his back to the men, his breath hard in his throat. "May I ask why?"

"We are interested in your research," Eberhardt said. "We would like to invite you to remain in Germany after your year is over."

Remain? When he was counting the days until the semester was over? Peter prayed for calm, sat in his desk chair, and spread his hands and his smile wide. "Ach, if only I could. But I must return to Harvard to finish my doctorate."

Eberhardt sat too, and a disarming grin transformed his long face. "We have spoken to the faculty. The University of Munich will accept your work and grant your doctorate."

Highly unorthodox. "Thank you, but—"

"You will join the faculty, a great honor at your young age. And we would hire you."

"The . . ." Peter's gaze darted between the officers. "The German army?"

General Richter's small eyes gleamed in his full face. "You can imagine how useful your skills would be to us."

Peter couldn't breathe. He had to look like a Nazi sympathizer—his life depended on it. But he absolutely could not take the job.

He managed to chuckle. "I'm sure your men would find an American accent useful when visiting the States."

"Yes," the colonel said. "Or England. The Americans and English are friends, ja?"

"Too much so," Peter said.

The officers laughed.

Peter shifted his shoes and found the perfect excuse. "Although I would love to accept your offer—it's an honor—I have another assignment for Germany."

Eberhardt frowned. "What sort of assignment?"

"I'm not at liberty to say, but it comes from high up. Sadly, it requires me to leave this fair land and return to America."

The general glared at the colonel. "High up?"

"Yes, Herr General," Peter said. "But thank you again."

The officers strode to the door, and the general turned to Peter. "I will make this happen. It is vital that you stay in Germany."

Peter forced himself to smile, thank them, and bid them farewell.

After he shut the door, he sank into his desk chair and ran his hands into his hair. "Lord, what have I gotten myself into?"

The last thing he wanted was to be trapped in Germany, training Germans to spy on America and Britain.

That would be treason. He wouldn't do it. He'd make excuses, say his widowed mother needed him. If that didn't work, he'd refuse outright.

And he'd be dead.

His head throbbed harder. He tore off his glasses and massaged his temples.

Better dead than a traitor.

He pushed up to his feet and paced the length of the office. He needed to go home now. Get away from this insanity.

The list of American Nazi sympathizers burned inside his shoe, under the insole where he kept it. He needed to turn it in to the FBI.

He couldn't mail it or cable it or phone it to the US—the Germans could intercept the message. He'd considered giving the list to an American military attaché in Germany. But what if the FBI questioned the people on the list while Peter was still in Munich?

He'd be dead.

Peter had to leave. He strode back to the desk and leaned his palms on his logbook. Could he abandon his research? His commitment to teach?

No. No. He had a fellowship. He had too many years invested. Too much of his heart. And Harvard would deny his doctorate.

His doctorate. Peter blew out a long breath. Even with generals pulling strings, the University of Munich needed a dissertation to grant a doctorate. And he wouldn't have the final data for his research until February.

"February," he whispered. A plea. A prayer. "February."

TWENTY-FIVE

Evelyn had never prayed so much in her life. Her heels clunked on the tile in the atrium at the University of Munich—hard, fast, desperate.

Libby said prayer made you stronger. But Evelyn's muscles quivered, she scrutinized every person, and she had to restrain herself from running to Peter's office.

Why had her thoughts flown to him first? If the consulate general couldn't help her, what good could Peter do?

However, she couldn't discuss this with her German friends. Libby was gone. O'Hara was gone. That left Peter.

She turned down the hallway and passed groups of students, laughing and chatting as if everything were right in the world.

Evelyn entered Peter's office. There he sat in a white shirt and a navy blue suit vest, his blond head bent over papers. Half the tension left her body.

He looked up, and his eyes widened with surprise, then concern. He pushed back his chair. "Ev—"

"Shh!" She jammed her finger to her lips, shut the door, and dashed behind his desk. She yanked off her overcoat, wrapped it around the telephone, and put the phone on the floor as far from the door as the cord allowed.

She returned to the door and peeked into the hallway. Empty. Good. No one had followed her, and she closed the door again.

Peter joined her, his forehead creased. "What's going on?" he whispered. "You think my phone—"

"I'm not taking any chances," she whispered back.

"What's going on?"

Evelyn fumbled open her purse and pulled out the passport.

Peter took it. "A German passport?"

"Open it."

While he did so, she pressed her trembling hand to her tumbling stomach. No, the passport hadn't changed.

Name: Brand, Evelyn Sara. At the top, a large red *J* had been stamped.

Peter looked up, his face stark and pale. "What is this?"

"Turn the page."

He flipped to the page with her photo on one side and personal information on the other—"Profession: Correspondent. Place of Birth: Dresden. Date of Birth: 15 January 1912."

"What is this?" he said.

"I found it in my purse today. My American passport—it's gone."

"Gone?"

She nodded to the document. "That's the photo from my passport. All the information is correct, except my middle name and birthplace. But my Grandpa Brand was born in Dresden."

Peter stepped closer, mouth agape. "It's one of the new Jewish passports."

"They—someone found out I'm three-quarters Jewish, and—and—" She leaned against the wall.

Peter fetched a chair. "You look like you're going to faint."

"I've never fainted in my life." But her vision darkened and sparkled, so she sat and slumped forward over her knees.

Peter knelt in front of her and rubbed her upper arms. "Deep breaths, Evie. Deep breaths."

She did so, in no mood to correct him. She'd never been an Evie. But at that moment, she wasn't even Evelyn Margaret Brand, citizen of the United States of America.

"Do you have any idea how this happened?" Peter's voice and touch worked calm into her.

"Helga. My cleaning lady. I've caught her snooping, but my landlord refuses to fire her. She must have read my mother's letter telling me I'm three-quarters Jewish."

Peter murmured and kept stroking her arms.

Evelyn's vision began to clear. "The other day—she was in my apartment when I awoke. She said she came early because she thought I was out of town, but I could tell she was lying. When I changed purses yesterday, my passport wasn't there. I assumed it was in another purse, but I was too rushed to look. I forgot about it."

"She took it."

"She must have. Then today. When I woke up, things were out of place. And I found that." She nodded at the offending document, lying beside Peter's knee.

"We know how it got there, but not why."

"The Gestapo." Evelyn looked up. Peter's face was too close, but closeness was necessary to speak low. "When they visited, I reminded them I'm an American citizen. If anything happened to me, it'd damage American-German relations. This—this passport changes everything. They can do anything they want to me."

"No." He squeezed her arms. "It doesn't change the *fact* of your citizenship. If they hurt you, it'd still create an international incident. The Gestapo knows that."

More than anything, she wanted to believe. But . . . "That's an official document. Look at all the stamps. Look how close the signature is to my own. Helga didn't make it. Someone in power did. Someone who researched my background. Someone who's out to get me."

Peter tucked in his lips, and his eyebrows bunched together. He didn't argue.

"All those antisemitic laws? Peter, they apply to me now." Her hands twisted into a knot. "Things are getting worse. Did you hear what they did last week to the Polish Jews living in Germany? Rounded them up—fifteen thousand of them—only one suitcase each. And they pushed them over the border into Poland at gunpoint. Actually pushed them. But Poland doesn't want them either. They're stuck in horrid refugee camps on the border."

"I heard." Peter's frown deepened.

Evelyn's breath came harder. "I need to leave now. But I can't. Not with that passport. I—I'm trapped."

"Shh. We'll take care of this. Let's head to the consulate gen—"

"That's the first place I went. They turned me away." Her fingers hurt from the twisting. "They think I'm lying. They think I'm one of the thousands of German Jews trying to escape."

"But your accent. You *sound* American." He looked so earnest, so outraged.

For the first time all day, she almost wanted to smile. "No offense to your research, but an accent is no proof of citizenship."

Peter lowered his head and let out a wry chuckle. "No offense taken."

"I—I showed them my press pass, but that means nothing. The ANS can hire people of any nationality."

"Let's start over." Peter raised his head, his gaze strong and assured. "Tomorrow we'll go to the consulate general. Speak to a different clerk. Say nothing about the German passport. Simply say you lost your American passport. They'll tell you what to do. Passports are lost or stolen every day. That's why we have consulates."

"That's true." Evelyn's eyes stretched wide. "Why didn't I think of that? Why did I—"

"So, tomorrow morning—"

"Bother. I can't." She scrunched up her face. "Tomorrow and the next day—it's the anniversary of the Nazi Putsch. Huge holiday. I have to report on it. And the consulate general will be closed."

"That's right. Okay. Thursday morning we'll take care of it. First thing."

"We?" Evelyn leaned back a bit. "You don't need to come. You shouldn't. We shouldn't be seen together. Even coming here today wasn't wise."

Peter released her arms and rested his hands on his knees. His gaze grew in quiet power. "I'll meet you there. We won't be seen together on the streets."

"But—"

"Not this time." He leaned forward. "This isn't the time to prove how independent you are. You're in danger. You need to get out of this country as soon as possible, but first you need a passport."

"Yes, but—"

"Like it or not, a male voice has more authority. As a fellow American, I'll lend your case some authenticity. And if they give you grief, I have a friend in the passport office in the US Embassy in Berlin. We'll call him right then, and things will happen."

Evelyn stared at her hands, which no longer trembled. If she hadn't wanted Peter's help, why had she come to him? Hadn't he come up with good ideas? And if he accompanied her, wouldn't he have the same calming effect he was having right now? "You're right. Please come. I'd appreciate it."

"Thanks." Peter sighed. "Listen, you might want to make plans to leave in a hurry. I have."

"You have?"

He shifted his glasses higher on that crooked nose. "After the general visited."

He'd told her about that in a note. How long had it been since she'd seen him? She'd . . . missed him.

Peter tilted his head toward his desk. "I keep things in my attaché case, more things in my rucksack at home. Map, compass, pocketknife, cash, a change of clothes. Things like that."

"That's a good idea." But where could she go? And how could she get away without her passport?

"It's going to be all right." Peter set his hands on hers and squeezed. "If you need help, if you need to escape, you call me, day or night. Understood?"

"Thank you." She had no intention of ripping him from his teaching and research, but his offer was exceptionally generous. "I—I should go now."

"I'll get your coat." He stood and went behind his desk.

Evelyn put the passport back in her purse. Not carrying papers was illegal, so the fake passport was better than nothing.

She rose to her feet. She felt calmer, less anxious.

Something inside her squirmed at how she'd leaned on Peter, how *he'd* made her feel better.

She could almost hear Libby comforting her after the Gestapo's visit. *"God didn't create us to be completely independent, but interdependent. That's why he gave us friends."*

Evelyn had prayed for help, and God had given her a friend. God had given her strength and calm and help—through that friend.

Peter returned with her coat.

She threw her arms around his neck and whispered in his ear. "Thank you."

"You—you're welcome." His hand settled on her waist.

She pressed a quick kiss to his cheek, grabbed her coat, and whirled out the door before she did something she'd regret for the rest of her life.

However short that might be.

TWENTY-SIX

Crammed in the gallery of Munich's Bürgerbräukeller, Peter leaned his forearms on the railing. Three thousand people filled the hall, with the "Old Fighters" from the early days of the Nazi movement seated below on the main floor and everyone else standing in galleries lining all four walls.

The room buzzed waiting for Hitler's big speech for the fifteenth anniversary of the launch of the 1923 Beer Hall Putsch. Every year the Nazis commemorated their failed attempt to overthrow the government that had led to the deaths of sixteen Nazis and four policemen. Hitler had been arrested but only served eight months in prison—time he'd spent writing *Mein Kampf*.

Peter's armpits felt sticky. Not just from the warm room, but from the predicament of having Otto von Albrecht and his Students' League friends to his right and George Norwood to his left. To keep Otto appeased, Peter had to talk like a Nazi—something he did not want to do in front of George, in case George mentioned it to folks back home.

Lord, help me speak out of both sides of my mouth. Peter cringed. It wasn't right to ask God to help him lie. Yet lying was necessary.

When Otto had invited him, he'd declined. But when Evelyn

said she'd be covering the late-night ceremony, he'd changed his mind. Then George had called to say he was reporting on the ceremony too.

What a mess. Around the corner in the gallery to his right, Evelyn watched with the press. She'd worn no red at all—gray from head to foot. With that passport, she needed to blend in. Her colleagues would protect her and vouch for her, but Peter felt better being present. He wore a navy blue suit to stand out for her in the sea of brown uniforms.

Otto leaned forward to catch Peter's eye. "Did you hear about that awful shooting in Paris yesterday?"

Peter frowned. "I did."

"Filthy Jew, shooting a German man."

Otto's friends muttered oaths, and Peter muttered an incoherent prayer.

Reading the newspaper article, he'd found some facts under the propaganda. Herschel Grynszpan, a seventeen-year-old German Jewish boy of Polish origin, lived in Paris. His parents were among the Jews forced from Germany into Poland the previous week. When the boy heard, he went to the German embassy in Paris and shot an official named Ernst vom Rath. The man clung to life in the hospital.

"The Jews would kill us all in our sleep if they had their way," Otto's friend Joachim said.

"Ja." Their friend Helmut clenched a fist on top of the railing. "Something needs to be done."

Peter glanced down to his own fists. The Nazis had already done something—many somethings. Laws after laws after laws, depriving the Jews of their livelihoods and freedoms, but the Nazis were never satisfied. Their hatred only grew.

George adjusted the knot of his tie. "I'm beginning to agree."

Peter snapped his gaze to his friend. "With . . . what?"

"Think of the problems we have in America. Our economy is in ruins, and who owns the banks?"

"The Jews," Otto said.

"Right," George said.

Peter stifled his alarm. His life depended on not showing his feelings.

George's chin edged forward. "Don't even get me started on the newspaper and radio and movie industries. You know who owns them all."

"Could it be the Jews?" Sarcasm distorted Otto's voice.

All the men laughed, and Peter wrenched his lips into the shape of a smile.

Otto clapped Peter on the back. "Peter's going to change that."

"What do you mean?" George asked.

Peter shot Otto a glare. His mission was secret. Even Otto wasn't supposed to know. Otto's gray eyes widened, and he gave a slight nod.

Peter turned a sheepish smile to George. "Otto thinks too highly of my future influence as a professor. But I will definitely tell everyone about my experiences here."

"Good," George said. "We have to counteract the lies in the papers. They manipulate what people hear, what people believe. They kick out clear-thinking men like me and sing the praises of hacks like her." He flicked his chin in the direction of the correspondents.

Peter chilled, but he feigned innocence. "Who?"

"Evelyn Brand. She shouldn't be here. She's supposed to be gone."

A kick in his gut. "Say, I know you don't like her, but wanting her to get expelled? That's too much."

George sent him a strange look—anger shifting to surprise—then he glanced away. "That isn't what I want."

"I'm glad to hear." But his friendship with George was at an end.

The band played. Arms shot out in salute, and voices sang, fervent and proud. Peter clasped his hands behind his back and sang not one word. Thank goodness, George did the same.

The speeches began, and Peter hated it all. Hated the pomp. Hated the role he played. Hated the hatred. If only he could escape the country when Evelyn did.

His gaze slid to her. She looked pale and quiet. It had to be difficult for her to feel helpless.

But in her crisis, she'd come to him. Of all the people she knew in Munich, she'd come to him. She'd embraced him and kissed him on the cheek. In any other circumstance, he'd have taken it as a sign to renew his pursuit.

Not now. Not when she feared for her life.

Across the void of the hall, she met his gaze.

Peter tapped two fingers under his chin, signaling her to keep her chin up.

The tiniest smile, and she glanced away.

More than anything, he wanted to draw her to his side forever. But to keep her safe, to show his love, he had to send her away.

Munich
Wednesday, November 9, 1938

The procession was so slow, Evelyn wrote out full copy as she walked, not just notes.

The clouds hung as low and gray as her mood. Hitler had just laid a giant wreath at the Feldherrnhalle, a memorial built a hundred years ago to honor Bavarian military leaders—now honoring street thugs gunned down by the police in 1923. Those thugs were entombed as martyrs at a shrine on Königlicher Platz.

She stuck close to the other foreign correspondents walking down the sidewalk under red-and-black swastika flags, as brown-shirted SA troops paraded down the street.

Across the road, Peter and Norwood kept pace with her. Once again, Peter's nearness calmed her. Everything was upside down lately.

"Is that George Norwood?" Cal Monroe said in front of her.

Behind Evelyn, Bert Sorensen snorted. "Man doesn't know he's licked."

"He's freelancing." Tony DeLuca of the Washington *Times Dispatch* screwed up his wide mouth. "The Nazi rags in the US need material too. I'll bet the German-American Bund is his best customer, and that fascist Father Coughlin."

"He's smart to stay on the other side of the road," Cal said.

"Smarter still to stay away from Brand." Tony grinned back at her. "She'd run him through. Making us think she was Goebbels's Girl."

Evelyn heaved a mock sigh. "Alas. Here I am, armed only with a hatpin."

The fellows laughed.

It felt good to be part of the group again. It felt secure. But that security was an illusion without her US passport. This morning she'd again debated which was more dangerous—the red-stamped passport or no papers. She'd decided to play by the rules and carry the passport.

To be safe, she avoided areas labeled *"Juden Verboten"*—no Jews allowed. Though she'd made an exception for the Putsch anniversary. She had a job to do. She needed the stories. Thank goodness, no one had asked for anything but her press pass.

The procession entered the expanse of the Königlicher Platz. As the band played "Deutschland über Alles," SA, SS, and army troops marched in formation, black boots thumping the granite pavement.

Tomorrow morning the consulate general would be open again, and she could start the process to get a new passport. How long would it take? Meanwhile, she had to lie low and avoid the Gestapo. How on earth could she do her job well?

Evelyn groaned and took more notes. Her situation was no different from that of Herr Gold and the other Jews in Germany. Except they didn't have the luxury of US citizenship to fall back on. Her situation was temporary, but theirs knew no end.

Cal nudged Tony with a scrawny elbow. "That Ernst vom Rath fellow had better pull through. These folks want blood."

Evelyn glanced around at the strident faces. The German rags this morning had been so rabid she couldn't read them. Violence against Jews had erupted in various cities the day before. What would happen if vom Rath died?

Next to the Führerbau, twin white mausoleums housed the sixteen coffins of the Putsch martyrs, and thousands gathered to pay homage. Evelyn and the other correspondents found the press area—but she lost sight of Peter.

Hundreds of black-uniformed SS men stood in rank by the neoclassical memorial, and a speaker sorrowfully intoned the names of the fallen over the loudspeaker. With each name, the crowd bellowed, "*Hier!*"—here!

The ceremony ended with the "Horst Wessel Song."

Cal and Bert sang their own comic version in a low voice—Evelyn could only pick out cuss words and a double entendre. Enough to know she didn't want to hear the rest. Not in her current mood.

When the crowd broke up, the correspondents headed out of the square.

Tony nudged Cal. "Hungry? Let's grab a bite at Osteria Bavaria."

Cal chuckled. "Hitler's favorite restaurant? Sure. Let's see if he shows."

"Count me in." Bert hailed a cab.

Evelyn would be left alone, and a strange panic squeezed her chest. "May I join you?"

"Sure, tootsie." Bert winked at her and opened the back door. "But you'll have to sit on my lap."

For once, she'd consider an offer like that. "Nonsense. We can all squeeze in."

A squeeze it was, and Evelyn perched on the edge of the seat, but she was in and safe.

"Say, Brand," Tony said. "Tell us how you got that scoop at the Munich Conference."

Cal pulled a newspaper from inside his trench coat and perused it. "Yeah, you scooped the world. Maids! Who'd have thunk?"

Evelyn allowed a moment to revel in her victory. "Only a woman."

Bert Sorensen rubbed his knee against Evelyn's backside.

"Say, Bertie." Evelyn patted her hat. "Ever imagine the damage a hatpin could do? I'm imagining it now."

Tony hooted. "Told you she's a firebrand. Watch it, or you'll get burned."

Bert grumbled and jerked his knee away.

"Bunch of garbage." Cal whapped the newspaper. "How these fellows can write this swill beats me. Look at this. They list a bunch of people beheaded as enemies of the state. They brag about it. Listen—Fräulein Magda Müller passed military secrets to foreigners, Herr Friedrich—"

Evelyn sucked in a breath. "Magda Müller? May I—may I see that?"

"Sure."

Her stomach frothed as she scanned the article. No doubt but it was her Magda Müller. Evelyn had stopped meeting her many weeks before, but the girl must have found another reporter—or a Gestapo agent posing as a reporter.

Her head and her stomach swirled, taunting her, haunting her. How could she go to a restaurant and eat and banter?

She gave Cal his paper. "Say, fellows, I don't feel well. I'm going to ask the driver to drop me at my place. It isn't far out of the way."

"What's the matter, Brandy?" Bert lifted his pointy chin. "That time of the month?"

Evelyn glared at him, fingered her hatpin, and leaned over the seatback to give directions to the driver.

For the next few minutes, the conversation floated around her, not entering her ears, but she held herself together.

When the cab pulled in front of her building, Bert didn't scoot out of her way. Evelyn climbed over him, and he fondled her bottom. She drove her high heel into his instep, making him yelp and the other fellows crack up.

She shoved open the door, dashed up to her apartment, and sank into an armchair with her head in her hands.

Magda. Poor Magda. Poor foolish Magda. Why hadn't she been careful? Why hadn't she followed Evelyn's instructions?

Then she clutched her stomach and doubled over. No. No. It was Evelyn's fault, not Magda's. The Gestapo had been watching Evelyn—she was the one who put them on Magda's tail. She'd as good as turned the girl in.

A chill sliced over the back of her neck, and she clutched it. If the Gestapo had followed Evelyn that day and found those papers, it would have been her under that guillotine and not Magda.

She moaned. "Lord, what have I done? I wanted a story, and I cost a woman her life."

What if the Gestapo had tortured Magda? Surely they had. Had she told them about General Gerlach and the others who had plotted a coup? The plot had fizzled after the Munich Agreement, but the Gestapo wouldn't care.

Germany needed the few remaining people who had courage to stand up to Hitler.

How many of those people had Evelyn condemned?

TWENTY-SEVEN

MUNICH
THURSDAY, NOVEMBER 10, 1938

Peter awoke in his dark bedroom. What was that noise? The phone?

He groaned and pulled the covers over his head. Who would call in the middle of the night?

Evelyn!

He threw off his bedclothes and stumbled into the living room in the moonlight.

Phone. Phone. Where was the phone? He'd told her to call any time of the day or night.

Peter grabbed the receiver. "Hello?"

"Hallo, Peter."

"Otto?" Peter sank into his desk chair. He could hear excited voices in the background. Otto and his buddies were probably drinking themselves under the table after the Putsch anniversary dinner. "Do you have any idea what time it is?"

"Ten after midnight. Do you want to have some fun?"

"I want to go back to *bed*. I'm teaching tomorrow morning—this morning."

"You do not want to waste this night sleeping. Tonight is for revenge. Revenge for the death of Ernst vom Rath."

The man had died, and the haze of sleep evaporated. Revenge? On the Jews. *Oh, Lord, no.*

"It's the moment we've been waiting for," Otto said. "We have orders from Goebbels to smash up Jewish businesses, burn synagogues, and arrest twenty thousand Jewish men throughout the Reich."

Peter was too horrified to know what to say. "A—a pogrom."

Otto laughed. "*Jawohl.* A good old-fashioned pogrom. It's supposed to look spontaneous, so we're in plain clothes, not uniform. We're not allowed to loot, and we're not to touch women or foreign Jews, but we'll still have fun."

Peter ran his hand into his hair. "Wow."

"Join us. They're torching the synagogue on Herzog-Rudolf Strasse. Meet us there."

"I—I can't."

"Why not?" Otto's voice hardened.

Peter glanced around as if his desk would furnish an excuse. "I—if word gets to America that I was involved, it—it would damage my reputation there. My mission for the Party."

"You think so?"

"I'm certain. I could ask your father if you—"

"No. We mustn't wake him."

"No. No, he wouldn't like that. Too bad. Another time."

Otto groaned. "What a shame."

Peter hung up. "Lord, now what?"

Evelyn—he had to warn her! And Herr Gold. The rabbi. The people he'd worked with in June when the main synagogue was demolished. "Lord, protect them. Show me what to do."

First, Evelyn. He dialed her number. He'd warn her to stay inside. She was a woman. The orders were to leave women alone. She'd be safe.

The phone kept ringing. "Come on, come on. Pick up."

Ten rings. Twenty. Where was she at ten after midnight?

George had mentioned a midnight ceremony—maybe she was reporting on it too.

He hung up. "Lord, I can't help her. Keep her safe."

Herr Gold. His café. Had the ownership transferred to his Aryan brother-in-law yet? Would the Nazis even care? Herr and Frau Gold lived above the café. They were in danger.

Peter dashed to his bedroom, stripped off his pajamas, and dressed.

What could he do? Fend off a mob? No, but if he arrived before the mob, he could hide the Golds in his apartment. The couple had just received their exit visas—so close to escaping.

Shirt, trousers, socks, the shoes with the list under the insole. The minimum.

But what if someone recognized him or his car?

Peter's breath slowed and stopped. He'd have to flee the country. He needed to dress for flight.

Suit vest, V-neck sweater, necktie stuffed in his pocket, suit jacket, overcoat with gloves in the pockets, glasses, hat. At the door he grabbed his rucksack.

He gave the apartment one last sweep. Anything else? No. He needed to leave.

Peter climbed into his Opel Admiral, tossed the rucksack in the back, and drove away. The street was silent, but the sky was brighter than usual for an overcast night, even with a nearly full moon.

He turned the corner. A reddish glow pulsed between buildings, and a column of silver smoke marred the sky.

Peter gripped the steering wheel. The Nazis had pledged to bring order, and they were burning and smashing and arresting innocent men. "It's chaos. Chaos."

He turned onto the deserted Gärtnerplatz. A star of David had been painted on the café's window, and Peter grimaced. It was only a matter of time.

On the side street, he parked by the door to the apartments upstairs. But there were three stories above ground level—which apartment was the Golds'?

"Lord, show me the way." The doorway wasn't locked, and he climbed the stairs. Names on the doors, thank goodness. The apartment directly over the café said "Gold."

"Herr Gold? It's Peter Lang." He knocked softly so as not to rouse the neighbors or their slumbering antisemitism. If he kept knocking long enough . . .

Herr Gold opened the door, fully dressed, his face grim.

Peter sighed. "You've heard."

"You must leave, Herr Lang. They will come soon and destroy my café and arrest me."

Peter ducked inside and shut the door. "We can't let them arrest you. You have exit visas."

Frau Gold sat in the golden glow of a single lamp. "It isn't meant to be."

"Yes, it is. I'll take you to my apartment. No one will look for you there. You can stay until it quiets down and you can travel."

She stared at luggage by the door, and her face puckered. "It will never quiet down."

"Then I'll drive you to the border." He gestured to the luggage. "Come on, you're already packed. Anything else you need?"

A light flickered in Herr Gold's brown eyes. "That might work."

"It's worth a try. Stay here, and you'll go to jail. Come with me, and you have a chance."

"Yes, yes. Miriam—quick, get what you need."

She shook her head. "It's no use, Jakob."

Herr Gold cupped his wife's chin in his hand. "It's our only chance. Come, *Liebchen*."

"My car's the black Opel. I'll start loading." Peter hefted up the trunk, maneuvered it downstairs, and set it in the trunk of his car.

Movement on the plaza caught his eye. People—but how many?

His stomach lurched, and he took the stairs two at a time. "Hurry! They're coming."

Herr and Frau Gold were scrambling into their coats.

Peter picked up two suitcases. "Anything else?"

"My purse!" Frau Gold grabbed it, then stopped and looked around the apartment.

"Come, *Liebchen*." Herr Gold took her hand. "There is nothing here for us anymore."

She set her chin and followed her husband.

Peter trotted down to the car and flung open the back door. "Get in. Get down."

In the light of the streetlamps, two dozen men approached, yelling and bearing torches.

Peter tossed the suitcases onto the passenger seat, loped around the car, jumped in, and started the car. "Come on. Come on."

The engine revved, and Peter pulled into the roundabout just far enough to turn around.

A man pointed to him and called out. Others hurled rocks through the café window and tossed in torches.

A sob rose from the backseat—Frau Gold.

"My café," Herr Gold said. "My beautiful café."

Peter cranked the car into a U-turn and tore down the street. His jaw clenched, and his eyes burned. "Justice! Mercy! Where are they, Lord?"

After the midnight swearing-in ceremony of new SS officers at the Feldherrnhalle, Evelyn stifled a yawn, once again jammed in a cab with Cal and Bert and Tony. "Why do so many Nazi festivities have to be in the middle of the night?"

"Because they're ghouls." Cal made a monster-like face. "Who-oo-oo."

Evelyn rolled her eyes. But the ceremony had indeed felt ghoulish. The men in black, the red flags, the searchlights, the sacred-to-the-Nazis blood flag—soaked in the blood of the Putsch martyrs. And the head ghoul himself—Hitler.

"Do you smell smoke?" Tony rolled down the cab window. "There's a red glow over there."

"On this side too," Bert said. "Something's burning."

The driver slammed on his brakes, and Evelyn braced herself on the seatback.

A crowd of men jogged in front of the cab, carrying sticks.

"Driver, wait." Tony leaned out the window. "What's going on, *meine Herren?*"

A burly fellow came closer, grinning. "We're getting back at those murderous Jews. All over town, all over the Reich."

Evelyn's chest squeezed, and she exchanged a glance with Cal.

Cal leaned over Tony. "Those fires—are they—"

"Ja!" The man slapped his stick into his palm. "Jewish shops, synagogues. It's time they pay. No more thieving and cheating and murdering."

"Oh no," Evelyn whispered. They'd already destroyed the main synagogue. Now the others too? What about Herr Gold's café? The stores and restaurants—the few that remained in Jewish hands?

Tony whipped out some Reichsmarks and flung them over to the driver. "I'm getting out here, boys. It's story time."

Cal and Bert scrambled to follow.

For the first time ever, Evelyn shrank back from a story. If she got separated from the others, if anyone asked to see her papers . . . "You know what, fellows? I'd better go home."

Bert plopped his hat on his head and grinned at her. "Yeah, a mob is no place for a dame."

Any other day, she'd argue. Ignoring Bert, she repeated her address to the driver.

Cal poked his head back inside, concern on his face. "Take care, Brandy. Stay inside and stay safe."

"Thanks."

The doors slammed, leaving her alone in the backseat, and the cab drove away.

Evelyn clutched her bulging purse in her lap, and it crinkled. After her talk with Peter at his office, she'd picked open the purse lining and stuffed it with her most damning story notes, Reichs-marks, and francs left from her time in Paris.

What had she just done? A story. A big story, and she was running away from it. If she didn't report on this violence because she felt unsafe as a woman, she'd undo all her hard work.

She gritted her teeth. She couldn't do that. Maybe she could dump the passport in her apartment and go back out.

Alone? Maybe she could call Peter. The thought of the big blond man at her side calmed her. But did she really want to wake him at one o'clock in the morning?

Evelyn groaned and rested her head back on the seat. *Lord, what should I do? Stay home or go out? Call Peter or not?*

The cab stopped beside her building. Some men walked down the other side of the street toward her.

Evelyn paid the driver, not waiting for change, and she rushed into her building and shut the door.

Voices came from upstairs, near her apartment.

Evelyn climbed the stairs. Not near her apartment—*in* her apartment.

Herr Falk, her landlord, rummaged through her kitchen cabinet, and Helga the cleaning lady went through Evelyn's desk drawers.

Evelyn cried out. "What do you think you're doing?"

Herr Falk stomped to her in the doorway, his round face red. "You lied to me! How dare you? I don't rent to Jews."

Her heart seized, and she took a step back from the large man. "I—I'm a Christian."

Helga joined him and spat at Evelyn. "Lying Jew. You said you were an American, but you're not. I saw your passport."

Evelyn swiped spittle off her chin and glared at Helga. "The only way you could have seen that false passport is when you *switched* it. You did it. You sneaky, lying—"

Helga shoved her into the hallway. "Jewish swine!"

"She stole my passport," Evelyn said to her landlord. "She switched it—"

"No more lies." Herr Falk made a circular motion with his beefy arm. "You're evicted."

Evelyn's heart beat hard and fast. She had to talk him down. She forced her voice lower, forced the fury out of her expression. "Very well, *mein Herr*. Tomorrow morning I'll look for a new apartment."

"Nein! You're not stepping another filthy foot on my property."

She moved to edge past him. "I—I need to pack."

He stepped in her way. "I said, you're not stepping foot on my property again."

Evelyn glanced past him to her typewriter, her clothing, her papers, her books. "But that—that's *my* property."

Helga smirked at her. "The Gestapo will confiscate it—and the papers you stole."

The rucksack rested just inside the door, right beside Herr Falk's leg. She reached for it.

He shoved her, and she fell to her backside.

"Get out! Before I have you arrested for trespassing—or spying."

Evelyn scrambled to her feet. Empty-handed. A voice in her head roared, *"Get out! Get out now!"*

She turned and ran down the stairs and out into the cold night.

"Lord, help me." She crossed her arms over her middle. She had nothing but her purse. The clothes on her back. A false and deadly passport.

"Now what?" she whispered. Small. Alone. Vulnerable.

And hunted.

TWENTY-EIGHT

Peter tucked in fresh bedsheets for the Golds.

Frau Gold slipped on a clean pillowcase. "You shouldn't have to sleep on your sofa."

"It's only for a night or two." Peter spread out a quilt. "If it still isn't safe for you to travel by Saturday, I'll drive you to the French border."

The phone rang.

Could it be Evelyn? To be safe, Peter motioned for the Golds to be quiet and shut the bedroom door before answering the phone. "Hallo?"

"Peter, it is Otto."

Peter put on a groggy voice. "What on earth? Waking me again?"

"This time you must join us. Your honor is at stake. You have been betrayed."

"Betrayed?" Still standing, Peter gripped the back of his desk chair. "By whom?"

"You know a woman named Evelyn Brand."

Clamminess crept down Peter's arms. "Ja. She is an American reporter. I feed her good stories about Germany."

Otto barked out a laugh. "She's played you for a fool. She prints garbage about us. We think she's been spying on you. She writes about things only Party insiders know."

Peter squeezed his eyes shut and fought to retain control. "I—"

"It gets worse. She is not an American. She was born in Germany—and she's a Jew." He spat out the last word.

How did Otto know? "That—that can't be. She grew up in America. She has an American accent."

"She has Jewish papers."

Only the Gestapo knew that, and Peter shuddered. "I don't know what to say." His voice came out choked.

"She lied to you. Tonight she will pay."

Peter frantically looked around, but for what? *Lord, help!*

"We have orders to rough her up," Otto said. "If she dies in the process, so be it."

He clenched the chair back. *God, help. Lead them astray.*

"I have her address. Meet us at the corner of Leopoldstrasse and Herzogstrasse in fifteen minutes."

"She isn't there," Peter blurted out.

"What do you mean? Where is she?"

Peter rubbed the heel of his hand on his forehead. She was probably reporting on some ceremony, but Otto might know where it was and intercept her on the way home. "She's staying at a friend's. The Gestapo visited her recently, and it scared her."

"As it should. If they'd known she was Jewish, they would have already stopped her lies. But it ends tonight. Where is she?"

Peter grimaced. "I don't know the address. But my friend knows. I'll call him."

"Good. We'll meet at your place in—"

"No." He had to keep them far away from Evelyn and the Golds. "She—yes, she said it was close to the main train station. Gather your friends. Meet me at the station."

"Jawohl. Tomorrow there will be one less scheming Jew in the world."

Peter waited for Otto to hang up, then dialed Evelyn's number. "Answer, answer."

It kept ringing and ringing.

His breath puffed like a bellows. He could see the mob descending on his father, the fists, the sticks, the blood. He could hear his father's cries.

Peter slammed down the phone. No! He would not be powerless again.

Where was she? Where was that ceremony? Munich was a big city.

"George!" He'd know. George might harbor a grudge against Evelyn, but he wouldn't want harm to come to her. Besides, who else could Peter call? Who else would know?

He dialed the Regina Palace Hotel, and they connected him to George's room.

"George Norwood here."

"It's Peter. Good, you're back."

"I just finished reporting on a ceremony. What's wrong?" Worry darkened his voice.

"It's Evelyn Brand. She's in trouble. Look, I know you don't like her, but I know you wouldn't want to see her harmed. I need to find her before Otto and his friends do. They have orders to kill her."

"What? What are you talking about?"

"The ceremony—where was it? Did you see her there?"

"At—at the Odeonsplatz. Yes, I saw her."

"Good." A nice distance from the train station. "She must be on her way home. I'll intercept her. At least I bought her some time."

"Bought her time? What do you mean?"

"I told Otto she was staying with a friend. Told them to meet me at the main train station. It'll take them time to get there, even longer to realize I lied to them, then to cross town to her apartment. I'll get there first."

"Wait! Let me. Let me make it up to her. Let me help. I'll get a cab, bring her to the hotel. She'll be safer here than at your place. Otto will look for you there after he figures it out."

"Thanks. That's kind of you. But I'm closer, can get there faster." He hung up.

Peter flung open the bedroom door.

Herr and Frau Gold stared at him. "What's going on?" Herr Gold asked.

"The Nazis have orders to kill Fräulein Brand. They know. They know she's Jewish."

Herr Gold pulled his wife close. "Oh no."

Peter pulled on his suit jacket. "I'm going out to find her, save her, bring her . . ."

He paused with his fingers on a jacket button. Oh no. George was right. In about an hour, Otto would realize Peter had lied. He knew about the list of American Nazi sympathizers. He'd come to Peter's apartment.

He'd be thirsting for blood.

Peter had led the Golds from one danger to another, and he slowly turned to them. "You won't be safe here. I must leave Munich tonight."

Frau Gold clapped her hand over her mouth.

"Now, now." Herr Gold patted her shoulder. "We will find a place."

Peter could take them along—but no. He couldn't drag them on his rescue mission, not with mobs on the streets. But where could he take them? Where would they be safe? "The Schreibers."

"Pardon?" Herr Gold asked.

"Professor Johannes Schreiber. I study under him. He and his wife are good people. They will hide you. I'll take you on the way to Evelyn's. It's close."

He tossed up a quick prayer that the Schreibers would be willing and courageous.

After everyone put on coats and hats, Herr Gold picked up the suitcases, and Peter slung on his rucksack and picked up the trunk.

He'd never come back. His gaze landed on his desk, his attaché case full of graded papers for tomorrow's class. A class he wouldn't teach.

A groan built in his chest, but this was no time for hesitation.

Peter and the Golds loaded the car, the Golds lay low in the backseat, and Peter drove a few blocks to the Schreibers' home. The neighborhood slept, unaware of the violence erupting in other parts of the city.

At the professor's home, Peter scanned the street, then rushed the Golds up the front steps and pounded on the front door.

In a few minutes, Professor Schreiber opened the door in a dressing gown, his hair mussed. "*Was ist los?* Peter?"

"May we come in?" Without waiting for an answer, Peter ushered his friends inside and shut the door. "Please pardon me for waking you, for barging into your home. This is an emergency."

The professor's eyes stretched wide as he took in his surprise visitors. "What is going on?"

Frau Schreiber appeared on the stairs, also in a dressing gown.

Peter removed his hat and bowed his head to her. "Please forgive me, Frau Schreiber. These are my friends, Herr and Frau Gold. You wouldn't know, but a pogrom is raging around the city. The Nazis are burning synagogues, smashing up stores, and beating people, killing people."

"Oh no." Horror and compassion raced through Professor Schreiber's eyes, and he turned to the Golds. "And you are—"

"Jewish." Herr Gold raised his chin in pride and defiance. "We are Jewish."

Professor Schreiber clutched the neck of his dressing gown. "I am—so sorry this is happening to you."

Time was ticking, and Evelyn was in danger. "May I ask a huge favor? The Nazis have orders to kill my friend Evelyn Brand. She's an American correspondent, and she's Jewish too. I need to find her and rescue her. I brought the Golds to my apartment, but they will not be safe there."

"Why not?" Frau Schreiber padded across the foyer in her slippers.

Peter juggled his words, aiming for clarity and speed and safety. "When the Nazis realize I rescued Fräulein Brand, they will come after me. I must leave town tonight. If I can, I'll return and take the Golds with me. But if I can't . . . well, the Gestapo will ransack my apartment. The Golds need someplace safe. You were the first people I thought of."

Frau Schreiber took her husband's arm. "Johannes, we must."

"We have exit visas, transit visas for France, and entry visas for Bolivia," Herr Gold said. "We would not stay long."

"Yes," Peter said. "They just need someplace to hide until the violence blows over. But I won't lie. It would be dangerous for you."

"Do not think of it." The professor set his hand on Peter's shoulder, and his eyes reddened. "Save Fräulein Brand. Your friends will be safe with us. If you do not return by morning, I will help them get to the border."

"Thank you." Peter shook his mentor's hand with deep gratitude.

The professor frowned. "The Gestapo will ransack your office too."

"Yes." The realization thudded like a rock in his stomach. His dissertation. His research logbook. His notes. Years of work. Tomorrow morning, it would all be gone.

"Herr Lang?" Herr Gold gave him a concerned look. "Do you have second thoughts?"

"Nein, my friend." Peter strode out the door to fetch the Golds' luggage. "None at all."

TWENTY-NINE

Evelyn pressed back in a cold stony doorway. Kitty-corner across the intersection to her right, a light shone from her apartment, where Herr Falk and Helga were looting Evelyn's possessions.

"They have the nerve to call the Jews thieves," she muttered.

She hugged herself, shivering. In the distance came sounds of sirens and shouts and glass breaking.

She'd always prided herself on her ability to handle anything on her own. But she couldn't handle this.

"Lord, I need help." Shielded in the doorway, she'd mulled her pitiful options. Of all the people she knew in Munich—reporters and artists and socialites and musicians—Peter was the one she could depend on.

He'd take her in tonight. Tomorrow, if this insanity had stopped, he'd accompany her to the consulate general. Then she'd find an apartment or hotel where she could stay while waiting for her new passport.

First, she had to leave the false security of the dark doorway and brave the half-mile walk to Peter's place.

Two headlights approached, and she pressed back as far as possible.

The car parked in front of her former apartment building, and a shadowy figure emerged and entered her building—without turning off the car's engine or headlights.

She didn't like the looks of that. Herr Falk must have called the Gestapo.

She pushed away from the building and turned left. Despite shaking legs, she walked at a crisp pace.

The shouts grew louder as she neared the intersection, and she hugged the building as she turned the corner.

Evelyn gasped and halted. Broken glass glinted on the sidewalk, on the street, as if the stars themselves had fallen.

A block away, dozens of people wielded torches and sticks, smashing windows, tossing out merchandise. Dragging people into the street. Beating them.

A moan rose in her throat. She had to find another route.

"You there!" A man brandished a torch in her direction. "Show me your papers!"

No! All she had was that passport stamped with a crimson *J*. Running away would be stupid, but standing still would mean a beating. Or worse.

Evelyn eased back, eyeing the mob, groping the wall beside her until at last it gave way. The corner—she turned and bolted back down the street where she'd hidden in the doorway.

Voices roared behind her. "Stop her! She's a Jew!"

Her legs flew, and her lungs screamed. Stupid skirt. Stupid pumps. Slowing her down. A map of the neighborhood ran through her mind. How could she get away? Hide? Get to Peter's?

She crossed her former street and kept running. Two blocks ahead of her, a car pulled into an intersection and squealed to a stop.

A man climbed out of the car and peered at her. "Evelyn Brand?" he called with a German accent, an accusing tone.

She stumbled to a stop.

"It's her! Get her!" The man swung his arm overhead, and the car doors flew open.

Evelyn stifled a cry. A mob behind her, hunters before her, a Gestapo car in front of her apartment to her left. She had to go right.

She wheeled back to her former street, rounded the corner, and ran in the opposite direction of her apartment.

Shouts and footsteps gained on her.

"Lord!" she cried. "Lord!"

Someone grabbed her arm. "It's me! Peter!"

A cry tumbled out, and she spun around.

Peter stood before her, hatless, with a fearsome expression. "Duck. I'll pretend to slap you. Then I'll drag you off. Play along."

"What?" Behind him, men pounded around the corner with torches.

Pain exploded in her left cheek, and she screamed and cradled that cheek.

Peter stared at her, mouth agape. "You were supposed to duck."

He'd slapped her, and fury welled inside. "How *could* you? I trusted you."

His jaw jutted forward, and he grabbed her wrist and turned to the crowd. "This one's mine. It's personal. Leave her to me."

"What?" She flailed her arm, but his grip clamped like a handcuff.

The mob stopped, and men laughed. "She's all yours."

Peter marched past them, jerking her arm. "Leave her to me. I'll take care of her."

"Let me go!" She lurched behind him, voice shaking, half in anger, half in grief. "Let me go!"

The crowd jeered as they passed, shoving torches toward her, calling her vile names.

Peter . . . he was rescuing her from them. Play along, he'd said.

Play along, she would. She shook her arm for show, but her feet followed willingly. "Let go of me!"

"Never! I'll never let you go." His voice fierce, his words calming.

He jogged toward her old apartment, toward that suspicious car—his car!

Then he stopped, and she barreled into him from behind.

"Otto," he said in a low voice.

A man stood silhouetted in the headlights. "I don't like traitors." The man from the car who'd called her name.

Peter released Evelyn's arm. "And I don't like murderers." He charged forward and swung his fist.

Otto ducked and slugged Peter in the ribs.

"Peter!" Evelyn cried.

He drove a fist up under Otto's chin. "Evie! Get in the car! Drive away!"

"What? No!" She couldn't leave him there.

"Get in the car! Drive away!" Peter took a punch square in the face.

Footsteps thumped on the pavement from where Otto's car had parked. Peter might be able to fend off Otto, but not three or four men. They'd kill him.

Peter's fist thudded into Otto's cheek, and Otto jabbed Peter in the gut.

Evelyn had to help. She raised her knee as far as her skirt allowed, and she drove her foot hard into the side of Otto's knee.

He yelled and collapsed to the side.

"Get in the car!" Peter slammed both fists down on the back of Otto's head, and the man dropped to the pavement.

Evelyn threw open the passenger door, jumped in, and slid behind the wheel. Thank goodness he'd left the engine running. "Peter! Get in!"

He scrambled in. Evelyn threw the car into reverse and stomped the gas pedal before he could shut his door.

Three men ran up, shouting, cursing.

Evelyn wrenched the steering wheel around, and the car spun backward, tires squealing.

Peter cried out and hung on.

When she faced away from the attackers and the mob, Evelyn

cranked the gear shift and punched the accelerator. The engine roared, and the car tore down the street.

Peter wrestled his door shut. "You okay?"

"Ye-yes." Evelyn careened around a corner and glanced in the rearview mirror. "What on earth?"

"They have orders to kill you."

"Me?"

"They know about the passport, think you're a German Jew, think you're a spy. They have orders."

"Oh my goodness." Evelyn wheeled around the corner, the tires screaming in protest, her mind aching in disbelief. They wanted her dead.

"How?" Peter clutched at his head. "How did they figure out I'd lied to them? So fast? Impossible!"

They'd lost the mob, and Evelyn let out a moan.

"You're all right, Evie. You'll be all right."

"I'm not . . ." How could she argue with him about her name after he'd saved her life? "You—you came for me."

"Thank goodness. Thank goodness he called. Thank you, Lord."

She had no idea what he was talking about. She just kept driving. Anywhere as long as it was away.

Peter's head sank back on the seatback. "When I went to your apartment and your landlord said he'd kicked you out . . . Then that mob—when I saw them chasing you . . ."

Evelyn shuddered and fought to keep her eyes from slamming shut—she had to watch the road. "I have never been so thankful to hear your voice."

"I'm sorry I slapped you. I didn't mean to. I meant for you to duck."

Her cheek stung, but she shoved back the outrage and the memories. Peter wasn't Howard or Clark or Warren. She forced the truth into her head. He'd done it to protect her. Not to hurt her. Not to silence her.

"Can you forgive me?" His voice sounded ragged.

He needed to see it, so she looked him in the eye. "All forgiven."

"Thank you." Dark rivulets ran from his nose.

"You're bleeding!" Evelyn shoved her purse to him. "There's a handkerchief inside."

"I have one."

Something was wrong with his face, but what? "Your nose—did he break it?"

"Maybe. I'll find out." He pressed his handkerchief to his nose and winced.

Evelyn stopped at an intersection. "Where to?"

Peter squinted at a street sign on a building. "What does that say?"

That was what was wrong with his face. "Your glasses. Where are they?"

"I lost them in the fight. You'll have to drive."

"Of—of course. To your place?"

"No." Peter settled in his seat. "Out of Munich. Out of Germany."

"What? We can't."

"We have to. They want you dead. Now they want me dead." He knifed his hand down the road. "Drive."

Evelyn's gloved hands gripped the steering wheel as if it were the only thing she had in the world.

And it was. That and her purse and a bleeding friend.

And the Lord. She let out a long breath.

Yes, she had the Lord. She pressed the gas pedal.

THIRTY

Peter got as comfortable as he could lying on the front seat of the car. He and Evelyn had driven south on the Olympic Road into the Alpine foothills, and they'd pulled off into a wooded area near Garmisch-Partenkirchen. "Get some sleep."

"I will," Evelyn said from the backseat.

They'd need clear heads in the morning to make plans.

If only he'd been able to return to Professor Schreiber's house for the Golds. But with Otto on his tail, returning would have put both the Golds and the Schreibers at risk.

Peter tucked one hand under his head and closed his eyes, but images of the night played out on the backs of his eyelids. The mob smashing up Herr Gold's café. The Schreibers in their night-clothes—fearful but resolute. The crowd chasing down Evelyn.

Peter's fingers curled into his hair. Only once before in his life had he been that terrified. Except this time, he was strong enough. This time, someone he loved hadn't died.

He breathed out a prayer of thanks that he'd arrived when he had, and that Evelyn had kicked Otto when she had. What a woman.

His nose throbbed, and he fingered it. Tender, but probably not broken again. The pain was greater in his ribs, where Otto had landed a few punches.

His only consolation was that Otto had to be in a lot more pain.

His mouth tightened. To think he'd called Otto a friend—a man willing, even eager, to beat a woman to death.

Evelyn had been devastated when he'd told her about the events of the night and Otto's orders.

Peter had moved past devastation to cold fury.

"Peter?" Evelyn said softly, as if she didn't want to awaken him.

"I'm awake."

"I'd like to go to Stuttgart tomorrow. My friend Renate Herzog moved there recently. She used to attend Frau von Forstner's parties. She'd let us stay at her place. And there's a consulate in Stuttgart."

Peter tugged his coat collar tighter. "You can't stay in Germany long enough to wait for a passport. Otto's father is an officer in the SS. We have to get you out of the country."

"I know, but the consulate might have some advice."

"True. And I can call Charles Norwood."

"Norwood?" The word twisted with disdain.

"Yes, George's older brother. He's an officer in the passport office in the US Embassy in Berlin. He'll know what to do."

"Can we trust him?"

Peter sighed. "I know you don't like George, but tonight he offered to help you, to take you—"

A thought crashed into his head, shattering everything he knew. "No. No, it can't be."

"What?"

He shoved himself up to sitting, but the change in position only made the pieces shuffle more quickly into place. "No. Please, no. He couldn't. He couldn't have."

A rustling sound, and Evelyn leaned against the seatback. "Couldn't what?"

"No. No." He pressed the heels of his hands against his forehead. "I wondered. I wondered how Otto got there so fast."

"What are you talking about?"

He massaged his forehead, searching for a different explanation but finding none. "When Otto told me about the plot against you, I called George."

"Why would you call him?"

"I needed to find you. I knew you were at some ceremony, but I didn't know where. I figured George would know, and he did. I told him about Otto's plot, how I'd bought you time by misdirecting Otto to the train station. I figured it would take Otto at least an hour to get to the station, realize I'd ditched them and lied to them, then get to your place."

Evelyn drew in a sharp breath. "You don't think . . . ?"

"I can't believe it. I can't." His forehead hurt, he was pressing so hard. "But how else? It took me less than half an hour to take the Golds to the Schreibers, then get to your place—more like twenty minutes. Otto couldn't have realized I'd lied so quickly. And he knew—he knew I'd lied. He called me a traitor."

"Norwood," she said in a voice as hard as George's heart.

Peter groaned. "He's staying at the Regina Palace Hotel, not far from the train station. It's the only explanation. He's the only one who knew where Otto was, knew what I'd done."

Anger simmered in his chest, boiled up his throat, roared out his mouth.

"Shh." Evelyn patted his shoulder.

She was right. They had to be quiet, and he restrained himself. But George's actions hurt worse than Otto's. Peter had known George most of his life, considered him one of his best friends. Yet he was willing to commit murder. Worse. He was a coward who sent a mob to do his dirty work.

"Do you think his brother—" Evelyn gulped. "Do you think he was behind my passport—no, that's too much. It was the Gestapo. I'm sure of it."

Peter wasn't sure of anything anymore. He dropped his hands to his lap and flopped his head back onto the seat. "Does the Gestapo know you're Jewish?"

"I assumed Helga found my mother's letter. But I had dozens of letters in that drawer."

Peter stared at the convertible roof of his car. "Who else knew? I did, Libby, Herr Gold. Anyone else?"

"I told Mitch O'Hara at the Berlin bureau. Reeves overheard. He and Norwood are pals."

Peter rolled his head back and forth as memories assaulted him. "He knew. George knew. I heard him call you—" He clamped his lips shut.

"Go ahead," she said.

"He called you a pushy Jewish broad."

"Hmm. Well, maybe I am."

"He knew. It all—it all makes sense." He let out another cry.

"You think he hired Helga?"

"He must have. He must have taken your passport to Berlin. Charles—I'm sure he knows people in the German passport office. Then George was in Munich this week."

How could George have done such a thing? Sure, he blamed Evelyn—falsely—for the loss of his job. But to trap her in Germany, force her under the antisemitic laws, and set Otto and his friends out to get her? Was he—could he have been behind the orders to kill her? Had he alerted Otto after they met at the Bürgerbräukeller?

"No . . ." he murmured.

"Peter?" Evelyn's voice sounded very small. "I don't think I should go to the consulate in Stuttgart."

"No." He twisted to face her, his elbow on the seatback. "We need to get you out of the country immediately."

"How?" Evelyn mirrored his posture. "I can't exactly sail from Hamburg with these papers."

An idea formed. He might get slapped himself this time, but he had to say it. "My passport is good. You could leave if we were married."

She glanced away and rested her chin on her forearm. "That

wouldn't work. The Nuremberg Laws forbid Aryans to marry Jews. Besides, by morning, the Nazis will have both our names on a list. We can't leave this country legally. We'll have to sneak across the border—to Italy, Switzerland, France, Belgium . . ."

Peter puffed out a breath. "Italy's too friendly with Germany lately. I doubt we'd be safe there."

"Switzerland? It's close, but that makes it obvious. And they have lots of Nazis."

"My original escape plan was to go to Paris. My friend Paul Aubrey lives there. But it's a long way. What do you think?"

Evelyn was quiet for a moment. "That's the best option. I have friends in Paris too, I speak French, and I have francs. I held on to them when I left Paris in case I wanted to visit."

"Good. Reichsmarks are worthless on the foreign currency market." And Reichsmarks were all he had in his rucksack.

"We can work out the details tomorrow." She yawned. "Now that we have a plan, I can sleep."

"Great." Peter stretched out again and tugged his overcoat against the growing chill in the car.

But how could he sleep when one of his best friends had tried to kill the woman he loved?

Peter's mouth hardened. *Lord, how can I ever forgive that?*

THIRTY-ONE

Arm in arm, Evelyn and Peter strolled down the street in the picturesque resort town, laughing and talking loudly in English as if American honeymooners. Today that's what they had to be.

A police officer headed their direction.

Evelyn's throat seized, and she whirled to the window of a toy store. She pointed to dolls dressed in dirndls and lederhosen. "Look, John. Aren't they darling?"

Peter leaned his head close to hers. "You know what I always say, Mary. Nothing's too good for my little wife."

The policeman passed behind them.

"Oh, Johnny, you're so sweet. Let's come back later. I'd like to take these to our hotel." She tapped the boxes in Peter's hand.

Out of the corner of her eye, she watched the policeman meander away, and her breath flowed freely again.

Evelyn and Peter continued, passing charming buildings in whites and pastels, many decorated on the outside in the Bavarian fashion with paintings of shields and folk in native dress. Views of the sparkling Ammersee flashed between the buildings.

The town seemed untouched by the violence. Maybe they didn't have a large Jewish population.

Evelyn hated to be out in public, but she needed supplies since she didn't have her rucksack. Their escape would involve hiking, so she'd bought a new rucksack and canteen, a warm dirndl skirt, sweater, thick stockings, and sturdy shoes. They'd also bought hard sausages and boxes of zwieback crackers.

She eyed every person they passed, but no one gave them a second glance.

At the clothing store, Evelyn had changed into her new hiking clothes and Peter had changed into the hiking clothes he'd packed. The second act of the day's performance required it.

They planned to arrive at Renate Herzog's house in Stuttgart late at night, saying they'd spent their honeymoon hiking the Black Forest and were too tired to make it all the way back to Munich.

Renate was no fan of the Nazis, but Evelyn didn't want to endanger her friend with knowledge of the truth.

Peter and Evelyn turned up a side street toward the inn on the outskirts of town where they'd parked the car, out of sight of the main streets.

If only she'd been able to snatch her rucksack from inside her apartment—she'd been so close. Then they could have avoided the risky shopping trip and could have driven all the way to the French border without stopping in Stuttgart.

Her jaw tightened. "They stole everything. Helga and Herr Falk—they're stealing my clothing, my jewelry, my typewriter."

Peter sighed. "I know. My apartment and office will be ransacked."

She gave him a sympathetic look. "All your books."

"My research." His voice ground out.

"Your research?" She gasped. "It isn't in your car?"

A shadow passed over his eyes. "It's in my office at the university. I didn't have time to get it."

Evelyn stopped and stared at him. Everything in her wanted to order him to go back and fetch it, but it was too late. "Oh no. What did you lose?"

He gazed over her shoulder toward Munich. "My dissertation, my notes, my logbook. My recordings have been shipped to Harvard, but they're labeled with randomized numbers. Without the key in the logbook, they're useless. I have nothing."

"Oh no." It was her fault. If he hadn't had to rescue her, he could have rescued his material. And if she hadn't been so hungry for stories, he wouldn't have dug himself so deep into the Nazi Party that he needed to escape. She kept destroying people. First Magda Müller. Now Peter. "I—I'm so sorry."

Peter's gaze rushed back to her, and he gave her a little smile. "None of that. We've lost a lot, but we have cash, a car, our two brains, and the Lord watching over us. We'll be fine."

At the inn, Peter unlocked the car and stashed the boxes in the backseat. Evelyn climbed in the driver's seat.

Peter slid in beside her, opened the map, and pointed to the main road. "Drive up to here, then I'll take over. Even without my glasses, I can't miss the Autobahn. You can take over again when it gets dark."

Evelyn started the car, pulled onto the street, and gave him a teasing smile, eager to lighten the mood. "What's the matter, Lang? You don't like having a dame drive your car?"

"That isn't it." He squinted out the window, but he didn't smile. "We have no idea if the riots are spreading or stopping. We'll get on the Autobahn west of Munich, but what if they've set up roadblocks? What if they're looking for Jews to arrest? With my blond hair, I won't be pulled over."

Evelyn turned onto a wooded lane. "I could lie on the backseat."

"You'll need to ride in the trunk."

She gaped at him. "The trunk!"

"It's roomy, and it'd only be for—"

"No!" Her stomach tightened like a fist, like Warren's fist that day in New York, closing around her coat, shoving her into the trunk of his car, locking her in. The dark, the stink of gasoline fumes, the fury of being caged. "The trunk? You've got to be kidding. Absolutely not."

Peter arched his eyebrows. "It's only for two or three hours."

"I wouldn't do it for two minutes." Her gaze whipped between the road and that man beside her. "You're crazy if you think you can lock me in the trunk."

He scrunched up his face and groaned. "Why are you—why do you have to be so stubborn?"

"I will never get in that trunk." She flung her arm in that direction. "I'll lie on the floor in the back, with our coats over me."

"It's too dangerous. What if they stop us and look back there? Absolutely not."

Evelyn stomped on the brakes, turned off the car, shoved open her door, and got out. "Good-bye, Mr. Lang. I refuse to go one more mile with you."

"Evelyn!"

She opened the back door to get her rucksack and purse.

"Where do you think you're going?" Peter leaned over the seat. "You think you can get there by foot? Alone?"

She could barely see. She threw open boxes and stuffed items in her rucksack. "Yes."

"Evelyn . . ." His voice softened. "It's at least a hundred miles to Switzerland. Over the Alps. In November."

"Better than traveling with a man who thinks I belong in the trunk." Her voice shook. Broke.

Peter sighed. "All right. Lie on the floor. I'll cover you up. And we'll pray—pray hard no one stops us."

"No." She yanked the cord on her rucksack to close it.

"Evelyn Brand." His voice firmed up again. "We need each other. You need this car to get to the border, and I need your eyes. Like it or not, our chances of survival are higher together than apart."

Evelyn hauled in a breath and met his gaze unfiltered by eyeglasses—the glasses he'd lost fighting for her.

Something earnest and vulnerable swam in the blue of his gaze. "I need to get that list to the FBI, and I need your help."

Her throat filled and clogged shut. This wasn't Howard or Clark or Warren. This was Peter Lang, who had sacrificed his research and risked his neck to save her life. "Oh, Peter. I'm an idiot."

He lifted one shoulder and one corner of his mouth. "Maybe."

Evelyn dragged her gaze to the trunk, swallowing her fear. "I'll get in the trunk."

"No." He got out of the car, opened the back door on his side, and unbuttoned his black overcoat. "Take off your coat and lie on the floor."

"No. I'll get in the trunk."

On the other side of the car, Peter flung his arms wide, but a touch of amusement played on his lips. "Just this once would you listen to me?"

No more arguing. Evelyn shrugged off her coat and wiggled down between the seats. She placed her rucksack under her head for a pillow.

Peter draped one coat over her feet and one over her head, and he tucked them in beside her. "It doesn't look bad. I'm glad your coat is gray, not red."

Evelyn retreated under the heavy wool, her hands clenched under her chin. The door slammed, shaking the car, then Peter climbed in and started the engine.

The car rumbled down the lane, then turned and sped up.

Evelyn squeezed her eyes shut, her mind shut, but it was no use. It was all too much. She wasn't just an idiot. She was sharp and pointy and hurt the only person in this country who cared about her and wanted to help.

How could she be so thoughtless?

Tears burned over the bridge of her nose and across her cheek.

The Norwood brothers had conspired to trap her in Germany.

George Norwood had turned a mob against her. Otto von Albrecht wanted her dead, and he'd never even met her. Herr Falk had stolen everything she owned and kicked her out onto the street, not caring if she lived or died. They all wanted to silence her forever.

"Are you all right back there?" Peter asked.

Evelyn bit her lip. Had she been making noise crying? No, he was just being nice.

"I'm fine." No, she wasn't fine. Not at all.

She'd lashed out at Peter for no reason, at least none that he knew of.

The rucksack grew warm and damp beneath her cheek, but she deserved to be uncomfortable.

Howard and Clark had slapped her to subdue her. Peter had done so to protect her. Peter had told her to get in the trunk, not to cage her but to protect her.

A sob gulped out.

"Evelyn?"

She burrowed into the rucksack. "He—he locked me in the trunk."

"What? No. No, I didn't."

"Warren." Her voice cracked. "Howard and Clark slapped me to shut me up, to put me in my place. Warren—he locked me in his trunk."

"Who—who's Warren? The others?"

"Old boyfriends." She tugged off her glove and swiped at her slimy nose with the back of her hand. "I dated Warren when I was working in New York. One evening he came to take me out to dinner—only he had a surprise. He wanted to take me away for a weekend in Connecticut. Except I had an article due on Monday, so I declined."

Where on earth had she stashed her handkerchief? Her hands were as damp as her face now. "Warren was livid. He opened the trunk and ordered me to get my bag. I refused. I wasn't about to lose my job for him. So he said he was going to teach me a lesson. He shoved me into the trunk and drove to Connecticut."

"What? What was he thinking?"

"He thought I'd be subdued, see the error of my ways, quit my job, and stop pretending to be a man. But oh no. When we arrived, I told the innkeeper to call a cab to take me to the train station. I never saw Warren again."

"He was a fool." Peter's voice was hard and forceful.

"Yes." She sniffed. "A fool. I won't be caged. I won't allow it."

"Of course not. But I meant he was a fool for *wanting* to subdue you. Why would anyone want to do that?"

Evelyn's eyes stretched wide in her dark burrow of satin-lined wool that smelled of Peter, sophisticated yet woodsy.

A man like her father, good and kind. Papa let her be herself. Papa took pride in her spunk and her accomplishments.

How could she have forgotten such men existed?

THIRTY-TWO

The silver light of dawn turned golden, and Peter sat up from his makeshift bed of blanket and pillow on the floor of the Herzogs' guest room.

Soft breathing came from above him on the bed. Good. Evelyn had slept.

Sleeping in the same room as her felt strange, but for the sake of August and Renate Herzog, they were John and Evelyn Williamson, returning from their honeymoon in the Black Forest. Peter was using a false name so the Herzogs could honestly say they'd never met Peter Lang if the Gestapo asked questions.

Peter rubbed at his bruised ribs over his bruised heart. Three boyfriends had hurt Evelyn. No wonder she wanted nothing to do with men. Now that Peter had slapped her and told her to get in the trunk, he'd never stand a chance with her.

If Peter loved her, he'd let her be, even if it meant denying his feelings permanently.

None of that would matter if they couldn't get to France. He pushed aside the blanket. In his shirt, trousers, and stocking feet, he crawled to his rucksack and pulled out his map of western

239

Germany. Quietly, he spread it on the floor and sat cross-legged before it.

After General Richter's visit, Peter had spent hours in the university library, studying topographical maps of the border region and making notes. Back in his apartment, he'd marked up his own maps.

Of course, none of the maps told him the most crucial information—where German and French troops were posted.

"Good morning." Evelyn sat on the edge of the bed in her white blouse and gray skirt, her hair mussed and begging for his fingers to muss it even more.

Peter managed a brotherly smile. "Good morning."

"Your map?" She sat beside him on the floor with her legs folded to the side.

"Now's a good time to discuss this," he said in a low voice. "While the house is quiet."

Evelyn studied the map. "The red circles are where you want to cross?"

"Yes. We can't cross by car. We'd never make it past the customs inspection. Our names are certainly on some list. We have two options—crossing the Rhine in the Black Forest region or crossing through the Pfälzerwald in the Palatinate Range. Can you swim?"

"Not well."

"Then we'll go through the Pfälzerwald. This looks like a good spot—not many villages on the German side, but several on the French side. It's hilly and wooded, so I doubt the German defenses will be strong—little chance the French would attack there."

Evelyn traced the border with her slim finger. "What about French defenses? The Maginot Line covers the entire border."

"I'm not worried about that. They'd stop us before shooting. Since we're wearing civilian clothes and you're a woman, we won't look threatening. Then we tell our story—American newlyweds, we got lost hiking, you lost your passport, so sorry."

Her finger tapped on the red circle. "How close can we get?"

"We'll find out when we get there. The maps don't show many roads close to the border, but we'll get as close as we can. Looks like we'll have anywhere from ten to twenty-five miles to hike."

She frowned at the map. She'd been quiet on the ride to Stuttgart. Then she'd acted perky for the Herzogs, a happy bride clinging to Peter's arm and beaming at him. Beaming back hadn't been difficult.

Now she was quiet again.

"Are you all right?" he asked.

She shook her head. "I hate this, not being free."

"I know." Even in this house, he didn't feel free. Renate had welcomed them, but August had looked at them with suspicion.

Evelyn folded her arms in her lap, and her shoulders hunched forward. "I never realized how much I depended on the rule of law to protect my freedom. But here there is no law—only the will of the Führer."

Peter nudged her shoulder. "In a few days, we'll be in France, savoring freedom *and* order."

She gave him a feeble smile. "They go together well."

"They do." So did he and Evelyn, but he didn't dare say it.

She got up to her knees. "When do you want to leave?"

"Right after lunch." He folded the map. "I want to reach the border area before dark."

"We should buy more food. There's a grocery two blocks down."

Peter slipped the map into his rucksack. "Good idea. I'll go out while you write your story and call it in."

"Story?"

"On the pogrom."

She pushed up to her bare feet and went to the bureau. "I missed the press conferences, the press release."

"You saw it firsthand."

In the reflection in the bureau mirror, her face clouded. "I—I can't write that."

That would be difficult for her, and he sighed. "Maybe not fully, but you can write some of what you saw and heard."

Evelyn fluffed her curls. "I can't call it to London or New York. I'd have to wait for the operator to arrange the call. It can take hours, and it's expensive. I refuse to stick Renate with that bill."

"What about the Berlin bureau? Could you call it to them and—wait, no. What if the bureau's line is tapped?"

"It is. I'm sure of it." She jabbed bobby pins into her hair. "Renate's might be tapped too. I'm not making a single call."

Peter sighed. The sooner they left Germany, the better.

"Kristallnacht," the headline of the *Völkischer Beobachter* proclaimed in vicious black letters. *Kristallnacht*—crystal night, they'd dubbed it for all the broken glass on the sidewalks throughout Germany.

Peter studied the paper as he walked down the street. Over twenty thousand Jewish people had been thrown into concentration camps, and dozens had been killed "resisting arrest." Now Joseph Goebbels had ordered an end to the violence.

Good, since he was the man who had ordered a *start* to the violence.

His hands coiled around the paper. He wanted to crumple it up and throw it in the trash, but Evelyn would want to read it.

He tucked the paper under his arm and adjusted the string bag full of apples and more zwiebacks over his shoulder. With the fruit shortage, he couldn't believe he'd found apples.

Across the street, a sign for a women's clothing store hung askew. The store's windows were knocked out, and the interior lay in darkness and disarray.

What had happened to the owner? Was he among the thousands who had been beaten and arrested? Arrested for no crime except being a Jewish man?

242

They'd join those arrested earlier for the crime of being communists or socialists.

Peter's stomach heaved, and he walked faster. Not long ago he'd thought that wasn't a half-bad idea. He'd been totally wrong.

Communists who murdered deserved to be arrested—as did fascists who murdered. But to lock someone up because they disagreed with you? No. Wrong.

His shoes thumped on the pavement. The Nazis wanted to arrest Herr Gold and to kill Evelyn.

What if Peter hadn't arrived in time at the Golds'? At Evelyn's? What if Otto and his friends had overpowered Peter? What if the mob had beaten Evelyn to death?

His breath came hard and fast. *Thank you, Lord, for being there, for helping me save her.*

Peter's feet stalled and his breath stilled. Was God more present and more powerful on Kristallnacht than he'd been that night at Father's factory?

Of course not. God never changed. He was always present, always powerful, always good.

"Why?" he whispered and resumed his pace. Why had the Lord saved Evelyn and not his father?

He didn't know, but he was glad the Lord had used him to save Evelyn and the Golds. He offered up yet another prayer that the Golds would get to Bolivia.

"Peter Lang?" a man called ahead of him.

Peter stopped, muscles tense. He didn't know anyone in Stuttgart. He struggled to focus his blurry vision on the man while his feet readied to run.

"Peter! It is you." It was Klaus Metzger, Otto's best friend, but his grin said he hadn't heard what Peter had done.

Peter forced himself to relax and grin back. "What are you doing in Stuttgart?"

"My uncle passed away last week. I'm home for the funeral."

"I'm sorry."

"Thank you." Klaus dipped his round chin. "What are you doing in my hometown?"

He scrambled for an excuse. "I'm here for a symposium at the university."

"Good. Did you have to miss the excitement in Munich too?"

Peter's smile came at a high price. He gestured to the smashed-up shop he'd passed. "Looks like you had some excitement here as well."

Klaus let out a high-pitched laugh, then he sobered. "*Jawohl*. We did. But I missed the Putsch anniversary."

Peter gave a sympathetic murmur. "When do you return to Munich?"

"I will catch the afternoon train. I don't want to miss Friday evening at the Hofbräuhaus." With Otto. Where Klaus would tell Otto he'd seen Peter in Stuttgart—heading west.

"Wish I could be there," Peter said. "I'll be back Sunday."

"See you then." He snapped up a salute. "Heil, Hitler!"

Peter tipped his hat. He hoped he never had to hear that greeting again. "Auf Wiedersehen."

He strode down the sidewalk to the Herzog home. Otto would send out the alarm. Peter and Evelyn needed to leave at once.

THIRTY-THREE

PALATINATE RANGE, GERMANY
FRIDAY, NOVEMBER 11, 1938

Evelyn looped her rucksack straps over her shoulders and joined
Peter behind his car among the beeches and pines. They'd driven
as close to the border as they dared, then as deep into the woods
as the forest permitted.

Peter stood with gloved palms flat on the trunk of his black
Opel Admiral convertible, head bowed as if before a coffin at a
funeral. "I hate to do this."

Evelyn tucked in her lips, longing to rub his slumped shoulders.
"I know. It's a beautiful car." The next in a long line of sacrifices
he'd made—and an expensive one.

Peter leaned over and braced his hands. "Push."

Together, they shoved the car over the edge of a shallow ravine.
The Opel rolled down, snapping vegetation as it went.

Peter uprooted a fern. "Let's cover it with branches, buy us
some more time."

"All right." She gathered leafy branches and handed them to
him.

It was almost five thirty, and Klaus Metzger would be in Munich
by now. Peter said Otto and his friends met at the Hofbräuhaus

every Friday at seven. How long until Klaus mentioned seeing Peter? Otto would immediately call the police. How long would it take the police to track Peter and Evelyn's route? To discover the car that pointed the way?

The farther they could get before the Opel was discovered, the better.

After the car was somewhat concealed, Peter pulled the map and compass from his rucksack. "The sun will set by six, and the moon won't rise until nine. Let's go as far as we can in the twilight."

"After dark, we can take turns napping until the moon rises. Otherwise, we might not wake until morning."

"Good idea. Then we'll hike until sunrise." He folded the map into a square showing their area of the world. "We're about fifteen miles from the border, about twenty from the nearest French town. Of course, that's as the crow flies. We have rugged terrain ahead. We'll just head south and pray."

Evelyn buttoned her overcoat up to her neck. "I've been praying a lot lately."

"Let's do some more." Peter removed his hat and bowed his head. "Almighty Father, please lead us. We don't know what lies ahead, and we don't know what's coming behind us, but you do. Please keep us safe, conceal us from the enemy, and lead us into freedom. Amen."

"Amen."

Peter put on his rucksack and draped a rolled-up blanket around his neck, the blanket that had kept Evelyn toasty the night they'd slept in the car.

He handed Evelyn the compass. "You're the eyes of this unit. Lead on. Pick a landmark on the route and head toward that and nothing else."

Evelyn cradled the compass in her palm, found south, and forged into the woods toward a gnarled tree. She'd been hiking countless times, but always on trails and always by daylight. This would be different and far more dangerous.

She set as fast a pace as possible. Every rustle of leaves sounded like approaching footsteps. Every icy breeze felt like the breath of the Gestapo. Every snap of a twig sounded like a gunshot.

When she reached the gnarled tree, Evelyn checked the compass in the dimming light. For her next landmark, she chose an unusual rock formation shaped like a fat letter *T*. She slipped the compass in her pocket in case she fell.

"In the past few days, I've broken more laws and rules than I ever imagined," Peter said.

Evelyn glanced over her shoulder to see his satisfied smile. "You're only doing it to help others. No danger of you becoming a true rogue."

His smile grew. "I'll have to work on that."

After she pressed through a stand of trees, she located the rock again. "Please don't. The world needs men like you—men of order and justice, who follow the rules and stand up for what's right."

Peter didn't reply. It was probably best to keep quiet anyway.

She headed down a slope, scanning the trees and hillsides for sentries or buildings or fortifications. At the bottom ran a little stream, and Evelyn looked for a good place to hop across. She could make it, but it would be close.

"I'll go first." Peter leaped over, then stretched his hand to her.

She took his hand and jumped, landing squarely where she'd planned. Although she hadn't needed his help, he'd been there in case she'd slipped. She met his gaze. "Thank you."

Peter tipped his black fedora, his manners out of place in the wilderness. "Onward."

Evelyn picked her way up the slope, bracing herself on trees as she climbed. The world did need more men like Peter Lang.

Maybe she needed him too.

Mother had always said Evelyn was too independent for a man, too hard to handle. Evelyn's previous boyfriends had proven Mother's point.

Loose leaves gave way beneath her shoe, and she grabbed a tree trunk to catch herself.

"Careful," Peter said. "I didn't pack crutches in my rucksack."

She forced a light laugh but didn't turn to him. The last thing she wanted was for him to see the turmoil on her face.

Peter wasn't like those men. He treated her with kindness. He asked her opinion and listened to her suggestions, unfazed by her intelligence or her strong views.

In a thinning, Evelyn paused and plotted the best route to the rock.

For so long she'd resisted depending on Peter, thinking it would make her weak.

But Peter depended on her—and he was far from weak. He leaned on her because he respected her and trusted her.

She respected and trusted him too. He'd earned it through his actions and character.

When Evelyn reached the rock, she rested her hand on the cool sandstone as she rounded its mass.

She could depend on the Lord for the same reasons and to a far greater extent. The Lord deserved her trust because of who he was and what he'd done.

Leaning didn't make her weaker. It made her stronger.

THIRTY-FOUR

Peter's breath puffed silver-white as he followed Evelyn over the shoulder of yet another wooded hill in the moonlight. In the past two and a half nights of hiking, how far had they come? Had they stayed on course?

The villages they'd passed were too small for his map, and they'd skirted around them from too far a distance to read signs that might orient them.

Evelyn held back a low-hanging branch for Peter. She was doing so well. She kept a solid pace and never griped about sore feet or the cold or fatigue. Since Peter suffered from all three, she surely did as well.

Several times on the journey, they'd heard suspicious sounds—people, animals, who knew? Each time, they'd taken cover and hunkered under the blanket until the sounds passed.

Peter stepped over a little ravine. How long would it take to reach France? He'd planned for four nights and they were rationing their food to last six, but what if it took longer? With a winding route through rugged terrain, picking their way in the moonlight, they only covered a few miles each night.

The moon was deserting them as an ally. Each night it rose about an hour later, and each night a fraction more had been shaved away. In about a week, it would rise too close to sunrise to permit sufficient hiking time. Then they'd have to choose between the dangers of hiking in full dark—or full light.

"Break?" Evelyn asked.

Peter angled his wristwatch toward the faint moonlight—one thirty. They'd been hiking for two hours. "Yes, it's time."

"This is a good spot." A cleft between hills, well wooded.

Peter sank behind a bank of ferns. His feet screamed to be released from his shoes, but if he listened to them, he'd never get his shoes back on again.

He'd moved the list of American Nazi sympathizers from his shoe to his shirt pocket in case he stepped in a stream. If the Nazis caught him, he was dead, whether or not they found the list.

Evelyn pulled an apple from her rucksack.

Peter sliced it with his Swiss Army knife and gave her half. "Lord, we thank thee for thy bounty."

Evelyn flipped up a smile. "Amen."

Every morning and evening, they each had a few zwiebacks and a slice of hard sausage. Twice during the night, they split an apple. If they didn't reach French civilization by the end of the fourth night, Peter would suggest half rations.

Evelyn nibbled her apple. "I've been thinking about your research."

"My research?" He thought of it as little as possible. Besides, right now the only thing that mattered was getting Evelyn and the list to the US.

"The recordings aren't a waste. You'll recognize the voices."

"Yes, except the control group under the other instructor at Harvard." He wiggled his toes. "But the fact that I recognize the voices introduces bias."

"At least you could assign them to the four groups—at Harvard or at Munich, with your instruction or without. You could pair each student's two recordings and have another professor label them as before or after."

Peter took tiny bites of apple to fool his brain into thinking the meal was larger. "I see what you're saying, but it requires assuming the students improved."

"A reasonable assumption."

"An assumption nonetheless. Also, if I assign students to groups, I could theoretically assign those who improved the most to my instructional groups. No. Without the logbook, it's all worthless."

Evelyn leaned back against the slope and stretched out her legs. "There has to be a way."

Peter had to smile at her optimism. "Even if I could assign the students to groups, I'd still be missing the fourth group, the current junior year students, those who would have both immersion and my instruction in their first semester abroad. I can only obtain that data in Germany, and I can never return to Germany until the regime changes. That won't happen anytime soon."

Evelyn scowled at the ferns. "They'll understand, won't they? The faculty at Harvard?"

"Probably." Peter shrugged, and pain zinged in his shoulder. He'd twisted it the day before when he'd slipped and grabbed a branch. "That won't change anything. My dissertation wouldn't stand up to academic rigor. They can't accept it. I'll lose my fellowship because I abandoned my teaching in Munich. I'll be removed from the PhD program."

"That isn't fair." Anger ruffled her voice.

"It is indeed fair." He kept his voice low, not hard to do with low spirits. "I can't finish this project, and I can't start a new one. Any research in my field requires time in Germany."

Evelyn turned the wedge of apple in her hand. "What will you do?"

Peter took another bite, although he'd lost his appetite. "I'll offer my language services to the US Army. But without a PhD, I doubt they'd be interested."

"The German army was."

"They saw my techniques in action." He poked a finger inside his left heel to relieve pressure on a blister. "I only have one option—get my teaching certificate and teach German in high school."

"That would be nice."

Peter nodded to convince himself. It wasn't the professorial position he'd worked for. He wouldn't write textbooks and lead seminars on how to teach diction. He wouldn't revolutionize teaching foreign language.

"I'm sorry." Evelyn's voice came out soft and soothing.

Maybe it was the fatigue or the hunger or the hopelessness of his situation, but something crumbled inside and left him exposed. "My father. He was a great man."

Evelyn murmured in understanding.

"He founded a successful company, got elected to the House of Representatives, and had enormous influence. My brothers . . ." Peter gnawed off a chunk of apple. "Richard has taken Father's seat in the House, Karl runs the company, and Albert will soon be a lawyer, a judge, on a high court someday. They're expanding our father's influence. But me? I'll teach small classes, and most of the students won't even care about the subject. My influence will be minuscule."

Evelyn dug a hole in the dirt with the heel of her shoe, and she buried her apple core. "You had quite an influence with your junior year students. I saw you getting to know them, and I saw how they looked up to you."

"There were only thirty-four of them." He bit off the last chunk of apple.

With care, Evelyn arranged leaves to hide the burial site. "My articles are read by thousands, but only for fifteen minutes or so. Most will forget what I wrote by the end of the day. I rarely change people's opinions, much less their lives. My influence is broad, but shallow."

Peter dug his own apple grave.

"But you, Peter Lang—your influence might be narrow, but it'll be *deep*. Deep and profound and for great good. With your character, you can change lives." In the moonlight, her eyes shone with conviction.

He stared at her as his insides shifted around. She might be correct, but would he ever be content with that life, with that narrow influence? If he failed to become content, that would be a sign of arrogance. And he hated arrogance.

"Are you all right?" she asked.

He poked the bitter apple core deep into the earth and covered it. Maybe it would grow to produce sweet fruit. "Someday I will be. Thanks for trying to cheer me up."

"Just returning the favor." Her smile gleamed warm, almost fond. Then she nudged his knee. "Come on, Lang. We have a long way to go."

"We certainly do." He pushed himself to standing and adjusted the rucksack and blanket. His leg muscles protested, but he hushed them. Those muscles would be dead along with the rest of him if German soldiers or police caught them.

Evelyn led the way through the forest of spindly bare trees. Leaves littered the ground, making it impossible to move quietly.

The moonlight dimmed, and gray clouds scuttled across the inky sky. No rain had fallen during their journey, but rain was inevitable in November.

A breeze fluttered close to the freezing point, and Peter shoved his fedora lower on his head.

A sound drifted ahead of them and above.

Human voices.

Peter tapped Evelyn's shoulder hard, three times, their signal. She faced him, eyes wide.

He unfurled the blanket and glanced around for cover—a clump of ferns. They sneaked over, worked their way in among the fronds, and pulled the blanket over them.

Peter hunched over his knees, over his clenched hands, his nose inches from the musty soil. *Lord, blind them. Blind them.*

The voices grew louder. Two male voices. Speaking German.

Peter grimaced. *Please, Lord.*

"I don't believe you, *Gefreiter*," a man said.

Gefreiter. A corporal. A German soldier. Peter sank lower into the dirt.

"I heard voices," the corporal said. "One was a woman."

Pressed to Peter's side, Evelyn trembled. Peter clutched her hand, and she didn't push him away.

"Who would be stupid enough to walk these woods at night? This close to the border, they'd get shot by both us and the French. You're hearing things."

"I'm not." Was the corporal's voice nearer or farther?

Peter squeezed Evelyn's hand and prayed the brown blanket and the ferns and the darkness and the hand of the Lord would conceal them.

"I heard them over there."

Probably where they'd taken their break. They'd buried their trash well, hadn't they? If the soldiers found a fresh apple core, they'd sound the alarm and scour the area.

"Come out and play, little French soldiers," the German soldier called.

"One's a woman."

"The French all sound like women."

They laughed together, but their voices sounded fainter and from behind them now.

The soldiers had passed Peter and Evelyn, and a long breath poured out. They needed to lie low for a while, then proceed as quietly as possible.

Evelyn's trembling diminished, but she didn't release Peter's hand.

He loved her more each day. They were good together. Did she notice it too?

However, she'd made herself clear. She wanted her independence. As soon as this journey concluded, she'd stop wanting him near.

Peter savored the feeling of her thin gloved hand in his. He'd never stop wanting her.

THIRTY-FIVE

Evelyn awoke, snug and warm, her pillow rising and falling in a gentle rhythm, and she smiled. Her head rested on Peter's shoulder, her arm draped over his stomach, and the blanket wrapped them in a cocoon.

The first day, she'd accepted the position only out of the necessity of keeping warm. It had been unbelievably, painfully awkward. But by now, the fifth day, it felt marvelous.

Soft afternoon light filtered through the fern fronds screening their spot under an outcropping of golden sandstone.

Despite the exhaustion and hunger and gnawing fear, something about the journey felt oddly idyllic.

Her lower arm cramped, and she shifted position. Peter's breathing hitched, and he rubbed his eyes with the rumble in his throat he made when he awoke.

"Good morning-evening." Evelyn pushed up to sitting. "Did my sharp points wake you up?"

"Huh?" Peter sat cross-legged, bowing his head under the stony roof, his hair tousled and only one eye open. Goodness, he was adorable when he was sleepy.

She didn't even want to know what her hair looked like. She

opened her rucksack and pulled out a half-empty zwieback box and a stump of sausage. They were on half rations now to extend their food another four days. "Would you like sausage now or at the end of the day?"

"Now." He flipped aside the blanket, pulled out his knife, cut off two slices, and said grace.

She passed him three zwiebacks and took two herself, careful to conceal she'd taken fewer. Although he was larger and needed more sustenance, he always split things in perfect halves.

"Coffee?" He passed her the canteen of cold water, one thing they never lacked.

"Thank you. Please pass the cream." She took a swig.

A smile dug into his cheek. "Don't worry. You aren't bony yet."

She passed back the canteen. "Bony?"

He took a drink and screwed the lid on. "You asked if your sharp points woke me. I'm saying you don't have any."

"It was a joke. Men always say I'm all sharp angles. They can't stand those points poking at them." Evelyn bit into a zwieback, careful not to lose precious crumbs.

Peter murmured and chewed on a cracker.

What a ridiculous thing for her to say, and she suppressed a groan.

He narrowed his eyes at the ferns shielding them. "That's why they wanted to tame you. To grind down those points."

"Yes." The word leaked out. As long as she'd known him, she'd wanted him to see she'd never be soft and rounded. Now that he finally saw it, sadness flooded deep inside her.

Peter popped the rest of the zwieback in his mouth, shoved the blanket under his crossed legs, and drew in the dirt.

What was he doing? She leaned closer.

He sat up straight. A star was engraved in the soil with five sharp points.

Peter traced the star again, deeper. "Stars shine. Why would anyone want to turn a star into a circle?"

And she loved him.

The knowledge lit up inside her, brighter than any star. Sliced into her, sharper than any sword.

"The sun's about to set." Peter packed his rucksack.

Evelyn had only half heard what he'd said, blinded and bleeding from the truth. "Oh. All right."

"I'd like to see how far we can get in the twilight. The moon won't rise until three in the morning if I estimated correctly. That'll give us only five hours of hiking before dawn." He motioned her off the blanket, and she scooted.

Crouching, Peter shook out the blanket. "I think we're close. Fewer pines and more deciduous trees. The slope is less steep, and the hills are opening up."

"I—I hope so." She fumbled for her hat, inspected it for bugs, and put it on.

"I'll scout. Be right back." He shoved on his hat and ducked out of their cozy hideaway.

Evelyn dug a hole, relieved herself, and buried the evidence. Then she packed and made sure they'd left no trace.

Only the star remained. She couldn't bear to erase it, so she spread leaves on top.

A rustling outside, and she stilled.

Peter pulled aside the fronds. "I think we're close. Let's go."

Evelyn passed him his rucksack and blanket, crawled out, and put on her own rucksack, much lighter than when they'd ventured out.

Peter pointed down a valley. "If that leads anywhere near south . . ."

Compass in hand, Evelyn waited for the needle to settle. "South-southeast. Let's follow it."

She set out in the golden light of the setting sun. When they passed the rock outcropping, she peered into the valley. "There's a road down there. Do we dare?"

"Let's get closer and travel in parallel. Roads lead to towns."

Evelyn perked up and forged ahead. "On a road we could travel even in full dark. Less risk of getting off course, of falling. If someone comes, we could take cover."

"Great idea. Let's do it." Enthusiasm lit Peter's voice.

They hiked as quietly as the undergrowth permitted, angling down to that very civilized road. But was it a French road or German?

Peter followed. Never once had he grumbled about a woman leading him.

No wonder she'd fallen in love. He accepted her, points and all. He used his power to protect her, not to restrict her. He was kind, but never condescending.

Evelyn stepped over a fallen beech branch. *But what do I do about him, Lord?*

If the American News Service didn't fire her for disappearing for so long, they'd give her a new foreign assignment.

With her crazy career, how could a romance survive? Much less a marriage. A family.

It wouldn't. She couldn't have both. She'd have to choose.

Evelyn glanced behind her in the graying evening. Peter gave her a smile and a flick of his chin, signaling her to carry on.

Why did she assume she even had a choice? Although Peter had once been romantically interested in her, their relationship had shifted to friendship, to a brotherly-sisterly closeness.

If only she hadn't pushed him away so many times.

A spot of white by the road, and she raised one hand. "I think that's a road sign. I'll take a look."

They eased down to the road, and Evelyn peeked from behind a tree—everything looked nice and quiet. She stepped out and read the sign in the distance. "Lembach. Wissembourg. Bourg with an *ou*, not a *u*. Peter! It's French!" She laughed for joy.

"Lembach? That's on my map. We're in France!" He scrambled to the road and scooped her into a hug, big and secure.

She never wanted to leave.

But Peter broke loose. "Race you." He took off running.

Evelyn chased him, laughing, but the blisters on her feet flamed. She slowed to a walk.

Peter spun to her, arms wide. "Come on, Brand. I want dinner and a bath and a good night's sleep."

"You need my francs to do it, so you'll have to wait for me." Thank goodness she'd never exchanged her francs for Reichsmarks. They probably had enough to make it to Paris. If not, they could wire home for more money.

They walked side by side down the road. The forested hills gave way to open rolling countryside, lightly wooded.

Peter walked backward and made a throwing motion. "Auf Wiedersehen, Deutschland! Auf Wiedersehen, you Nazis and Otto von Albrecht and George Norwood. Good riddance."

A sudden shiver, and Evelyn tucked her hands in her coat pockets. "You don't think they'll follow us, do you? They must have figured out we're going to France."

Peter marched down the road, his jaw forward. "The Nazis have no jurisdiction here. George might suspect we're going to Aubrey's, but he won't follow. He isn't stupid enough to take us on. Or brave enough. He's a coward." His voice registered the hardness once reserved for communists, for the men who'd murdered his father.

Evelyn's heart sank. One more thing he'd lost—a good friend and a lifetime of trust.

Peter nudged her with his elbow. "Just think. In only a few days, you can go to the embassy in Paris and this nightmare will be over."

She smiled for his sake, but her heart drifted even lower. Peter needed to sail for America to turn in the list to the FBI, but Evelyn would have to wait for her passport and to hear whether the ANS would reassign her or fire her.

They rounded a corner, and lights shone in the distance. A town.

Blisters or not, she picked up speed.

"You'll have to do the talking, since I don't speak French," Peter said. "Remember our story."

Lost honeymooners. That story might allow the two of them to travel with only one good passport. Of course, they'd have to share a room to bolster that story and to save francs.

They entered the town, full of quaint white buildings with half-timbering near the rooflines. Signs in French soothed her.

An older couple strolled toward them.

Peter sucked in a breath, then let out a self-conscious chuckle.

Evelyn grinned at him. After being on alert so long, it was difficult to act normally.

She turned her smile to the couple. *"Bonsoir. Où est un hôtel?"*

The gentleman eyed her from bedraggled hair to snagged stockings, then gave directions.

The inn was a half-timbered darling of a building, and Evelyn rang the bell.

A plump little man with a wreath of silver hair opened the door.

Evelyn launched into her story. They were Americans on their honeymoon. They'd gotten lost while hiking, and she'd lost her passport—how could she have been so careless?—and they needed to get to Paris as soon as possible to straighten it out. She had money—thank goodness, she hadn't lost that. Did they have a room?

"Oui, madame." He introduced himself as Monsieur Staebell and ushered them inside, where an equally plump little woman joined him.

Evelyn let herself fall apart, and she poured out her story again, how they were so tired and hungry and filthy.

Peter kept his arm around her shoulder, murmuring consolation to her.

The couple fussed over Peter and Evelyn, and within minutes they'd paid for a room and found out how to get to Paris.

Madame Staebell led them into the kitchen, sat them at a table, and served up fragrant bowls of stew and bread. Peter thanked the Lord for his bounty with fervor, and they ate. The stew filled the cold, empty places inside her.

After they finished, Monsieur Staebell led them up steep, winding stairs to their room, tiny but already warmed by a stove.

When the innkeeper left, Peter closed the door. "You are an exceptional actress. Slightly scary."

Evelyn laughed. "Go take your bath. Madame Staebell promised to bring clean nightclothes, so toss your dirty things out of the bathroom and I'll start laundry."

Peter hung his hat and coat on a peg. "I can wash my own things."

The relief of the day flicked up a smile, and she set her hands on her hips. "Stop being so stubborn and independent. Just once would you listen to me?"

A brilliant smile of recognition broke free. He sat on a chair, tugged off his shoes with a loud groan, and transferred the dangerous list from his shirt pocket back into his shoe.

Why was he so slow in crafting a comeback? She cocked her head to the side.

Peter opened the door and shot her a mischievous smile. "What a good little wife you are." He ducked out as if he expected her to throw something at him.

Maybe she should have. Just for fun.

After she took off her coat and hat, Evelyn opened the rucksacks and pulled out their suits, last worn on Kristallnacht and badly rumpled. She'd have to press them. For now, she shook them out and hung them up.

She peeked into the hallway. A pile of clothing rested outside the bathroom door, and she fetched it.

Madame Staebell came up the stairs with white linen folded over her pudgy arm. "Here are nightclothes for you and your husband."

"*Merci*. You are so kind." Evelyn took the fragrant clean garments. "May I borrow an iron?"

Madame Staebell clucked her tongue. "Let me. I will press your clothes."

Evelyn stared at her, and her throat swelled. After so many people had tried to hurt her, kindness from a stranger felt foreign.

Madame Staebell clucked again and motioned with her fingers.

"*Merci.*" After Evelyn passed the woman the wrinkled suits, she locked the door and shed her stinking clothes. She threw away the shredded stockings and slipped on the nightgown. Voluminous white folds fell to her knees.

She hated to put on a clean nightgown before her bath, but she needed to start the wash. She filled the sink in the room and washed the underthings, her good stockings and blouses, and Peter's socks and shirts.

When she'd scrubbed away the smell of Germany and the journey, she hung the laundry around the stove to dry.

Poor Peter would hate the mess, but she had no choice.

The doorknob jiggled. A knock. "Evelyn?"

She unlocked it.

Peter stepped in, damp and clean smelling and clad only in a towel about his waist.

Evelyn couldn't breathe. It was like standing in front of one of the statues in the Munich art museum, perfectly sculpted Aryan masculinity, but alive and breathing and Peter.

"Something to wear?" she heard him say.

"Oh yes." She darted to the bed and handed him the nightshirt.

"Thanks." He went off to the corner and turned his back to her—just as impressive as his front—and pulled on the nightshirt. "No pants?"

"Uh, no."

"It isn't very—pardon me." He dropped the towel. "It isn't very long."

No, it wasn't. It covered everything that needed to be covered, but only fell mid-thigh. She chuckled. "You're showing more leg than you did in your lederhosen."

He sent her a mock glare. "Go take your bath. You stink."

"What a sweet little husband you are." She blew him a kiss and headed to the bathroom.

Soon she sank into warm, soapy heaven. She scrubbed her itchy scalp and nursed her battered feet. Only when the water cooled did she dry herself and put on the tent of a nightdress.

In their room, Peter lay on his back on the floor in a makeshift bed of blanket and pillow, his hands behind his head and his eyes closed.

She had a big soft bed, which wasn't fair to him. Sitting on the side of the bed, she took off the towel around her head and squeezed her hair dry.

"Lights?" Peter said, his eyes still closed.

Evelyn pulled the chain on the bedside lamp. "Good night."

"Good night."

She climbed into downy softness with layers of blankets and quilts and warmth. Yet not as snug as she'd been lying beside Peter.

Peter, who was lying all alone on the hard floor.

"You don't have to sleep on the floor," she said. "There's plenty of room up here."

A long, silent moment. "Thanks. I'll stay down here." His voice sounded pinched.

Goodness gracious! In the darkness, she clapped her hands over her face. What on earth had she been thinking? "I am so sorry. I don't know what I was thinking. That was completely, horribly inappropriate—"

"Sweet," he said. "It was completely, horribly sweet of you."

Her face scrunched up under the pressure of her hands. "Thank you." Her voice squeaked out.

"Besides . . ." His voice took on a teasing lilt. "I'm flattered that you invited me into your bed."

Evelyn gasped and slapped her hands down onto the covers. "That is not what I meant. Aren't you sure of yourself!"

He laughed, long and rolling and hearty, the first good laugh she'd heard from him in weeks.

"You stinker." She wrenched her pillow from under her head and threw it at him.

"Two pillows. My, my. You really *are* sweet. Thank you."

"Peter!" She managed to talk through the laughter. "Give it back."

"Good night, Evie."

She settled back onto the mattress. "My name isn't Evie."

"It suits you."

No, it didn't. An Evie was soft and rounded. An Evie would climb out of bed, kiss him, tell him she loved him, and thank him for all he'd done for her. Evelyn couldn't do that.

She rolled onto her back. Even if she couldn't do all of that, she could do the most important part. "I haven't thanked you enough for all you've done."

"You don't have—"

"Yes, I do. You saved my life, you've given up everything you own, you've lost your research and your career, and you've been kind and good to me each and every minute. I want you to know how much I appreciate it." Her mouth dried out. "How much I appreciate you."

He lay so still for so long.

She grimaced. Had he fallen asleep? Or had he realized she'd fallen in love and was figuring out how to let her down gently?

"You're welcome." His voice sounded gravelly. "It's been an honor, and I'd do it again in a heartbeat."

He would, wouldn't he? She nestled down with her head flat on the mattress. She didn't mind the lack of a pillow. Not for him.

A whishing sound, and the pillow landed on her hip. "Good night, Evie."

"Good night, Peter." *Good night, my love.*

THIRTY-SIX

HAGUENAU, FRANCE
FRIDAY, NOVEMBER 18, 1938

In the train station, Peter stood with his hand on Evelyn's shoulder as she rattled off a flurry of French. For a composed woman, she played a flustered damsel with remarkable ease.

Every time the poor ticket agent started to turn the page in Peter's passport, probably looking for the French transit visa Peter didn't have, Evelyn set her hand on the passport and launched another litany, most likely about newlyweds and lost passports and—were those tears in her eyes? My, she was good.

The ticket agent looked as flustered as Evelyn, and soon he handed her two tickets.

"*Merci!*" Evelyn pressed her hand to her heart and looked up to Peter. "We have tickets to Paris."

"Thank you. *Merci*." Peter deliberately sounded as American as possible. He might not speak French, but he could hear the diction and music of the language, and he could probably reproduce the accent without much effort.

"Come along, darling." Evelyn took his arm and led him out of the depot.

A streamlined locomotive pointed its rounded nose west. On

the platform, passersby gave Peter and Evelyn second looks—their grungy rucksacks didn't belong with their neatly pressed suits. Thank goodness it was warm enough not to wear their overcoats, which were filthy.

After Evelyn purchased a newspaper, they climbed the steps to their car, stashed rucksacks and coats in the overhead rack, and settled in.

"I've been thinking," Evelyn whispered. She slipped her hand in his and peered down the aisle. "We should act like newlyweds in case the conductor asks for our papers along with our tickets."

"Agreed." He squeezed her hand and gave her a loving look, which she returned.

His heart strained. For her, it was pretense, but Peter could finally drop all pretense.

In a few minutes, the train pulled away from the station.

Evelyn disengaged her hand and opened the newspaper. "Shall I translate for you?"

"Yes, please." He draped his arm around her shoulder, and she nestled up to his side. So natural and comfortable, yet it wasn't real.

"Stop me if a headline grabs you." Evelyn flipped pages and read headlines, all about France. "Here! Something about Germany. Oh! You won't believe this."

"What?" He tried to make sense of the words—so many vowels.

"Boy, I'm glad I'm in a free country again and can speak my mind." She jabbed her finger at a headline. "Germany has blamed the Kristallnacht violence—on the Jews! They're fining the Jews for the damage—one billion Reichsmarks—one-fifth of all Jewish assets. That's why they wanted the Jews to register their assets back in April—so they could steal them. I can't believe it."

A groan collapsed Peter's chest. "Sadly, I can." Hatred was never satisfied. The more it ate, the more it hungered.

"Oh no." Her voice diminished. "More—even more antisemitic laws. The Decree on the Exclusion of Jews from German Economic Life. They're banned from operating stores or businesses and from the trades."

Peter squeezed his eyes shut. They'd already been banned from the professions. They'd be left with manual labor, if they could get it.

"That's not all. They're banned from Aryan cultural events and theaters and hospitals and . . . and schools. I can't stand this. I can't." Evelyn turned a page and frowned at the articles. "The world is doing nothing. Look—Britain and France clucked their tongues, and Roosevelt—all he did was recall our ambassador."

"That's better than nothing." Peter shrugged. "Hitler wants recognition on the world stage, and the president is depriving him of that."

"We need to do more." Embers burned in Evelyn's eyes. "Germany's economy is highly dependent on American cash and resources and industry. We need to cut them off."

"I agree, but American companies would disagree."

"You have to talk to them. You have friends in business, in government. Talk to them."

"I will." Her belief in him inflated his chest. He smiled, enjoying the nearness of her pretty face. "And you have to write about it."

Her shoulders shrank in his embrace. "I don't know if I can."

"You can and you must. I've never known you to shy away from a challenge. You're a star. Stars shine."

And those eyes shone at him, wide and luminous, searching for confidence—from him.

He pressed a kiss to her nose. He couldn't help it. Besides, it fit with the role of husband. "Your articles on the Munich Conference were insightful and thought-provoking. You'll write something great about Kristallnacht."

Evelyn glanced out the window to the wooded landscape whishing by. "It's too late."

"For a news article, it is. But you have a bigger story. You no longer have to appease Goebbels and his propaganda ministry. You're free to write the stories you had to repress. I envision one of those features you see in *Collier's* or the *Atlantic Monthly*. A book even."

"A book?"

"I'd read it. Pretty exciting stuff. Especially the part about the dashing graduate student playing spy."

Evelyn laughed and elbowed him in the ribs. Lightly. Then her mouth firmed, and her gaze darted around. "I do have your notes."

"My notes?"

"From the Nazi Party meetings. I couldn't use most of the material, but I transcribed your notes and reworded them and burned the originals to protect you."

"Thanks. I hadn't thought about that." He frowned. "You have them? Where?"

"In my purse, in the lining with the cash. After the passport switch, I transcribed your notes in the tiniest shorthand I could manage. It fit on a few sheets of paper."

"You're incredible." It was all he could do not to kiss her for real.

Evelyn patted the purse by her side. "You took a lot of risks getting this information."

"Now you can use it. Say, that really would make a good book, complete with an exciting ending with Nazis and Norwood on our tail."

"No." She shook her head hard. "I can't write about Norwood unless he's convicted. We don't even have enough of a case to get him arrested."

Of course, they did. His mind whirled over the evidence—how George blamed Evelyn for his job loss, Charles's position in the passport office, Peter's phone call to George on Kristallnacht, the timing of Otto's attack on Evelyn. Motive, means, opportunity.

But nothing else. The only concrete evidence was the false passport—with no proof of where it came from.

Peter let out a long groan. "It's crystal clear to us, but it wouldn't stand up in court."

"No." She folded her arms around her stomach. "We can only pray his anger simmers down, and that he never realizes we figured out what he did."

Peter's own anger bubbled to a boil. George had better pray he never saw Peter again.

Evelyn drew her purse onto her lap and pulled out a notepad.

"Taking notes?" Peter asked. "That's my little star."

She glared at him from under the brim of her hat.

Peter gazed at the ceiling of the passenger car. "I think I shall call you Twinkles."

"Twinkles?" The word warped with disgust.

"Twinkle, twinkle, little star."

"Absolutely not. It's bad enough you call me Evie."

He glanced around at the passengers. "Newlyweds should have pet names for each other."

"Then I'll call you Baloney, because you're full of it."

Peter laughed. "You write. I'll nap." He leaned his head on the seatback and slipped his hat over his face.

"Go ahead. Your snoring has a soothing effect."

He lifted his hat enough to scowl at her. "I don't snore."

She smiled. "If that's what you want to believe . . ."

Peter lowered his hat and filled it with a contented sigh.

If only this were real. But it wasn't. When they reached Paris, the marriage charade would end, and she'd leave his arms. When they reached America, she'd leave his life.

Evelyn Brand needed freedom, and out of love for her, he'd grant it.

Paris

In Paris's tony 16th *arrondissement*, golden lights shone from the windows of a four-story house of creamy stone. Paul Aubrey came from money, married into money, earned money—and it showed.

"I think he'll have room for us." Peter led Evelyn up the steps to the front door.

She clung to her rucksack. "I hope so, because we're out of cash."

Peter rang the bell. In a moment, a butler opened the door.

The man came straight from central casting, with sleepy dark eyes, slicked-back dark hair, and a thin mustache. *"Bonsoir, monsieur et madame."*

Peter stilled. For some reason, he'd thought everyone in the Aubrey home would speak English.

"Bonsoir," Evelyn said. Then a string of vowels and "Monsieur Aubrey" and more vowels and "Peter Lang."

"Oui, madame." The butler admitted them to a high-ceilinged foyer of gleaming marble, then disappeared into a room to the left.

Soft conversation, then footsteps, then Paul Aubrey appeared in the doorway wearing a sweater and a big grin. "Peter? What on earth are you doing here?"

Peter shook his Harvard chum's hand. Aubrey stood only an inch or two shorter than Peter, with smooth brown hair and the kind of smile that made others smile even when they didn't want to. "You haven't changed a bit, old boy."

Aubrey laughed and eyed Peter from head to foot. "I can't say the same about you. Where's our old bean?"

"Bean?" Evelyn asked.

"String bean," Peter grumbled. "Evelyn, this is my friend Paul Aubrey. Aubrey, this is Miss Evelyn Brand, a correspondent with the American News Service."

"It's a pleasure to meet you." Aubrey shook Evelyn's hand. "Come on in. Simone's kissing the baby good night. She'll be down shortly."

Aubrey led them into a large sitting room with a parquet floor and tall windows framed by golden drapes. "Have you eaten?"

Peter and Evelyn sat on a dark red sofa and exchanged a glance.

On the train they'd eaten their last zwiebacks and apple, but this late at night, asking for dinner would be rude.

"Your silence means no." Aubrey chuckled, returned to the foyer, and summoned the butler. More French, then he sat on the other sofa and frowned. "I wish you'd called. We would have prepared rooms for you. You're staying with us, aren't you?"

"I hope so." Peter resisted the urge to put his arm around Evelyn—he no longer had an excuse. "We're out of money."

The frown deepened. "It isn't like you to be unprepared."

"We left Germany in a hurry."

Aubrey leaned his forearms on his knees. "What's going on?"

Peter hesitated, lacing his fingers together. "Have you heard from George Norwood?"

"Peter, you shouldn't," Evelyn said.

"From George?" Aubrey leaned back in his chair and studied them. "Not in several months. Why?"

"Peter . . ." She all but growled at him.

He patted her hands, folded on her knees, but kept his gaze on Aubrey. "If he should call, don't tell him we're in Paris. Don't mention us at all."

"What is going on?" Aubrey's voice hardened.

"I thought I heard voices." An elegant brunette strolled in, speaking English with a French accent and an amused tone. "Why did you not mention having guests, my dear?"

"I didn't know they were coming." Aubrey stood and introduced Peter and Evelyn to his wife, Simone. "They'll be staying with us."

Simone clasped her hands together. "*Magnifique!* I shall find Claudette and have her make up your rooms."

"I'll go with you." Evelyn grabbed both rucksacks and headed out.

Peter took his seat again. Something told him Evelyn didn't want to hear the story any more than Peter wanted to tell it.

But tell it he did, and while he did, Aubrey's expression turned from confusion to disbelief to shock to horror. Peter shared those feelings.

At Harvard, Peter and George and Aubrey and Henning had been inseparable, a fraternity within the fraternity. And Peter's friendship with George ran back to childhood summers at the shore. To think an old friend was capable of such cruelty—it shredded him inside.

Aubrey sat with his fingers splayed across his mouth. Slowly, he lowered his hand. "You and Miss Brand may stay with us as long as you need."

The butler stepped into the sitting room and addressed Aubrey.

"Your dinner is ready," Aubrey said to Peter. "Xavier will summon the ladies."

"Thanks." His stomach protested the emptiness, especially with savory smells wafting from the adjacent room.

Aubrey showed Peter toward that room, then stopped and held out his hand for a handshake.

Odd at this point in the evening, but Peter obliged.

Aubrey grasped his hand hard, his brown eyes full of emotion. "I'm proud to know you."

"Me? Why?"

Aubrey chuckled and led Peter into the dining room. "That, old bean, is exactly why."

THIRTY-SEVEN

"Where have you been, Miss Brand?" Hamilton Chase's voice boomed through the wires from London to Paul Aubrey's bookshelf-lined study. "No one's heard a word from you in almost two weeks—not Keller, not New York, and certainly not me. Do you know how many big stories you've missed?"

Evelyn leaned her hip against the massive wood desk and glanced at Peter in the corner chair. "I've been rather busy living out a story myself."

Leaving out Norwood's role, she related everything—the switched passports, the eviction, the attack, Peter's rescue, and the flight to Paris.

After she finished and Chase gave the appropriate expressions of shock and concern and gratitude for her safety, he drew in an audible breath. "That is indeed a good story, but not for the ANS."

"No, sir. It isn't news."

"One of the ladies' magazines is sure to buy it."

Evelyn rolled her eyes. Only women would read a story by a woman and about a woman? Ridiculous.

"Meanwhile," Chase said, "you're useless to us."

Evelyn winced. "Can I help at the Paris bureau while waiting for my new passport?"

"Without papers? Absolutely not. Once you have your passport, we'll discuss your new assignment. Meanwhile, with you gone, I'm down yet another reporter in Germany. I'm almost desperate enough to hire back George Norwood."

"Norwood! Anyone but him." She bit her lip. She'd promised herself not to mention him.

"I have no intention of doing so, even though he's called several times in the past week."

Evelyn's fingers coiled hard around the cool black phone. "Has he now? Almost as if he knew I was on the run." Oh, why couldn't she control her tongue?

Peter sat up straighter, his gaze riveted on her.

"No, but he said he'd been trying to reach you," Chase said. "He wants the pen you borrowed at the Putsch ceremony—it was a gift from his father. He asked if I'd heard from you."

"A pen? I didn't borrow anything from him." She pushed away from the desk, but the cord stopped her from pacing. Due to Peter's phone call, Norwood knew she was in danger, and yet he'd said nothing to Chase. More proof that Norwood had tipped off Otto.

And he wanted to find her.

Evelyn set her hand on her hip. "Do not tell that man where I am. Don't even say you've heard from me. I have nothing of his, and I never want to hear from him again."

The European bureau chief laughed. "Neither do I. Listen, write a killer story for *Ladies' Home Journal*, and call if you need my help with the passport office."

"Thanks, sir. Any idea where you'll send me next?" Evelyn cut her gaze away from Peter and out the window to the back garden.

"I have no idea. Other than Germany, I have no positions in Europe. I do know we have openings in the States—New York, Boston, DC."

Evelyn's heart drifted low. She'd loved being a foreign correspondent. But how could she complain? At least she had a job. Peter had lost his entire career.

Evelyn hunched with Peter and the Aubreys at the top of the Eiffel Tower, all holding on to their hats in the stiff, cool breeze. Simone had lent Evelyn a dress and coat while her suit and overcoat were being cleaned.

Simone had also given Evelyn powder and lipstick. After living in Nazi Germany, where makeup was considered immoral, wearing it again felt deliciously defiant.

Aubrey pointed to the northeast. "Across the Seine, right off the Place de la Concorde, there's the US Embassy."

"I wish it were open today," Peter said.

"Monday morning, first thing." Evelyn leaned against his arm. For warmth, she told herself. Out of habit, she reasoned. Out of the sheer pleasure of it, she had to admit.

"Now that you've seen Paris from above, let's see it from the ground," Aubrey said to Peter, who had never been to the City of Lights.

They edged through the crowd to the elevators. One was waiting, and the foursome squeezed in.

As the elevator descended, Simone smoothed her brown curls. "Remember, you two are welcome to stay with us as long as you want."

"Thank you." Peter turned sideways to make more room. "I hope we won't inconvenience you long, but it can take weeks to get a passport replaced."

"We?" Evelyn gaped at him. "Not you. Right after we visit the embassy, we're getting your ticket home."

Under the brim of his fedora, twin furrows split Peter's brow. "I'm not leaving until you do."

"You have important business. It can't be delayed." She gave him a significant look. She didn't dare mention the list.

"It can wait until you're safe." The set of his jaw said he'd be hard to sway.

Pressure built in Evelyn's ears, and she yawned to pop them. This evening she'd talk to him in private.

The Nazis wouldn't care about Evelyn anymore—they'd only wanted to kick her out of the country, which they'd done. But they couldn't afford to let Peter take that list to the FBI.

Evelyn hadn't thought it wise to leave the safety of the Aubrey home to sightsee, but she'd been outvoted. According to Aubrey, the French fascists weren't connected to the German Nazis, and their nationalism inspired them to hate Germans as much as they hated communists. Because of that, Peter insisted the French fascists wouldn't care if German agents in the US were compromised. They might welcome it.

The elevator doors opened to the crowd in the plaza, and Evelyn stuck close to Peter's side. Never would she have believed she'd be the voice of caution.

They passed the giant slanting steel legs of the tower and crossed to a broad walkway along the Seine. Across the river, the magnificent Palais de Chaillot stretched long in the cool hazy day. The men walked ahead, and Evelyn and Simone fell behind.

Evelyn scrutinized each person they passed, but everyone focused on the Eiffel Tower, not on her. She forced herself to relax.

She was free. Not as free as she'd be when she had a US passport again, but freer than she'd ever been in Germany. France and the United States had huge problems, but in each nation, the government served to safeguard liberties, not strip them.

Simone tapped Evelyn's arm. "You must tell me about being a foreign correspondent. It sounds exciting."

Since Peter wasn't part of the conversation, Evelyn switched to French. "It is, but lately it's been too exciting, even for me."

"A woman of adventure." Simone's mouth tipped in a smile. "As am I. I raced autos. That is how I met my Paul. He was testing his company's latest model."

Evelyn grinned. "I've never met a woman race car driver."

"I wore my hair short and dressed as a man. No one knew."

"Has anyone written your story?" Evelyn scrounged in her purse for her notepad.

"*Non, ma chère.*" She touched Evelyn's forearm. "It is a secret. I am proud of my trophies, and they would take them away if they knew."

Evelyn closed her purse. "It must have been difficult to give it up when you married."

"I only stopped when Josephine came along. It is dangerous, and Josie needs her mother." She gave Evelyn a conspiratorial smile. "But Paul takes me to the track and lets me drive as fast as I want. No more races though."

Evelyn eyed the two men. "Your husband likes having a daring wife."

"*Oui.* Your Monsieur Lang likes daring women too."

"You think . . . ?" Evelyn blinked at her. "*Non.* Peter and I are only friends."

Simone stopped, grasped Evelyn's arm, and leaned close. "Which is it? Do you not return his affections? Or does he not return yours? Because you two are as one."

Evelyn glanced at Peter's broad back in his tailored gray suit, his profile angled to Aubrey, his mouth wide in laughter, his fedora shading his eyes. Everything in her longed to hear every word from that gorgeous mouth.

She faced Simone. "We've spent every minute together for almost two weeks. We've placed our lives in each other's hands. That is what you see."

Simone lifted one dark eyebrow. "I see love."

"Ah, you French."

"Ah, you Americans. Tell him you love him. What do you have to lose?"

Evelyn's mind whirled. She hadn't said she loved him. It was new and fresh—too new and fresh to voice to anyone, much less Peter.

"Come now." Evelyn resumed walking and flung one hand to the gray sky. "It is too dreary a day to talk of *l'amour.*"

Simone laughed, and she didn't press.

They rounded the bend of the Seine, and Evelyn frowned at the tourist boats and the perfectly spaced chestnut trees.

What *did* she have to lose?

Her independence? She no longer cared about that, not when she'd seen the benefits of interdependence.

Could she lose Peter if he didn't return her feelings? She'd lose him anyway when he sailed for New York.

No, her fear ran deeper. What if he *could* return her feelings? What then? Marriage wouldn't work with her career and her personality. What if she destroyed everything they had together?

Simone walked beside her, as straight figured as Evelyn and with a square jaw any man would be proud to own. A race car driver.

And a beloved wife.

"Simone?" Evelyn whispered. "Tell me how you and Monsieur Aubrey make your marriage work."

Simone gave Evelyn a knowing glance. "Gladly."

SUNDAY, NOVEMBER 20, 1938

Hearing a sermon in English sounded good to Peter's ears. He'd stopped attending church in Munich when it became clear the pastors only preached the few portions of the Bible sanctioned by the Nazi Party.

The soaring sanctuary of the American Church in Paris felt like home, although he'd never set foot inside before. Dark wood, an enormous organ, and bright stained-glass windows stood out against the whitewashed walls.

Evelyn sat beside him, with Paul and Simone and eighteen-month-old Josie on his other side.

Gratitude welled up, thickening his tongue and tightening his throat. The Lord had gotten them safely to France, and tomorrow Evelyn's nightmare would start to come to an end.

Leaving her would be excruciating, but she was correct. The

sooner he turned in that list, the better. The FBI needed to capture those German agents and make sure no one else organized the Americans partial to the Nazis.

Like Charles Norwood Sr.

Peter's chest burned. The Nazis had killed dozens of people on Kristallnacht, and they could have killed Evelyn and the Golds. And George Norwood didn't care. George had wanted Evelyn dead. Probably still did.

Would she be safe in France after he left? The warmth from her arm stretched to him across the half-inch gap between their shoulders.

France was in disarray with crippling strikes, high unemployment, strife among countless political factions, and at least twenty prime ministers in the past decade. Before the Munich Conference, thousands had fled Paris, convinced German bombs were about to fall.

Chaos and fear left the nation vulnerable to the promises of both communism and fascism.

Evelyn murmured at something the pastor said, and she wrote in her notepad.

Peter peeked over her shoulder. A jumble of notes crossed in all directions. He couldn't make sense of it, but she could. She worked best that way, just as he worked best when things were orderly.

Evelyn understood, and warmth flowed through him. The night they'd arrived in Paris, while he'd told Aubrey their story, she'd unpacked his rucksack in his room. He'd come upstairs to find his clothes neatly folded and his toiletry items in a straight line on the bureau.

That empty room had suddenly felt less lonely.

Reverend Thompson finished the sermon with a prayer, and Peter gave himself a little shake. He'd missed most of the preaching—a shame since he'd enjoyed what he'd heard.

Then the pastor announced the closing hymn, "We Gather Together," appropriate with Thanksgiving in the coming week.

Peter stood and shared a hymnal with Evelyn.

> We gather together to ask the Lord's blessing,
> He chastens and hastens His will to make known.
> The wicked oppressing now cease from distressing,
> Sing praises to His name, He forgets not His own.
>
> Beside us to guide us, our God with us joining,
> Ordaining, maintaining His kingdom divine;
> So from the beginning the fight we were winning,
> Thou Lord, wast at our side: the glory be Thine!

The lyrics couldn't have been more appropriate. The Lord had indeed been beside them to guide them, and Peter's voice roughened as he sang.

The pastor spoke the benediction, and the congregation dismissed.

Evelyn looped her purse over her shoulder and looked up at Peter. "Do you remember when we were hiking at the Partnach Gorge and you said you sing horribly?"

"Yes." The memory of that day brought up a smile.

She stepped into the aisle. "That was a gross understatement."

He laughed and followed her, with the Aubreys behind him. "I don't remember granting you any more insults."

"You need them after how I've been singing your praises lately." A grumble ran through her voice.

"I promise I won't misinterpret that praise." He patted her shoulder and gave it a squeeze.

Evelyn glanced back with a smile, not even shrugging off his hand. For half a second, he thought he saw something in her eyes. Something beyond affection.

One last pat, and he motioned her to the door.

Boy, did he need new glasses.

THIRTY-EIGHT

Paris
Monday, November 21, 1938

Evelyn paused in the doorway to the passport office in the US Embassy. A long counter manned by half a dozen clerks opposed her, but she could do this.

"Ready?" Peter asked by her side.

Evelyn straightened her shoulders and selected an available clerk on the far right by the wall, an older gentleman who might be sympathetic to a young lady's plight. "I'm ready."

Peter found an empty seat. "I'm here if you need me."

Evelyn packed a lot of gratitude into her smile. He trusted her to take care of herself, but he'd step in if she couldn't.

Her ankles wobbled as she approached the counter, but she gave the clerk a smile she hoped looked both friendly and pitiful. "Good morning, sir. I'm an American citizen, and I've lost my passport."

The man's lips thinned. "Must everyone be so careless?"

"It was stolen, sir. Carelessness had nothing to do with it." Oh dear. She had to avoid sharp words. Time to play the helpless female. "I apologize. I—I've been through such an ordeal."

The clerk slipped her a card and a pencil, and she began filling it out.

"I'll warn you, miss," the clerk said. "This is a long process. With so many Jews trying to sneak into America, we have to be careful."

The pencil almost snapped in Evelyn's hand. They weren't sneaking—they were fleeing for their lives.

"You're not one of them, are you?" He narrowed eyes as gray as his hair, as if Evelyn's dark eyes and hair were condemning evidence.

Evelyn turned the card to him, the top half filled out. "Name—Evelyn Margaret Brand. Birthplace—Chicago, Illinois. My passport number, which ought to speed the process. I cabled home this morning, and my parents will send a copy of my birth certificate to my Paris address. Also, my employer will vouch for me. I'll write my boss's name and number on the card."

He harrumphed and picked up the card. "Evelyn . . . Brand?" His gaze snapped to her. "The reporter?"

Someone recognized her byline? Every reporter's dream come true. "Why, yes. I'm with the American News Service."

The clerk took a step back and gave her a strange, twitchy smile.

Did that mean he liked her writing? Or hated it?

"Excuse me, Miss Brand. I'll be right back." He darted along behind the counter and flagged down a middle-aged gentleman standing to the far left in the back of the office.

Peter rose and picked up a discarded newspaper on a chair.

The reporter in her hated to see anyone reading a paper without paying for it, but she couldn't blame Peter for wanting to pass the time.

He went to the far end of the counter, leaned against it, and raised the newspaper.

The clerk and the man who had to be his supervisor were in deep discussion, studying her card and glancing at her. Then the supervisor pulled a slip of paper from his pocket, handed it to the clerk, and motioned him toward the side offices.

The clerk entered an office door, not five feet from Peter, and he picked up a phone and dialed.

Evelyn drummed her fingers on the gleaming wooden counter, but what was another five minutes in a process that would take weeks?

Might as well keep busy while she waited. She took out her notepad and found her notes on the article Hamilton Chase had earmarked for *Ladies' Home Journal* but Peter had earmarked for *Collier's* or the *Atlantic Monthly*. She had plenty of material for a feature article. Over the next few minutes, she sketched an outline.

"Evelyn." Peter's voice came from behind her—low, firm, strident. "Do not look at me. Do not talk to me."

What on earth? Her breath caught in her throat. She lifted her head but resisted the impulse to face him.

The clerk was talking to the supervisor again. Then he turned and approached Evelyn with a wide smile.

"Leave now," Peter said. "Pass me without a glance. I'll follow a few minutes later."

Everything in his voice spoke of urgency and danger, and Evelyn couldn't breathe. What on earth was going on?

"Miss Brand?" The clerk returned to the counter, his smile even wider. "We've found a way to expedite the process. Please come with me into the back office."

Expedite the process?

Something ripped inside her. Follow the clerk and his promise of an early escape home? Or follow Peter's odd warning, without explanation, without reason?

Evelyn stepped back, bobbling her purse and notepad. "I—please pardon me. I need to find the powder room."

The clerk's smile flattened. "Your powder looks fine. Come with me, please."

"It's urgent. I'll be back in a minute." She headed for the door. Out of the corner of her eye, she spied Peter seated, the newspaper hiding his face.

Her heart beat a wild pattern, and she strode down the hall and down the stairs past a Gilbert Stuart painting of George Washington, past the seal of the United States, the promise of freedom—why couldn't she find it?

In the lobby, she pressed back against the wall close to the door, with the staircase in view. If she spotted the clerk or his supervisor, she'd flee. "Please, Peter," she murmured. "Hurry."

Had he meant for her to leave the office or the building? To return to the Aubreys' or find another refuge? Was she supposed to wait for him?

Her breath bounced in her mouth. She hadn't felt this scared since Kristallnacht, but this time she couldn't name the danger. She only knew it existed.

Two women came downstairs. Three gentlemen entered the front door. No Peter.

Prayers bumbled around in her head, and she shoved her notepad in her purse so she wouldn't lose it if she had to run.

Never once did she break her gaze with the staircase. One hundred—she'd count to one hundred then take a cab to the Aubrey home.

A man's legs came into view—Peter, sauntering downstairs, taking his time.

Evelyn pushed away from the wall to rush to him, but he held up one hand before his stomach and made a little pushing motion. He looked at the door, not at her.

He wanted her to stay back and pretend she didn't know him, so she gazed around as if waiting for someone else.

About six feet from her, he squatted, yanked his shoelace undone, and tied it again. "George knows you're here," he said in that low and intense voice. "Go to Aubrey's. Take the first cab you see. I'll go separately. Go—now."

Her mind whirled with questions and confusion and stark, cold fear. She glanced at her wristwatch and heaved a sigh as if her appointment were late, then she opened the wooden door and left.

At a brisk clip, she crossed the courtyard and exited through wrought-iron gates flanked by stone eagles on pillars. Blind. Powerless.

The open expanse of the Place de la Concorde faced her, the plaza named after harmony and agreement, where hundreds had been guillotined in the French Revolution.

Evelyn stumbled on a cobblestone, then pulled herself together.

A black cab sat at the curb, and Evelyn slipped in the back door. *"Sacré-Coeur, s'il vous plaît,"* she said to the driver. The church lay to the north while the Aubrey home lay to the southwest. If George Norwood was watching, she'd lead him astray. In a few blocks, she'd give the driver the correct address.

The cab drove north. Evelyn restrained herself from looking out the back window for Peter.

Oh no. He didn't speak French, he didn't know Paris, and she was leaving him.

Her heart strained for him. For his safety. For his presence.

Now that she knew the power of partnership, being alone had lost its appeal.

THIRTY-NINE

Hunched low in the backseat of the cab, Peter surveyed the boulevard outside Aubrey's house as best he could with his faulty eyesight. An elderly couple. A mother with a baby carriage. No sign of George.

Peter peeled off a bunch of francs for the driver—far too many, judging by the man's happy exclamations.

"Au revoir." Peter tipped his hat and bounded out of the cab and up to the front door. Locked. He rang the bell.

When Xavier opened the door, Peter ducked inside. "Is Miss Brand back? Mademoiselle Brand?"

"Peter?" Her voice came from the dayroom to the right.

He loped in. There she was, rising from the sofa with relief and joy all over her beautiful face. In half a heartbeat, he went to her and took her in his arms. "Thank God. Thank God you're safe."

"I was worried about you," she said, crushed to his chest. "You don't speak French. You don't know your way around."

"I pronounced the address the way you did the night we arrived and added *s'il vous plaît.*"

Evelyn planted her hands on his waist and pushed back, her expression piercing. "What's going on?"

"Bad news, I'm afraid." He sank onto the sofa, and Evelyn joined him. Simone sat in an armchair. "Oh, hello, Simone."

"Hello, Peter." She gave him a sly look, then excused herself into her husband's study.

"What's going on?" Evelyn asked.

Peter stretched his arm along the back of the sofa behind her. "When the clerk talked to his supervisor, I heard him say your name. The supervisor clearly recognized it and wasn't pleased. I wandered closer, but I could only hear fragments. I thought I heard 'Norwood,' but I wasn't sure."

Evelyn's eyes flashed. "Charles Norwood placed an alert on my name, didn't he?"

"It looks that way." He rubbed his fingers together, longing to embrace her. "The clerk went into the office and made a phone call. Evelyn, it was a local call. He didn't speak to an operator."

"To Norwood?" She twisted her hands together.

Peter nodded. "The office was near, and I heard almost everything the clerk said. He asked to speak to George Norwood."

She gasped. "He's in Paris? How did he follow us?"

"It isn't illogical. He and Otto are in contact. Otto could have told him I was seen in Stuttgart, probably headed west. And you and I both have friends in Paris."

"This house." Evelyn glanced around, eyes wide. "He'll know we came here."

"I don't think so. After the clerk told him you were in the passport office, he said yes, you were alone."

Evelyn's brows drew together. "Norwood wanted to know if you were with me."

"That's why I insisted we leave separately. If he thinks you're alone, he won't look here."

"But he has to know we left Munich together. Otto saw us."

"Yes, but maybe George will think we went our separate ways. We're fine here for now, but not for long."

Evelyn crossed her arms in a strange mixture of defiance and vulnerability. "Did you hear anything else?"

Peter mashed his lips together. He hated to alarm her, but she was strong and she needed to know the seriousness of the situation. "The clerk repeated back instructions from Norwood, probably because they sounded strange. He agreed to delay you for an hour, and then let you go home. Apparently George was adamant that it be a full hour."

Evelyn's lip curled. "If he wanted me to be detained, I'm sure he could have made up a reason. He's good at lying. Why only an hour? Why send me home?"

The words congealed in his throat, but he shoved them out. "An hour would give George time to get to the embassy."

Her eyes hardened, agates in a face of marble. "Or to send thugs to intercept me and knock me off."

Peter lowered his head and nodded. Then he met her gaze again. "We have to get you home immediately."

"How? With an alert on my name, I can't get a new passport, even if I show up with my birth certificate. No. You need to leave France now. The list—you need to get out of here."

He stood and marched the length of the room. "I'm not leaving until you're safe. That's final."

"I can't get home legally. You can and you must."

Peter whipped around. "Then we'll get you home illegally."

"How?" Evelyn spread her hands wide. "Do you want me to stow away on a freighter? Swim across the Atlantic?"

Peter groaned. "We'll get you forged papers."

"You? Peter Lang?" She arched one eyebrow. "You know how to obtain forged papers? The most law-abiding person I know?"

He ran his hands through his hair. "I don't care anymore. The law has failed us. We have to—I don't know—I just want to smash down the walls."

Evelyn pursed her lips, and the corners of her eyes turned down. "No, Peter. No more."

"No more what?"

"It was one thing when we were breaking unjust laws of an unjust nation. Now we're talking about breaking just laws of a just nation."

"Just?" Peter flung his hand westward. "What's just about these laws? These quotas? Hundreds of thousands of Jews are suffering, and some bureaucrat—"

"No, Peter." Evelyn shook her head. "We can't decide for ourselves which laws we want to obey and which we don't. That's . . . chaos."

He pressed his palms over his eyes, his fingers digging into his scalp, as desires and principles warred with each other.

"Sit down, Peter. Sit down," she said, her voice soft and low. "It's all right. You've done everything you could. Now go home. Talk to your brother in Congress and to the ANS in New York and to my parents. Straighten things out for me. It'll be easier on that side of the Atlantic. You can get me home."

Peter collapsed onto the sofa. "That could take months. No. I can't do that. I won't leave you in danger."

Evelyn rested her hand on his. "I'll be fine. I'll go into hiding with a friend Norwood doesn't know. My parents can wire money, and the Aubreys will help, I'm sure."

All resistance drained out of him. All hope. He clutched her hand in both of his. How could he leave the woman he loved? Leave her alone and in danger?

What a horrible decision. He had to leave her to save her.

"Please, Peter," she said. "It's the only way."

Simone strolled back into the room with a smug expression. "I can think of three other ways."

"Three?" Peter scrunched up his nose. "I can't think of one."

Simone settled into the armchair. "I made some calls. Paul's on his way, and so is Reverend Thompson."

"The reverend?" Evelyn asked. "Does he know what to do?"

"He can help with one of the solutions."

"Solutions? What have we missed?" Peter glanced at Evelyn, but she shared his confusion.

Simone crossed long legs. "Paul and I have been discussing this. Evelyn could travel with my passport. I have an active visa for America—we visited Paul's family this summer. We're about the same height and coloring, and Claudette could cut your hair like mine. Just mail the passport back when you reach New York."

It didn't sit right with Peter. "If Evelyn is caught, you'd both be in big trouble."

"I'll take that risk if Evelyn will." Simone gestured to Peter. "We're also concerned that Monsieur Norwood might have placed an alert on your name too."

His jaw set hard. "He'd be stupid to do that. I have a valid passport. The only law I've broken is entering France without a visa. He doesn't dare start that fight, because I'll win, and he knows it."

Simone dipped her chin in acknowledgment. "In case he has, Paul and I could buy tickets under our names. You two would board the ocean liner with us as if to wish us bon voyage, then Paul and I would disembark. You would sail under our names, then sort everything out in New York."

"No," Peter said. "That'll cause problems for both of you, guaranteed."

"I don't like it." Evelyn clenched Peter's hand even tighter. "I don't like either of them. I don't want to cause any more problems for the Aubreys than we already have."

"The third option is obvious." Simone draped her forearms along the armrests. "Marriage."

"Marriage?" Evelyn's voice squeaked, and her hand went wooden in his grip.

Peter slid his hand off of hers, refusing to trap her. "That isn't an option."

"It's an excellent option." Simone placed one hand on her chest. "I am a French citizen, but as Paul's wife, I can obtain a visa outside of quotas. If you two were married, Evelyn could obtain a visa with her current passport, the German one. All—as you Americans say—above board."

It made a lot of sense, but Peter shook his head, shaking his emotions away from logic. "There's still an alert on her name."

"At the passport office." A light dawned on Evelyn's face. "Not in the visa office. George would never suspect I'd try for a visa on the German passport, not with a waiting list several years long. I think . . . that might work."

Peter shifted his jaw back and forth. More than anything, he wanted to take Evelyn as his wife. But not this way. Not without her love.

"Would it be so bad? Marrying me?" Evelyn's voice wavered. "We—we work well together. We like each other."

"True." The word rasped over his dry tongue.

Evelyn gazed into her lap. "It's our best option."

Everything she said made sense. But how could he wed a woman who feared being caged by a man? Maybe if he didn't lock the cage. He wet his lips. "All right. But as soon as your paperwork is straightened out back home, we'll get an annulment. I don't want to trap you in marriage."

She flinched but nodded.

Simone huffed. "I'm glad my Paul is more romantic than the rest of you Americans."

She was right. Evelyn deserved better. He slid off the sofa and onto one knee before her. Her fingers were tangled together, but he pried one hand free and held it in his.

"Evelyn?" He waited until she raised her head, her gaze hesitant and wary. Peter let a smile creep up. "Would you do me the honor of being my wife, even if only for a few weeks?"

Her hand relaxed, and she lowered her face so he couldn't see her expression. "Yes, I'll marry you. I'm the one who's honored."

Peter clung to her hand, small and warm and soon to be his. Marriage would make their eventual separation even more painful. But it would be worth it to save her life.

FORTY

Simone hustled Evelyn upstairs. "We will find you something to wear for your wedding. All you have is your suit. It is a handsome suit, but *non*."

Evelyn followed Simone into her bedroom. "Thank you, but this is only a formality."

"No, it is an opportunity." Simone flung open the doors to a large closet. "You love him, *n'est ce pas*?"

Evelyn clutched the buttons of her suit jacket. She'd only known she loved him for a few days, and she'd never voiced it. But the truth fell out. *"Oui."*

"He loves you too. Did you not see his joy when he returned from the embassy?"

"He was worried." Evelyn unbuttoned her suit jacket, the memory of Peter's joyful expression ingrained in her mind.

"His bliss when he embraced you, and the way you kept holding each other's hands. How's this?" She held up a long mossy green gabardine dress.

"Not green." Evelyn tossed her suit jacket on the bed. "And you're mistaken."

"Never. Oh, this." She held up a floor-length gown with cap sleeves.

Rejection sat on the tip of Evelyn's tongue. Dove gray silk crepe flowed in a slim, draped silhouette, accented with half a dozen embroidered bouquets of pink and blue flowers scattered on the bodice and hips. Silk rosettes wreathed the neckline.

The dress was too feminine. Yet something about it seemed new and right for her. "That's the one."

Evelyn shed her blouse and suit skirt, and she shimmied into the smooth silk.

Simone did up the buttons in the back. "Not only will marriage take you home, but it will take you where you belong—with each other."

Peter's stiff words pounded Evelyn's ears. "You heard. He wants to annul the marriage."

"Convince him not to." Simone rummaged in a bureau drawer and pulled out a nightgown of slinky cream silk. "This would work."

Evelyn gasped and laughed. "I'm not going to seduce him!"

"I don't see why not." Simone inspected the negligee, what there was of it.

With a flap of her hand, Evelyn laughed her off. Even if she were capable of seducing Peter, she wouldn't want to persuade him that way. She'd want him to choose her because he loved her and wanted to spend his life with her.

Simone came behind Evelyn and fluffed her curls. "I'm glad you let Claudette style your hair this morning. It looks lovely. Now go to your chamber and powder your nose."

In her own room, Evelyn freshened her makeup.

In her reflection in the mirror, her grandmother's cross glinted, the only piece of her family that would attend the wedding. What if Evelyn had never asked the jeweler about the cross? She wouldn't know she was three-quarters Jewish, and neither would Norwood. She wouldn't have been evicted or hunted on Kristallnacht. She'd still be reporting in Munich, and Peter would be teaching and writing his dissertation.

Her fingers folded around the cool gold, and her heart folded in half. Everything had been upended because she was inquisitive and persistent and headstrong.

She blew out a breath. Nonsense. It was best to know the truth. It was always best.

Norwood could have found another way to exact his revenge—and he might not have failed.

With a shudder, Evelyn tucked the cross under the neckline of the gown.

Downstairs in the sitting room, Peter sat with Paul Aubrey and Reverend Thompson, and they rose when she entered.

Peter raised a smile as appreciative as when he'd greeted her on their first and only date, but softer. "You look . . . radiant."

The same words he'd spoken that night, and she bit back a joke. Not today. Not when he was looking at her as if Simone were right and he did love her. "Thank you."

"Good day, Miss Brand." Reverend Thompson shook her hand. "Mr. Aubrey and Mr. Lang have told me about your situation."

"I told him everything," Peter said. "Even about George."

Evelyn joined Peter on the sofa, Aubrey excused himself, and the reverend sat in an armchair.

In his sixties, with salt-and-pepper hair, Reverend Thompson spoke with a Midwestern accent. "So, Miss Brand, Mr. Lang says you're from Chicago. I went to college there." He asked about her favorite restaurants and museums and her home church. Then he asked what her father did, and she told him.

The reverend's thick eyebrows rose. "Ernest Brand is your father?"

"Yes, and he and my mother moved to Chicago in 1908, before I was born. Do I pass?"

"Pardon?"

Evelyn sent him half a smile. "Have I convinced you I'm a Chicago native and not a German Jew trying to bamboozle you so I can obtain a visa to America?"

Peter chuckled.

The reverend's eyes crinkled around the sides. "Yes, Miss Brand. You pass. Do you have the passport? May I see?"

Evelyn opened her purse and handed him her papers. "All the information on the German passport is correct except my middle name and my birthplace. The press pass has the correct information, but it can't be used as official identification."

"No, it can't." Reverend Thompson frowned at the papers. "Marrying you two would be unorthodox under these conditions."

"Yes, sir," Peter said. "But her life depends on it."

The reverend's gaze shot to Peter. "Marriage is not a decision to be made rashly. I understand your hurry, but the institution of marriage is sacred."

Evelyn's stomach crushed along with her best hope of escape.

Peter rested his forearms on his knees. "Sir, I love her with all my heart. This crisis sped up the process, but I've wanted to marry her for some time." His voice shook with what sounded like conviction and urgency.

The beauty of his words bloomed inside her, but those words were for the reverend's benefit, not hers.

Reverend Thompson's gaze shifted to Evelyn.

She'd voiced the truth to Simone, but now it was time to voice it to the only person who mattered.

Peter looked at the reverend, his face tense and his hands clasped between his knees.

"I love you, Peter." Her voice shook too, from the release and the joy and the pain of it. She threaded her arm through the crook of his arm. "I never want to be apart from you again."

Peter's gaze sped to her, his eyes wide. Then one corner of his mouth indented with a touch of amusement. He took her hand and pulled it through and gripped it in both his hands. "Please marry us, Reverend. I promise to love her all the days of my life."

Reverend Thompson laughed. "Slow down, son. We haven't reached the 'I dos' yet. But your eagerness counts in your favor."

Evelyn's fingertips tingled from the pressure of Peter's grip.

The reverend rubbed his forehead. "Since you'll present this passport at the visa office, I'll have to issue the marriage certificate with the information on the passport. After you obtain your new passport, I'll issue a corrected certificate. Either way, it's legally binding."

"You'll marry us?" Evelyn asked.

"Yes."

"Thank you, sir." Peter sprang to his feet. "Aubrey! We're ready!"

With her hand lost in Peter's grip, Evelyn had no choice but to stand.

Paul Aubrey leaned into the room. "A little while longer. Simone sent Xavier to buy rings about an hour ago. She guessed at your sizes."

Peter frowned at the reverend. "Do we need rings for the ceremony?"

"Well, no, but—"

"Then let's get started." Peter played the role of eager groom quite convincingly.

Simone rushed into the room. "Here you go. Claudette has a way with flowers."

Evelyn took a bouquet from Simone. The sprays of pink and blue flowers complemented the embroidery on the gown. "Thank you. It's beautiful. Please thank Claudette for me."

"I will." Simone swept her arm to the windows framed by golden drapes. "Let's have the ceremony here, overlooking the garden."

Reverend Thompson took his place, with Peter and Evelyn before him and Paul and Simone by their sides.

Thoughts and emotions tumbled in Evelyn's mind as she took Peter's arm. Marriage? She'd never seriously considered it until recently. Mother had always said Evelyn was too much for any man to handle. But Peter "handled" her just fine.

Now she was marrying him.

A formality to save her life? Or an opportunity for a new life together?

The reverend took out his Bible and began the service, intoning about the beauty of marriage, and Evelyn prayed along, praying that she and Peter could find that beauty, that they could lean on each other for life.

Was it too much to ask? Too much to hope for? The more she accepted her love for Peter, the more she wanted to make it work. If only he could be convinced.

Reverend Thompson asked them to face each other for the vows, and Evelyn passed Simone the bouquet and took Peter's outstretched hands. The sincerity in his eyes weakened her knees, but she forced them straight.

Peter repeated his vows with earnestness. He'd keep those vows for the duration of their marriage, honoring and cherishing her for better or for worse, same as he'd been doing for several weeks already.

Evelyn infused her own vows with the same earnestness, the same honoring and cherishing, the same for better or for worse, but with forever in each word.

A flurry of activity beside her. Simone conferred with Xavier and held out a box. "We have wedding rings, just in time."

Peter thanked the butler and pulled a ring from the box. As he repeated the reverend's words, Peter slipped the ring onto Evelyn's finger, a bit big, but it stayed in place.

Evelyn worked Peter's ring over his knuckle. "With this ring, I thee wed."

"I now declare you man and wife," Reverend Thompson said. "You may kiss the bride."

With those lips. Those perfect lips.

A question flashed in Peter's eyes, an apology.

No, they couldn't hesitate now. If he didn't initiate, she would.

But he leaned in, his gaze never leaving hers until the last moment. Then those lips met hers in a perfect fit. And she gave back, thanking him with her kiss for his care, his protection, his sacrifice, his kindness, his Peter-ness.

A giggle sounded behind her. Simone.

How long had they been kissing? Peter pulled away with a sheepish smile and turned to Reverend Thompson.

Evelyn tried to focus her eyes on the reverend. If Peter had meant for that kiss to convince the pastor of their love, it had to have worked. Because it had almost convinced Evelyn.

Her legs failing her, she leaned against Peter's side.

If only it were real.

If only it could last.

FORTY-ONE

Suitcase in hand, Peter opened the door to the US Embassy for Simone Aubrey and followed her inside. Evelyn stood in the foyer with Paul Aubrey and Reverend Thompson. No one else in the foyer, and the tension in Peter's lungs released.

Evelyn slipped her arm in Peter's as freely as any wife would. "You made it. Any problems?"

"No, but Simone saw some suspicious characters on their street." In case Norwood was watching the Aubrey home, Paul had left in his car as if on his way to work, with Evelyn low in the backseat. Half an hour later, Simone's chauffeur had driven her in the opposite direction as if out for a day of shopping, but with Peter hiding in the backseat.

"Suspicious characters?" Evelyn's fingers dug into Peter's arm.

Simone adjusted her hat. "Two men leaning against lampposts, reading newspapers, not even close to a bus stop."

Aubrey's expression grew dour. "I saw George."

"You did?" Evelyn said. "You didn't say anything."

"I didn't want to risk you raising your head to verify." Aubrey

299

gave her an apologetic look. "I pretended I didn't see him, but I could tell he saw me."

Peter's grip on the suitcase tightened. "Did he follow you?"

"I didn't see any cars behind me."

Regardless, Peter and Evelyn couldn't return to Aubrey's house. If she obtained her visa, they'd take the train to Cherbourg and sail on the RMS *Aquitania* on Friday. If not, Evelyn would ask one of her Parisian friends for a new hiding place.

Reverend Thompson gestured to the staircase. "Are we ready?"

"We'll be in the waiting room," Aubrey said. "If you need help, give us a thumbs-down behind Evelyn's back, and we'll create a diversion so you can leave."

"Thank you for all you've done for us." Evelyn's eyes looked watery, and she hugged Simone.

Peter shook Aubrey's hand. If things went badly, this could be farewell. "Thanks again for the loan. I'll pay you back as soon as we reach New York. And thank you . . ." Peter pressed his hand over his heart, over the small pistol hidden in his suit jacket. Aubrey had bought it to defend himself from communists rioting in his factory, and now Peter carried it to protect Evelyn from fascists.

"Let's go." Chin high, Evelyn took Peter's arm again, and they headed upstairs and down the hallway to the right. "Remember, I want to do this legally and honestly."

"I know." But if he had to lie to get her home, he would. Technically, he wasn't breaking the law, since Evelyn was an American citizen and had every right to enter the United States.

They paused inside the visa office, laid out like the passport office, with a long counter and six officials. No one sat in the waiting room, which would make escape easier if necessary. The Aubreys and the reverend took seats.

Peter turned to Evelyn. To his wife. "Ready?"

She looked up at him, her expression brimming with strength, but with an undercurrent of fear. His chest ached with his love for her, with his need for her, and with the knowledge that she needed him too.

In that moment he felt the weight of the vows they'd spoken the day before, felt like a true husband to her, felt the pleasure of that single heart-filling, heart-shattering kiss.

"I'm ready," she said.

Peter led her to an official, a heavyset man in his thirties. Peter set the suitcase by his feet, where he could grab it in a hurry, and he gave the official a friendly smile. "Good morning. I'm an American citizen, and my wife needs a tourist visa. We were married yesterday."

"Congratulations." The official gave Peter a card. "Please fill this out."

After they filled out the card, they handed it back, along with the marriage certificate and passports, with Peter's on top.

The official scanned Peter's passport and set it aside, exposing Evelyn's. He gave her a suspicious look. "You're German."

Evelyn's smile was so sweet, Peter's teeth ached. "I was raised and educated in Chicago, and my entire family lives in Chicago. But yes, that is the passport I carry right now."

Not a single untrue word, and Peter smiled.

The official opened Evelyn's passport, and alarm flashed in his eyes. "You're Jewish."

Evelyn slid over her press pass, her fingers concealing her actual birthplace. "I won't be a burden on American society. I'm a reporter with the American News Service. You can verify my employment with the bureau here in Paris or with the European bureau chief in London."

Peter gave the man a look heavy with meaning. "You've heard of the problems in Germany. She ran into difficulties with the Gestapo and had to leave in a hurry."

The official frowned and flipped through her passport. He'd reacted—but not to Evelyn's name. Maybe the alert hadn't crossed from the passport office to the visa office after all.

The official studied a blank page in the passport. "If you've lived in the US so long, why don't you already have a visa?"

Evelyn's hand went stiff on his arm. She didn't have a truthful answer to that, did she?

He could still see the panic on her face the day she'd discovered that false passport. Once again, she needed his help. And the memory of that day gave him the answer.

Peter tapped the document that had sent them running for their lives. "You heard how the Nazis revoked the passports of all Jewish people. This one is brand-new."

"Oh." The official's face fell. "They didn't transfer the visa, did they?"

"The Nazis aren't known for either compassion or fairness." He'd honored her wishes and hadn't told a lie. Yet.

The official's brown-eyed gaze bounced between Peter and Evelyn, narrowing to a slit. "So, you saw marriage as your solution?"

Peter forced a lighthearted chuckle. "I wanted to marry her. This just sped up the process."

Evelyn relaxed against his side. "My parents will kill me for not having a big wedding at home, but all will be forgiven when they meet my darling Peter."

Well, now she'd lied, so she couldn't fault him if he did likewise.

The official studied the marriage certificate. "I'll need to verify this."

Peter beckoned to Reverend Thompson. "The pastor who officiated is here."

"Reverend Thompson?" the official said.

"Good morning, Mr. Goodwin." The reverend joined them at the counter. "I was pleased to see you in church on Sunday."

"The sermon was excellent, Reverend." Mr. Goodwin stood taller. "Did you indeed marry this couple?"

"Just yesterday." He set a hand on Evelyn's shoulder. "Rarely do you see two people more loving and dedicated to each other than Mr. and Mrs. Lang."

Evelyn cast a gaze up to Peter, as loving and dedicated as the pastor said, and Peter squeezed her waist. Lying with her eyes, the rascal. Well, he could tell a truth with his lips, and he kissed her forehead.

"Thank you, Reverend." The official made notes on the card. "This will expedite the process. Mrs. Lang, we should have your visa in a few weeks."

Peter and Evelyn gasped together. "A few weeks?" Peter said.

How long would it take for the alert to pass within the embassy building? Not long once George figured out their strategy.

"Sir?" Evelyn's voice trembled. "We can't wait that long."

"We need to leave now." Peter patted the counter, not a slap, but firm. "I had to abandon my teaching position in Munich due to my wife's emergency, and I need to meet with the faculty at Harvard right away or I'll lose my position. We need to sail on the *Aquitania* on Friday."

Mr. Goodwin gave him a sympathetic look. "You may sail on Friday, but your wife can't."

"Oh, Peter." She slumped against his side.

"I won't leave without her."

"Excuse me, Mr. Goodwin." Reverend Thompson leaned his elbows on the counter. "Forgive me for intruding, but isn't there some way to get these two on the *Aquitania*? It's their honeymoon."

"I can't. You under—"

"What more do you need?" The pastor's smile carried both warmth and authority. "You have two valid passports, one for an American citizen. You have a valid and verified marriage certificate. Why, you even have proof of employment for the bride."

"We—we have procedures." Mr. Goodwin shuffled the documents. "We—we need—"

Reverend Thompson set his hand on the papers. "If anything on that form proves false, you could wire New York and have her detained when the *Aquitania* docks. You may hold me personally accountable."

Peter saw the official's wavering, felt his struggle between rules and mercy.

"Please, sir," Evelyn said. "It would mean so much to us. Why, we'd name our first child after you."

An empty promise, but Goodwin wouldn't know that. The official frowned at the passport for a long moment, then he pulled a stamp from a drawer and stamped Evelyn's visa. "My name is John."

Peter laughed with relief. "John is a fine name."

"It is. John Lang. I like it." Evelyn gazed up at Peter in such a way that he could imagine her holding a chubby, curly-haired babe with coffee-and-milk eyes.

He pressed another kiss to her forehead. How could she hold it against him when she was looking at him that way?

"Here." Goodwin slid the paperwork to them. "Go catch that ship. I expect baby pictures within a year."

"Lord willing, sir. Thank you from the bottom of my heart." Peter grinned, shook the man's hand, and spun Evelyn to the door. "Come on, sweetheart. Let's go home."

FORTY-TWO

Evelyn descended the embassy stairs with her purse clutched to her side—her purse holding the passport with that glorious visa. "We did it."

He grinned at her. "You were incredible."

She sent him an arch look. "Were?"

That grin grew in brilliance. "Are. You *are* incredible."

In the foyer, they thanked Reverend Thompson thoroughly, and the pastor departed.

Evelyn turned to Peter. "Next stop—the train station."

"You can't take the train without transit visas," Aubrey said. "We're driving you to Cherbourg."

"Driving us?" Evelyn pictured a map of France in her head. "That's a long way."

"Three hundred miles," Simone said. "I could do it in three hours if Paul let me."

"Which I won't." He raised an amused smile. "It'll take all day, possibly all night. We have an overnight bag in my car, and Josie's nanny will take good care of her at home."

Evelyn's stomach clenched. He'd already taken two days off for them. "That's a lot of time to take off work."

"A benefit to running the company." He led them across the lobby.

Evelyn felt the weight of someone's gaze, and she looked over her shoulder. A man in a dark suit ducked into a corridor. Was that . . . ? It couldn't be.

"Peter?" That weighty sensation grew ice cold, prickling down the nerves of her fingers. "I think I saw Norwood."

Peter's gaze sharpened to a point, following the direction she indicated. He handed Evelyn the suitcase, motioned for her to stay put, and beckoned to Aubrey.

The men dashed to the corridor.

Evelyn's prayers wrestled with each other, one prayer for Peter to find Norwood and have it out with him, and the other that she'd been mistaken and Peter and Aubrey would be safe.

Simone came to Evelyn's side. "You do not think George is armed, do you?"

"I don't know." But any man desperate enough to chase them this far was dangerous.

In a few very long minutes, the men returned, shaking their heads.

"We checked all the offices we could down there." Peter took the suitcase back. "We didn't see anyone who looked like George."

Evelyn squeezed her eyes shut. It wasn't like her to imagine things. "What's wrong with me?"

"Nothing. It'll take time to get used to being free and safe again." Peter placed his hand on the small of her back. "Let's get you home."

In Aubrey's car, Peter wormed down onto the floor in the back-seat. "It won't hurt to lie low until we're out of Paris."

"Good idea." Evelyn stretched out on the backseat. Today was Tuesday. On Wednesday they'd be in Cherbourg, on Thursday they'd board the ship, and on Friday they'd sail.

Aubrey started the car and pulled into traffic.

On the floor, Peter rested his hat on his belly and winked at Evelyn. "Travel with me, sweetheart, and you travel in style."

Darling Peter, making her smile, helping her see the freedom and safety at hand. Time to grab hold of that assurance and stop being anxious, which wasn't like her anyway.

Evelyn removed her hat and rested her chin on her forearm. "You know what would be fun? Instead of hiding, we could wear disguises."

"Disguises, eh? I'd look dashing in a beret, a boater sweater, and a mustache."

With his German looks? She chuckled. "I could dress as a man."

He snorted. "That would never work."

"I almost pulled it off two years ago, right here in Paris. Did I ever tell you that story?"

Disbelief rolled over his face. "You could never pull it off."

"I did. Well, almost. One of the government ministers doesn't allow female reporters into his press conferences. So I wore a man's suit and pinned my hair under a fedora."

"It worked?" Peter's eyes widened.

"I got in. But my hair . . ." She fiddled with a curl. "I should have used more pins and pomade. Curls sprang from under the hat. They kicked me out. It was a fiasco."

Warm laughter floated up. "That's why they call you 'Firebrand.'"

"You're the only one who calls me that to my face." She reached down and poked him in the chest. "Good afternoon, Miss Firebrand," she said in a manly voice.

He poked her shoulder, grinning like a schoolboy. "Is that the voice you used? No wonder you got caught."

"Nonsense." She snatched his hat from his belly and set it on her head, low over one eye. "I make an excellent man."

He snorted. "You couldn't walk five feet without giving yourself away."

"Hardly." All Evelyn's life, Mother had moaned about her clomping about like a boy.

Peter shook his head. "You sway."

"I sway?"

"Your hips. They sway."

"They do not."

"I just spent a week walking behind you. Yes, you sway and nicely." He plucked his hat off her head and set it over his face. "Now, if you'll excuse me, I'd like a nap."

Evelyn rolled away and leaned her head against the seatback. Her spinning head. Peter thought she walked like a woman, swaying. Nicely.

A groan built in her chest, but she trapped it before it could escape. She was already so deeply in love she could never escape. Why did he have to dig her in even deeper?

The way he let her lead in the visa office. The way he sprang to protect her. The teasing and ease and familiarity they shared. And the tenderness he affected for the benefit of the pastor and the official. What would it be like if that tenderness were genuine? If he could love her?

She set her jaw. Could marriage work?

Male foreign correspondents like Mitch O'Hara often had happy marriages, but every female foreign correspondent she knew was either single or divorced. What man would be willing to follow his wife around the world? What man would put up with the type of woman who could succeed as a correspondent? A firebrand?

Simone had given Evelyn insight into how she, as a strong and independent woman, made her marriage work. Compromise and sacrifice and humility and forgiveness and humor.

Would Peter be willing to try? The only way to find out would be to ask.

She rolled onto her stomach to gaze down at him. He lay squished between the seats with his long fingers laced over his belly.

Her hand stretched toward him, craving the feel of his fingers. Was it too much to ask? A lifetime of compromise and sacrifice and humility and forgiveness?

She tucked her hand back under her chin. *Lord, please show me the way.*

Cherbourg, France
Thursday, November 24, 1938

Peter gathered his clothing and shaving kit and stood beside the bed in the hotel room.

Evelyn lay on her side, fast asleep, one arm draped across the mattress. Everything in Peter ached. If only he could slip under that arm and draw her near. Kiss her awake.

He'd have to wake her in a more conventional manner. He grasped her shoulder. Why had she worn both nightgown and dressing gown to bed? The room was plenty warm. "Evelyn?" he murmured.

Thick dark lashes fluttered and rose, revealing sleepy eyes. "Hmm?"

The ache intensified. "I'm going to the restroom to shave and dress. Lock the door behind me."

"Mm-hmm." She pushed up to sitting, unsteady, and she brushed curls off her face.

Lord, help me. Peter strode out the door. Spending another week sleeping in the same room as her might just kill him.

After the lock clicked behind him, Peter padded down the hall in the tiny hotel. He and Evelyn were the only guests, which suited him fine.

They'd arrived in Cherbourg at dawn the day before. After Peter had purchased tickets on the *Aquitania* without a blink of concern from the ticket agent, the Aubreys had returned to Paris.

Peter and Evelyn had checked in to the hotel and spent the day playing cards with a deck in the bureau. Competition certainly stoked the fire in Evelyn's eyes.

Peter grinned and entered the bathroom. After he took care of business, he removed the pajamas Aubrey had given him, set them on top of a large wooden cabinet by the door, and put on his trousers. Simone must have given Evelyn the nightgown and dressing gown. Peter would need to wire his friend a substantial sum when he arrived in New York.

When—he liked the sound of that word.

He lathered and shaved. Today was Thanksgiving, and Peter had plenty to be thankful for. Within a week, Evelyn would be safe in New York and that list of American Nazi sympathizers would be safe in FBI hands.

Peter rinsed his face, praying thanks with each splash of icy water.

Something wasn't right.

A strange sensation crawled over his scalp, and he raised his right hand to stop it.

A rough hand on his shoulder.

Hot pain slashed through his right arm.

Peter cried out, jerked up straight.

In the mirror—a small, dark-haired man. A raised knife.

"No!" Peter spun and drove his left fist into the man's gut.

His attacker doubled over, and Peter shoved him away.

The man's head banged on the open door of the cabinet—he must have been hidden inside! He tumbled to the floor. Dazed but conscious. Still holding the knife.

Peter had to get out! But the man and the open cabinet door blocked the bathroom door.

The gun! In his jacket pocket.

He snatched his jacket from the clothes rack by the bathtub, and he backed to the wall, eyeing the man.

"Who are you?" Peter fumbled for the gun, his hands wet and slippery, his arm hot and stinging from the knife wound. "Who sent you?"

The man wore a blue shirt with dark trousers and tie and beret, almost like a German SA uniform, but in blue. He pushed up to his knees, spitting out French words.

Peter's hand closed around steel. The safety! Aubrey had shown him—how did it work?

More angry French, and the man stumbled to his feet.

Even if he couldn't shoot, he might be able to scare him off, get out of the room. Peter thrust out the gun, his right hand numb, groping for anything mechanical that might be the safety.

The man roared and charged, knife raised.

"No!" Peter squeezed the trigger.

An explosion of sound, and the man reeled back and slumped to the ground.

"Oh, Lord. No." Peter slammed his eyes shut, but the image wouldn't leave.

The attacker was so short, Peter had shot him in the head. He'd killed a man.

Who was he? Where had he come from?

Peter squatted beside the body, angling away from the carnage. A tie clip caught his eye—a sheaf of wheat on top of a cogged wheel, with a double-edged battle-ax above it.

The smell of blood and other vile things filled his head and turned his stomach. "Oh, Lord. I killed a man."

The gunshot. The innkeeper would have heard it. Called the police.

Peter grabbed his shaving kit, pajamas, shirt. He couldn't leave anything behind, any evidence.

Even though he'd acted in self-defense, when the police came, Peter would be held for questioning, detained during the investigation. He wouldn't be allowed to board the ship today. He wouldn't be able to get Evelyn home.

Evelyn.

Sweat tingled on his upper lip.

Evelyn. Alone in the room.

"Good Lord, no!" He struggled to open the door. "Evelyn!"

FORTY-THREE

Evelyn zipped up her skirt. With Peter in the bathroom, she could dress in privacy.

After she slipped on her jacket, she stashed away the slinky nightgown Simone had sneaked into the suitcase. Evelyn would throttle that woman if she ever saw her again. At least Simone had also packed a dressing gown. Yes, Evelyn wanted to convince Peter not to annul the marriage, but not by sashaying around in creamy satin.

As best she could, she straightened the suitcase. Neatness was foreign to her, but since it was important to Peter, it was important to her—especially in close quarters.

Hands on hips, she surveyed the room. Only her toiletries remained. As soon as Peter returned, she'd take her turn in the bath—

A loud crack sounded outside the room.

Evelyn startled. A gunshot?

No . . .

All her thoughts and all her blood drained from her head.

"Peter?" she whispered. He didn't have a gun. That meant . . .

"Oh no. Oh no. Lord, help." Something to use as a weapon—anything!

She grabbed the fireplace poker and flung open the door.

"Evelyn!" Peter cried from inside the bathroom.

He was alive! Thank God! "Peter!"

The bathroom door banged open, and he lurched out, shirtless, clothing in one hand, and in the other—a gun!

Crazed eyes met hers, then his face flooded with relief and he strode to her. "We need to leave."

"What happened? I heard—"

Crimson streaked across the arm with the gun, dripped to the floor.

"You're bleeding!" She reached for him.

But he shepherded her to their room. "Now! We need to leave now. A man tried to kill me. I shot him. He's dead."

Evelyn stumbled through the doorway. "A man? Who? How did—"

"I'll explain later." He dumped his clothing into the suitcase and swung the lid shut. "Let's go."

She grabbed his arm above the wound and thrust her face in front of his. "Stop. You're bleeding hard. You need a bandage. You need to get dressed."

He straightened, his eyes as wild as the night the synagogue was destroyed but as focused as on Kristallnacht. "We have to get on the ship before the police arrive. A man was killed. It was self-defense, but I'll be detained. We *must* get home."

Her stomach caved in. He was right.

She grabbed a linen towel from the rack by the sink. "Fine. But a bleeding, half-naked man will draw attention. Understood?"

Peter groaned in resignation.

"Put on your shirt." She whipped the towel around the wound—deep and ugly and in need of stitches—and she bound it tight. "Keep your sleeve above the elbow and drape your overcoat over the bandage."

While Evelyn packed the suitcase, Peter finished dressing.

"I can't believe the innkeeper isn't up here. The gunshot . . ."

313

Peter eyed the door as he struggled into his suit jacket. "I'll fight him off if I must."

With her heartbeat reverberating in her ears, Evelyn threw on her hat, coat, and purse. A sick feeling wormed in her stomach. They'd used their real names on the hotel registration card since they had to show their papers. "Peter? We should call the police. If we run, we'll look guilty."

"Absolutely not." Peter slapped on his hat, tossed his coat over his injured arm, and picked up the gun with his good hand. "They want us dead. We aren't safe in France. Let's go."

Evelyn clamped her tongue between her teeth, picked up the suitcase, and followed him. She'd have to convince him to call the police along the way. Somehow, her law-abiding Peter had turned into a gunslinger.

Leading with that gun, he stepped out of the room, looked both ways, and dashed down the hall, light-footed. "Don't look in the bathroom."

Evelyn averted her gaze. Not only did she not want to see a dead body, but she also didn't want to be reminded that she needed to use the restroom.

Peter made his way downstairs. Everything was quiet. Why was there no shouting? No phones ringing?

At the bottom of the stairs, Peter held up one hand to signal Evelyn to wait, then he crept forward and peered behind the front desk. His shoulders drooped. "Lord, no."

"What?" She rushed to join him. Behind the desk—two feet— legs sprawled—

Peter tugged her into an embrace. "Don't look. His throat is slit. The innkeeper—he's dead, Evie. He's dead."

"Oh no. The poor man." She pressed her face into Peter's shoulder, her mind convulsing.

"Not to be callous, but that means he hasn't called the police."

Evelyn pulled herself together. She had to think straight. "Someone else in the neighborhood . . . surely someone heard."

"We have a little more time though." He guided her toward the front door.

"Wait." She spun away to the desk, to the box of green registration cards. Evelyn riffled through, found theirs, and stuffed it in her coat pocket. "Now we're clear. When we reach New York, we'll contact the authorities and tell them everything."

Peter stared at her pocket. "The registration card. I didn't even think—"

"Put away the gun. We'll stroll out as if nothing were amiss." Evelyn took his arm above the wound and led him outside.

Two women and a man stood in the street, calling to each other, pointing in different directions. Was it gunfire? Something else?

"Did you hear that too?" Evelyn put on a worried expression and pointed across the street. "Over there."

"*Oui, madame*," the gentleman said. "My wife is calling the gendarme."

"Good. Thank you." Evelyn gave him a grateful nod and led Peter to the south.

"The docks are the other way," Peter whispered.

She assumed a low voice. "We'll circle the block. If they report seeing us leave, they'll say we headed south, toward the train station."

"Good idea." Peter set the pace, brisk but unhurried.

"So . . ." She affected a cheerful voice and gazed at the row of pastel homes with windows rimmed in brick. "It looks like rain. Can you tell me what happened casually, as if we were discussing the weather?"

"Sure." Peter smiled at the gray sky. "A man was waiting in the bathroom, hiding in the cabinet. When I was at the sink, he tried to slit my throat. I raised my arm just in time."

Evelyn's stomach heaved. That could have been Peter sprawled dead on the floor. But she propped up her smile. "Did you recognize him?"

Peter turned the corner, tipped his hat to a young couple, and stayed silent until the couple was well behind them. "Never saw him before. He wore a uniform—like the SA, but with a blue shirt and a beret. His tie clip had a strange design—a sheaf of wheat, a wheel, a battle-ax."

"What?" Evelyn worked hard to maintain her neutral expression. "I know that badge. He was a Blue Shirt, a member of the *Mouvement Franciste*—it's a fascist group, antisemitic. They were banned a couple of years ago, but . . . obviously Norwood is working with them."

"Maybe. Or through Otto's connections. Or George and Otto working together. Doesn't matter who—it only matters that they want us dead."

An elderly man approached, hand in hand with a tiny girl, and Evelyn worked up a *"Bonjour."*

Was it her imagination or was the street more crowded, the people more menacing, the clothing bluer? "How do they know we're here? Did Norwood follow us?"

Peter shrugged and turned another corner, now headed north to the docks. "Or he simply realized we want to leave the country. Not many ships sail this time of year."

"What if . . ." She smiled at a lady with a baby carriage and waited a bit. "What if I did see Norwood at the embassy? What if he hid from you? What if he realized we came from the visa office and talked to the official? We mentioned the *Aquitania*."

"We did," Peter said in a low voice.

At the end of the street, the RMS *Aquitania* rose into view, her massive black hull, her elegant white upper decks, and four giant stacks painted red and tipped with black.

Evelyn had thought the ship would be a refuge. "We won't be safe on board."

"Yes, we will." Peter gave her a powerful look. "We have a first-class stateroom with a private bath. We'll have the steward bring our meals. We'll never have to leave. And in New York, we'll tell the police the whole story. If Norwood follows us, they can arrest him—or at least bring him in for questioning."

As they drew closer to the majestic ocean liner, a sad smile rose. "All those sumptuous dining rooms and lounges and swimming pools, and we'll be cowering in our stateroom."

Peter let out a dry chuckle. "Some romantic honeymoon, eh, Mrs. Lang?"

She gave him a gentle smile and a squeeze of the arm.

But her goal had careened from romance to survival.

FORTY-FOUR

RMS *Aquitania*
Tuesday, November 29, 1938

Jeffries, the steward, stood in the stateroom doorway holding a tray of late-night coffee. "I say, sir," he said in his British accent. "You have but two more nights at sea. You should enjoy a beautiful evening of dining and dancing."

"I'm on my honeymoon." Peter grinned and took the tray. "Thanks to your attentive care, I'm able to spend every second basking in my bride's presence."

Jeffries gazed past Peter to Evelyn, who was writing at the little desk between the two beds. "Women enjoy such evenings."

Evelyn sent the steward a mischievous smile. "I'm not most women."

Indeed, she wasn't, and Peter chuckled.

Jeffries released a deep sigh. "I'll return in half an hour for the tray—at midnight."

"Thank you." Peter locked the door behind him and set the tray on the bureau.

For the past five days, Peter had almost been able to forget they were on the run. The stateroom was comfortable, and Jeffries

318

brought everything they needed. He'd even brought the requested bottle of aspirin.

No need to worry Evelyn about the fever he'd felt rising all day. Peter popped two pills in his mouth, washed them down with coffee, and slipped the bottle in his trouser pocket.

Despite Evelyn's nursing, the knife wound was infected.

Peter brought Evelyn her coffee. "How is the story coming?"

She took a sip. "I finished another ten pages today. I hate writing longhand, but it'll do."

"Good." He sat on his bed with the book Jeffries had brought from the ship's library.

They'd passed the days leisurely, sleeping late and staying up late. But they'd spent their days well, reading, playing cards, and discussing her story. Evelyn had decided to write it truthfully, including George's role, then she'd edit it down for publication to avoid slander. She'd finished her feature-length article and was now working on a book.

Peter would have to wire half his savings account to Aubrey to pay for the first-class accommodations, but it was worth it to keep Evelyn safe and see the light return to her eyes.

His arm throbbed with heat. After he finished the chapter he was reading, he headed into the bathroom, where he rolled up his sleeve and unwound the bandage.

The redness this morning had concerned Evelyn. Now it was worse. But medical care had to wait until they passed customs in New York.

At the sink, Peter ran cold water over the wound and flinched from the pain.

"What do you think you're doing?" Evelyn leaned against the doorjamb.

He should have shut the door. "Changing the bandage."

"By yourself."

"I can do it."

"Let me see." Evelyn leaned around him. "Oh dear. It's so red."

Peter patted his arm dry with a towel. "It's fine. I must have exerted myself too much."

"How? Turning the pages of your book too vigorously?" She took his arm and gasped. "You're burning up."

"It's warm in here. It'll pass." As soon as the aspirin kicked in.

Evelyn pulled out a dry bandage and wound it around Peter's arm. "It's time to call the ship's doctor."

"We can't. He'll ask how it happened and why I didn't seek care earlier. They'll detain us on this side of customs, maybe send us back to France."

"We won't arrive in New York for two more days." Her voice trembled as she secured the bandage with a pin. "If this spreads . . ."

Her meaning was clear. In two days, it might be too late. "I'll be fine."

"I thought you looked flushed." She pressed an icy hand to his cheek. "Oh, darling, you're burning up."

Darling? Her voice, so tender. Her touch, so gentle.

Peter swallowed hard. "Maybe it's the fever making me imagine things, but I thought I heard you call me *darling*."

Her eyebrows jolted. Denial sparked in her eyes—then extinguished, replaced by a new fire, soft and content as a hearthside.

Could it be? Was she falling for him? After all this time? After he'd given up?

Evelyn dropped her hand and her gaze, and she rolled Peter's sleeve back in place. "The last few weeks, we've been together constantly, day and night." Her voice came out breathy.

Only one thing mattered—he needed to gather her in his arms right that moment.

A knock on the door.

"Oh!" Evelyn darted out of the bathroom. "That's Jeffries, returning for the tray."

Groaning, Peter clenched the rim of the sink, the fire now in his belly. Fever or no fever, as soon as Jeffries left, he'd tell Evelyn he loved her. *Show* her he loved her.

The stateroom door clicked open. Evelyn cried out—short and gulping.

"Shut up!" a man said. The door banged shut.

No! Peter dashed out of the bathroom. His gun—it was in his jacket—hanging by the stateroom door.

In the doorway, George Norwood held a gun to Evelyn's head.

Lord, no! Peter stopped short. "Put it down! Get your hands off her!"

George scowled at him. "Raise your voice again, and I'll put a bullet through her brain and gladly. Put your hands where I can see them."

Peter's breath raced, but he raised his hands to waist level. How had he let his guard down? How could he get his gun?

Evelyn stared at him, wide-eyed and pale, but her chin jutted forward. She wouldn't fall apart.

George looked ruffled. An overcoat draped over his raised elbow, and his homburg sat at an awkward angle. "The three of us will take a stroll on the deck, and you'll give me the list."

Peter had to delay him, think of a plan. "List? What are you talking about?"

"Don't play innocent. You know what I mean."

Peter's mind whirled, trying to outthink his former friend. Why did George want to go up on the deck? If Peter gave him the list, George would have to shoot them both to keep them quiet. If Peter refused, George would also have to shoot them. A gunshot in the cabin would rouse other passengers, and George would be apprehended. But the deck would be empty at midnight. George could kill them, throw their bodies overboard, and never be caught.

Swallowing hard, Peter spread his hands wide. "What list?"

"Otto told me all about it. You betrayed them. They trusted you with the list, trusted you to bring those people together for the good of America."

Every option Peter could think of ended in death, but he kept his voice calm. "I do plan to do what's best for America."

"You betrayed us." George's voice went hard. "I won't let you give that list to the FBI. My father's name is on that list."

Peter raised a little shrug. "He has nothing to fear if he hasn't done anything wrong."

"He hasn't. He just wants to put the communists and Jews in their place, bring back prosperity. But you—you want to drag my family's name through the mud, destroy the family company, make my father lose his seat in the House. I won't let you do that. You'll give me that list, and I'll use it for its intended purpose. I'll be the one to organize and lead, to do what's right."

"Don't give it to him," Evelyn said, her fists clenched at her sides.

He didn't intend to, but he needed time to think. That meant pacifying George.

"Let's go." George backed Evelyn away from the doorway, scooted the gun barrel down to her ribs, and jiggled his arm until the overcoat slid down to conceal the weapon. "Open the door, Lang. You'll walk in front. If you make any sudden moves or signal anyone, I'll shoot her, then you."

Peter eased forward, hands raised. His jacket hung on a hook by the door, but reaching for it would be a sudden move.

"Peter?" Evelyn said. "It's cold outside. Don't forget your jacket."

Just the excuse he needed, and he reached for it.

"Don't," George said with a growl.

Peter's hand hovered over the jacket. "Do you want the list or not?"

"It's in your jacket?"

It was still in his shoe. "Do you want it or not?"

"Give me the jacket."

No. No, he couldn't. His fingers agitated, yearning for the wool, the steel, their only chance. "It might be in there. It might not. I might be handing you the jacket to burden you or distract you and gain the advantage. Want to take that chance?"

"Fine. Put it on. But remember the gun is pointed at your wife's heart." His voice twisted around the word *wife*.

Peter's hand coiled like claws into his jacket. If only he could put a fist through George's face.

He stepped out into the empty passageway. Even if he saw someone, how could he signal without alerting George?

"We're right behind you," George said. "Remember—"

"I remember." Peter spat out the words, walked down the passageway, and pulled on his jacket. He slipped his hand into the inside pocket, to the cold steel over his heart. But by the time he could release the safety, turn, and aim, Evelyn would be dead.

"Hands by your side," George said.

Peter obeyed.

"Say, Georgie," Evelyn said in a taunting voice. "Too bad you don't have a silencer. You could have taken care of this whole nasty business in our nice toasty cabin."

"Shut up." George's words ground out. "Not one more word."

Thank goodness Evelyn wasn't ruffled. Because Peter was.

He had to figure out a plan—but what? On the deck, George would ask for the list. If Peter refused, George would search his dead body—the list wouldn't be hard to find. No matter what Peter did, in a matter of minutes, he and Evelyn would be dead and George would have the list.

His insides writhed, and his feet dragged. Maybe he should get it over with and make a sudden move in the passageway. The gunshots would bring people out from their rooms. Peter and Evelyn would die, but George would have to run. He wouldn't get the list. He might get caught.

No. He couldn't do that. He couldn't give up.

The ornate staircase neared, broad and open, with wrought-iron banisters.

"Up to the boat deck, to the badminton courts."

Peter trudged up the stairs. Once again, someone he loved was under attack, and he was powerless. What good were muscles against a gun? *Lord, show me what to do.*

It couldn't end this way. Not now. Evelyn had an important story to tell, a lifetime of stories. And Peter? Even though his life's work was destroyed, he could still use his talents for good.

On the landing, he turned and climbed the next flight.

Evelyn stared up at him, and her expression sank into his soul. She believed in him, not as a damsel in distress awaiting rescue, but as a partner. She trusted him. She'd work with him. She'd follow his lead.

Peter shoved away his despondency, and he mirrored her look. He trusted her too. He'd fight for her. And he'd gladly follow her lead if she had any ideas.

Because he had none.

He continued to climb, and each time he turned, he met her gaze, each time stronger. Only the Lord had power. Only the Lord would decide who lived and who died.

A strange and determined peace settled into his soul.

"Here we are," George said. "Open the door and go thirty paces down the center badminton court, then stop and face me."

Peter let out a sharp laugh. "Like a duel? Hardly an even match when only one of us has a gun."

"Too bad for you."

Peter shoved open the door, itching for his gun, but with his poor eyesight and the darkness, he'd be as likely to hit Evelyn as George.

Icy air buffeted him, and he resisted the urge to cross his arms against the cold. No sudden moves. At least he had his jacket. Evelyn wore only a wool dress.

Lifeboats hung to the side of the badminton courts, and the rush of waves sounded below.

He strode down the center court toward the mast strung with lights, counting out loud, just to irk George. The air cooled his fevered cheeks, but then the chills came. As if he needed anything else to throw off his aim.

To get in a good shot, he'd need a distraction so he could draw his gun unnoticed, and he'd need Evelyn to get out of the way.

"Thirty." Peter faced George, hands high. "Shoot."

George stopped about fifteen feet away, and he shifted the gun up to Evelyn's head. "Give me the list."

"Don't," Evelyn said. "He'll shoot us both."

George glared at her. "Shut up."

She'd distracted him, and Peter's mind spun, a needle whirling, pointing to possibilities. *Show me, Lord.*

"Give it to me." George jabbed the gun into Evelyn's cheek.

Peter had implied the list was in his jacket. He could grab the gun, but he'd still need a distraction. "It's in my jacket." With his left hand raised, Peter eased his right hand inside his jacket, around the steel.

Evelyn's eyes widened, and she shrank back from George. She knew what was in that pocket, knew how blind he was without his glasses—and fevered and shivering, to boot.

George yanked her back to his side. "Now, Peter! Give it to me."

The list was in his right shoe, and the spinning stopped, the needle pointing down—to that shoe.

"That's right," Peter said as the plan coalesced. "I moved it to my shoe."

"Your shoe?"

"Yes." In one fluid move, Peter swiveled to his right and went down to his knee, drawing out his gun and sliding it down the side of his right leg to the outside of his foot, away from George.

"What are you doing? Get where I can see you."

"I need light." Peter tilted his head to the mast to his right. "I can barely see without glasses, and I have a knot in my shoelace."

"Hurry up."

With his left hand, he fiddled with his shoelaces to conceal his manipulation of the gun with his injured, shivering hand. The safety would make a click. He needed noise to cover it.

"Don't give it to him," Evelyn said, her voice sharp.

His firebrand could create a distraction. "I have to, Evelyn. Don't be dramatic. You're always so *dramatic*." He emphasized the word and shot her a signal of a glance. Would she receive it?

"Dramatic?" Her voice rose. "I have every right to be dramatic. You can't give him the list. You just can't."

Smart, smart woman. Peter clicked off the safety.

"He'll shoot us both," she cried, wringing her hands. "He'll do awful things with that list. I know it."

"Shut up," George said. "Be quiet."

Peter slipped his finger into the trigger, but his right hand was weak from the injury, so he wrapped his left hand around the gun too.

"It's all my fault," Evelyn wailed. "Oh, Peter, you wouldn't be in this mess if it weren't for me."

"Shut up!" George gripped her harder, his gaze darting between Peter and Evelyn.

One more signal to send, and he prayed she'd receive it. He'd only get one shot before George turned the gun on him. And he needed to make sure he didn't hit Evelyn.

"Calm *down*, Evelyn." Peter made his voice disdainful, and he fixed a hard gaze on her. The more he sounded like a cad, the better. "Remember that time I slapped you? Remember why it happened? Because you didn't listen to me. Because you didn't do what I told you to do. I told you to calm *down*."

Even in the dark, he saw the anger on her face—but also the questions.

"Calm *down*." He jerked his head down in emphasis—signaling her to get down. "Calm *down*, Evelyn. Now!"

Her brows shot high in comprehension.

Down on one knee, Peter swung the gun toward George.

Evelyn dropped to the deck.

George yelled and turned the gun to Peter.

Shots rang out. Noise exploded in his ears. Light exploded in his eyes. Fire exploded in his right shoulder.

Peter fell to his right hip, his elbow, and fire snaked through his arm and chest. He'd been hit, and he cried out.

George! He was still on his feet, wobbling, clutching his side, raising the gun again.

"Peter!" Evelyn screamed, down on all fours.

He couldn't move his arm, couldn't feel his hand, the gun.

George aimed at him.

"No!" Evelyn swung her leg forward in an arc and knocked George's foot out from under him.

He went down flat on his back, and the gun skittered across the deck.

"Get it!" Peter cried. "Get the gun, Evie."

She scrambled after it on hands and knees, grabbed it, and pointed it at George.

"Shoot him!" Peter said.

Evelyn shook her head. She got to her feet and stood over George, who writhed on the deck, clutching his belly. Was he hit too?

"Help!" Evelyn screamed. She backed toward the door, the gun trained on George, and she flung the door open and called inside. "Help! We need help! My husband's been shot! We need a doctor!"

Relief and pain swamped him in equal measures. Peter rolled down to the wooden deck and felt his shoulder—hot and wet—and he groaned.

"Peter?" Evelyn edged toward him, the gun pointed at George. "Peter? Oh no. You're hit. How badly?"

"Just—my shoulder. I'm—fine. You—you're all right?"

"Yes." She swung her head back and forth between the two men. "My goodness. My goodness. My goodness."

Peter stretched a smile up to her, wanting to soothe her and thank her. "You were incredible. You—you saved my life."

Footsteps pounded over the deck.

"Over here!" Evelyn beckoned. "This man! He shot my husband. Take him into custody. And get a doctor."

"Give me the gun, ma'am."

"With pleasure. It's *his* gun." She kicked George's foot.

"What happened here?" a man asked.

Evelyn rushed to Peter's side, down to her knees. "I'll tell you everything, but first, get a doctor. He's been shot. And lock up that man."

"This fellow needs a doctor too," a second man said. "He's shot in the gut. Looks bad."

More footsteps, and men darted around above him, knelt by him, peeled away his jacket, his shirt.

All Peter could see was Evelyn's beautiful face, leaning over him, murmuring her worries, calling him her darling, her hero, her love, kissing his forehead over and over.

Was she delirious? No, he was. That was the only explanation.

Was the delirium from the fever? The gunshot wound? The tension?

Peter didn't care. Delirium was delicious.

FORTY-FIVE

Eight o'clock. Outside sick bay, Evelyn tapped her foot and adjusted the belt of the burgundy gabardine dress Simone had given her.

Dr. Schwartz meandered down the passageway with a teasing smile on his jowly face. "Ah, Mrs. Lang. What a surprise to find you here," he said in his German accent.

"How is he?" Evelyn pushed away from the wall. "You didn't let me see him all day yesterday. I haven't seen him in over thirty hours."

Dr. Schwartz opened the door to his examination room. "Only a new bride counts the hours."

The longest thirty hours of her life. "Please, sir. We're docking in a few hours, and it's vital that I speak with him before we disembark."

"I'll talk to the night orderly. Please have a seat." He slipped into Peter's room so quickly, Evelyn couldn't see past his portly frame.

She stared at the offending closed door. How could she sit? The ship's captain had wired ahead to New York. As soon as they docked, FBI agents and police would board to take testimonies and to arrest George Norwood. After that, Evelyn would be caught up in a flurry of cables and interviews and paperwork, the long list of tasks she'd assembled yesterday while staving off worry for Peter.

The coming hour might be her last time alone with him, to tell him how she felt and to lay out her case for a future together.

"Oh, Lord." Her foot resumed its frenetic tapping. "Show me the way to tell him the truth so we can have a life together."

She was mangling the Bible verse again, but this time it felt less self-serving.

Dr. Schwartz returned. "Your husband is much better today."

Every pent-up muscle uncoiled. "Thank goodness."

"He slept well. He's recuperating from his surgery."

"His fever? The knife wound?"

"He's responding to the sulfanilamide and the debridement. Other than nerve and bone damage, I expect him to make a full recovery."

Evelyn's eyes slid shut, and she pressed her hand to her mouth. "Thank goodness. Thank you, Doctor. May I—"

"Yes, you may see him." The doctor's eyes shone with kindness. "Then you both will stop pestering me."

"Has he—he's been asking for me?"

"Every minute. Go in. The orderly is in the operating room attending to—our other patient."

Norwood. She tensed, but Norwood was incapacitated by the gunshot wound and major abdominal surgery. Plus, they'd handcuffed him to the operating table for good measure.

Dr. Schwartz held open the door, and Evelyn stepped into the recovery room.

Peter lay in a bed against the right wall, and he craned up his head. "Evelyn."

"Oh, Peter." She pulled up a chair close beside him. He looked pale, but his eyes and smile were brilliant, and she stroked his brow, so blessedly warm and alive, yet so blessedly cool. "You're all right. Thank God you're all right."

"And you?" He searched her face. "You're all right?"

She smoothed back the golden waves of his hair. "A little shaken, but mostly worried about you. How do you feel?"

"Much better today."

"Your arm?" Gauze bandages wound up from his wrist and over his shoulder, crossing his bare chest. "Does it hurt?"

"Not as much as you'd think, but they give me morphine, so it's hard to tell." He gave her a lopsided smile. "Knowing you're safe is the best medicine ever."

She was indeed safe, but she'd still taken her meals in the state-room to avoid attention in the dining room. "Jeffries says the whole ship is talking about us, about the shooting."

Peter glanced past her toward the door to the operating room. "I'm glad you didn't listen when I told you to shoot him. I'm glad he's alive."

Sweet, compassionate Peter. Evelyn twiddled a blond curl around her finger. "I'm glad too, because he gave a full confession."

"He did? I thought I heard the doctor say something yesterday."

Her gaze roamed the curve of his eyelids, the sandy lashes, and the Wedgwood blue she loved. She nodded to reset her brain on the conversation. "Norwood heard Dr. Schwartz's German accent and assumed they were on the same side. Dr. Schwartz played along and brought in one of the ship's officers, who pretended to be a German agent."

"Clever," Peter said.

"Yes. Norwood told the officer everything. How he worked with the Gestapo, first to frame Mitch O'Hara and then to trap me. How he paid Helga to steal my passport, how his brother had a friend in the German passport office make the false passport, how he told Otto where I was on Kristallnacht so the mob could kill me."

Peter grunted, as close to a curse as she'd heard from him.

"Norwood had a list of French fascists in his pocket," Evelyn said. "He asked Dr. Schwartz to dispose of it. Those were the thugs he hired to shadow us in Paris—and the man he hired to kill us in Cherbourg."

Peter's eyes darkened. "The man I killed."

She raked back the curl she'd been playing with. "You acted in self-defense, and Norwood's confession sweeps away all doubt. You'll be questioned, but only as a formality. Norwood's going to prison. It'll be a mess of a case with so many countries and nationalities and a British ship on international waters, but he'll go to prison. So will his brother."

Peter shook his head on the pillow. Sadness turned down the corners of his eyes. "I never thought—never thought I'd have to shoot one of my oldest friends."

"Shh." She stroked his hair. "He shot too, remember? He planned to kill both of us. You acted in self-defense—and to protect me."

Her throat clamped shut. If she hadn't already been in love with him, she would have fallen that night.

Watching him stand up to Norwood, strong and resolute. Watching him communicate with her in a way only she would understand. Watching him down on one knee taking down the man who planned to murder her.

"I'd do it again." His voice rumbled in a way that turned her insides every which way.

"I know you would." She needed to kiss him. Right then. Her lips softened at the thought, yearning for him. But her body resisted, stiffened, disobedient.

"Thank you for understanding my signals." His gaze penetrated deep, as if reading the struggle within her heart.

"We make a good team." She was still playing with his hair, and her fingers stilled. They did make a good team, and that was the segue she needed, the one she'd searched for in vain during the entire voyage.

Did he return her feelings? The only way to find out would be to open her mouth and tell him.

Now was the moment.

A frustrated scream built up inside her, and she strangled it.

Evelyn pushed up to her feet and spun to the cabinet by the door, her back to Peter. His belongings lay strewn along the top, the books and toiletries she'd sent the day before. "What a mess. You poor thing. You need things in order."

"It's fine. We're arriving in New York soon anyway." His voice sounded distant. Sad.

Evelyn cringed as she straightened the books. What was she doing? Why couldn't she speak?

"New York," Peter said. "You can get your passport and your next assignment."

She tried to put his comb in the leather shaving kit, but she couldn't see, the window of her vision darkened. "Yes. Yes, I can."

"Where do you want to go?"

Wherever Peter was. Her lungs and her eyes and her mind opened wide, to the way, to the solution.

And the glass cleared.

She tucked Peter's comb into the kit. "As soon as you find a job, I'll ask for an assignment there."

Silence hung, thick and weighty, and Evelyn held her breath, her fingers tense around his toothbrush.

"What do you . . . ?" Peter coughed. "What do you mean?"

In went the toothbrush, and she raised one shoulder. "I couldn't figure things out, but I was going about it backward, trying to figure out how you could teach while I gallivanted around the world. But I'm a reporter. A reporter can work anywhere. No matter where you go, I can write."

"I . . . I'm missing something."

Yes, he was. The something about her loving him and wanting to be his wife forever. She zipped the shaving kit shut. "We're a good team, don't you think?"

"Yes . . ." A question turned up the end of the word.

"I never really thought of marriage as a trap. The person traps, not the institution. And you—I trust you."

The bed creaked behind her, and bedclothes rustled. "Evelyn, please turn around so I can see your face."

Evelyn plopped the kit on top of the books. "For heaven's sake, Lang. I read your signals on the deck in the dark. Why can't you read mine now?"

"Evie . . ." His voice drew her, warm and inviting, but firm. "I want—to see—your face."

That face scrunched up, and she turned to him, peering out of one eye.

Peter sat up, leaning against the headboard, his expression as tender as when he was pretending to love her. Only now he had no reason to pretend.

All her reservations melted, and her mouth fell open. "I love you." She slapped her hands over her face. "Oh, for heaven's sake. Of all the trite—I'm a writer! Surely I could find a better way to say—"

"Evelyn Lang!"

Her hands slid down to her chin, and she stared at him.

Peter beckoned with his good arm, bare and sculpted in masculine perfection. "Would you get over here so I can kiss you?"

"You want to kiss me?"

He grinned and beckoned again. "Yes, I want to kiss you, because I love you, and I want to have and to hold you till death us do part. And I'll follow you to Timbuktu, or you can follow me to Podunk Falls. I don't care as long as we're together."

He loved her? Oh, he did!

Evelyn rushed to him, perched on the side of the bed, her hands on his cheeks, his arm around her back, her lips on his, his lips on hers, her heart big and full in her throat, throbbing with joy.

His mouth widened under hers in a smile. "I should get shot more often."

"No. No, you shouldn't." She shook her head, rubbing her nose against his, careful to keep her weight off his injured arm. "Never again, you darling, darling man."

He worked his hand into her hair, cupping the back of her head, his eyes smoky. "I like it when you call me darling."

She kissed his adorably crooked nose. "I like it when you call me Evie. But no one else can call me that. No one. Just you."

"My Evie. My darling Evie." He pulled her to him, to those perfect lips, to his marvelous kiss, his wonderful love.

This was no trap, but freedom—true and ordered freedom, leaning upon and being leaned upon, giving and receiving, speaking and listening.

"Come here." He guided her over him, to sit with her hips on his good side and her legs draped across his lap. "That's better."

She tugged the blanket higher on his bare chest. "Don't want to scandalize the doctor."

"Why not? We're on our honeymoon." He gave her a playful smile, a promising smile, and he nuzzled his face in her neck. "It turned into a romantic honeymoon after all."

She laughed and cradled his head, relishing the warmth of his kisses. "A shootout and a garbled declaration of love in sick bay. Oh yes—what could possibly be more romantic?"

Peter's lips traveled up over her jaw toward her mouth. "I have a lifetime to make it up to you."

What a delectable thought. But she let a chuckle escape with one more barb for old times' sake. "Good, Lang. You'll need it."

FORTY-SIX

COLUMBIA PRESBYTERIAN HOSPITAL
MANHATTAN, NEW YORK
SATURDAY, DECEMBER 10, 1938

With each sit-up, Peter eyed the closed door to his room at Columbia Presbyterian Hospital. The doctors urged him not to do calisthenics and said he'd never have full use of his right arm again. But he was determined to regain as much strength as possible.

The private room helped conceal his activity.

The first few days, police had guarded his hospital room. But the FBI was convinced Norwood had acted alone, since none of the French fascists on his list were on board.

As for the German agents on Peter's list, one had already fled the US during a recent FBI investigation and the other was now under arrest because of Peter. The American Nazi sympathizers had broken no laws, but the FBI would keep an eye on them.

After he finished his sit-ups, Peter slipped his pajama top over his left arm and draped it over his right arm in its sling. Visiting hours started soon, and Evelyn never missed, despite the busy week she'd had.

At the sink, Peter dipped his toothbrush in tooth powder and scrubbed oatmeal and orange juice from his breath.

In the past week, Peter and Evelyn had testified to the FBI and the police and had given interviews to newspapers and the ANS. Evelyn had called Peter's mother to tell her Peter was all right—and to introduce herself. She'd called her parents in Chicago to send her birth certificate, which they'd brought in person. She'd visited the passport office and the ANS bureau, and she'd ordered new eyeglasses for Peter from his optometrist back home.

In addition, she'd signed with an agent and had met with magazine and book editors eager for her story.

A knock on the door. "It's me."

"Come in." Peter took a quick rinse of water.

Evelyn tossed her coat and purse on the bed and met him halfway across the room. He gathered her in a one-armed embrace and kissed her long and well.

She slipped her arms around his waist—under his pajama top. "I missed you, darling."

How could he speak while she was caressing his back? He cleared his throat. "Missed you too. I can't wait until they discharge me."

"Me too." Her coffee eyes darkened with longing, not a hint of milk at all.

He drew her close for another kiss. Three weeks they'd been married. Ten days they'd known they loved each other. But he couldn't take her to bed until they released him from this prison of a hospital, so he cut the kiss short.

Besides, the door was open.

He leaned back to look her in the face. "How was your morning?"

"Wonderful. Libby and I went shopping." She pulled out of his arms and twirled, displaying a gray suit with red trim and a matching hat. "Still replacing my wardrobe."

"I like it." He beckoned with one finger. "But I like it better up close."

"Not now. Libby wants to say hello. She's waiting in the hallway for us to finish."

Peter leaned close. "I'll never finish." But then he raised his voice. "Come in, Libby. It's safe."

Libby White entered the room wearing a dark green suit and a pretty smile. "Hi, Peter. It's good to see you on your feet again."

He pressed one finger to his lips. "Don't tell my doctor."

"What have you done to him, Evelyn?" Libby heaved a sigh, then shook her head at Peter. "I was counting on you to keep her in line."

"Are you kidding? Now she has to keep me in line."

"Hopeless." But Libby smiled. "Well, I can't stay. I have to get ready for tonight's concert, and Evelyn has a full schedule for you today. I'll see you later."

Peter shook her hand, said good-bye, and turned to his wife. "Schedule?"

She glanced at her watch. "We have one minute. Let's make you presentable, although it's a shame to cover you up." She closed his pajama top and did up a few buttons.

"Promise to unbutton me later?" he murmured.

"No." She laughed and guided him to a chair by the window. "You'll sit here and our guests here."

Peter smiled as she scooted chairs around, caring for him, busy and purposeful, her shapely legs flashing beneath the hem of her skirt.

She stepped into the hallway and waved. *"Guten Tag!"*

German? Peter raised his eyebrows. He hadn't heard the language since they'd entered France, and for the first time in his life he hadn't wanted to.

A young man in a snappy gray suit entered—Hans-Jürgen Schreiber!

"Hans-Jürgen!" Peter sprang from his chair and pumped the boy's hand—the man's hand. "It's so good to see you."

"It is good to see you too, Herr Lang."

Another man stood behind Hans-Jürgen—Professor Kurt Wagner, Peter's faculty advisor at Harvard. Peter's heart sank low again. *"Guten Tag*, Herr Professor."

"*Guten Tag*, Herr Lang." Wagner smiled as if he hadn't come to close the coffin on Peter's career. "Frau Lang told me about your ordeal."

Peter gave her a sad smile. She'd done so to gain sympathy, but sympathy couldn't replace research.

"Please come in, gentlemen." Evelyn showed everyone to their seats. "Thank you for coming out from Cambridge. We're honored by your visit."

Professor Wagner set a suitcase beside his chair—he must not have had time to stop at his hotel.

Etiquette demanded Peter address the older man first, but burning curiosity turned his attention to the younger. "Any word from your parents? Are they all right?"

"Yes." Hans-Jürgen settled his fedora in his lap, revealing a shorter haircut in the American style. "They send letters. We have a code."

Professor Wagner smoothed what remained of his graying blond hair. "After Kristallnacht, Jim Purcell's parents convinced him to cut his junior year in Munich short and return to Harvard. He brought messages from Professor Schreiber."

Peter's chest muscles tensed more than when doing one-armed push-ups. "Hans-Jürgen—any word about the couple I brought to your parents' house? Did the Gestapo visit?"

A smile spread on the young man's face. "My father escorted the Golds safely over the French border. They have tickets to Lisbon. My father gave them my address, and they promised to write me when they reach Bolivia."

"What good news." Evelyn clutched Peter's hand. "Please thank your father for us."

"Yes, please do." A month-old sigh leached out. "I'm so thankful. Please let me know when they write."

"I am glad you helped them, Herr Lang. I am ashamed of what my country is doing." Hans-Jürgen's mouth thinned. "After Kristallnacht, students at Harvard and Radcliffe started a committee to aid student refugees. But I can only help quietly. Most of the German exchange students are ardent Nazis. If I speak out, my parents will be in danger."

Professor Wagner nodded. "Or the German government could recall you and make you return."

"That is the last thing your parents want," Peter said.

"I know. But I do tell my American friends about life in Germany. They need to know."

Peter exchanged a look with Evelyn. They were both determined to declare that truth as well.

"You asked about the Gestapo," Hans-Jürgen said. "They did not visit my parents, but they did raid your office."

"I knew they would." No grief accompanied those words. He'd accepted the loss.

"But not before my father did." A grin burst onto Hans-Jürgen's face.

"Pardon?"

"Jim Purcell told us what happened, straight from Professor Schreiber." Professor Wagner stood, set the suitcase on the bed, and opened it. "After you brought the Golds to his house, the good professor went to your office and filled this suitcase. When Mr. Purcell sailed from Hamburg, he told the Gestapo the papers were his own."

"My . . . papers?" Peter gripped his jaw with his good hand, his fingers splayed over his mouth.

Wagner riffled through the contents. "The logbook for your recordings, what looks like a rough draft of your dissertation, notebooks and folders—all neatly labeled. Your organization made it easy for Professor Schreiber to know what to pack. He did leave some papers—mostly lesson plans and tests. He wanted the Gestapo to feel successful."

Peter pushed himself to standing, numb inside. "My research?" he murmured between his fingers, staring down at what he'd thought forever lost.

"Isn't it wonderful?" Evelyn's eyes glistened.

"You knew?" His voice came out throaty.

She clutched her hands before her chest. "I called the professor on Tuesday. It's been so difficult to keep secret."

He gave her shoulder a quick squeeze, then stroked the leather of his logbook. "I can't believe it. I can't—but I still—I'm still missing the last set of data. I won't be able to complete my research."

"My father is your research assistant."

Peter whipped his gaze to Hans-Jürgen. "Pardon?"

"He took over teaching your classes, of course," Hans-Jürgen said. "Jim said he promised to use your methods as best he could. He will record the students at the end of the semester and send the data. That night when he rescued your papers, he moved the Dictaphone into his own office."

Peter's throat felt swollen, and he forced a cough to clear his airway. "He'd do that for me?"

Hans-Jürgen's expression turned solemn. "After what you did that night, he feels it's the least he can do."

Evelyn stood and hugged his arm. "It's an appropriate reward for your courage and compassion."

Wagner pulled a slip of paper from his jacket pocket. "Mr. Purcell said the professor was adamant that you hear this precisely, so I wrote it down. He said, 'Sometimes a reed must choose to become a rod and risk the breaking in the storm.'"

Peter closed his eyes and prayed hard for the professor, his friend, because the storm would only build in intensity.

"Of course, we'll accept Professor Schreiber's data on your behalf," Wagner said. "Mrs. Lang seemed concerned that you'd lose your position at Harvard, but your worries are groundless. We're glad you're back. Professor Kramer is in poor health, and if you're willing to take over his classes next semester, we would be most grateful."

Peter lowered himself into his chair, but he didn't trust his voice.

His research, his life's work, his hoped-for career—all restored. He squeezed his eyes shut and thanked the Lord.

"What my husband means to say is, 'Yes, thank you. I'd be delighted, and I'll be ready first thing in January.'"

Peter nodded and smiled, closed lipped, thanking his wife with his eyes that she'd spoken when he couldn't, thanking Professor Wagner for the gift and the opportunity.

"Well." The professor slapped his hands to his thighs and got to his feet. "I promised your wife we wouldn't take much of your time. We need you healed so you can teach."

Peter stood and shook both men's hands. "Hans-Jürgen, please tell your parents—in code—that my wife and I are safe and that we're most grateful."

"I will, sir." He and the professor departed.

Peter drew Evelyn to his side. "I can't believe it. I can't."

She squeezed his waist. "Now I can tell you my other news. I start at the Boston bureau of the ANS in January. I'll also work on my book while we're in Cambridge. And then—" She spun away and looked at the clock on the wall.

"Then what?"

She raised an enigmatic smile, straightened his pajama top, and stepped out of the room again—and waved again.

"How many appointments do I have?" Peter asked.

"This is the last one."

"I'm glad to hear that." Good news was strangely depleting.

His oldest brother, Richard, strode into the room in a pinstriped navy suit.

Peter laughed and crushed him in a hug. "What brings you up from Capitol Hill?"

Rich gripped Peter's good shoulder. In his mid-thirties, Rich looked so much like their father, Peter's chest ached. "It isn't every day your little brother makes the papers as a big hero."

Peter rolled his eyes, feeling about ten years old.

"Mutti said your *wife* called—that was a surprise. Then lo and behold, the newest Mrs. Lang called my office the very next day."

"You did?" Peter asked her. Then he noticed an Army officer in the doorway, and he stood a bit taller. "Good day, sir."

Rich beckoned the man inside. "Colonel Collins, this is my brother, Peter, and his wife, Evelyn. Peter, this is Colonel Bill Collins."

Evelyn ushered the men to their seats. "I told Representative Lang about the interest the German army and the Abwehr had shown in your language instruction skills. I assumed our own military would be just as interested."

Rich removed his homburg and took his seat. "I knew just the man to call."

"I had a long discussion with the faculty in the German department at Harvard." The colonel spoke with a gravelly voice that matched his chiseled face. "I'd like to talk to you."

"Yes, sir. I'll do whatever I can to help." Peter didn't hesitate.

"Good. We'll let you finish your PhD first, of course, but I'm glad you're interested. I'm sure you can see how useful your skills could be."

Somehow those words didn't sound sinister this time. "Yes, sir. War is coming."

Rich dipped his head as if his little brother had embarrassed him on the playground.

"It is, Rich," Peter said. "Hitler keeps snatching, and he keeps getting away with it. Each time he gets bolder. Someday he'll cross a line and there will be war. We might fool ourselves into thinking it's only Europe's concern, but it isn't. The way the Nazis treat people is a concern to all humanity, and therefore, to us."

The colonel blew out a sigh. "I hope you're wrong, but I fear you're right."

Peter laid a hand on his bandaged shoulder. "With this arm and my bad eyesight, I'll be no good with a gun. But the skills I have—if they can help in any way—I gladly offer them."

Colonel Collins chuckled. "Ah, Mr. Lang, don't you know pacifism is in vogue this season? You're behind the times."

Peter lifted a sad smile. "Or ahead of them."

"Either way, we're glad you're on our side." The colonel rose and shook Peter's hand.

Rich did likewise. "You'll have to come to DC for a visit. My wife and kids want to meet the newest family member."

"Thank you." Evelyn looped her arm around Peter's waist. "I can't wait to meet them."

"And . . ." Rich's expression sobered. "My friends on the Hill need to hear about your experiences in Germany. Whether or not war is coming, we have to be aware of what's happening."

"I'd be glad to."

"I can't believe the Norwoods . . ." Rich shuddered. "Representative Norwood is under pressure to resign. He doesn't stand a chance in the next election."

"Not surprising." Scandal had hit the Norwoods hard, with an FBI investigation, one son under arrest on multiple counts, and the other son summoned home to face charges.

Peter frowned. "I wonder what Father would say to all this."

Rich clamped his hand on Peter's shoulder, and his eyes misted over. "Father would say he's very proud of his third son."

Peter's throat swelled shut again. He just nodded and let Evelyn say the appropriate good-byes and thank-yous and see-you-soons.

After Rich and the colonel left, Evelyn hugged Peter and laid her head on his shoulder. "I'm proud of you too and so very happy for you."

All his life, he'd longed to have an influence in the world. Now he'd have a true influence for good, deep and broad, aided by the Lord and by the incredible woman in his arms.

He placed a kiss on her temple. "Ready, Mrs. Lang? Let's shake up this world."

FORTY-SEVEN

Notes from Libby's flute danced to the high Gothic arches of the church on Fifth Avenue. Evelyn pressed to Peter's side in the pew, their entwined hands resting in the valley between his black tuxedo trousers and her red velvet gown.

Peter had been discharged from the hospital the day before, and the Christmas Eve concert just barely managed to entice them out of their suite at the Plaza.

Evelyn closed her eyes and soaked in the final song. A chorale sang "Silent Night" while Libby's flute wafted above, embellishing and enlightening.

A German song, and her head dragged low. But she had to remember people like the Schreibers and General Gerlach and "Frau Engel" were doing what they could under the threat of death. Evelyn prayed for their continued strength and courage.

The conductor lowered his baton, Libby and the chorale bowed, and Evelyn applauded.

She glanced at Peter, and he grinned, the gorgeous blue of his eyes framed by glasses again.

Only nine months earlier, she'd sat beside him at Libby's concert, admiring his eyes and his crooked nose and contemplating two, three, four dates. Now she contemplated twenty, thirty, forty years, or more.

They filed out of the sanctuary with the festively clad crowd. Peter fetched their coats from the cloakroom, and she helped him arrange his coat over his sling.

Outside, the previous day's dusting of snow had evaporated, but frostiness tingled Evelyn's face.

She tucked her hand in the crook of Peter's good arm and strolled by his side. Christmas lights and displays decorated the tall buildings, and Salvation Army bells rang on the other side of the street.

Peter tilted his head, the top hat making him look especially dapper. "On a night like tonight, with music like that in your ears, it's almost possible to believe in peace on earth. If only . . ." He sighed. "Well, at least Herr and Frau Gold are finding peace on earth."

"I'm so glad." Hans-Jürgen Schreiber had called. Herr Gold had written from Lisbon, where he and his wife were about to board a steamer bound for South America.

"If only it were possible for all the others." A frown dug into Evelyn's cheeks. Hundreds of thousands of Jews remained in the Greater Reich, and still more antisemitic laws had been passed. "It gets worse and worse over there. It's horrible."

"It is." Peter nudged her. "But let's think of happier things tonight. It's Christmas, and we're on our honeymoon."

Evelyn's parents had treated them to a week at the Plaza for a Christmas present. After that, they'd go to Albany, where Peter's mother was throwing a wedding reception. Then to Boston.

"You're still frowning," Peter said.

They passed Feldman's Menswear, the plate-glass window shiny and intact, and Evelyn sighed. "The glass won't stop shattering."

A traffic cop waved them across the street with a Merry Christmas—a policeman enforcing order and freedom, not trampling them.

"The thing about glass . . ." Peter's eyes narrowed in the thoughtful way she adored. "It may shatter, but you can melt it down and create something new and good."

"Yes, but that requires high heat. Just how hot will this world have to get?"

The Plaza stood tall and majestic on the corner of Fifth Avenue, but Peter passed by the door.

Evelyn gave him a curious look. Considering how difficult it had been to get him clothed and out of their suite, she assumed he'd be eager to reverse the process.

Instead, he led her across the street and into Central Park, where a gilded statue of William Tecumseh Sherman guarded the park entrance, with Nike, goddess of victory, leading the general's horse.

"Where are we going?" Evelyn asked.

"To find clarity." He stopped in the square just past the statue, came behind Evelyn, and wrapped his arm around her waist. "Come here."

She relaxed back against his solid chest, mindful of his healing arm in its sling.

"The night is coming, isn't it?" His voice rumbled low in her ear.

Evelyn hugged his arm to her stomach. "It is." Her voice caught.

"Look up, my love. What do you see?"

"Buildings, lights . . ."

"Past that." He pressed his cheek to hers. "What do you see in the sky?"

Evelyn peered into the inkiness. "Stars. I can barely see them with the city lights though."

"But they're there. They're always there. Clouds may conceal them, but they're still there. Even in the darkest night, the stars always shine."

Light in the darkness, peace in the chaos, and a smile rose. No matter how dark the world became, there would always be some light, some music, some hope. She had to seek it and coax it out.

Evelyn leaned against the man she loved. They'd help each other seek the hope and speak the truth.

"You're a star, you know." Peter kissed her cheek. "Use those beautiful points of yours to prick people's consciences, to poke holes in their preconceived notions and their complacency. Then flood them with brilliant light."

Why had she taken so long to fall in love with this man? He didn't want to silence her voice but to magnify it. And she wanted to magnify his voice as well.

Evelyn twisted to face him, and she kissed his chin. "You're a star too. You're going to share truth with your students and the faculty and in those lectures everyone wants you to give."

Peter leaned his forehead against hers. "Well then, let's shine together."

Read On for a Sneak Peek of
Another Captivating Story From

SARAH SUNDIN!

COMING SOON

Paris, France
Wednesday, May 29, 1940

As long as she kept dancing, Lucille Girard could pretend the world wasn't falling apart.

In the practice room at the Palais Garnier, Lucie and the others in the *corps de ballet* curtsied to Serge Lifar, the ballet master, as the piano played the tune for the *grande révérance*.

Lifar dismissed the ballerinas, and they headed to the dressing room, their pointe shoes softly thudding on the polished wood floor, but more softly than ever. Since Germany had invaded the Netherlands and Belgium and France earlier in the month, dancers were fleeing Paris.

"Mademoiselle Girard?" the ballet master called in his Ukrainian-accented French.

Lucie's breath caught. He rarely singled her out, and she turned back with a light smile full of expectation and a tight chest full of dread. *"Oui, monsieur?"*

Serge Lifar stood with the erect bearing of a dancer in his prime and the casual authority of the innovative choreographer who had returned the Paris Opéra Ballet to glory. "I am surprised you are still in Paris. You are an American. You should go home."

Lucie had read the notice from US Ambassador William Bullitt in *Le Matin* that morning. Yes, she could sail with the other expatriates on the SS *Washington* from Bordeaux on June 4, but she wouldn't. "This *is* my home. I won't let German soldiers or bombs scare me."

351

He glanced away, and a muscle twitched in his sharp-angled cheek. "The French girls would gladly take your place."

"*Oui, monsieur*. Thank you for your concern for my safety." Lucie dropped a small *révérance* and scurried off, over boards graced by ballerinas for over sixty years, by the dancers in Edgar Degas's paintings, and for the past sixteen years, by little Lucie Girard.

In the dressing room for the *quadrille*, the fifth and lowest rank of dancers, she squeezed onto a bench with all the young girls. After she untied the ribbons of her pointe shoes, she eased the shoes off, folded in the sides, and wound the ribbons around the insteps as she inspected the toes for spots that needed darning.

Somber faces and quiet conversations filled the dressing room, so Lucie gave the girls reassuring smiles and words as she shimmied out of her skirted leotard and into her street dress.

Lucie blew the girls a kiss and stepped into the hallway to wait for her friends in the *coryphée* and the *sujet*, the fourth and third ranks, where most of the ballerinas Lucie's age were.

She leaned back against the wall as dancers breezed down the hall. After six years at the Paris Opéra Ballet School, Lucie had been admitted to the *corps de ballet* at the age of sixteen. For ten years since, she'd felt the sting of not advancing to the next rank, tempered by the joy of continuing to dance in one of the best ballets in the world.

"Lucie!" Véronique Baudin and Marie-Claude Desjardins bussed her on the cheek, and the three roommates made their way out of the building made famous by the novel *The Phantom of the Opera*.

Out on Avenue de l'Opéra, Lucie inserted herself between her friends on the sidewalk to create a pleasing tableau of Véronique's golden tresses, Lucie's light brown waves, and Marie-Claude's raven curls.

Not that the refugees on the avenue would care about tableaux, and Lucie ached for their plight. A stoop-shouldered man in peasant's garb pulled a two-wheeled cart loaded with small children, furniture, and baggage, and his wife trudged beside him, leading a dozen goats.

"What beasts the Germans are," Marie-Claude muttered about the soldiers who had frightened these people out of their homes.

"Did you hear?" Véronique stepped around an abandoned crate on the sidewalk. "The Nazis cut off our boys in Belgium, and now they're driving north to finish them off."

Marie-Claude wrinkled her pretty little nose. "British beasts. Running away at Dunkirk and leaving us French to fend for ourselves."

"Let's go this way." Lucie led her friends to a side street too narrow for the refugees. "And it's such a lovely spring day. Let's not talk of the war."

"What else can we talk about?" Véronique frowned up at the blue sky as Parisians did nowadays, watching for Luftwaffe bombers.

At the intersection ahead, a blue-caped policeman carrying a rifle—still a jarring sight—checked a young man's identity papers.

"Do you suppose he's a German spy?" Véronique whispered, her green eyes enormous. "I heard a parachutist landed in the Tuileries yesterday."

Lucie smiled at her friend. "If we believed every reported sighting of a parachutist, the Germans would outnumber the French in Paris. We mustn't be disheartened by rumors."

In the next block, a middle-aged couple in expensive suits stood beside a sleek black car and barked orders at servants who were loading the car with boxes.

Marie-Claude brushed past them, forcing the wife to take a little step to the side. "Bourgeois beasts."

Lucie's mouth went tight, and she nodded. Typical businessman who lobbied for war so he could get rich and now fled when that war threatened those riches.

The ladies passed the Louvre, crossed the Seine, and entered the Latin Quarter on the Left Bank, home of artists and writers and others of like mind.

The cheery green façade of Green Leaf Books quickened Lucie's steps.

"We'll see you upstairs." Véronique blew Lucie a kiss. "We know you want to visit the Greenblatts."

Lucie blew a kiss back and entered the English-language bookstore, a home for American and British and French literati since Hal and Erma Greenblatt founded it after the Great War. When Lucie's parents moved to Paris in 1923, they'd become fast friends with the Greenblatts.

"Hello, Lucie." Hal peeked out of the back office. "Come join us."

"Okay." Lucie flipped back to English. Why was he in the office? Hal liked to greet customers and help them choose books, while Erma did the bookkeeping and other tasks.

After Lucie greeted Bernadette Martel behind the cash register, she made her way through the store, past the delightfully jumbled bookshelves and the tables which fostered conversations about art and theater and the important things in life.

Boxes were piled outside the office door, and inside the office Hal and Erma stood in front of the desk, faces wan.

"What—what's wrong?" Lucie asked.

Hal set his hand on Lucie's shoulder, his brown eyes sad. "We're leaving tomorrow."

"Leaving? But you can't."

"We must." Erma lifted her thin shoulders as she always did when her decisions were etched in stone. "The Nazis don't allow Jews to run businesses."

"They won't come to Paris, I know it." Lucie gestured to the north where French soldiers lined the Somme and Aisne Rivers. "Besides, you're American citizens. They won't do anything to you. Our country is neutral."

"We can't take any chances," Erma said. "We're going to Bordeaux and sailing home. You should come too."

Lucie had already told them she'd never leave. But as a Christian, she could afford to be brave and remain in Paris, come what may. She could never forgive herself if she persuaded the Greenblatts to stay and they ended up impoverished—or worse.

An ache grew in her chest, but she gave them an understanding look. "You're taking the SS *Washington*."

Erma stepped behind the desk and opened a drawer. "If we can."

"Hush, Erma. Don't worry the girl."

"*If* you can?" Lucie glanced back and forth between the couple.

"We don't have the money for the passage." Erma pulled out folders and stacked them on the desk. "It's all tied up in the store."

Lucie's hand rolled tight around the strap of her ballet bag. "You can—you can sell the store, can't you?"

Hal chuckled and ran his hand through his black hair threaded with silver. "Who would buy it? All the British and American expatriates are fleeing."

"What will you do?" Lucie's voice came out small.

"We have friends." Hal spread his hands wide as if to embrace all those he had welcomed over the years. "We have lots of friends."

Erma thumped a stack of papers on the desk, her mouth tight. "I refuse to beg."

Hal dropped Lucie a quick wink. He'd beg his friends.

What if those friends didn't have the means or the heart to help? What if the Germans did conquer all of France, including Bordeaux?

No. No. A shiver ran through her. Lucie couldn't let anything happen to them, not when she had both the means and the heart. "I'll give you the money. I have enough."

"What?" Erma's gaze skewered her. "We can't take your money."

"Why not?" She entreated Hal with her eyes, as if she were thirteen again and asking him to dip into the allowance from her parents for a new pair of pointe shoes. "I'm practically family. I lived with you for three years. Because of you, I could stay in the ballet school when my parents returned to New York. You've always said I'm like the daughter you never had."

Hal patted her shoulder. "If we took your money, how would you get home?"

"I'm not going home. I told you."

Erma flipped through a folder. "You'll change your mind when the bombs start falling. Look what Hitler did to Warsaw and Rotterdam."

It wouldn't happen to Paris. It couldn't. "I'll be fine. I want you to have my money."

Hal turned Lucie to the door. "Don't worry about us. Now, I know you're hungry after practice. Go. Eat. We'll talk to you later tonight."

Out into the warmth of the store, her home, but it was all falling away, falling apart. The Greenblatts—leaving. The store—closing.

Green Leaf Books was their dream, their life, and they were giving it up.

Ballet was Lucie's dream. Her life. All she knew. Could she give it up? If she did, what would she have? Who would she be?

She rose to demi-pointe and turned slowly, taking in the shelves and tomes and the rich scent, and she knew what she'd have, who she'd be.

Lucie whirled back into the office. "I'll buy the store."

Erma looked up from the box she was packing. "Pardon?"

"I'll buy the store. Not a gift. A business transaction."

Hal's chin dropped. "Dear, sweet Lucie. You are so kind. But you—you're a ballerina."

"Not anymore." Although she did stand in fifth position. She breathed a little prayer for forgiveness for lying. "Lifar plans to cut me. I need a job. I'll run the bookstore."

After twenty-five years of marriage, Hal and Erma could speak volumes to each other with a glance. And they did. Then Erma sighed and stood up straight. "But Lucie, you're a *ballerina*."

Lucie's cheeks warmed. True, she wasn't terribly smart, especially with numbers, and she wasn't well read. But she kept her chin up. "I'm good with people, with customers. And Bernadette helps you with the business end of things. She knows how it runs. She and I—we can run the store."

"Lucie . . ." Hal's voice roughened.

Her eyes stung. Her lashes felt heavy. "And when we kick the Germans back to where they belong, this store will be here, waiting for you. I promise."

Erma stared at the folder in her hands, her chin wagging back and forth. Wavering.

"I want to do this." Lucie swiped the moisture from her eyes. "I need to do this. Please. Please trust me with your store."

Erma set down the folder and came to Lucie, ever the stern one, the practical one, the one to say no. She gripped Lucie's shoulders and pressed her forehead to Lucie's. "It's yours. You dear, dear girl."

Lucie fumbled for Erma's beloved hands and tried to say thank you, but she could only nod. Then she broke away and ran out, ran upstairs to her flat.

Now she couldn't change her mind about leaving Paris, even if the Germans came. Now she had to resign from the ballet. Now she'd have to figure out how to run a bookstore.

But she wouldn't change a thing.

Dear Reader,

Sometimes it's difficult to pinpoint where a story idea begins, but for this novel it began when my family visited Ellis Island. To my surprise and joy, I found a listing for my grandfather's voyage home from Germany in 1936. I knew he had studied in Germany, but it hadn't sunk in that he'd studied in *Hitler's* Germany.

Peter is not—I repeat *not*—modeled after my grandfather. But many elements of his career are based on my grandfather's. John F. Ebelke studied in the Junior Year in Munich program in 1935–36, received his PhD in German from the University of Michigan, became a professor at Wayne State University, and cowrote a textbook with Conrad P. Homberger. Their work, which included pronunciation diagrams of the mouth, lips, and tongue, was unusual for its time and helped many students over the years—including me.

During World War II, John Ebelke served with the US Army Specialized Training Program to teach American soldiers the German language and culture. After the war, he was instrumental in reinstating the Junior Year in Munich program. Sadly, he died in 1960, and I never had the chance to meet him.

You'll see many of these elements in Peter's story, but everything else about Peter's story is entirely fictional, *especially* his ethical struggle.

However, Peter and Evelyn display the two most common reactions to prewar Nazi Germany (1933–39) seen in American and British visitors—students, tourists, businessmen, correspondents, and others. Some were impressed with the cleanliness, order, and prosperity, while the rest of the world struggled with the upheaval and economic troubles of the Great Depression. Others were horrified by the persecution of Jews, political opponents, religious leaders, and the disabled—years before the horrors of the death camps and gas chambers. Those visitors felt the oppressive atmosphere of living in a police state, where saying the wrong thing to the wrong person could land you in a concentration camp.

General Gerlach is fictional, but he represents real German military officers who plotted to arrest Hitler when he gave the order to invade Czechoslovakia. We can only speculate what might have happened if Britain and France hadn't appeased Hitler in Munich. As for Kristallnacht, ninety-one people were killed, and over two thousand of those arrested that night are estimated to have died in concentration camps. Sadly, as Peter noted in the story, the hatred was never satiated—it only grew.

The RMS *Aquitania* was a real ship—the ship on which my grandmother sailed home from her "grand tour" of Europe, also in 1936. The American News Service and all American newspapers in the story are fictional, as are all characters, except the historical figures—and the historical figures mentioned include pioneering female correspondents Dorothy Thompson and Sigrid Schultz. Herr Gold's café is fictional, but his *Gemütlichkeit* was inspired by an innkeeper we met in Garmisch-Partenkirchen in 2007.

If you're on Pinterest, please visit my board for *When Twilight Breaks* (www.pinterest.com/sarahsundin) to see pictures of events and places mentioned in the novel, fashions, and other inspiration for the story.

Acknowledgments

With each book I write, I become ever more thankful for the people in my life who enable this crazy pursuit—from my family to my small group to my writer buddies. I love you all, and I couldn't do it without you.

Deep thanks to my critique partners, Marcy Weydemuller, Sherry Kyle, Lisa Bogart, and Judy Gann. And special thanks to author friend Michelle Ule, who gave this novel a read-through as a journalist. Any journalistic errors are mine alone!

The key to looking smart as an author is knowing smart people. Thank you to Vinnie Angelo, an excellent Bible teacher at my church, for the transliteration of Hebrew. And overflowing thanks to my sister, Martha Groeber, an outstanding flautist and flute teacher. Not only did she provide pieces appropriate for Libby to play, but my memories of growing up with Martha's dedicated—and gorgeous—flute practice infused those scenes.

As for Libby White—her name is a thank-you present to Libby Weisman, one of my former Sunday school students. Libby's mother told me she described my books to her friends as "warmance." Isn't that perfect? Such cleverness deserved a character nod, and I hope Libby White's sweet and enthusiastic spirit reflects my young friend's.

Although I've told some of my grandfather John Ebelke's story in my "Dear Reader" letter, I would be remiss to omit him here. His textbook *Foundation Course in German*, cowritten with Conrad P. Homberger, helped me with Peter's diction lessons, provided a song for the Hofbräuhaus scene, and bolstered my rusty German skills. Also, his article "An Experiment with Recording and Play-back Machines in Academic Foreign Language Teaching" in the December 1948 issue of *The Modern Language Journal* (the wonders you can find online!) inspired Peter's Dictaphone research.

As always, I'm indebted to my incredible agent, Rachel Kent of Books and Such, and the phenomenal team at Revell—Vicki Crumpton, Kristin Kornoelje, Michele Misiak, Karen Steele, Gayle Raymer, and countless others who take my little stories and make them look good!

Thank you also to my wonderful readers! Your encouragement and support are an indescribable blessing. Please visit me at www.sarahsundin.com to leave a message, sign up for my email newsletter, and read about the history behind the story. I hope to hear from you.

Discussion Questions

1. The year of 1938 was momentous in Germany. Which events in the story did you already know about and which were new for you?

2. Evelyn Brand prefers freedom, while Peter Lang prefers order. How does Evelyn change during the story—and why? How does Peter change in the story—and why? Do you lean more toward freedom or order? Has this changed during your life?

3. Peter is impressed with the order, safety, and prosperity in Germany, especially given the condition of the rest of the world—a position shared by thousands of American and British visitors in the prewar years. What would you have thought in the same circumstances? How does the loss of his father color Peter's views?

4. As a female foreign correspondent, Evelyn "was held to loftier standards, paid higher dues, and took stiffer punishments." How do you see this in her story? How does she work to overcome these obstacles? Have you ever faced problems due to gender, race, or other factors outside your control?

5. Coming from an influential family, Peter has a strong desire to have an influence in the world. How does this shift during the story? What did you think when Evelyn contrasts her broad influence with Peter's deep influence? Which would you prefer?

6. Evelyn and Libby have been longtime friends, as have Peter and George. How have these friendships shaped them? How do these friendships affect the decisions they make?

7. Evelyn dislikes depending on other people, but events force her to do so. What does she learn in the process? How does this affect her relationship with the Lord? Are you more like Evelyn or like Libby when it comes to independence?

8. Early in the story, Professor Schreiber tells Peter, "When the storm comes, the reed bends but the stick breaks." What do you think he means by that? Which characters act like "reeds" in the story, which like "sticks," and which like "rods"? If you lived in Nazi Germany, which do you think you'd be?

9. Herr Gold represents the many German Jews who slowly lost their freedoms and livelihoods, and who had great difficulty leaving their homeland. What struck you about his experience? What would you have done in his circumstances?

10. Evelyn sees men as hunters determined to cage her. Then Peter challenges her not to put all men in the same box, comparing her dismissive attitude to how men treat her as a female reporter. How does this change her views?

11. An important Bible verse for Peter is Micah 6:8: "He hath shewed thee, O man, what is good; and what doth the Lord require of thee, but to do justly, and to love mercy, and to walk humbly with thy God?" How does this verse change him? What does it say to you?

12. Although Evelyn and Peter have widely differing views, they're willing to listen to each other and they learn from each other. Is this something that is easy or difficult for you?

13. Evelyn is frustrated that the German people have sacrificed liberties to have jobs and security and national strength, and Peter comes to realize that they "drew the line in the wrong place." Where would you draw the line?

14. Peter felt powerless to save his father. How does he compensate for this? How does he grow in this respect?

15. Peter and Evelyn share many interests, such as classical music and hiking. How do these build their friendship? What interests do you share with your friends?

16. At the end of the story, Peter tells Evelyn, "Even in the darkest night, the stars always shine." How do you think that will affect them going forward? What does it mean to you?

Sarah Sundin is the bestselling author of *The Sea Before Us*, *The Sky Above Us*, and *The Land Beneath Us*, as well as the WAVES OF FREEDOM, the WINGS OF THE NIGHTINGALE, and the WINGS OF GLORY series. Her novel *The Sky Above Us* is a finalist for the 2020 Carol Award, *The Sea Before Us* received the 2019 Reader's Choice Award from RWA Faith, Hope, and Love, *When Tides Turn* and *Through Waters Deep* were named to Booklist's "101 Best Romance Novels of the Last 10 Years," and *Through Waters Deep* won the 2016 INSPY Award. In 2011, Sarah received the Writer of the Year Award at the Mount Hermon Christian Writers Conference.

During WW II, one of her grandfathers served as a pharmacist's mate (medic) in the US Navy, and her great-uncle flew with the US Eighth Air Force. Her other grandfather, a professor of German, helped train American soldiers in the German language through the US Army Specialized Training Program. Sarah and her husband live in northern California, and they have three adult children. She enjoys speaking for church, community, and writers' groups, and she serves as codirector of the West Coast Christian Writers Conference. Visit www.sarahsundin.com for more information.

One fateful night drove three brothers apart.
One fateful day thrusts them together... D-day.

"The author of *When Tides Turn* kicks off a new wartime series, mixing her usual excellent historical research with fast-paced, breathtaking suspense."
—*Library Journal*

War is coming.
Can love carry them through the rough waters that lie ahead?

"Sarah Sundin seamlessly weaves together emotion, action, and sweet romance."

—*USA Today's Happy Ever After* blog

GET TO KNOW

SARAH SUNDIN

To Learn More about Sarah,
Read Her Blog, or See
the Inspiration behind the Stories
Visit

SARAHSUNDIN.COM

LET'S TALK ABOUT BOOKS

- Share or mention the book on your social media platforms. Use the hashtag **#WhenTwilightBreaks**.

- Write a book review on your blog or on a retailer site.

- Pick up a copy for friends, family, or anyone who you think would enjoy and be challenged by its message!

- Share this message on Twitter, Facebook, or Instagram: **I loved #WhenTwilightBreaks by @SarahSundin @RevellBooks**

- Recommend this book for your church, workplace, book club, or small group.

- Follow Revell on social media and tell us what you like.

RevellBooks

RevellBooks

RevellBooks

RevellBooks